19

3⁸

The
Memory of
Elephants

The Memory of Elephants

by
Boman Desai

ANDRE DEUTSCH

For Soonamai and for Granny

Thanks to Cheryl Rozycki for the use of her house, her Apple, and her countless cups of tea – and thanks, also, Mom, for the translations and the time.
I would also like to thank Anil Dharkar, editor of the Bombay magazine *Debonair*, in which excerps from this book were published: his support came at a time when it was much needed

First published 1988 by
André Deutsch Limited
105–106 Great Russell Street London WC1B 3LJ

British Library Cataloguing in Publication Data

Desai, Boman
The memory of elephants.
I. Title
823 F

ISBN 0 233 98313 9

Printed in Great Britain by
St Edmundsbury Press, Bury St Edmunds, Suffolk

Contents

Rusi

Homi

Seervai and Cama Family Trees

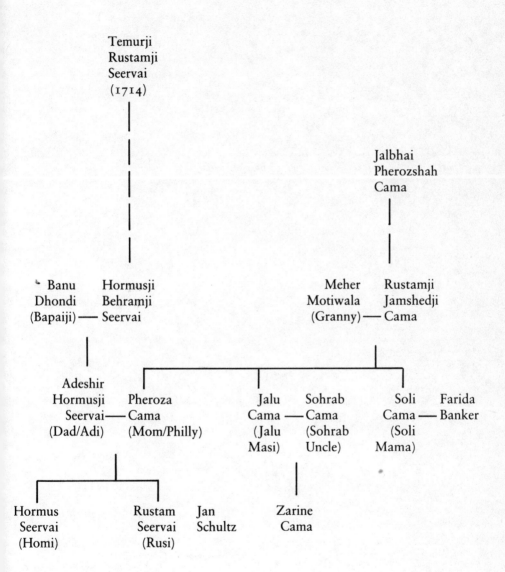

Prologue

I am bawaji, the son of the son of and so on and so on of a bawaji;
but as my bapaiji, my paternal grandmother, whom everyone
(including her son) called Bapaiji, as if it were her name, recently
said to me: You are a bawaji, Hormusji (she spoke ironically, using
the exalted form of my name, Hormus – or Homi as everyone called
me), but you yourself do not know what it means to be a bawaji.
You should be ashamed.

I was not ashamed; I was perhaps too ignorant to be ashamed;
but I was bewildered. I thought I was going crazy. I saw people, the
dead (Bapaiji, Granny, Dad) and the living (Mom, Jalu Masi, Sohrab
Uncle, Soli Mama, Rusi, Zarine – Myself!) as if they were acting out
the scenes of their lives by my bedside. Worse, I saw armies, hordes
and phalanxes of warriors, Arabs and Persians, on foot, on horseback, camelback, elephantback, engaged in battle, showers of
descending arrows, a constant swarm of adverse activity as might be
witnessed when rival ant colonies collide; the dead and the living
were brought together, the ancient and the modern, sometimes in
closeups as if someone had zeroed in on a scene with a zoom lens,
sometimes from afar as if with a wide angle lens, in short bites of
motion as if in a badly edited movie; my understanding of what I
saw was perfect, infallible, but the source of my understanding, still
a mystery, fed my terror of imminent insanity.

I wanted to get up but I could not move; I might as well have been
bound like Gulliver by the Lilliputians even to his hair twined
around stakes hammered into the ground, but my hair was not that
long; there was a throbbing in my head as if threads were being
drawn by needles from the right to the left, from the left to the right,
sometimes in both directions at once, sometimes in more. My

conscious states blurred with my unconscious like everything else happening all at once. "Hello, Homi? Can you hear me?" People in white stood all around me, some faces grim, others anxious.

"Yes. Who are you?"

"It's Dr Edward Horvath, Homi. You are in good hands. You are getting better. Can you tell me exactly how you feel?"

I tried to focus on the voice but couldn't. "My head hurts."

There was a shuffle. A new face loomed in the foreground. "Homi, do you know who I am?"

I recognized the voice, even the face though it had a heavy black beard. "Rusi, my brother."

The face smiled. "Yes, yes. How are you feeling?"

"My head hurts."

He could not stop smiling. I must have been unconscious a long time. "They will give you something for that. Are you hungry?"

"Yes."

"What would you like?"

"Anything. Tell Mom I want sali boti for dinner."

"Mom isn't here. We are in a hospital, still in Aquihana, in Pennsylvania. I flew in from Chicago when they said you were sick. Mom is still in Bombay. They have a choice of beef stew and baked chicken in the hospital today. What do you want?"

"Chicken."

Someone left for the chicken. I was still in Aquihana, Pennsylvania, USA, where I had accepted the scholarship from Aquihana University. I could have gone to Harvard, I could have gone to Yale, I could have gone to Princeton, they all offered scholarships and others did too, but they were not for me; I preferred the low profile; I preferred to create my own prestige; I preferred, if you wish, to be a snob in reverse.

"Can I get you anything else?"

"Rusi?"

"Yes?"

"I want to go home."

"When you are better I will take you home myself."

"When?"

"Soon."

A nurse gave me some pills to swallow with a glass of water. I went through the motions of drinking, when the food arrived, of being fed, still feeling as if I were supine, immobile, but the throbbing in my head lessened. Rusi pushed his scraggly black hair behind his ears; they were long like Bapaiji's ears, and as I watched Bapaiji materialized in entirety, as if from his ears, where Rusi had been standing. "Hello, Bapaiji."

"I am not Bapaiji. I am Rusi. Bapaiji is dead." The voice was Rusi's.

"Array, listen to me, no? It is Bapaiji only. I may be dead as you know the dead but I am trying to show you something. Look now, pay attention." The voice was deeper than I remembered but unmistakably Bapaiji's. The throbbing in my head got worse as I looked for what she wanted to show me.

A desert appeared, and a group of Arabs on camelback approaching at a leisurely pace through the loose stones and thickets of thorny bush that grew around them; behind them the earth was arid, dirty yellow, without even brush to be seen; before them stood two sentries, spears held ready, guarding a bridge; to left and right of them stood other sentries, similarly ready, guarding adjacent bridges. It was spring and the river – actually, a canal from the Euphrates River – was full. When the summer reached its zenith the canal dried up and could be forded easily, even at its fullest, on horseback. Trees full of figs, pomegranates, oranges, dates, and lime grew on the Persian side of the river before the walls of the city of Madayn. The foremost sentry waited for the caravan to stop; when it was almost upon him and showed no signs of slowing down he shouted, "Halt!" The camels were immediately reined to a halt. The sentry counted their number, fifteen, to himself. "Dismount!"

The Arabs commanded their camels to their knees and sprang off unwrapping the white flap of cloth across their faces. They were hardier, bred in the desert, than the Persians, taller with gaunt faces, sand encrusted stubble, thin noses like beaks, and eyes narrowed by continual squinting against the wind and sun; the space around the eyes was more wrinkled and darker like a mask owing to the lesser protection provided the eyes by their cowls.

3

When the last Arab had dismounted the sentry spoke again. "State your business."

One of the Arabs, standing ahead of the others, spoke with scarcely concealed contempt. "We are bedouin, a deputation from our Caliph Omar to your King Yezdigard III. My name is Noman Makarin. We are expected."

The sentry knew they were expected. He had been appointed to stand by the gate because during his adventures as a soldier he had learned a little Arabic. "You are expected," he said. "We are to escort you to the throne room of King Yezdigard III – but you must leave behind your camels and arms."

One corner of Noman Makarin's thin mouth curved sharply down. "Has the great Persian empire been so debilitated by its wars with Byzantium that it now fears the arms of fifteen bedouin?"

The sentry's face grew taut as if it had received a slap. "You must leave behind your camels," he said.

Noman Makarin smiled and raised his arm to gather the Arabs around him. One of the Arabs stayed with the camels; the others were escorted across the bridge by the sentries. They walked with long measured strides and the old Persian sentry was struck immediately by their difference from the Arabs he had known, a skulking subservient nomadic people, lacking culture, lacking education, barely above the rats of the desert upon which they fed, but these bedouin walked as if they were nobility – as if they were conquerors and the Persians were their lackeys; they looked as smug as their camels.

They entered the city through an arched brick gateway guarded at each end by giant stone mastiffs. (Jamshed, the legendary Persian hero, had kept two mastiffs whose powerful vision could drive away demons invisible to men.) The houses within the walls were of brick, some with flat roofs of timber and packed earth, others with vaulted domes of brick; the walls around the doorways were plastered, painted shades of tan and blue; the wealthier homeowners had pillared porches; fire temples stood apart from the residences, square buildings of limestone blocks embedded in mortar, roofed by domes over four arches, built for the worship of Ahura Mazda and His prophet Zoroaster, their entablatures supported by winged bulls with human faces. The Persians, sleek and olive skinned – the men in colourful blouses open down the front fastened by girdles and breeches reaching their knees, the women dressed similarly but in longer wider garments with blouses closed down the front except for a slit at the breast – gathered to make fun of the curved Arab scimitars, their dirty burnooses, and weather-beaten features; someone suggested, to the crowd's immense amusement, that they acquire new wardrobes by using their bows as distaffs for spinning flax. There were enclosures with horses, donkeys, cows, camels, and fat-tailed sheep; goats, dogs, and cats roamed freely; a brightly clothed juggler thrust his rump at the procession juggling oranges between his legs. The Arabs remained inscrutable, looking neither left nor right, appearing oblivious to everything, even the magnificence of the palace ahead.

The palace was so sumptuous it might have been a mirage; the entire face of its main staircase was covered with sculptures in low relief, of Persian guards, armed with spears, swords, shields, others carrying bows and quiversful of arrows, lions attacking bulls, hunting parties, mythological beasts combining lions and bulls and eagles and men, and more; a border of rosettes adorned the parapet on which was carved an inscription commemorating the founder of the palace, the Great King, Khushrow II, shahanshah eran ud aneran, the King of Kings of Iran and non-Iran. A tall, wide, barely-tipped central arch indicated the main entrance; on either side of the arch the façade, divided into string courses and pilasters, was ornamented. Inside were huge square rooms with barrel vaults of baked bricks which opened one into the other, the largest of which, the Great Hall, the throne room, was in the centre, large enough to hold thousands of ministers, noblemen, guards, and attendants; the interior walls were stuccoed and ornamented with paintings, embroidery, and hanging weapons glittering with jewels; the Paradise carpet, 70 cubits long and 60 broad, so richly embroidered that it seemed like a garden with walks of gold, meadows of emeralds, streams of silver, and trees, flowers, fruits, and birds of diamonds, rubies, sapphires, and pearls, formed the backdrop to the golden throne, its ruby supports, and the priceless crown, encrusted with gems, which had to be suspended over the head of the Great King, Yezdigard III, owing to its insupportable weight.

The throne was set on a platform behind curtains embroidered with gold; knights and princes stood thirty feet to the right of the throne, governors and tributary kings in residence a similar distance farther, and jesters and musicians a farther distance yet; guards stood on the left; but despite the remoteness of his throne, despite his fine trappings, Yezdigard III, the grandson of Khushrow II, could not appear to be more than he was, a boy king with a thick cluster of black curls, the more barefaced for the men of his court with well trained beards tied in a knot below their chins; his necklace of stones only gave him a more pearlfaced rubycheeked cast. Since the death of Khushrow II in 628 AD by his son, there had been a succession of eleven rulers, two of them women, in the span of four years, before Yezdigard's accession had been masterminded by the Persian general, Rustam, who had removed Purandakht, daughter of Khushrow II, from the throne. The regal bearing of the Arabs despite their beggarly raiment surprised him; he knew they had taken Damascus from the Byzantines and won decisive battles against them, but the Byzantine forces had been enervated by his own wars against their emperor Heraclius; he knew the Arabs had won some battles against even the Persian forces, but he couldn't think of them as more than jackals harrassing an old lion; something had happened to give the Arabs their uncustomarily dignified bearing.

The sentries escorting the delegation prostrated themselves before Yezdigard but the Arabs remained standing. "Down, fool," the old sentry whispered sharply to Noman Makarin, "if you wish to live."

Noman Makarin said nothing; he did not look at the sentry; he had ignored all the wonders of the palace, concentrating instead on his purpose, fixing Yezdigard with his stare from the moment he had entered his presence; he made his obeisance without servility, with deference to etiquette more than the threat of the sentry, and the other Arabs followed.

The Persians were known for their humanity; vanquished kings were dealt with honourably, enemy towns left unmolested, their ranks welcomed into the services of Persia, and land given them to administrate; Zoroastrianism was the religion of the royal house of Persia, but Judaism, Christianity, and even paganism were tolerated with equanimity. Yezdigard assumed the Arabs wanted clemency for their excursions against the Persians, permission to mingle, and perhaps some land. He officiated the ceremony by satisfying his curiosity about some of their accoutrements. The old sentry continued to serve as interpreter. "We call this *burd*," said Noman Makarin when the sentry asked what they called their cloaks. Makarin's eyes never left Yezdigard's while he spoke and the boy king felt threatened because the Persian word *burdan* meant "taking". Similarly, when he asked about their whips and sandals Makarin said *saut* and *na'l* whose homonyms in Persian, *sukhtan* and *nalidan*, meant "burning" and "lamenting". Yezdigard blanched, then spoke angrily because Noman Makarin continued to appraise him inscrutably, imperturbably. "What is it you want, then?"

Noman Makarin replied: "Allah has commanded us, by the mouth of His prophet Mohammad, to extend the dominion of Islam over all nations. This order we obey. We invite you to become our brothers by adopting our faith – or pay tribute if you wish to avoid war."

Yezdigard knew of the prophet Mohammad; the prophet had died in the year Yezdigard had come to the throne; but he had not felt the power of the prophet before. He was outraged that the representative of a people who had no precedent for organizing, holding, and ruling an empire, who were acknowledged in the common parlance as desert rats, would dare to speak as Makarin had done to the shahanshah eran ud aneran. His eyes flashed, his hand went to the gem-encrusted hilt of his sword, he almost rose from his throne – but he fought to regain his composure and spoke calmly though with his hand still on his sword. "Your minor victories have made you bold indeed – but Byzantium has fallen, and if Persia sets aside her internal dissensions for only a day she will drive you deep into the desert again with the rats and the snakes upon which you feed. You have been known to bury your daughters to avoid sharing food with them, you have been known to feed on carcasses and drink blood; of all the world's nations you are the poorest, the least united, the most ignorant, the most estranged from the arts. Who are you to dictate what Persia should do? If misery and want have driven you from the desert, if you open your eyes and cease deceiving yourselves, we will give you food and clothing and freedom of worship. We have welcomed Jews to live peaceably among us, we have welcomed Christians, we will welcome you – for that is the way of Persia."

Noman Makarin remained silent for a moment as if with respect, but when he spoke his tone was condescending as if he spoke to a child. "What you have said about our former condition is true. We ate lizards, we buried our daughters, we drank blood, such was our state – but Allah, in His mercy, has sent us His prophet Mohammad, and through the organ of His prophet has instructed us that He is the only God, that the earth belongs to Him, that we are to spread His dominion, to exact tribute from those who would keep their faiths, and to exterminate all others."

The Arab stopped as if to appraise his effect. "This is our destiny; those of us who fall will obtain Paradise, those who survive, victory. Now it is for you to choose."

Yezdigard recognised it would be hopeless to talk further. "If I had less respect for your offices as emissaries," he said, "I would have you instantly deprived of life." He ordered a bag full of earth to be given to Makarin. "This is all the tribute you will get from me," he said. "Return to your Caliph and tell him that my general Rustam will bury his general and his entire army in a few days at Kadesia."

Yezdigard did not understand why Makarin had accepted the earth so eagerly but Rustam understood immediately that he had taken it as a pledge of future success; Rustam ordered the bag retaken as soon as he learned what had happened, but the Arabs had proved too quick. Makarin deposited the bag before his general, Sa'd, exclaiming, "The soil of Persia is ours."

Kadesia was a village on the edge of the desert with a fort, some cultivation, and palm groves. It lay within a plain bound on the west by a stream and on the east by a canal from the Euphrates. Sa'd, the Arab leader, and his troops camped by a spring near the desert; Rustam and the Persians camped by the canal. The Persians were weary from their long wars with Byzantium; they had forty thousand men to the Arabs' thirty thousand, but Rustam did not want to attack as long as the Arabs could escape into the desert and attempted negotiations instead to determine the Arabs' grievances, their ultimate goals, and their reasons for raiding Persian frontiers – but to no avail. After four months, against his wishes, Rustam opened the battle.

I heard the scrunch of marching feet, the thud-de-de-thud of galloping horsehooves, a soft slow heavy regular pad, pad, pad, which, as the glorious horrific spectacle unfolded in front of me I recognized as elephant footsteps. The plain was flat as far as it was visible; the hazy early morning rendered the sunlight into trapezoidal shapes, casting long shadows. The Persian cavalry wore helmets, coats of mail, buskins reaching up to their knees; they wielded swords, shields, lances, maces, bows, and arrows; even their chargers were protected by armour not unlike the chargers of medieval knights. The sun grew brighter picking highlights from the abundance of metal in the field so that the charges resembled a glistening turbulent river. Archers, trained to shoot with accuracy and rapidity from behind wattled shields, formed the most important part of the infantry; the rest of the infantry supported the archers with spears and swords. Vaults of arrows flew like monster predatory birds casting ominous moving shadows on the ground until they found their prey. The Arabs, in their desert robes, with only their shields for protection, were easy targets; the numbers of their dead mounted quickly and their bodies lay with clusters of arrows sticking out of them like the quills of porcupines. Men screamed like children and ran wildeyed to and fro like trapped animals striking at one another. Two mounted Arabs squeezed Rustam's mount between them; one held him so the other might find a vantage point for his blade, but Rustam spurred his horse forward breaking the first Arab's hold, held his shield against the second Arab's scimitar, and swiped backward with his sword slicing the centre of the first Arab's face from the crown to the chin; someone else swung at the second Arab so that his head flew through the air with wide white bulging eyes; Rustam smiled, nodding a quick acknowledgement to his compatriot.

More than anything else the Persian war elephants scattered the Arab horses and threw their riders in the air. The victory for the first day belonged to the Persians, and Sa'd sent for reinforcements from

Syria. If the Persians had followed up their advantage through the night they might have checked the Arab expansion for all time, but the numbers were still great on both sides and they returned to their camp instead.

On the second day the field was already cluttered with the bodies of the dead, the ground still damp and dark with blood; rats and snakes gnawed at the bones of the corpses and the stench of rotting flesh was everywhere getting stronger as the day deepened into a hot afternoon. The Arab leader, Sa'd, with two arrows in the back of his left shoulder, felt as if his arm would fall off from its weight alone; he wanted to leave the field so he could have his shoulder bound, but didn't want to undermine the Arab morale; he was grateful for whatever lack of foresight had prevented the Persians from bringing their elephants onto the field again, but he couldn't tell which way the battle was going yet. His arm was almost too heavy to hold up much longer when the Syrian reinforcements arrived. Sa'd rallied, fastened his arm within his girdle to relieve its weight, shouted the takbeer, Allah Akbar (God is Great), to invigorate his men, and renewed his onslaught with such fervour that the Arabs won the second day.

On the third day an elephant plucked an Arab from his mount and held him high under the armpits with his trunk, but before he could throw him the Arab drove his lance firmly into the elephant's eye. The elephant gored the Arab into the ground, stamping his body into puddings of flesh, but he couldn't shake the hateful shaft protruding from his eye. Dark red blood spread like a wash across his armoured trunk; trumpeting his pain above the cries of the battle he invited a volley of Arab arrows to be fired at his good eye. The blinded elephant went berserk and wheeling around madly charged the Persian troops, disrupting their centre. The Arabs pushed them back with renewed cries of Allah Akbar, not letting up even when the night fell. The armour of the Persians worked to their disadvantage in the close quarters of the night, a sandstorm blew in their faces, and more reinforcements arrived from Syria. By the fourth day the Persians had been driven against the canal, their forces disorganized, and their general Rustam killed.

For two months the Arabs rested and rejoiced, then Sa'd led them on to Yezdigard's capital, Madayn. The bridges across the canal to the city had all been destroyed; when the guards saw the Arabs they ran through the city shouting, "The devils, the followers of Ahriman, have come!" Yezdigard had already fled to the east with a retinue of four thousand noncombatants including secretaries, cooks, women, children, old people and as much of his treasury as he could take with him. Madayn fell after token resistance and the wealth of Persia passed into Arab hands – carpets, dresses, arms, jewels, even a horse of pure gold. Fifty thousand Arabs, many of whom had never seen gold before, never lived in more than a tent, wandered as if in a dream through the palaces and gardens taking whatever they wished; each received a booty of twelve thousand dirhams (one thousand dollars); the prophecy of the prophet, that the treasure of the Khushrows and the Caesars was destined for the Arabs, was coming true.

"Did you like the fish?"

The white fish, served with a lemon sauce with French beans (green beans as they were called in America), had not been bad, but I was not partial to fish; nor, it seemed were most of the residents of the hospital – they had run out of the alternative choice, roast beef with a baked potato, before noon. "I like chicken," I told Rusi.

"I know. I'm sorry – but there was no chicken on the menu today." The tiny uplifted nose in his tiny oval face fringed by his wild black hair and beard wrinkled with his regret. "Maybe they'll have chicken tomorrow."

"Rusi . . . I want to go home, Rusi."

"Yes, yes – soon. The doc says you need more rest. You have to build up strength for the trip."

"I'm well. I feel well. Look." I sat up in bed. I tried to get out but Rusi stopped me. "I'm fine. We can go tomorrow."

Rusi held my shoulders and pushed me gently back again. "Only a little longer. Let me tell you what the doc said. Do you follow me?"

It was strange to have him speak to me as if I were a child; I was the older brother. "Yes, yes, of course I follow you. What do you mean?"

"Listen," he said, looking at me carefully for my reaction. "You've been in the hospital for a month now and the doc says you're recuperating well – but your system has had a severe shock and he wants to be sure there will be no relapse. He's given you all the tests and the results have all been negative. The only problem is your memory has been damaged because of the experiments you performed on yourself – something to do with a memory machine he said, something you invented, a memoscan I think he called it. At least we don't have to feed you intravenously any more like when you were unconscious – but even when you're conscious you don't remember what you've eaten or even whether you've eaten at all."

My memory? damaged? I was recalling things I didn't even know I knew – in vivid detail!

"The doc thinks there might be some permanent damage to your long-term memory as well because you keep talking to Bapaiji as if she were still alive; he thinks that if I took you back to Bombay the familiarity of childhood associations might be the best thing to spark your memory – but he wants to be sure you're well enough for the trip because otherwise you might slip back into your coma. Are you still following me?"

I think I nodded. I wanted to say Yes but I couldn't. I understood what he was saying – but there was so much I did not understand about which I could not even begin to ask him. How did I know what I knew? see what I saw? hear what I heard? when it was so evidently fantastical, so alien to my life?

Rusi segued once more into Bapaiji. "Array, but my dear Hormusji, what is so very fantastical about this? You said so, yourself, that you are the son of the son of and so on and so on of a bawaji? So sonorously you put it – and what is bawaji but a name we Parsis call ourselves? and what is Parsi but the pure form of Farsi – the Arabic form because there is no P in Arabic? and what is Farsi but the people from Fars, the province in Persia once called Parsa by our people who were driven from their homeland to India by the Arabs? The Europeans called Persia after the province Parsa to represent the whole of Iran; it wasn't until 1935 that the Europeans called Persia by her true name Iran (land of the Aryans) at the request of the Iranian government, home of the Arabs, the Musalman as we Parsis call them; the Musalman did not allow freedom of worship like the Persians, Iranis as we Parsis call them, and all Zoroastrians, Jews, and Christians, called dhimmis by the Musalman, had to pay an extra tax, the jizya; on paying the jizya the dhimmis were marked with seals of lead to advertise their inferior status; they were not allowed to ride, carry weapons, drink wine openly, show signs of their religion, wear Musalman clothing, speak to Musalman women, nor build houses taller than Musalman houses. At first dhimmis became Musalmans so they wouldn't have to pay the jizya; but the Musalmans' gain in 'true believers' was proportional to their loss in taxes, so converted dhimmis were called mawalis, the jizya was reinstated on them, and their inferior status put in effect once more. Most of the original, the pure Persians, whose numbers have fallen below ninety thousand, now reside in India, mostly in Bombay. The battle of Kadesia was the beginning of the end of the Persian empire, of the Sasanian dynasty which had flourished for four centuries of which Yezdigard III was the last monarch; it was the turning point between the ancient and the modern world. Two more battles were fought before the fate of the Persians was assured; Yezdigard raised armies wherever he could but he lost the battle of Jalula to Sa'd in 637 AD and the battle of Nihavand, the 'Victory of Victories' for the Musalman, in 642 AD. After that Yezdigard fled from province to province until he was murdered by a miller in Merv in 652 AD. The major battles had long been over but raids continued interminably; the towns of Fars put up the strongest resistance of all the provinces, but the inhabitants were insecure, never knowing when to expect the raids. . . .

"But enough of this buk-buk. Let me show you so you can see for yourself. This is the village of Sarosh, typical of the villages in the Fars province."

I saw a cluster of flat-topped brick houses enclosed by a high solid wall with a thick heavy wooden gate. The houses were essentially single rooms opening onto courtyards which were linked by narrow alleys to the gate. Green poplar and sycamore trees grew in the courtyards and outside the walls. Sheep were herded in pens in the courtyard, a few horses were tethered near the houses; as much as was possible was kept within the walls because when the Arabs couldn't break down the gate they had destroyed all the orchards, livestock, and crops on the outside; a watch stood continuously on a tower at the gate.

The scene changed suddenly as if someone had edited a strip out of a movie reel; the perspective remained the same but the gate had been destroyed, a battering ram lay beside it, equestrian Arabs swarmed across the courtyard, and domestic animals scattered in terror looking for cover. In one of the houses a man pushed his wife and child under a rope bed covered with sheepskin. As he turned an Arab burst through the door. The man held out his sword to parry the Arab's swipe, but he stumbled over a scurrying dog and the Arab's blade struck the arc of his neck and shoulder slicing almost through his chest; blood spurted like a fountain; his wife heard the sound of the spray hitting the ceiling, walls, and floor, even over the sounds of fighting outside, as harmless as the sound made by spattering the frontage of a house with water to flatten and thicken the mud for chalk patterns, or using a garden hose on a lawn. The Arab turned his attention immediately to the bed which had engaged the man he had killed and dragged the woman out from underneath. With a single violent motion of his hand he yanked at her bodice pulling her forward so that she fell on her face. The child dashed out to its mother as she fell and the Arab, unaware of the child till then, swung his scimitar reflexively in an arc. He missed the child's head by a fraction but sliced off its nose. He kicked the woman so that she turned on her back and raised his sword arm again when a blade cut his hand off at the wrist from behind. The woman scurried with her bleeding unconscious child to a corner and squatted holding it close to her torn bodice which soaked up the blood like a sponge. The Arab's severed hand twitched in the dirt and his scimitar clattered to the ground as he turned with a howl to face his assailant. The woman watched as the man severed the Arab's second hand and one of his legs at the thigh; when the Arab fell on his back the man pinned him through his groin to the ground; the Arab's howls could hardly be heard above the clamour of the screams outside. The man thanked God the Arabs had brought a battering ram; he had never wished to hide behind the gate like a woman; he wished he could have got home before his father had been killed. His mother, rocking

14

with horror, sticky with blood, hardly recognized her son in his fury; why did he not simply finish off the Arab? When he looked in her direction she felt only hatred. The man was aware of his mother's feeling but he did not understand it. Had she not seen her father killed? her sisters raped? and now her own husband killed? Could she not understand that revenge – the more vengeful the better – was everything? He turned to the squirming body on the floor again, jealous as if his mother favoured the Arab, and hacked at the arms and legs, careful not to touch the torso or head, until slivers of flesh and blood raced like striations in the wake of his sword. He only stopped when a cheer rang through the courtyard; the Arabs had been routed; then, with a careless look in his mother's direction, he ran the Arab through.

The survivors of the battle left Sarosh the same evening; they had lost too many men to withstand another Arab onslaught; they followed the trail of other Zoroastrians who had made their way to the coast to sail to the island of Hormuz in the Persian Gulf where they would be safe from the Arabs. The woman made preparations in silence, speaking only when she had to. The older son, Bahman, respecting her silence, said nothing. The younger son, Xerxes, who had bled for more than an hour, lay pale and exhausted.

The journey to the coast took almost a month, the older people on horseback, the others walking alongside; the mother rode on Bahman's horse holding Xerxes in her arms while Bahman carried a leather sack with their clothes and other belongings; she did not talk to Bahman and she would not leave him alone with Xerxes for even a little while. Bahman wanted her comfort; once, dreaming that she held him, he had not wanted to wake up – but he had awakened and continued to respect her silence.

The caravan proceeded to the coast without further misfortune. Bahman took courage from the cool night, the clear brooks, the fruit trees, the clean air, and put an arm around his mother, smiling encouragement. "Soon we will be safe, it will be over, we will start again."

She remained still, like a sack, in the circle of his arm; then she narrowed her shoulders and stepped out. "Safe?" she said without looking at him. "Safe from what? I have seen my father killed, my husband killed, my sisters defiled. What is safe? Who cares about safe?"

Her voice was flat, distant; his smile felt painful. "I care, Mamma," he said, his voice trembling. "Tell me, no? What is it? Why are you like this? I am your son, no?"

"My son," she said, looking at Xerxes asleep against their sack on the sand before them, "is only a boy. When he is a man he will till the ground, he will make things grow."

"But I am also your son, no?"

"I do not know my son," she said. "He is like a wild animal who has had its first taste of blood. There will never be enough blood for him. He will kill the Musalman only to become the Musalman himself. I am afraid of my own son."

He took her by the shoulders and shook her. "What was I to do, Mamma? They killed Pappa. They killed your pappa. What was I to do?"

She remained unmoved. "Is it right to kill the man who kills your father? to kill the father of the man who kills your father? Does that give him the right to kill you? to kill your sons? First, it is sweet, yes, revenge; but then it begins to justify all forms of corruption – mutilation, murder, assassination; it becomes your master, and you become your own enemy. There is more honour in death than in such a life. How can I make you see this thing?"

Bahman turned away from her. "I do not understand. This much I know – if I did not kill the Musalman he would have killed me, and I did not want to die. More than that I cannot understand." She saw his back shaking as if he were crying, she saw in him once more her son; she understood he was a man now, he had to find his own way; she wanted to hold him, to say she was sorry, but she did not know how to do it.

The village in which they settled was less than half a mile from the coast; it was built in a rectangle comprising conical tents of felt and huts of willow and mud with thatched roofs supported by wooden rafters, and fortified by high mud walls and corner towers. Further inland from the village, within a grove of date palms, Xerxes, nervously tracing the ridge of his gaping unprotected nostrils with his forefinger, hid his shadow within the long evening shadow of the tree against which he leaned as he waited for Bahman to bring Yasmin to him – "a present," Bahman had said with a wink, "for your fifteenth birthday. An hour with Yasmin and you will grow hair on your behind, yes. She has slept with camels – it's that crazy Musalman blood in her." Xerxes had winked back because he wanted to please his brother, but he was afraid. Yasmin was a year older than him; she had round black eyes, the dark skin of her Arab father, and the wide brow of her Persian mother. She had come to Hormuz five years ago with her aunt after her mother had been killed by the Arabs.

Xerxes snatched his hand from the ridge where his nose should have been; he touched it constantly, particularly when he was nervous, but he didn't want Yasmin to think he was nervous; he wanted her to think of him as she must of his brother. The others had long stopped teasing him about his nostrils, his pacifism, primarily out of respect for his brother's soldierliness, but he continued to feel strange among them. He wished he had learned how to fight; Bahman could have taught him much; but for eight years after they had come to Hormuz his mother had not let him out of her sight, and when Bahman taught others how to use the sword and shield, the bow and arrow, his mother had taken him away. They were savage arts, she said, of no use to civilized people; of the four parties of Arabs that had landed on the island none had been victorious over the Persians. The Arabs were not shipbuilders, not seafarers; although the Persians kept a continuous watch she did not fear any more invasions – Hormuz was too petty; but she knew she would not feel secure again until they reached the shores of India, the land of the Hindus, with whom the Persians had traded. She could hardly wait for seaworthy ships to be built, but there were signs of her growing optimism even before then – she had begun to trust Bahman alone with Xerxes.

Bahman would not teach Xerxes how to fight – he did not wish to cause their mother more pain than he had already – but he explained her to Xerxes once. "Nothing ever felt so right," he said, "as when I killed the man who killed Pappa, when I slashed his body and his flesh flew like ribbons. I had breathed water; now I breathed air. I had seen only grey; now I saw bright, bright red. If you feel something strongly enough to kill for it, killing is the sweetest feeling in the world. I only did what Mamma wanted with all her heart to do – but my anger went into my sword and hers into fear and helplessness and resentment. I had crossed the line; she was jealous; she did not want to lose you the same way; that is all there is to it."

Xerxes understood; he felt it was true; his own anger had become like his mother's; she had been a woman, he a child – but Bahman too had paid a price. When you looked deeply enough into his eyes they became hollow, as if his memory had been arrested. If you killed too hard to rid yourself of the feeling of a moment you rid yourself of feeling altogether.

"Xerxes? Are you there?"

The voice came from behind him. He stepped out from behind the tree. "I am here."

Bahman had chosen the place because it afforded more cover than any other. "Good, good," he said. "I have your present."

Xerxes smiled but he did not see Yasmin. Bahman stood alone with a leathern sack in his hand and the rolled pelt of a black sheep on his shoulder which he carefully placed on the ground at Xerxes's feet.

Xerxes would have found such a pelt a handsome gift, but with Yasmin on his mind he barely looked at it. "Where is she? Where is Yasmin?"

Bahman only laughed and quickly unrolled the pelt; Yasmin lay on the black fleece wearing nothing but the veil of the Musalman women, her black well-oiled hair splashed shining behind her, her small breasts and black nipples heaving from her tumble. Bahman grinned, said "Happy Birthday, Brother," and left, leaving behind also the leathern sack he had carried.

Xerxes remained where he stood, his hand fingering his nostrils again, until she held out her hand to him and he knelt by her side. Her clear black eyes became cloudy over the veil as if she sought to hide something, but that did not prevent him from quickly removing his tunic and lying naked beside her. He wanted to rouse her feeling but the cloud never lifted from her eyes. When he tore her veil from her face in desperation to see what she was feeling she smiled as if it were a joke. He wanted to talk but she got up quickly, dressed from the sack Bahman had left behind, rolled up the pelt, and left him saying only, "It's getting cold."

Xerxes's brief contact with Yasmin fed the helplessness he had learned from his mother; he followed her wretchedly everywhere, even watching her lie with other men, until he saw her once with Bahman, her eyes shut tight like fists, her breath like that of a runner, and sweat from her forehead wrinkled with her self absorption as if she had been out in the rain. He recognized their difference then; Bahman and she were the same, but not he. He felt shrunken as if the largest part of him had been removed. His recourse became, as his mother's had become, to prayer, to inquiries into truth, the nature of things, and the will of God.

I saw a silhouette of ancient ships, their masts, spars, yards, booms, and rigging, rising like black spires against a rising sun, against sleek streamlined clouds over the horizon, their underbellies filling with gold. Around the ships the sea was still but in the distance fishermen cast nets into the water. Groves of poplar, myrtle, acacia, willow, plum, and mulberry trees lined the coast. Outside the village a group of women drew water from a well, storing it in pearshaped earthenware vessels for the day while chanting a song together like a mantra. Xerxes emerged from one of the huts, wrapped in a pelt, and made his way through the narrow alleys, and past the women at the well. He knew the women stared at him but he ignored them; he wanted to say something but couldn't; he had always felt strange among them, and since he had immersed himself in prayer for the past year his strangeness had grown; he passed the grove where he had lain with Yasmin and his hand moved instinctively to his face but he held it down; two dogs followed him amiably until he reached the end of the grove, then they turned back; he wanted to reach the well at the edge of the Great Sand to pray to Ahura Mazda for guidance in his dilemma: Truth appeared like a kaleidoscope instead of like the sun, one twist and it changed instead of remaining dependable, eternal, impartial; for a year he had been so sure of his vocation, but a single statement from his mother the night before had twisted the kaleidoscope around once more. Bahman understood that the cause of the Persians in Fars was lost, but he still liked to fantasize. "It is our land. The Musalman takes what is not his. We must get it back." His mother had laughed. "And what do you think the Musalman says about that? He does not want the land for himself; he wants it for Allah. This is the blindness that destroys the world. Everyone kills for God. What do you think? The Persian empire was built by penitents and martyrs? No – no, Bahman, my son. You are like a lion in your valour – but peace will come only when the lion becomes the lamb and" (she had looked at Xerxes then with a stare that went through him like a shaft of ice) "the lamb becomes the lion."

Bahman had muttered something under his breath and let the matter go because he did not like to upset his mother over these matters; Xerxes had remained silent but felt his mother's statement like an accusation. In wartime things happened quickly; answers were scarce; blind actions such as Bahman's kept them one step ahead of the Musalman; thought paralyzed and feeling became perhaps only a luxury, a retreat from the world, the crutch of a boy who had not the courage to become a man.

By the time he reached the well the sun was much higher, he had begun to sweat under his pelt which he removed, folded, and placed by the side of the well. Underneath he wore a lhega and the two primary articles of the Zoroastrian faith: a thin white cotton vestlike garment, the sadra, and a woollen thread, the kusti, wound thrice around the waist, secured in front and behind by simple knots, during prayers. He removed his sandals and arranged them neatly by his pelt; he drew water from the well and washed his hands (the ritual before praying), put on a skull cap he had tucked into his girdle, and faced the sun. In front of him the sands shifted constantly so that the horizon appeared hazy; he could not see clearly because of the dunes in the way but the haze of sand to his right appeared to get larger, rising like a cloud. Xerxes knew there were horsemen coming his way, but he could not tell how many and he could not tell what kind. Fearing the worst he hid behind the well; he knew they would surely stop by the well but he needed time to think and it was easier to think knowing he was hidden. It was too late to escape unseen and he didn't want to lead them back to the village. He wished he were a fighting man; he might then have died valiantly instead of cowering behind a well.

He knew he had to get up but couldn't; a sour taste climbed in his throat; however coarse this human cloth, his mother had said, a thread of dignity will make it fine – but who cared about dignity when there was no one there to see? Courage was a public virtue, more easily performed for posterity than for itself, an exercise to prove to others that one was not afraid. Who would know the difference if there was no one there to see?

Xerxes swallowed hard, breathed deeply, and got up. The riders would know; he himself would know; Ahura Mazda would know. There were only three riders; he smiled because in his panic he had imagined at least twenty. He felt colder; he didn't know if it was the wind or the increasing certainty of the habiliment of the Musalman.

When the foremost horseman raised his spear he was still too far to throw it, but Xerxes was ready to greet it. He filled his lungs deeply with breath, closed his eyes, walked with slow measured steps toward his malefactors, and intoned in a rich strong voice a prayer in Avestan:

Ashem Vohu	Blessed Is Virtue
Vahistem Asti	The Highest Good
Ushta Asti	The Greatest Happiness
Ushta Ahmai	He Who Loves Virtue
Hyat Ashai	For Its Own Sake
Vahishta Ashem	Will Find Virtue Is Bliss Untold

There was a rumble of hoofbeats behind him but his thoughts were already too much with Ahura Mazda to notice. Having made the initial effort the rest was joyful. Blood filled his head, his neck, his arms as he held them to the sky; his heart pounded as if he were in love; he felt the wind blow through his hair as if it would bear him aloft; if Bahman had been there he would have told him that the sweetest feeling in the world was when you felt something strongly enough to die for it. His body appeared to rise in the air, breast extended, like that of a huge fish surfacing from the sea. He withstood the spear so firmly that it passed right through him before he fell. If he had survived another minute he would have seen all three riders felled, the first with an arrow through his eye, the second with a spear through his chest, the third beheaded by a sword.

Bahman's mother knew her premonition had been too late even before she saw him return with Xerxes's body slumped before him on his horse. He told her what he had done, but not how he had treated the bodies; she wanted to tell him that he had done the right thing to kill his brother's murderers, but couldn't. "He died with courage, Mamma," Bahman said, "with his hair in the wind like a lion's." She held him for the first time since they had come to Hormuz, and she cried in his arms until he thought her heart would break like a twig.

"Listen, Homi. Great news!"

"What?"

"The doc thinks you're well enough to go home. We're going home tomorrow."

"Home? Where? Aquihana or Bombay?"

"Tomorrow, Aquihana – in a week, Bombay. You still need a lot of rest. You move around too much even in your sleep. The doc says your dreams are too vivid – but he thinks the best thing for you is to be in secure surroundings. The sooner we get to Bombay the better."

They thought I was dreaming – I stumble over a vine in a lime green jungle and my leg twitches in my hospital bed, that sort of thing. My tales of Arabs and camels and elephants might have been interpreted as a relapse into dementia.

"Tell Mom to get an air conditioner ready."

"I did already. You never stopped asking for it."

I didn't remember asking for it but I said nothing.

"Actually, your timing is perfect," Rusi continued. "Jan is two months pregnant. What do you say, Homi? You are going to be an uncle in seven months."

"Jan is here? Where is she? I have never met her."

"No, no, she is not here. She is still in Chicago. She is enrolled in a course for the summer, but like I said, your timing is perfect. If you had got sick next semester I would have had to drop out, or Jan might have been ready to deliver – but your timing was too good."

Prologue

There was a Turneresque stormscape-on-the-sea-with-ships mounted on the hospital wall in front of me which appeared to spill out of the borders of its frame and fill up the room. The water slapped the floor around me, sharp as the crack of gunfire, rising, spiraling, sucking everything into its vortex; through the black water walls I saw the ships being tossed like toys – one, capsized, its hull dancing madly as nerves of lightning struck it from the sky – another, lying on its side, its oars sticking helplessly into the air like the legs of a giant dying insect – still others, bobbing like buoys, occasionally thrown clear of the sea; within the hulls, sailors and passengers, clinging to rafters, benches, posts, kneedeep in rank water and debris, had long given up attempts at guiding the ships, when the hull of one ship came to a scraping jarring sudden stop against an abrupt rise in the sea floor; Bahman hit his head against a rafter and lost the hold he had maintained on his mother; some ships went beyond the first before coming to a similar stop, others stopped behind it; some of the hopeless voyagers lay unconscious where they had fallen, some asleep, but the hardier among them ventured onto the decks once more and stared, amazed, at a long white beach, bright with the sun, and a soft green forest beyond; birds skimmed the sea, driftwood approached them, blackfaced monkeys chattered and screamed from tall swaying coconut trees, and brown skinny fishermen with white cloths wrapped around their loins stared back at them from the shore; to the left a bay held an armada of dhows, sails furled. The fishermen launched canoes, climbed into them from the water, and paddled noisily toward the ships which had run aground. The Persians girded themselves at first for an attack, noting, despite their travails, the advantage of their war weapons over the fishermen's harpoons, knives, and paddles – but the first canoes greeted them like heroes with hosannas, flowers, coconut milk, invited them to the shore, and provided shelter and food, a feast of rice, a fish curry, and toddy.

Jadhav Rana, the rajah of Sanjan, the fishing village near which the ships had been beached, met officially with the Persians less than a month after their arrival. A darbar was conducted on a wide flat maidan. Jadhav Rana wore a long violet satin robe, red satin slippers,

23

and a diadem of gold with a ruby centerpiece. He sat on a covered throne with embroidered drapes surrounded by noblemen in satin and velvet robes and turbans and guards in white with spears glittering in the sun. He raised his hand and the Persians were brought into the centre of the assembly and invited to tell their story. The most senior of the dasturs, each of whom wore a white cotton turban and robe bound by a red sash around the waist, had been elected spokesman. Jadhav Rana felt sorry for the Persians but was uncomfortable with their stern warlike appearance. "This is a sad story," he said when the dastur was finished. "What you wish – a place to stay where you may worship freely, where you may cultivate the soil so that you are not burdensome to others – is fine and honourable, but it is not that simple. Let me show you how it is."

He clapped his hands twice and a jug of milk, filled to the brim, was brought out. "Sanjan is like this jug of milk," he said. "There is no room for more."

The old dastur reached into his robe for a coin. "Your Highness," he said, slipping the coin carefully into the jug without spilling a drop, "we Persians will be as the coin is in the milk. You will not even know we are there."

The crowd applauded the dastur; Jadhav Rana was impressed but did not smile. "This is well," he said, "but a coin is tribute, and the hospitality which can be bought with a coin is not the hospitality of Sanjan. How will you repay our hospitality?"

The dastur dropped a pinch of sugar into the milk, taking care once more not to spill even a drop. "Your Highness," he said, "as the sugar sweetens the milk so shall we endeavor to sweeten your lives with our industry."

Members of the crowd jumped as they cheered. Jadhav Rana smiled and gave his consent but also named five conditions: the Persians were to give him a full explanation of their religion, they were to adopt Gujarati (the language of Sanjan) as their own, they were to adopt the local forms of dress, to surrender their weapons, and conduct their ceremonies after nightfall to avoid influencing the Hindus. Bahman hated to give up his sword but his mother gaily took it from him. "We have finally come through the long tunnel of war," she said. "For what do you need this now?"

Bapaiji

Navsari

Seen from above Bombay is a doglegged peninsula jutting into the Arabian Sea. It is hot, as much of India is hot, but were it less of a peninsula, were it further inland like Dehli, it would be at least less humid. Dehli is hot, but dry. In Bombay, no sooner has one taken a bath than the last drops of water, no matter how cool, mingle with the first drops of sweat so that even the most absorbent clothing becomes immediately damp. Even the green in the landscape looks a denser green as if swollen with the humidity.

I hate the hot season, but that is not the only reason I insisted that Mom buy a new air conditioner before we arrived. When we were young, Rusi and I would lug the mattresses from our beds every night during the hot season to Mom and Dad's bedroom because it was air-conditioned. We laid the mattresses on the cool tile floor between Mom's bed and the Grundig radiogram. The black rubber strip around the doorframe, clearly visible to me on the floor, insulating the cool air within the room, insulated us even more cozily from the outside world. Sometimes, after the lights were out, I would listen quietly as Mom and Dad talked; sometimes, Rusi and I would join in; it made us feel grown up. The low hum of the air conditioner, the clean clear cool air, the warmth of the blanket, the friendly darkness with Mom and Dad nearby, lulled me into a deeper sleep than I would get in my own room.

Mom got rid of the air conditioner soon after Dad died, by which time I was already in Aquihana. She had always mistrusted it as she mistrusted anything that had not been a part of her childhood, from the Grundig radiogram to the pocket calculator Rusi brought back for her from the States – she preferred to do her hisabs in longhand.

The new air conditioner meant more to me than relief from the heat, more than a return to what I had before the womb. How can I explain it? Sealed into my air conditioned room, with its preternatural hum, I imagined myself in the belly of a whale, journeying through an amniotic ocean as ancient as an Indian age. I closed my eyes and the Kingdom of God appeared, greater, more rewarding, more appealing than anything in my life – but I won't say anymore about it yet because saying too much too soon I would only lose credibility.

The first time Bapaiji "spoke" to me she said, "Array, my American grandson, Homi, this is your bapaiji speaking, not your mamaiji – or are you too much of an American now to remember what little Gujarati you learned so eagerly from me?" I recognized her immediately by her irony: I hated Gujarati. I hated it because she was the only person with whom I spoke it and that was the only reason I had to learn it; she should have learned English if it meant that much to her to speak with Rusi and me. After all, I spoke English with my parents, other relatives (my mamaiji, whom I called Granny, could not praise the English enough), friends; and Hindi with the servants, banias, and whoever else didn't speak English; Bapaiji wouldn't even speak Hindi.

But Bapaiji lived in Navsari, a small town about two hundred miles north of Bombay, we visited her for just two weeks during Christmas every year, and Mom said it wasn't too much to ask to humour her during that time. So I sat with Bapaiji in the long enclosed front verandah with a black slate in my lap and a hard chalk pencil in my hand for an hour every morning of our visit. Rusi was exempted from these sessions because at first he was too young, and by the time he was old enough Bapaiji had realized what I could have told her all along: two weeks a year is not enough to learn a language.

In the afternoons I would be in the same verandah with Mom, she on the bench swing, I with my cane (because of my polio) on one of the innumerable couches, with my *Fundamental English* text, except now I would use a notebook and a lead pencil, and, after my tenth year, a fountain pen. Bapaiji slept in the afternoons, otherwise she might have had something to say about it; she hated to waste anything, even paper when I could have used a slate. I remember her house, Hill Bungalow, best for its chairs and its photographs. Chairs of all kinds, recliners, rockers, upright chairs, with cushions, without, upholstered chairs, upholstered couches, spring couches, settees, loveseats, wooden benches, stools, footrests (my favourite was an upholstered elephant's foot for a low stool; it was just my size; it even had toenails), lined the perimeter of the verandah (the bench swing was in the middle), also of the sitting room. Bapaiji's favourite chair was a cane recliner with slats under its arms which came out to provide leg rests so that she could lie back as if she were in a hammock. Some of the chairs, the ones beyond the doors to the sitting room, were never used. I hated this part of the verandah because the chairs (the photographs, too) were covered with dust. Once, when I was five, I wrote my name in the dust on the seat of a wooden rocker, in English; I erased it immediately thinking Bapaiji would have wanted me to write it in Gujarati. Suddenly, the rocker seemed too clean, and I thought I might have to dust the entire section of the verandah to hide the evidence of my crime – but the clean seat of the rocker went unnoticed and by the end of my visit the rocker looked as if it had never been disturbed.

For every chair there were at least five photographs on the walls, each bordered by an elaborate wooden frame, of *all* our relatives (which meant *all* the Parsis in Navsari; all Parsis in Navsari have photographs on their walls of all the Parsis in Navsari), single portraits, duos, trios, larger groups, at navjotes, weddings, standing like schoolchildren in single file along stoops, seated like prophets on the chairs lining the walls in the sitting room, arranged in studios with dramatic jungle backdrops, ruin backdrops, the men wearing white ceremonial dress with high collars (satin daglas, cotton daglis), and ceremonial headgear (paghris, fehntas), the women covering their heads with their saris, gazing into the distance as if they had weightier matters to consider than photographs, the children with large round eyes as if they had something to hide. The wedges of space hidden between the photographs and walls were thick with dust and cobwebs.

Bapaiji knew her irony about my affinity for Gujarati was not lost on me. "I was only kidding," she said, "as you Americans like to say." She cleared her throat loudly, like a man, and spat. I wondered what she had spat into; I couldn't see her, just hear her. In Navsari she had kept a tin plate under her bed full of ash into which she spat periodically through the night.

"Don't be surprised that you understand me so clearly," she continued. "I know as much English as you know Gujarati, but here words don't mean a thing, only the thoughts. Whatever is said is clear, as if by magic, to whomever it is addressed. You would understand me if I spoke Zulu."

What surprised me was not that I understood her, but that I heard her at all; my problem was not understanding her, but overcoming my delusion (I was sure that was what it was); but she continued speaking as if she had read my mind.

"Just to put you at your ease," she said, "to convince you that this is really me, though I am dead as you know the dead, and not someone playing a trick, let me remind you of the time of your operation."

I knew immediately that she was referring to my first tonsillectomy. I had been four; I had been given an injection; the doctor had asked me to count to ten; I had thought that too easy and counted down instead of up, from twenty instead of ten; the doctor had been surprised; Mom had said brightly, "He's a very intelligent child." The next thing I remembered a clock struck five; it was a pendulum clock, across the room from my bed, which struck just as I regained consciousness. Everyone was smiling; the doctor said I shouldn't say anything unless there was something I wanted; he showed me my tonsils in a water glass, said everything had gone well; there was all the ice cream I wanted because it was good for my throat; but all I wanted was to gargle. "Kogra," I said, or tried to say, to Bapaiji, the Gujarati word for "gargle", but she kept shooing away a crow cawing at the window, thinking he was bothering me – the Gujarati word for crow is "kaagro". The charade was repeated tirelessly until she recognized what I really wanted. The incident never ceased to amuse her, particularly since the crow had proven too stubborn to be shooed away. She repeated the incident once more to prove to me that she was whom she said she was.

"Things seem different here, wherever this is, but they're not. Everything is spirit – by that I do not mean there are souls flashing around like fireflies. Everything is as you want it but nothing is tangible. I am a man here; I wear pants, I walk more quickly, upright, directly forward without that ridiculous waddle with which so many women are afflicted, without those huge breasts like a cow elephant's which always got in my way; I even have a deeper voice – you will doubtless find this comical, but it is what I had always wanted, to be a man, to do the things men did – but, and here's the irony, I did more in Navsari as a woman than I can do here as a man. Here I have no effect, only illusions.

"Your mamaiji, Granny as you called her, has her own illusions too. Here you can have anything you want – anything, as long as it doesn't interfere with what someone else might want – and what does she choose? A house with high ceilings, crystal chandeliers, custom-made furniture, paintings on the wall, a verandah just like the one from which she stared at Bombay everyday – the same house, Zephyr, in which she lived so much of her life, even the dust is the same.

"Your pappa is also here. You know how much he loved the UK – well, here he dresses as if he'd never left, as if he were always going to the the-A-tah, with his top hat and tails, twirling his stick as if he were an Englishman. When I first saw him in London I laughed so hard my sides hurt. After that he didn't put on any airs with me; he even hid his stick behind himself as if he thought I would not notice; I noticed, of course, but didn't say anything. I had made my point.

"And if he's not twirling his stick he's skipping around in his kilt playing bagpipes, jumping in the air like a dancing girl at the cinema. I hated that music – I still do – it sounds like snake-charming music; and the problem with those kilts is you wear nothing underneath. I could never stand show-offs, but who would even want to look at *that*?

"It is a strange numbing feeling when you know everything there is to know about everyone but remain unable to do anything about it. I am a man but without the power that goes with being a man, your mamaiji thinks she has what she wants but it's the same as what she had before, and your pappa chose to be in the UK so he would be far from me but he's closer to me now than when he was in Bombay. Be careful what you ask for; it is not always the same as what you might want.

"But I am not getting through to you, Homi. You are still fighting me, still thinking I am a delusion. I thought it would be clear to you now, but for a scientist you are not thinking very clearly. When you invented your memo-machine you cut into the Memory of the Soul. What I showed you, the Arabs and the Persians, were scoops from this memory. I have heard you say so often that the brain is like an iceberg – the tip holding the living memory, the submerged the Memory of the Soul. A drop of water can become lost in the ocean; it can also become the ocean; I am giving you the chance to become the ocean. You were so obsessed with reliving the times you spent with your American muddum that you didn't even care about the cost to yourself. You would have sacrificed your gift, the brain of an Einstein, for a muddum who slept with waiters and barkeeps. She saw in you an exotic, a scientist, a cripple, someone – some*thing* – different, nothing more, and once she had added you to her collection she lost interest, but you, of course, could not let her go."

I began to understand, to recognize the importance of the memo-scan, what Bapaiji had called my memo-machine. It can be used to scan memory traces recorded in convolutions in the brain, rather like a movie projector can be used to scan a movie on a screen, speeding it up, slowing it down, until the required episode has been located, until the required memory has been located to be relived as if it were occurring for the first time – but there is a catch: the memory traces are recorded within convolutions in the brain; the deeper the convolution the more vivid the memory, and the more frequently the memory is replayed the deeper the convolution becomes; the process can be repeated an indeterminate number of times depending on how vivid the memory is to begin with – how deep the convolution is to begin with – before the depth of the convolution becomes like an incision in the brain. Beyond that point the brain cells decay with, understandably, deleterious effects on the rest of the body.

A man in baggy white pants, a smooth white dagla, and shining black fehnta, sat on a grey wooden chair, leaning aggressively forward, one arm outstretched, the hand resting confidently on the head of a walking stick, its metal tip standing by a black, well polished, patent leather, out-turned boot, the other arm akimbo with its fist turned outward at the waist. His face was smooth, fair, with the skin of a young boy, but his expression, particularly the barely perceptible lift at the corners of his wide mouth, indicated a deeper, broader experience. I didn't know who the man was but I knew I had seen his face, certainly his mouth, before. I recognized his surroundings more easily: he was seated in Bapaiji's sitting room with all the chairs and photographs, the clock behind him whose weights had to be adjusted daily so the cuckoo would call at the appropriate times from behind one of the two tiny doors followed by the German boy fiddler behind the other, the swing doors one might expect to see in a wild west saloon to the left of the clock, leading to the dining room, and the old Murphy radio in its wood and glass case to his right giving out the news in Gujarati. The man smiled as if he knew I was watching him, held his walking stick in one hand, and turned off the radio with the other. I recognized Bapaiji's walking stick as soon as I saw its ivory-knobbed handle. The man's smile deepened as if he understood my deepening comprehension. "You are doing well, Homi, very well. Your faith is stronger than I thought. You can see me now as well as hear me. It only took a little rest, a little trust. Don't look so surprised. I told you I was a man here. We can have whatever we want here as long as it does not interfere with what someone else wants, so here I am. Take a good look. How do you like my fehnta? You think it is just another fehnta, but you know so little. All fehntas were individually made. So much care was taken. But now there are no more fehnta makers; there is no money in it. Men are all wearing paghris now instead which they buy from the store. What they gain in money what they lose in majesty. But take a good look, no? at my dagla, at my pants. Convince yourself who this is. There is no rush. After all, this is not the first time I have worn pants."

But as I watched the panorama changed, almost as if to defy my attempt to place it in a familiar context. An unseen camera appeared to pan from Bapaiji's face to the window, to the mango and tamarind trees outside, to a ragtag bunch of children playing Pakadav,

Catching Cook as we called it in English, Tag in American. There was only one girl among them; I didn't have to look hard to know it was Bapaiji; her wide sharp jaw was unmistakable. As I watched, one of the boys lunged at her and she fell. That was when I became aware of another girl, standing to the side, pretending not to see, appearing more embarrassed than Bapaiji as Bapaiji's dusty skirt rode to her thighs. "Come on, now, Banu," the second girl called. "Food is ready. Mamma is waiting. Come, all of you, Jamshed, Jehangir, Savak, Kavas. Food is ready. It will get cold."

Bapaiji laughed, punching the boy who had knocked her down, who tagged her again so she would chase him. "Are you coming or no, Banu?" the girl persisted, her brow furrowing as if she were annoyed. "Food is getting cold."

"Then let it get cold." Bapaiji tagged the boy again, laughing so she was almost out of breath.

The game was over. The others started going home. "We are going, Banu," the girl said, her hands on her hips. "If you are coming, then come now."

"Coming, coming, Dhunmai. Wait, no, you all? I am just coming."

Bapaiji caught up with the others walking back to the house. "I swear, Dhunmai, sometimes you are like an old woman."

"At least, I have some shame," Dhunmai said, her voice shaking. "Just wait until Mamma hears about this."

"About what?"

"Just wait."

"About what?"

"I said no? Just wait."

Bapaiji mimicked Dhunmai. "I said no? Just wait."

Dhunmai remained obstinately – ominously – silent after that during the walk home through narrow wadis, over mud roads, with the smell of dust and dung and hay in the air. Bapaiji and her brothers happily ignored her. But Dhunmai's silence broke as soon as they got home. "And she was just lying there with her skirt up and all the boys laughing at how shameless she was." Her brothers said they were all just having fun, no one thought about shame, but Dhunmai wasn't finished. "And who has to keep the time while everyone is having fun? Who has to go and call them when food is ready as if I don't have something better to do? Who does all the work while everyone is playing the fool?"

"Wah-wah," Bapaiji said, shaking her head primly. "As if only you do work around here. Who puts the dung on the floor in the morning? And who lets down the mosquito nets at night?" Dhunmai was too squeamish to line the floor with dung which was purchased every day for two or three pice a basket from vendors at the door and mixed with sand from the talao, or to kill the mosquitos within the nets at night as Bapaiji did by clapping her hands so that they became red splotches on her palms.

"And who does the sweeping every morning?" Dhunmai was screaming. "And who fills up the matkas with water from the well?And who puts the chalk patterns on the doorsteps? Do you think we can afford dubras to do all the work or what?" All these chores were done by the women before the men awakened. Their mother burned sandalwood in the looban, took it around the house, and kept it burning all day so the house would always be full of its smell.

Their father, who had been waiting with their mother, looked at their mother as if this were her concern alone. She had long accepted that his primary interest was his work, the experiments he conducted as a perfumer and chemist discovering new cosmetics and medicines, which made most people avoid him because he smelled constantly of chemicals. "Be quiet now, Dhunmai," she said. "What is all this screaming? And, Banu, you are not to play with boys. You are a girl. You have to wear skirts. You cannot do things boys do. Now, everyone, be quiet. Food is getting cold."

The next day Bapaiji wore her closest brother's pants, bunching her dress into its waist, making more holes in the belt to make it fit, rolling up the cuffs. The boys laughed; Dhunmai scowled; their mother smiled; their father was in a room to the side pouring a bubbling green liquid from a beaker into a test tube.

Hu-tu-tu

Bapaiji took a deep breath, crossed the line into the dusty combat zone of the game, and began her "Hu-tu-tu-tu" in a barely audible tone. The object of the game was to step behind the enemy line, touch one of the enemy, and return behind your own line without losing your breath. If the "Hu-tu-tu-tu" of the invading member was cut short the enemy scored a point. Bapaiji had her eye on Adi; if she could get away with touching him it would be a coup. He pretended not to care about the way he looked, but took a lot of trouble to look that way; he never cut his hair, but washed it and oiled it and combed it to make it look as if he had just been in a fight; he had no brains but all the girls liked him because he was the tallest person in Navsari, almost six feet, and the school's best athlete; the girls' parents liked him because his father was rich, a sweets merchant, the owner of *Ghadiali ni Mithai* in the Mota Bajar. Bapaiji knew all these things, she had even seen Dhunmai staring at Adi when she thought no one was looking, but Bapaiji liked Adi most for something else: he also did wood carvings, delicate work, faces and animals and landscapes in relief, ornamented frames for photographs with frogs and snakes in the borders, and figurines of elephants, camels, and buffaloes. He always kept four whittling knives with him for degrees of fineness, and any chance he got he would dig into the small burlap sack he carried, pull out a piece of wood, and carve it.

Bapaiji was wearing Kavas's pants as usual, but she no longer moved as easily as she used to. Her hips were still skinny enough to fit into a boy's pants, but her breasts were too big for comfort; they hurt just bouncing up and down so violently during the game. The boys' attitude toward her had changed as well. They spoke to her less and

36

touched her more, particularly when it was time for them to drag her back across the home line. They were rougher with her, they hurt her more, but she didn't know what to do about it. It was becoming increasingly difficult, even for her, to ignore herself as a woman.

Adi was watching her through narrowed eyes under an untidy mat of curly black hair plastered with sweat to his forehead, but she couldn't be sure that his watchfulness owed everything to the game. "Tu-tu-tu-tu-tu-tu," she continued under her breath, an inch away from the enemy line, an armslength away from Adi, a caterpillar of sweat beading her upper lip; once she had stepped across the line she would lose the element of surprise and have to move quickly to touch one of the enemy and get behind her own line, but the longer she waited the sooner she would be out of breath. She looked at Adi as if to size up her chances, but she found herself noting instead how fine his skin was, how sleek and thick his eyebrows, how delicate and pink his lips, how red his tongue which slid over his lips as if they might have been too dry. He puckered his lips, "Tu-tu-tu-tu," as if he were mocking her, but she saw in those puckered lips the promise of a kiss. She puckered her own lips more firmly, raised her voice, "Tu-tu-tu-tu," but she didn't want to cross the line because that would be the signal for everyone to start grabbing her again. She couldn't say when she had begun to resent the touch of their hands; it was as if a favourite shirt had suddenly grown too small for her to wear; in the same way this game which she had enjoyed had developed an undergame which made her queasy, what had once been fun had developed into a pretext for something else. "Tu-tu-tu-tu," she concluded, almost spitting the last syllable at Adi, and walked away from the game. "I don't want to play anymore," she said.

Both sides were bewildered: "Array, but you must finish the game"; "Array, but you are our best player"; "Array, but we were just winning"; "Array, but what is the matter, no?" She said nothing was the matter, she didn't want to play, she was going home. Adi said he would walk home with her, then the game could go on with one less player on each side. She said, "Okay." On the way he said. "It is still early. Let us walk by the Lunsi Kui talao." She said "Okay" again. She had become uncharacteristically quiet and acquiescent since he had offered to walk her home. The gul mohor trees seemed more orange than she could remember, the lotuses on the talao more pink, and the vines under them more densely green. Adi said little other than to ask her if she wanted to go deeper into the wilderness. She knew there were monkeys, jackals, snakes in the forest beyond, but she said, "Okay." She felt safe with Adi; besides, the animals would not bother them, especially not in the daylight, unless they bothered them first. She stumbled over the underbrush as Adi, striding firmly, led her along a narrow beaten path, until they came to perhaps the largest of the banyan trees in the forest with sturdy brown vines from which they could swing and thick high widespread roots within which they could be enclosed. "I come here when I want to be by myself," Adi said. He seemed shy, unable to meet her eyes, as if he were showing her something private and precious. She nodded. "It's very peaceful." He pulled a knife from his pocket, a piece of roughly carved wood from his sack, and began working on it. She saw it was a squirrel but said nothing, seating herself on a high root, watching him work, listening to the birdsong of the koels and sparrows and mynahs and bulbuls and crows. She didn't notice the passage of time until he suggested going home. As they approached the town again he said, "Would you like to come to the forest again sometime?" She said "Okay" without looking at him, without giving him even a smile to show how she felt.

When she saw him again the next day in the school playground he held something in his hands behind him. "I have got something for you. What is it, do you think?" Bapaiji tried to dart behind him but he was too quick. "You must guess," he said. "Sun chhe?" ("What is it?")

Bapaiji ran around him again, chanting a foolish rhyme that children used when playing:

Sun chhe?	What is it?
Saru chhe.	It is fine.
Dunda leke	With a stick
Maru chhe.	I'll break your spine.

Adi eluded her easily again because he knew she was only playing, but he didn't make her guess anymore because he could see she didn't want to. "It is a walking stick. I carved it myself."

Bapaiji had been boisterous before only because she didn't know how to show her pleasure that he had brought her something. When he showed her the stick she grabbed it from him, still nervous, and walked around him, bent and hobbling like a cripple. "Why is this? What is all this?" she said, talking so quickly he could hardly understand her, walking so quickly around him because she couldn't face him that he could hardly follow her. "Do you think I am an old woman? Is that what you think?"

"No, no," he said, laughing at her craziness. "It is for clearing the underbrush when we go to the forest. Look, no? It has got a metal stop at the end. And look at the handle. It has got a fine grip. Try to swing it. You will see what I mean."

Bapaiji looked at the stick more closely; the bottom was stopped with iron, the body was smooth and cylindrical, the handle was carved with a snake head with grooves along its neck for grip. "It is beautiful," Bapaiji said, stealing a quick look at Adi. "Thank you." He was smiling. She touched his cheek with her hand.

They said nothing about their meetings to anyone and no one said anything to them; Bapaiji's parents were too preoccupied – her father with his experiments, her mother with the household – to keep a lookout on each of their children; but Dhunmai's suspicions were aroused and she came into the forest once to look for them. "Are you there, Banu?" she called. "Food is getting cold." She hadn't meant to call out loud; she had wanted to surprise them; but as she got deeper into the forest she got scared and wanted their reassurance, so she called, telling herself that she didn't want to embarrass them by catching them unawares. "Are you there, Banu? I thought I saw you going in."

They were not far when they heard her call. Adi threw everything into his sack and jumped into the tree; Bapaiji followed him immediately. They didn't mind being found together but they didn't want to give Dhunmai the satisfaction of finding them. Too late they realized they had left one of Adi's whittling knives on the ground; there wasn't enough time to get it before Dhunmai came; there was a chance Dhunmai might not see it, but sometimes when the shadows changed in the wind, the steel glinted in the sunlight.

Behind Bapaiji, from the thick of the foliage, hung the tails of three monkeys. She would not have paid them any attention; there were hundreds of monkeys hidden in the foliage, their tails hanging like brown furry ribbons; but on this occasion Bapaiji thought differently. She grabbed the three tails and yanked as hard as she could. The idyll of the forest was slashed as if by a bolt of lightning: the monkeys shrieked *oop-oop-oop*, setting the birds screaming, and in the distance a wolf howled as if it were nighttime; but woven with their screams, as brilliantly as the centrepiece of a peacock's fantail, was Dhunmai's screech as she turned and ran the way she had come. The monkeys continued shrieking, *oop-oop*-OOP-OOP, baring their teeth, whooping around Bapaiji and Adi as if the trees had suddenly grown too hot to touch; Adi laughed so hard he fell out of the tree, and when Bapaiji reached to catch him he pulled her down with him, but they kept on laughing even when the air was knocked out of them by their fall.

The forest was much denser in Bapaiji's time than when I was growing up; the talao is still full of lotuses like a floating pink and white garden, but Navsari is far more industrialized now, its major industry being diamond and ruby cutting; the ground was as thickly matted with leaves and grass as a rug; there were more wolves, water buffalo, snakes, reptiles and wild birds then, but whereas the animal kingdom was very much in retreat in my time I still remember the monkeys and one rather frightening incident associated with them.

There is a fountain in the park near the Lunsi Kui talao with frogs on lily pads, warty toads, tadpoles, and goldfish. I enjoyed watching them and playing with them so much, pushing my cane after them in the water, that I invariably gave Rusi's Goanese ayah, Julie, a difficult time when she said we must go home. She was almost too patient, so much so that on one occasion we were the last to leave the park. We had to cut across a forested area to get to the main road. It was twilight and there were no lights along the narrow beaten path, but we could see the distant street lamps toward which we were headed. Julie carried Rusi in her arms since he was only two, while I hobbled along by her side suddenly subdued by the dark, the solitude, the sound of the crickets, and the gaze of perhaps a hundred monkeys gathered on either side as if we were rulers parading for subjects; I felt their hatred as if they knew we had diminished their forest. It was a relief to reach the main road; it was even more of a relief when, at a later date, the monkeys were all exterminated (as the forests shrank they had become bolder, stealing things from houses, leaving their odour in the rooms) – my imagination, running amok, had conjured a monkey revolution in which they had all chased the wicked little lame boy who had chased goldfish with his cane.

"You were still young when Dhunmai died, but you must remember her. You must remember at least the kharia party at which you told the fox story I had taught you." Bapaiji's voice-over faded; the panorama of herself and Adi laughing, out of breath from their fall, undulated like a backdrop, until that too faded and we were back in her sitting room with the photographs and chairs. A boy stood with his right leg in braces (myself!), holding a cane in a space that had been cleared for him amidst about twenty guests, some of whom were still eating the kharia and chori on banana leaves on the rough grey tesselated stone floor. I was smiling, well pleased with myself, hardly able to stand still while Mom wiped my mouth and face still sticky and brown from the kharia. When she was finished I started the story, speaking with confidence, turning around periodically to include all my listeners.

I remembered the story easily as I watched myself tell it, of Mr and Mrs Fox who were hungry but had no firewood with which to cook puris. They visited Mr Tiger in the forest promising to make him a puri if he would give them some firewood. Mr Tiger gave them the firewood, but the Foxes were so hungry that they ate his puri as well and hid in baskets of straw when he came. While Mr Tiger was prowling about their house the Foxes felt they had to fart, the consequence of the puris, and cautioned each other to do it quietly-quietly. Mrs Fox farted quietly-quietly, but Mr Fox could not. He had to fart BOOM-BANG FATAANG! The straw baskets in which they were hiding exploded so violently that Mr Tiger was scared away and the Foxes lived happily ever after.

41

"You had told the story many times, but at the kharia party you added a twist: when the fox's wife made the fart you said she made it quietly-quietly – like Dhunmai! And when the fox made his fart he made it BOOM-BANG FATAANG like Bapaiji! I did not mind of course; it was so funny; but Dhunmai sat with a smile like a rubber band.

"Dhunmai never learned anything. Her name was Dhun, of course, but she thought we called her Dhunmai out of respect; it never occurred to her it was because she behaved like an old woman. Everyone, even our father who hardly even spoke to us, called her Dhunmai from the time she was six. No one – except perhaps our mother – even felt sorry for her, and when she died you couldn't have filled even a thimble with everyone's regret for her.

"After the incident with the monkeys in the forest Dhunmai became the least of my problems. No one said anything but in a town like Navsari nothing remains a secret long; everyone is a newspaper. They saw Adi's stick in my hand and that was enough. When my parents heard about it they wanted us to get married, to save my reputation. I hadn't even thought about marriage but I would have suggested nothing else myself – every girl in Navsari wanted to marry Adi – but his parents objected. The Ghadialis were of the priestly class and we, Dhondis, were not. My mother was so offended that she immediately found someone else for me to marry, your bapavaji, your grandfather, Hormusji Behramji Seervai. Not only were the Seervais also of the priestly class but they were richer than the Ghadialis, and Hormusji had a degree in law from a university in Bombay – but I still wanted to marry Adi. Hormusji was nice looking but he was twelve years older than me, his father and his grandfather had elephantiasis, and his mother and sister were hunchbacks; I was afraid my son would be deformed. I tried to explain to my mother that I was going to talk to Adi, that the class difference would not be a problem if he stood his ground firmly; I could not understand why she refused even to listen to me because her own marriage had hardly been orthodox; she had been widowed at fourteen by her first husband to whom she had been married when she was only six months old, before she had married my father, the family's apothecary, against the wishes of her own family (he was only a tinkerer, they said, not a real doctor)."

A young girl in a thin bright short-sleeved dress, white socks, and dusty heavy-heeled brown shoes, rapped sharply on the frosted glass of a sliding window on which was printed:

DHONDI
DISPENSARY

She felt her heart pound as loudly as she had rapped on the glass. She chewed the tip of one of her pigtails in anticipation, absently admiring the tiny pink ribbon she had tied into a bow at the end. When the window was slid to one side she looked first at the weathered bricks in the wall visible where some of the yellow powdery plaster had cracked.

"Yes? What is it?"

The voice behind the window was gruff, but it was one she frequently played back for herself. Looking into the narrow rectangle of the open window she saw his thin long face with the sparsely cultivated goatee, the hurricane lantern hanging from the ceiling behind him, and handed him a folded piece of paper. "My mother is sick," she said.

He took the paper, hardly unconscious of the low neck of her blue dress, her fingers caressing the silken red ribbon in her hair, turning away to hide his smile as he recognized the prescription on the piece of paper once more. He had lost count of the number of times she had brought him the same piece of paper; he had mixed a compound into a harmless solution with water each time; he had also returned the prescription each time because he didn't think she knew how to write and he wanted her to come back. He had followed her on more than one occasion and seen her pour the solution by the roadside when she thought no one was looking; he had been intrigued enough to find out more about her. There was no one else in the dispensary when he gave her the solution that day. He didn't know when he might get another chance. "Wait," he said. "Don't go. I am having something to say."

"What?"

43

"Wait. I will come out."

When he came through the door she was surprised how short he was, but it made him appear more approachable; there was a step up going into the dispensary. There was a smell of chemicals about him, but that only made him appear different. He didn't waste any time. "Will you marry me?" He had thought it all over. Most parents found his interest in perfumery too eccentric a hobby to be tolerated in a son-in-law; it commanded too much of his time and affection and might adversely affect his ability to provide for a family with both love and money. But this girl was compromised too; her chances were no better than his because she was a widow – but she had pursued him, flattering him, allowing, however discreetly, for no misunderstanding of her intentions.

The girl smiled but turned away, blushing as if she, not he, had proposed. He touched her for the first time, by her waist with both hands from behind. She turned again to face him, her face full of light. "Yes," she said. "Yes, I will marry you."

Bapaiji went on a fast to change her mother's mind. On the third day of the fast she arranged to meet with Adi at their usual place in the forest to talk things over. If they kept up a strong front she knew there was nothing their parents could do, but Adi was less sure. "If our parents are against it, then it is hopeless," he cried.

"Why? If we just get married they will come round to our way of thinking. Once it is done they are not going to hold a grudge for the rest of their lives."

"They might do that, no? What we will do then?"

"What is to do? We will be together, no? We will have our friends, no?"

"But they will cut me off from the sweet shop. What I will do then?"

"You will start another sweet shop. You will do whatever you want to do."

"But *Ghadiali ni Mithai* has been going a long time. If they keep me I will be able to open more shops. I will go to Surat and Bombay and Delhi and Kashmir on business. I will go to UK for a holiday."

Bapaiji knew then his mind had long been made up. She said, "If we want to do something we will do it, whatever comes in the way," but she knew it was a losing battle.

"But there is no guarantee," he said. "This is a guarantee."

Bapaiji saw how he was; she had only been fooling herself about how he really was. "There are no guarantees," she said. "Only cowards live by guarantees." She felt a sudden emptiness. Adi stood waiting as if for her blessing to leave, but she was too angry, too disgusted, to give him what he wanted. "Then go, no? Why you are still here? Go to Bombay, go to UK, go where you want, go to hell. But do not look for me again. I will not be here. Go, no? Why you are not going? What is there now?"

He left with a forlorn look, as if he had been misunderstood, as if she had wronged him. She waited until she could no longer see him, then thrashed the trees and bushes around her with her stick. Her rage had just begun to die when she realized she had knocked a cobra from its rest. The snake raised its small black hooded head to strike. Bapaiji was transfixed momentarily by the wicked glinting beady eyes, the narrow flickering ribbonlike tongue, but she struck first with the snake-headed handle of her stick, hitting the cobra on the side of its head, and then again at its head where it fell on the rock. She broke its head with her second blow but kept beating it until the head of her stick broke off and rolled behind the rock. The snake was dead but it still moved amidst the carnage of its own blood and white flesh. Bapaiji hit it two or three more times to be sure it was dead, then threw away the stick. She went home, broke her fast with a slice of bread and jam and a drink of toddy, and told her mother she was willing to marry whomever she wanted.

Things became clearer: in the evenings Bapaiji and Mom went to the club together in Bapaiji's green two-seater cycle rickshaw, which would then return to the house for Rusi and me. The evenings were uncomfortable for us because we spoke little Gujarati and hated the fuss the old ladies made over Bapaiji's grandchildren when we arrived or during their turns as dummies at bridge. Bapaiji and Mom, intent on their games (canasta, samba, rummy, whatever), hardly noticed us then. Eight card tables and two carom tables were arranged every evening behind the club by the badminton courts, or, if it rained, on the verandah in the back.

The club was a long single-storey stone and brick bungalow with a tiled gable roof, long verandahs in the front and back, a long room in the middle with two table tennis tables set lengthwise, cupboards along the walls for the decks of cards, badminton racquets, shuttlecocks, table tennis racquets and balls, draughts boards, draughtsmen, and carom men, and Bapaiji's portrait conspicuously in the centre of the wall (she was the president of the club), a library on one side of the room and an all-purpose room and bathroom on the other. One caretaker, Thakor, a bony hollow-cheeked man in a white Nehru cap, who always said "Yes-yes, of course-yes" to anything Bapaiji asked of him, managed everything.

I spent much of my time on the swings because they were furthest from the club, or reading a book I had brought with me in the library of the club: Rusi would either join me on the swings or play badminton or table tennis. We never ceased to procrastinate when it was time to go to the club; often, to the chagrin of our rickshawwallah, we would ask him to take us via detours, around the Lunsi Kui talao or through the Mota Bajar. The bajar was always crowded at that time; bicycle bells rang and motor rickshaws hooted incessantly; people, cows, goats, and dogs moved around the stalls, shops, and caravans of vegetables, fruits, stationery, clothes, luggage, tools, building materials, and the homes of the hawkers who often lived behind their shops, so that seen from above the ensemble might have resembled a continuously shifting kaleidoscope, and when the occasional automobile came by the crowd parted and swallowed up the path behind it like the Red Sea might have done for the Israelites. On one such occasion the rickshaw developed a puncture, and Rusi and I were waiting for the rickshaw-wallah to fix it, when a tall man with a long face called us into his sweet shop. He was the tallest man I had seen until then, but his face was even more memorable — as if filled with regret for innumerable lost opportunities, and old with a bristly white stubble as if he had lost interest in his appearance. He looked happy to see us, but it was a transparent happiness that might have dissolved had someone questioned its cover. He said nothing but got behind the glass cases filled with pyramids of round laddoos, fat pendas, and squares of burfees ornamented with spangles of silver paper, big puddings of red and green and orange and yellow halvahs, brittle khatais wrapped in tissue paper with the ends twisted like the crepe paper ends of party firecrackers, balls of ghulab jamans and white rasgullahs in thick honeyed syrups, interlocking concentric circles of gleaming orange knotty deepfried jalebis with sugary casings and syrupy centres, and sweet white suttarfanis like flattened birdsnests with badams and pistas, and began heaping the various sweets onto two plates which he offered us. We ate the sweets as much to please him as ourselves; he might have cried had we refused them.

I remember the shop best for all the wood carvings of animals on exhibition: monkeys, elephants, camels, buffalo, deer, even dogs, cats, and mice. I picked a walnut-sized sandalwood elephant when he asked me which piece I wanted (Rusi picked a tiger); I kept the elephant for good luck even after the veneer came off when I accidentally washed it along with the pants from which I had forgotten to remove it in a washing machine years later in Aquihana. I gave it finally (it might have been just last month, but I cannot be sure of such things anymore) to Candace Kirchner as a token of my love.

When the rickshaw was ready he filled two blue rectangular boxes with a picture of the blueskinned Prince Ram drawing his bow and the lovely voluptuous Sita by his side with more sweets, and insisted we take them with us. We took the boxes and, at a discreet distance from the shop, gave them to the rickshaw-wallah to take home to his family. Bapaiji would have been annoyed with us for accepting food from a stranger (she was annoyed even when we accepted refreshments from friends of hers whom we visited because she was afraid her friends would think she did not feed us enough – which she didn't, doling out portions at dinner as if we lived in a Dickensian workhouse) – except now he seemed less of a stranger than I had thought at the time.

Hormusji Behramji Seervai

A whirlwind of images followed, not unlike those sped up in silent movies, culminating in a series of fierce looking, bushy-browed, clubfooted men seated in wood and wicker chairs and sour-faced hunchbacked women leaning over them from behind. The last image was the most horrific of all: a baby, crying, so small it was nestled in the palm of someone's hand, being immersed in a bucket of milk, barely the suggestion of a struggle as the hand held it under, just bubbles of air breaking the surface of the milk for less than thirty seconds before the surface appeared undisturbed again.

"Do not be so shocked. The baby was made to drink milk. It was illegitimate; it was unwanted; it was the accepted way to get rid of such babies. You didn't think a Seervai would marry a Dhondi unless there was something wrong with him, did you? During the centuries after the Parsis settled in Sanjan to escape the Musalman they wanted only citizenship and commerce; they had had their fill of war. They stayed in Sanjan for three hundred years; their numbers increased; they became farmers, weavers, carpenters, fruit growers, toddy planters; they spread to Cambay, Variav, Ankleswar, Navsari, Surat, Udvada, Bulsar, and finally Bombay. When the Musalman came to India he vanquished their Hindu friends and subjugated the Parsis again, but the Indian Musalman was more benign than the Arabian; he even rewarded the Parsis with land for their industry — what was lost by the sword was won back by the sickle. The sixth Moghal Emperor, Aurangzeb, the son of Shah Jehan the builder of the Taj Mahal, rewarded your great great great great great great grandfather, Temurji Rustamji Seervai, in 1714, with land in Navsari and all the revenue that came with it. That is how the Seervais came by their money. But when they became rich they also became

48

exclusive and for generations they married only their first cousins – which accounts for the deformed ancestors you just saw. Your bapavaji, Hormusji Behramji Seervai, was better looking than the other Seervais, but he too was married first to his first cousin – but she had a baby by someone else, the marriage was annulled, and the baby was made to drink milk. There was little to be said for Hormusji's prospects after that: he was much older than the other eligible Navsari bachelors because he had been married for three years and had spent four years before that in Bombay getting a degree in law; even more important, there were no first cousins left to marry and his name had been touched by scandal after the annulment so that the Seervais were willing to allow even a Dhondi into their family."

When Bapaiji moved in with her in-laws I had a clear picture of the house, Hill Bungalow, with which I was familiar having visited Bapaiji enough times, but the in-laws themselves appeared gnarled, seated in chairs at isolated points in the front compound, clattering their teeth, khut-khut-khut-khut, and shaking twisted walking sticks in the air, reminding me of the Mother Goose rhyme I had played frequently on my old, black, boxlike, wind-up HMV gramophone, whose needle had to be changed every six 78 rpm records:

> *There was a crooked man*
> *and he walked a crooked mile.*
> *He found a crooked sixpence*
> *beside a crooked stile.*
> *He bought a crooked cat*
> *which caught a crooked mouse,*
> *And they all lived together*
> *in a little crooked house.*

Bapaiji's house was not crooked (the images and the rhyme come to mind because of the elephantiasis and hunchbacks in the family – even my own deformities appear less incongruous in this context), but it was not well planned either. It looked fine: double-storeyed, with brick walls, stone floors, a hipped tiled roof, and teak balustrades with cordate and paisley motifs in shades of tan and chocolate enclosing verandahs on each floor; but there were no corridors and sometimes the only way to get from one room to another was through someone else's bedroom.

The toilet was an even stranger feature, built on top of a tower twenty feet from the house but connected to the second floor by a passageway bordered by balustrades and covered by a tiled roof: a four foot square room with a hole in the centre and a wooden collapsible seat hinged onto the wall; a wicker basket, changed every morning by one of the dubras, collected the waste on the ground at the bottom of the deep hole. Bapaiji complained unceasingly of the chhabar created by everyone (first her in-laws through Hormusji, then her in-laws through her son) when cleaning themselves in the room – there was a matka of water outside the toilet and a tumbler to be filled and used for cleaning. I was more concerned that a single tumbler of water would not be enough to clean myself than that the water would splash around the toilet creating the chhabar instead of pouring itself straight into the hole. I sometimes amused myself in the toilet counting the seconds between the release and the cannon-like volley of contact that reverberated up the shaft running the gamut of sounds from SPLAATTT to BOINNGG depending on how full the basket was. Even the fainter of heart – Mom, for example – were forced to laugh. She hadn't much choice, of course; to be or not to be constipated was the question. Even so, she generally emerged from the toilet with a sheepish look.

In front of the house was a goldfish pond, with lily pads, frogs, tadpoles, snails, and of course goldfish among other pond creatures, built around a fountain which spouted periodically from a single metal stalk in the hand of a two foot Cupid on a pedestal. Dragonflies and mosquitoes hovered constantly over the pond. A narrow beaten track passed by one side of the pond coming up a gentle incline (the hill in Hill Bungalow); on the other side was a gravel path wide enough for a rickshaw.

Beyond the paths slim-leaved mango trees stood lined like sentinels along the borders of the compound. Sometimes, stray cows and goats would slip through a gate left unlatched by a careless hand and graze until Bapaiji was sent to turn them out again. Bapaiji had not anticipated the many ways in which marriage would make a woman of her. Being the youngest female in the house she was expected to stay home all day, cook everyone's meals, wash their clothes, keep the house clean; she had the dubras to help but the responsibility was hers if something went wrong, and she hated it. Hormusji was too much of a rabbit to trouble her, but his father became a bull elephant if things went wrong, and his mother watched her like a mongoose to see that she did everything that was expected. The constant vigilance irked her; her own mother had watched her less as a child. Her mother had spoiled her in other ways too: being a careless housekeeper she had constantly left loose change around the house providing Bapaiji and her brothers with unexpected windfalls; they had to watch for Dhunmai who told on them, but that only added to the fun. The Seervais, on the other hand, even watched the money she was given. The only time she had to herself was at the end of the day when the work was finished and the old people talked before going to bed. They would not miss her then until someone wanted something – a pillow, a glass of water, a newspaper, slippers, to close a window, to close a door.

On one such evening Bapaiji sat, upright and crosslegged, sideways on the long wooden swing in the front verandah, pushing herself lightly from the wall, her sari bunched into her lap, a shawl wrapped around her shoulders, waiting for Hormusji to come home from his club. She had brought a kusti with her to weave and a hurricane lantern for light. She hoped Hormusji would get home before his father realized she was sitting out with the lantern and told her not to eat up all the oil. She was beginning to trust Hormusji; he made no demands on her, he taught in the school, he went to the club, he was polite; she disliked him most for the awe he continued to hold for his father; she felt it made him less of a man. She kept her ears tuned for the sound of Hormusji unlatching and latching the gate as he came in but all she could hear, interspersed with the sound of the crickets and the frogs, was the BOINNNGG BOINNNGG of her father-in-law whom she recognized by the loudness and the rhythm of his BOINNNGGs and his PARP-PARP farts. She missed the sound of Hormusji at the gate, but she saw his tall lanky shadowy frame emerge soon after from the darkness of the incline by the pond into the light of her lantern in the verandah. "Array, you, Banu, here, all alone?" he said. "Are you not getting cold?"

It was November. Bapaiji pulled her shawl more tightly around her shoulders. "Array, bawa, what is a little cold? I am not cold. Sit, no? I want to talk first before you go in."

He came up the stone steps and sat beside her on the swing. She liked how handsome he looked in his shirt, sweater, coat, and puffy long white pants; she liked even more the concern in his eyes which narrowed behind the black full moon frames of his spectacles and his brow furrowed beneath the sharp black rim of his skullcap. "What is it?" he said. "Something has happened?"

"Nothing has happened. That is the trouble. I need more money for the house. You must do something."

Hormusji shook his head slowly as if he spoke with regret, as if he had given the matter much thought. "That is out of my hands. For that you will have to talk to Pappa."

"But why? It is your money, no? You have earned it, no? Why you must give it all to him?"

"He is my father. He has spent on me all of my life. I cannot be so ungrateful."

There was a BOINNNGG-BOINNNGG from the toilet tower but they both ignored it. "So give him, but don't give him everything. Give him for his needs. We will keep the rest for ours."

"But he is my father. He expects me to give everything."

Bapaiji hated that argument but she kept her patience. "My father has got four sons," she said, "but he expects nothing. He knows they would give if needed."

There was a PAAAARRRPP but again they ignored it. Hormusji remained silent. He looked unhappily away from his wife. "I hate to ask him for money," Bapaiji said, "but I need for the house. If you give it to me it will be the same thing but I will not have to ask him all the time for it. Why you can't trust me? I am your wife, no?"

Hormusji shook his head. "It is not done. I cannot do it. But you are making more money from the kustis now, no? Mamma has shown you how to make them? That is more money, no?"

"That is ten annas for one kusti, but you know how much time that is taking?" Her voice rose as she spoke. "But that is my money

– for my work. Why I should spend that on the house when I have a husband who also works?"

She caught the rising pitch in her voice to impress him with her effort. "Today was your payday, I know," she said, squaring her shoulders, speaking with a deliberate tone. "If you give me the money now it will be the same thing."

Hormusji shook his head. "I cannot do it. He is my father. I am his son."

Bapaiji picked up her things, swung her feet from where she was sitting into her slippers on the floor and got up as if she couldn't argue anymore. "He is a donkey who loves to bray, ghonchi-ghonchi, and you are a goat going ben-hen-hen-hen all the time." She stamped away and was almost gone before Hormusji could compose himself to say something, but as she turned the corner of the house to the main entrance on the side there was a loud BOINNG-SPLATT-BOINNG, followed by a trumpetlike PARP-PARP-PARP-PART-PAARRRPP! She turned back to Hormusji right away. "See? What I told you?"

She spoke so triumphantly he had to laugh. She had never heard him laugh so loudly; it made her smile. He motioned her with his hand to come back. "Wait, no, Banubai? You are always in such a hurry. Whose life you are going to save? I, also, have something to tell."

She came back, a little shy; he had never criticized her before. She sat where he patted the space beside him on the swing. "What?"

He clasped his hands in front of him and spoke more seriously. "I am thinking of going to Bombay. I am a solicitor but there is no need for solicitors in Navsari. Here I can only be a schoolteacher. Do you think that is a good idea?"

She was flattered he had asked her. Men did not ask women such things. He was giving her the same respect as to a man. "Yes," she said. "I think that is a great idea. I think that is the best idea. I think we should go tomorrow. I think we should go this night only, but I have got to pack up still."

As the two of them went into the house the soundtrack provided by Bapaiji's father-in-law reached supersonic proportions, accompanied by images of fireworks blazing nobly like comets, convincing me that the scoop from my collective unconscious comes to me muddied as much by Bapaiji's direction as by my own associations and imagination; perhaps her in-laws were not the clutch of hobgoblins she presented, but a purer view demanded more objectivity than my brainsickness, the product of my lovesickness, allowed.

The Light of a Million Stars

In Bombay Hormusji slept on a wooden bench in the verandah of his great uncle's huge house on Grant Road. It was cold in December but he took two blankets and stayed there because he wanted to please Bapaiji. He knew she had not wanted to marry him, there was only one bed in their room, and he wanted to make things easy for her. He did not know that Bapaiji sometimes came to the verandah to look at him while he slept. One clear night she studied his face in the light of a million stars; it was long, thin, smooth, noble, and so sad she wanted to hold and caress it, but she didn't dare; his chin was pointed almost like a pencil, and his cheeks, brow, and temples were composed of flat planes like the facets of a crystal. When he wore his stately black fehnta he was tall enough and imposing enough to turn anyone's head – except Bapaiji's; she had walked with Adi, the tallest man in Navsari, and for the longest time Hormusji's purely physical charms had been wasted on her – but the tenderness with which he treated her had already made an impression; and now, in the light of the stars, other attractions were becoming visible. She herself, as she readily acknowledged, was no beauty; her jaw was wide and sharp like the edge of an axe, her ears were long, and her lips were thin like a boy's, but her breasts were huge and she enjoyed the attention they commanded – but Hormusji, inexplicably, thought of her as his wife only from the neck up. They had separate beds in his father's house in Navsari, and he had not touched her even once except socially even though they had slept in the same room for a year now. At first it had been a relief because she saw him as an intruder in her life more than a husband, but once she was secure that he would not touch her she wondered why he didn't, then curiosity led to anxiety that he found her unattractive, and then to frustration because she had too much pride to tell him what she wanted. She had thought things would change in Bombay, particularly when she saw the single bed in their room, but he now slept in the verandah and she sometimes stood by and watched him. On the starry night she watched him for two hours before going back to her bed.

The next night Hormusji's great uncle heard a noise in the sitting room. He suspected it was Bapaiji because he had seen her the night before looking at Hormusji in the starlight, but she must have heard him coming because by the time he was in the sitting room she was back in her bedroom. He had seen her on other nights too but had said nothing because he was a shy man who had never found the courage to marry. But now he felt the situation was getting too strange; if he didn't do something it might get worse. He woke Hormusji from his sleep. "What is this, Hormus?" he said. "It is cold. The bench is hard. Why you are doing this?"

Hormusji blinked his eyes like an owl. He was too astonished to speak.

"You should sleep with your wife, Hormus. You should sleep inside where it is warm. Here you will only catch cold."

"I am not cold. I am comfortable. I am all right, really, Motabawa."

"What you mean you are not cold? You are shivering like a rat in a trap."

"It is okay, Motabawa, really. I am all right."

"No, it is not okay. I do not like for people to sleep on my bench. A bench is for sitting. You should be with your wife. Go to Banu, no? She is waiting for you."

"Tomorrow! Tomorrow, I will go to Banu. Tonight I will only disturb her."

"How you will disturb her? You are her husband, not a killer. You must go tonight. This is all nonsense."

Bapaiji heard the entire exchange but pretended to be asleep when Hormusji approached her bed loaded down with the blankets and pillows he had brought in from the verandah. "Banu, you are sleeping, yes?"

She was turned away from him and groaned as if she were deep in sleep. He asked again if she were asleep, but she was enjoying herself; she groaned again, louder, turning to face him, but still saying nothing.

"Motabawa does not want sleeping on the bench. The bench is for sitting only he says."

Still she said nothing, simulating instead a breath that was perhaps too deep for credibility in an attempt at a breezy snore. When Hormusji remained quiet for a while she cracked her eyes just enough to see what he was doing. He had unrolled his blankets on the floor beside her and was puffing up his pillow getting ready to lie down. "Hormus," she said, opening her eyes. "What you are doing?"

"Motabawa says there is no sleeping on the bench. And I did not want to disturb you."

"Array, come, come, no? Sleep in the bed. What is this sleeping on the floor? You will catch cold." She moved to one side of the bed, making room for him.

He looked at her uncertainly from the floor. "It is all right? I will not disturb you?"

"Disturb-disturb! What disturb? I am your wife, no? What is to disturb? Come, no? Sleep, sleep with me. You are my husband."

He would have been happy enough just to sleep in the bed beside her, but she put a hand behind his head and pulled him to herself, reassuring him all the while, "It is all right. I am your wife. This is how it should be."

Bapaiji would have shown me everything; she, apparently, had no shame about these matters; but I wasn't quite as willing a voyeur as she might have supposed. I hid in the only place in the room from which I could not see them – under the bed, on the cold mosaic floor, two sets of slippers to my side, and the wooden slats of the bed rattling above me telling the story I dared not see for myself.

When the slats stopped rattling Bapaiji was disappointed that she had had to take all the initiative. "Hormus," she said, "if I had said nothing, you would have slept all of the night on the floor?"

Hormusji smiled suddenly as if he had a secret. "No," he said, offering no more explanation.

"What you would have done? Tell me, no?"

57

"I would have waited. I knew you heard everything. You were smiling all the time I was talking. I said, Let her have her fun. I will have my own."

Bapaiji was surprised, delighted, with his playfulness; perhaps he felt more comfortable with his parents far away. "Robber!" she said fiercely, pushing him out of the bed, "You stole your way into my bed."

"I stole nothing," he said, pushing her back. "This is also my bed. You are the robber for keeping it all these nights."

Soon after that the slats started rattling again and I kept my focus on the two holes for ventilation in the black rubber slipper in front of my face on the floor.

Bapaiji was determined with the first stirrings of her son in her womb that he would be in the railways; Motabawa was an engine-driver and made nine hundred rupees a month (it was a new profession then) and Hormusji, a solicitor, made only ninety, most of which he sent home to his father. Bapaiji was able to persuade Hormusji to keep at least enough for tramfare to and from work, even though his father thought he should walk as he had done in Navsari. "Bombay is not like Navsari," Bapaiji said, "where you can walk everywhere, jut-phut, in a minute."

As she developed her intimacy with Hormusji she prevailed more frequently over his father. Hormusji had seen how efficiently she managed the thirty-five rupees Motabawa gave her monthly for their household expenses and felt confident about entrusting her with his own money, particularly when she spoke about saving it for their son (if it were a daughter, Bapaiji swore, she would make it drink milk; all good women, so she contended, hated their sex).

They stayed in Bombay less than a year because there was no one but Bapaiji to care for the baby there, and she did not want to be cooped up with it all day in the house. She insisted that the baby would be named Adi, after her sweet-shop sweetheart whose family had refused her before; it was her way of finally resolving the situation for herself. Hormusji did not mind, though his father wanted the child named after himself, but Bapaiji stayed with the child at her parents' house (it was the custom for a mother to stay with her parents again until the child was at least six months old, though Bapaiji didn't stay even six months), and after that it was too late to call the child anything else. Hormusji returned to his parents and taught once more at the same school at which he had taught before they had left for Bombay.

When Adi was born Bapaiji's mother yanked his arms and legs fiercely, methodically, turned his head one way, then the other, until it seemed he would never stop crying. When Bapaiji had first voiced her objection to marrying Hormusji by recounting the deformities in the Seervai family her mother had said, "Go, go, you are making only excuses," but now she wanted to be sure for herself.

The baby was fine and Bapaiji let her mother and Dhunmai take care of it. She had hated the pregnancy and she hated motherhood; it was just one more way, perhaps the most diabolical, of tying down a woman. It was not that she did not love her baby, but she resented having to show it in the conventional womanly ways; besides, with both sides of the family making such a fuss over the baby there was no need for her to do anything – if anything, someone was needed to be strict just to strike a balance. She let the baby stay with Dhunmai most of the time, even at night, to make her point. "Dirty, nasty, smelly, noisy, crying thing," she said of Adi, as much to antagonize the family as to establish that she was only incidentally a woman, reminding me of the times I had seen her poke and pinch children who had come within her reach when we had gone to the movies. She wished she could have been a grandmother without being a mother (then she could have done what she wished, not what was expected), which prompted Hormusji to call her Bapaiji for the first time, and what began as a joke grew into a sign of respect; even Adi called her first Bapai, then Bapaiji.

One afternoon, when Adi was three months, Bapaiji found Dhunmai nursing Adi at her breast. She had a smile on her face as if she were the mother. Bapaiji strode up to her and pulled the baby away. "What you are doing?" she said.

Dhunmai looked embarrassed. "I have milk. It happens with sisters like that sometimes."

"What milk? Where you have milk?" Bapaiji tweaked Dhunmai's flaccid, still exposed nipple sharply with her fingers, digging with her nails. "What lies you are telling."

Dhunmai screamed, the baby started crying, their mother came rushing. "What is it? What is all the noise?"

Bapaiji related the story in outraged tones, rocking the baby to make it quiet, while Dhunmai quietened down herself and covered her breast. To her surprise, their mother said, "So what is the fuss? Even if there is no milk the baby is quiet, and what is the harm?" She felt sorry for her youngest daughter who would never marry; this was the closest she would come to motherhood; she didn't want to take that happiness from her, particularly when it was so clear how much Bapaiji resented her own motherhood.

Dhunmai smiled again; the baby was still crying and reaching for her. "Give him here," she said. "I know how to make him quiet."

But Bapaiji held Adi away from her. "Sometimes it is better to let him cry," she said.

"Banu, think, no?" her mother said. "You have got bread, but you want butter also. You should be thanking Dhunmai for how much time she is spending with Adi."

"I am not thanking her for anything," Bapaiji said, rocking the baby violently to keep it quiet. "She is stealing away my baby. I am packing up and going back to my husband tomorrow." She strode from the room, rocking Adi as if she wanted to stun him into silence.

Things did not work out as Bapaiji planned. The Seervais were not willing to overlook the six month period, but when she said, "I will die on the roadside first of hunger and thirst with the baby with me," they took her back on the condition that she was not to step in the house itself but stay in the room where the women went during menstruation. The room was adjacent to the house but had no direct access to it. During menstruation the Seervai women were isolated in the room, their food was cooked separately, they used separate utensils and an outhouse which was a few yards from the house. Bapaiji would have to stay there for the remainder of the six months.

She hated her life during that time. She hated living in such cramped quarters with bedbugs, spiders, cockroaches, lizards, and mice; no matter how much she cleaned the room it remained muddy and full of cobwebs. She could hear the wolves howling in the sugarcane fields. She felt unsafe because the door had a faulty latch, and slept with a string tied from her wrist to Adi's cradle.

One night she heard a twig crack as if something large had stepped on it. She immediately got a firm grip on the thick wooden stick with the weighted knob at the end which she kept by her side. There was a furtive tapping at the door. "Who is it?" she said in a loud voice.

"Do not shout. It is only me." It was Hormusji. "Let me come in."

She unlatched the door. He had brought a thin rolled mattress and pillow with him. "Why you are bringing all this?" she said. "I already have."

"Not for you," he said. "For me. I am staying here for the night."

"But why?"

"I heard you crying before."

"I was not crying."

"I wanted to be with you."

"But why? You will be with me tomorrow."

"You are my wife."

"But this room is only for women in their menses."

"So what do I care?"

She liked the way he looked in the dim light of her candle. She liked the way she felt, isolated with her baby and her man and the sound of the frogs and the crickets outside. She wanted him to stay but she liked what he was saying and would have continued the conversation except for a sound in the back of the room. She turned and swung her weighted stick without warning, striking three times before she was satisfied. She smiled; she could see, even in the flickering light of the candle, that Hormusji had turned pale. He was afraid of mice and continually amazed at how easily she killed them. "I killed my first mouse when I was four," she had told him. "I don't even remember, but Mamma said." She picked up the dead mouse by its tail and flung it with a swing from the door. "Still you are wanting to stay?" she said.

"Yes."

"Then let us go to sleep now. It is late."

He unrolled his mattress across the room from where she had killed the mouse. She watched him as he prepared for the night, facing the candle, saying his prayers as he wrapped his kusti around his waist in three loops, and lying down at last to sleep. She wanted to cry then because he was going to stay with her all night in that room even though he was afraid of every little thing that moved. Her heart felt big and she sat by his side for a while caressing his face in the dark.

The next morning he was gone with his mattress and pillow before anyone could miss him in the house – he was even more afraid of his father than of mice – but he was back the following night and every subsequent night until it was time for Bapaiji to enter the house again.

Bapaiji's violin teacher was a Musalman. He wore a red fez with a black tassel and a coat which he kept buttoned to his neck even in the hottest weather. He had a face like a chicken with a tiny beak of a nose and no chin. It was ten o'clock on a Tuesday morning and he stood in the Seervais' sitting room with his violin case under his arm, waiting for Bapaiji, almost afraid to sit down because the other Seervais glared at him like tigers as they passed in and out of the room without saying a word. When Bapaiji came he took a deep breath. "Are you ready, Maiji? Shall we begin?" he had his violin out of its case in an instant.

"Wait, no?" Bapaiji said. "You would like something to drink? Some water, no?"

"No, it is all right. It is not so hot today."

There were trails of sweat running down his thin brown face to where his chin should have been. "It is no trouble," Bapaiji said. "Mamma," she called loudly, "get some water, no, please, for me and the teacherji? It is so hot today."

Her mother-in-law shouted from the kitchen. "Today there is no water."

"What you mean there is no water? Bring us water, no?"

Her mother-in-law appeared at the door, bent, stout, ferocious. "What I said? I am talking to the wind? There is no water. You want some oil to clean your ears?"

Bapaiji was furious but the violin teacher said, "It is all right. I am not hot. I have got to go soon. I have got another lesson far away at half past eleven."

During the lesson the Seervais talked loudly to one another; at one point Bapaiji's father-in-law shouted to Bapaiji that she and her teacher were making too much noise; Bapaiji bit her lip but when the lesson was over she wasted no time. "What is it with all you today? What is this business 'Today there is no water'? We are living in the Sahara Desert or what?"

Four bent old frowning women, tapping sticks angrily on the floor, responded like Jack-in-the-Boxes in a row: "How you can let a Musalman in our house?" – "We could get diseases from him." – "We do not want to keep a separate glass for his water anymore." – "Also, he smells."

Her father-in-law spoke last. "Give up this vilin-filin, Banubai. We do not want Musalmans in our house all the time. Adi could get germs from him."

Bapaiji knew what the real issue was. Everyone liked to play with the baby, but no one wanted to take care of it. She had started violin lessons to provide herself with a regular respite from the baby, but they had seen through her scheme. "All right," she said, "from next week I will go to teacherji's place instead. I am not so afraid of diseases like you are."

They said nothing to her, they grumbled among themselves, but the next Tuesday, when Bapaiji was ready to leave the house she found herself all alone with Adi. The others had all left, jut-phut, as Bapaiji might have said. The image she provided for me was memorable: dozens of gnarled old men in wheelchairs holding twisted sticks, and hunchbacked women with long noses and chins on broomsticks, ejecting themselves like rockets from the doors and windows of the house.

After lunch on Sunday afternoons most of the Seervais took a nap. Bapaiji rarely napped; she preferred to read or weave kustis; the money she made from the kustis she saved for Adi. She had just settled herself with a kusti on the swing in the verandah one afternoon when her mother-in-law came to her with Adi, who had peed in his pants, in her arms. "Our Lion needs to be changed," she said.

They called him the Lion, the King of the Jungle, because he received so much attention in the house. "So change him, no?" Bapaiji said coolly without looking up from her kusti.

With her hunched back, her mother-in-law was almost eye level with Bapaiji seated on the swing. "I have to clean myself," she said, her voice low, threatening to turn ugly. "Who is the mother?"

"Who is the grandmother?" Bapaiji said. "A grandmother is not helpless."

"A mother should not leave her son dirty," her mother-in-law said, and left without waiting for a response.

"And a grandmother should leave her grandson?" Bapaiji shouted, but she knew the old lady would not come back. Adi was crying; she flung her things on the floor and picked him up roughly. He was just an excuse for them to tell her what to do.

On the evening of the same day her father-in-law lay in his armchair in the sitting room, his legs raised on the slats which slid under the arms of the chair, his pajama bottoms pulled up so that his calves were bare, playing with Adi. He liked the armchair because it was good for his elephantiasis to rest his legs up high; his legs were swollen and pierced at points so that they seemed ready to ooze pus. Adi liked playing on his grandfather's huge torso, particularly to reach up and squeeze his lightbulb nose, but on this occasion he was crawling from his stomach to his knees when Bapaiji picked him up without a word and took him to her room. "Array, Hormus," the old man shouted. "Your wife is gone crazy at last. She has snatch my grandson from my own hands. What she is thinking? Go and bring back our Lion from her clutches."

When Hormusji went to see what was wrong she said, "Adi will catch a disease from his legs. If Pappa will not keep the bandages on his legs like the doctor said, then he cannot play with Adi."

Poor Hormusji, caught between his love for his wife and his fear of his father, relayed the message. "What?" his father shouted, sitting up in his chair. "What she said? To me? In my house? Tell her to send Adi at once! You hear? At once!"

But Hormusji didn't move. He replied in a small voice. "Pappa, why make such a fuss about such a small matter?"

The old man said nothing at first. His mouth opened, his lightbulb nose appeared to shine as it did when he was angry, and he looked at his son as if he were someone else. "So," he said, smiling, sinking into his chair again. "The goat has finally climbed the hill." He seemed to shrink, literally, as if there were no need for him to appear so large anymore.

A series of images followed: a skinny six year old Dad in his khaki and white school uniform trotting to school with Hormusji who was now the headmaster; alone on another occasion buying chana and sing from a chana-wallah in the schoolyard; bending over Hormusji's desk in his office for a caning for setting a bad example as the headmaster's son (schoolboys were forbidden to buy food from hawkers because the food might have been polluted); a skinny fifteen year old, recognizable as Dad from the snapshots I had seen, in white pants and shirt, walking with friends along Bombay's Chowpatty Beach from the Wilson college where he was studying for his Inter-Science, buying bhel puri; skipping in a kilt with bagpipes in a stone room with a fireplace and a view of a castle near the University of Edinburgh where he was studying Engineering; leaning on a walking stick, wearing tails and a bowler in Picadilly Circus, waiting for Bapaiji; Bapaiji in the cabin of the *Strathaird*, lying on an unmade bed, looking out of a huge porthole at the choppy water striking the hull barely a few feet below her, over a pile of sweaters on the wide curving sill; the two of them at the Folies in Paris, Dad smiling at Bapaiji's wide-eyed admiration of the nude kaleidoscopic formations on stage; the two of them sprawled luxuriously on the plush green seats of the privileged quarters of a railway engineer as a steam engine pulled them through a flat dry Indian landscape; Dad, back in Bombay in the uniform of an army captain, a young darkhaired woman on his arm as sleek as a freshwater fish, standing by a jeep in the driveway of a palatial house; Bapaiji, back in Navsari, addressing a group of men from the head of the long wooden table at which they sat; Bapaiji, behind a nucleus of microphones in an auditorium, addressing an audience, and then behind more microphones in a maidan addressing a crowd.

Bapaiji was easily recognizable behind the microphones; she had told me once how she loved making speeches, she loved the attention, to tell people what she thought, and I had seen her often enough behind lecterns, podiums, at heads of tables, on daises, stages, platforms, even standing once on a chair, to recognize her stance as easily as her features. Even the image immediately prior to Bapaiji at the head of the table was familiar; the woman sleek as a fish on Dad's arm was Mom, recognizable from the photographs I had seen of their engagement. Her sari, wide at her hips, swirled to a pinstripe at her knees before flaring to a fantail covering her feet below. Bapaiji had said it was her low centre of gravity, nothing else, that had attracted Dad, but she was happy enough with his choice because Mom was the great-niece of Jalbhai Pherozshah Cama, the industrialist, capitalist, and philanthropist, who was in all the history books. Jalbhai had been born in Navsari, and had gone to college in Bombay and stayed there, but his sister, Tehmina Cama, had started the movement for the emancipation of women in Navsari; I had heard of her but knew little of what she had done because she had died long before I had been born and her accomplishments had been overshadowed entirely in the history books by those of her brother. I moved backward through the images until I found the one I needed: Tehmina Cama unlatching the door within the gate leading up to Hill Bungalow, Bapaiji and Hormusji reclining on the verandah talking to one of the dubras, the older people inside the house, sitting by the windows, praying, eating, talking among themselves, to themselves. It was morning, it must have been Sunday for everyone to be at home, chalk patterns had been laid in the mud in front of the stoop, two goats grazed in the compound to the side of the house, the two-foot Cupid on his pedestal spouted water from the stalk in his hand into the pond. "Look," Bapaiji said, rising from her chair, "someone is coming. They came in a ghora gari."

Hormusji stopped talking to the dubra but did not get up. "In a ghora gari they came? Who is it?"

"Wait, wait, no? Let me put on my spectacles." Bapaiji raised her full moon, wire rim spectacles to her eyes. "It is Tehmina Cama."

"What? You are sure?"

"No, it is the king of England. Of course, I am sure. I have seen her before, no?"

Hormusji got out of his seat and came to the front of the verandah.

"Nagin," Bapaiji said to the dubro. "Go make a plate of sweets from the pinjda, little bit of everything. Go now." Bapaiji kept sweets, wafers, and khari biscuits in glass jars for expressly such occasions in the pinjda, which was mounted on earthen vessels filled with water to keep away termites.

Mrs Cama was within earshot as Nagin disappeared. "Array, Mrs Cama," Bapaiji said, "it is good to see you at our house. How are you?"

"We are how we are," Mrs Cama said with a smile. "So nice a day we are having, no? And how are you, Mr Seervai?"

Hormusji opened the balustrade gate as Mrs Cama came up the steps. "Nothing to complain," he said. "The day is very nice, yes. Come, come inside the house."

Mrs Cama preferred to stay on the verandah because it was such a fine morning, so the three of them sat down again. "We are always hearing great things about your brother," Bapaiji said. "How he is doing?"

"Jalbhai is always okay – but I have my own business to conduct. That is why I have come. I cannot stay very long."

"Array, stay, stay, have some food, no? Have some water. Nagin, bring food, no, for our guest?"

Mrs Cama protested she had just breakfasted, she would soon be lunching, but Bapaiji insisted she eat something, "just to make your mouth sweet, nothing more," and Mrs Cama complied, nibbling on a single long stem of jalebi while she got to the point of her visit. Her organization for the emancipation of women needed a solicitor to draw up their constitution and not only was Hormusji the only solicitor in Navsari but he had a reputation for being sympathetic to the cause of women.

Hormusji's older brother, the first of the inmates to find the courage to present himself to Tehmina Cama, made his appearance on the verandah as if he were about to leave the house on an errand, but his ruse was painfully transparent when he sat instead by Hormusji and gaped foolishly at Mrs Cama. "Go, no," Hormusji said, "if you have got something to do."

"It is nothing," the older brother said with a smile. "It will take only a very little time."

"Mrs Cama and I have got important things to discuss," Hormusji said. "If it will take a very little time, then go and come back. We will still be here."

The older brother left but then Hormusji's hunchbacked sister appeared, smiling, then his mother, then an aunt; the older brother kept waving goodbye from the gate, the others sat smiling in chairs around Hormusji eating the sweets Bapaiji had brought out for Mrs Cama. When Hormusji protested his mother pointed at Bapaiji. "Why she is staying if you have got important business to discuss? Who is the mother? Who gets the respect?"

Bapaiji said she would go inside if everyone else came with her and so, grumbling between their smiles, they followed her in. Hormusji concluded his business quickly. Too shy to do much for himself he had always encouraged Bapaiji to express herself, and was ecstatic at this chance not only to be working as a solicitor but also to develop Navsari. When Jalbhai himself later offered Hormusji a job in Bombay as an industrial solicitor at a much higher salary, Hormusji declined. He often said he preferred to work for the rights of women than the wrongs of industry – but would immediately profess his admiration for what Tehmina and Jalbhai were doing for both women and industry.

But when he asked Bapaiji if she would like to be on the governing board she turned him down. Adi, already in college in Bombay, was no longer a pressing responsibility, but fifteen years of domesticity had tamed Bapaiji to the point of questioning a woman's role outside the home. She was embarrassed to discuss it with Hormusji, but she asked their closest neighbor, Framroze, what he would do if his wife started working outside the house. "I would throw her from the window," Framroze said. "Throw her from the window and forget it." When she presented this argument to Hormusji, Hormusji put on his coat and fehnta, picked up his stick, and strode to Framroze's house, an inflated Ichabod Crane, a rooster fluffed with wrath, his customarily twiglike frame appearing to swell as his customarily limp arms became bowed and firm by his sides, and his customarily white pencil-thin face turned puffy and red.

When Framroze recognized the source of Hormusji's rage he capitulated easily. "It was only a joke. I was only joking. I am sorry." Hormusji felt almost foolish after his majestic entry, but drawing himself to his full height he said, "If you throw your wife from the window then you don't deserve her in the first place."

Bapaiji was inspired. For himself Hormusji might remain a mouse for the rest of his life, but for her he had risen like a giant.

Bapaiji sat silently on one side of the table where the Committee of Eleven had met to vote on the subject of a dance workshop. She knew there were more men at the table who would have voted differently had they not been intimidated by the chairman, Mr Patel, a tiny brown man who chewed paan constantly and scowled. She was afraid to say anything herself but if she was to be more than a token woman on the committee she knew she would have to assert herself. "Wait," she said, "I think before we put this subject to rest we must think about something else."

Mr Patel spoke impatiently. "What is it, Bapaiji? What are you trying to say?"

"I am saying," Bapaiji said, looking around the table, "that we should have a secret ballot. Otherwise, people do not vote what they think."

"What nonsense is this, Bapaiji?" Mr Patel spat the red paan spittle into a dish full of ash on the floor by his chair. "You are wasting time. The matter has been settled."

"Wait, Mr Chairman, Mr Patel, sir. Let me suggest a different issue for voting. Who over here thinks we should keep the vote open like it is now, raise your hands."

The men looked from Mr Patel to Bapaiji. "What you are all looking at?" Mr Patel said. "Raise your hands, no? whoever agrees."

Eight hands of the eleven went slowly up.

"Now I will pass this box around," Bapaiji said, picking up a shoebox from a windowsill behind her. "Write on a piece of paper what you think, Yes or No, and then let us see."

Nine ballots voted for a secret ballot. Mr Patel fumed, "That is not the way, Bapaiji," but he had been outmanouevered; the dance workshop was voted in with the next ballot.

More images: Bapaiji in the newspapers; Hormusji compiling a scrapbook of clippings of Bapaiji; Hormusji, one of his last appearances, fine white hair like webs of gossamer in his ears, stepping with Bapaiji from the back seat of our chauffeur-driven Ford at the gate of Hill Bungalow, the first car in Navsari, draped in marigolds, surrounded by throngs of open-mouthed villagers, presenting it to Dad in his Captain's uniform and Mom in a calf-length dress on the occasion of their fifth wedding anniversary; Hormusji dying of cancer, Bapaiji holding back tears by his bedside.

Rajya Ratna

Bapaiji settled herself in her favourite armchair in the verandah of Hill Bungalow, resting her feet up on one of the slats, to read the daily *Jam-e-Jamshed*, the six page Gujarati newspaper she had co-founded with Tehmina Cama almost thirty years ago. I remember it best for its only English features: Ripley's Believe It or Not, and comic strips of Dagwood and Blondie, The Phantom, and Mandrake the Magician. She was proud of the newspaper as she was of so many of the projects sponsored by the Women's Committee. They had classes in sewing, dance, music, drama, embroidery, Hindi – whatever someone could teach someone else wanted to learn. The Maharajah of Baroda had come to one of the annual presentations of their work which they supplemented with music and a skit written by Bapaiji, and had been impressed enough to initiate an annual donation of five hundred rupees, making it fashionable to donate to the cause of the Women's Committee, which enabled them to build a library and a club for the women. Bapaiji was the club's first president and remained so until she died. She wished Hormusji could have been with her for the next day's event, when the Maharajah of Baroda conferred upon her the title, Rajya Ratna, the Jewel of the State, and awarded her the solid gold medal embossed with her name and new title; he had been so proud of all her honours and medals. She wished Adi would come with Pheroza; the ceremony was to be held in the school compound where Hormusji had been the headmaster and Adi the pupil, but her relations with Adi were not like they had been with Hormusji; Adi resented everything about her that Hormusji had encouraged; he had even chosen a docile, pleasing, pretty wife, everything she was not – but if Pheroza had been more like herself they might have had arguments about everything; there wasn't room for more than one Bapaiji in the family and Pheroza was wise enough to know it; but Bapaiji wished she understood Adi's discontent better.

The pendulum clocks in the different rooms whirred almost simultaneously and tolled their single bell-like tones, the cuckoo called once to mark the half hour and the German boy fiddler in the door next to the cuckoo's played the first two lines of his quatrain. It was half past eight o'clock. I heard laughter from the dining room past the wooden swing doors from the sitting room. Mom and Dad were finishing breakfast. Dad was eating scrambled eggs while Mom stood behind him, her hands on his shoulders, her head lowered to his, nuzzling his face from the side, as close (Bapaiji might have said) as two cats in a bag.

Bapaiji cleared her throat to warn them of her presence; Mom jumped immediately away, her face suddenly pink. Dad continued as if nothing had happened, but his shoulders became rigid and he kept his eyes on his breakfast. Bapaiji felt something shrink inside her as if a screw were being tightened. She saw they had bought an extra loaf of bread when she had told them one would be enough; she had even sacrificed her own two slices that morning, but Adi had to have four slices with each egg and Pheroza had to slice them four fingers thick as if she were afraid she might cut herself. Bapaiji sat down heavily at the head of the table. "Who is drinking this tea?" she said, pushing away the cup and saucer in front of her.

"I was," Mom said, approaching the table again, "but I'm finished. I'll clear it away."

"First, finish it," Bapaiji said. "There is still at least two annas of tea in it. We are not all rich like Camas here. We cannot afford to waste."

Mom sat down next to Dad. She said, "Yes, Bapaiji," but made no further attempt to take the cup.

Dad looked up suddenly. "There is nothing to waste. There is not even two pice of tea in the cup. But why not just let it be now, Bapaiji? Too much has been said about it already."

Bapaiji took a deep breath. "Array, yes-yes, too much has been said. I will let it go. You have bought an extra loaf of bread also, do not think I have not seen, but I will let that also go. But one thing I must ask you again." She paused to inject gravity into what was to come, to allow her querulousness to smoothen into plaintiveness. "Will you not please just reconsider about tomorrow, no? How it will look if my own son is not there when the Maharajah presents me with the Rajya Ratna? What I will say when people ask, Array, but Bapaiji, where is Adi today? You only tell me what I should say then?"

Dad paid more attention to his eggs than to Bapaiji as he replied. "Say the truth. Say he has work in Bombay. Say he has his own sons. Say he cannot come every time his Bapaiji is given a medal. Otherwise, he would have to live in Navsari only."

"Array, but Son, there will be pehlwans. They will do wrestling and gymnastics and weight lifting. Come, no, to see them if not for me? There will be Kolah's ice cream. You like ice cream, no?"

Dad spoke, still without looking at her, his voice shaking with anger. "The pehlwans are for you only, Bapaiji. I do not care about pehlwans. I do not like ice cream so cold like you like it." When Bapaiji had begun having trouble with her teeth she had had them all removed, and now she liked her ice cream so cold that only she could eat it; it chilled everyone else's teeth. "I have got work in Bombay to do," Dad continued. "Let us leave the subject now, let us just leave it."

"It is still about the gate, no? You are still angry about the gate money, no? That is what it is, no?"

"It is not about the gate. If I did work I should have been paid, but that is all over. Just say I had work in Bombay."

The school gate had been in need of repair. Bapaiji had volunteered to donate the money if she were recognized for her donation by a plaque bearing her name mounted on the arch over the gateposts. Her way of cutting costs was getting Dad to engineer the project. When he asked what he would be paid she said, "We will see." When he submitted his first design she said she wanted a much larger plaque with her name in bolder letters so it could be seen from a great distance; the extra cost meant nothing to Bapaiji. Dad completed the job, even when he realized he would not be paid because he felt obligated professionally to finish the job and to obey his mother; besides, as she never ceased to remind him, it was his old school, where his pappa had been the headmaster, where he himself had been the pupil; and she was his mother, not just any client; but he continued to feel she had used him again as she had times before.

Bapaiji knew she had taken advantage of him, and she knew she would continue as long as he allowed her to do so; how else would he learn? She received no satisfaction when she bested him, only frustration. He knew how she was; he should have refused the job or settled the money problem from the beginning. "Why you cannot understand?" she said. "Everything I have is yours only. What difference it makes if I pay you? For who I am doing this? For me?"

"That is not the point, Bapaiji. You know that is not the point."

"Then what is the point?" She waited for an answer, but when he remained silent she said, "Never mind. What is done is done. But stay for tomorrow, no? What difference one day will make? Bombay will not fall into the sea. Stay, no, Son?"

But Dad shook his head. He understood vaguely that he was refusing her now to make up for his earlier inability to refuse to design her gate and other occasions when his sense of duty had overawed his commonsense, that his irritation was directed as much at himself as at her, that leaving her on this important day would give him no more satisfaction than it would her, but he couldn't help himself. "No," he said. "I have got to go. I have got business in Bombay."

Bapaiji might have said more, but the doorbell rang. "That will be Thakor," she said. "Think what I have said, no? Just think. I am asking nothing else."

After she left Mom spoke first. "Perhaps one of us should stay, darling," she said, stroking Dad's head. "It would mean so much to her to have family there."

He knew she was right, he knew he should stay himself, but he said, "Perhaps you're right, Philly. Would you mind very much staying by yourself? I would, but you know how it is. I have so much work in Bombay."

They both knew how it was; there was no work that could not wait; but the sacrifice of a night apart would ease Dad's conscience and enhance Mom's sense of her worth. "Not at all. I'll be happy to stay. It will make Bapaiji so happy."

Bapaiji had already forgotten about them on her way back to the verandah, thinking instead of the things she had to tell Thakor. Thakor arrived about that time every weekday morning. He always stayed in the verandah unless he had brought something to be put in the house or Bapaiji needed something moved or fixed, but mostly she needed him at the club to set up the card tables, board games, badminton courts, sweep the floors, dust the furniture, fill the matkas with water – in short, he was indispensable.

He always dressed the same – a white cotton Nehru cap, white shirt, baggy white pants clamped at his ankles so they wouldn't get in the way of the chain of his bicycle, black leather chappals, a grey sweater in the winter; he even looked the same to me – hollow cheeks, hair shining with brylcreem, a few longish hairs on his chin which he called a beard, a constant sweet boyish look – except that in time his hair became greyer. When he saw Bapaiji he bowed his head immediately. "Saebji, Bapaiji, saebji. How are you?"

Bapaiji nodded her head. "Saebji, Thakor. We are fine."

"Everyone is fine? Seth? Bai?"

"Everyone is fine."

"Good-good. Very good."

"Some things I want to do first, Thakor. Then I will tell you what to do about the Maharani tomorrow."

"Yes-yes, of course-yes, of course-yes."

Bapaiji knew he worshipped her and she loved it. After she had run through the regular errands she said, "The Maharani is coming first class in the Baroda Express tomorrow at half past eleven. She is coming here for lunch. The Maharajah will come later straight to the school; he is busy. You must keep a ghora gari ready for the Maharani and bring her here straight away. I will be waiting here."

"Bachubai has said she will send her motor. After all, she is a Maharani, no?"

"She is a Maharani, but we are ordinary people. We will show how ordinary people live. Tell Bachubai to keep her motor-fotor. Bring our Maharani in the ghora gari."

Bapaiji's democracy delighted Thakor. He gave one of his loco-motive laughs which seemed to go on forever. "Hyuh-hyuh-hyuh-hyuh-hyuh. Yes-yes, of course-yes, as you say only, it shall be as you say only. Hyuh-hyuh-hyuh-hyuh-hyuh."

Then it was time to go, but Thakor stayed, an embarrassed look creeping into his face. "There is something else?" Bapaiji asked.

"There is one thing."

"What is it?"

"It is like this. I have work for you now how many years?"

"Who is counting? We are all getting old."

"I have a wife, three daughters, one got married, but I need dowries still for two, or who will marry them?"

Bapaiji understood what he was saying. "Everyone needs money," she said. "I had a son. I sent him to UK to study. You think I pulled money from the wind? I had to live within my means. It is the only way to learn what money means."

Thakor looked embarrassed as if he had somehow appeared ungrateful, but his mouth set in a pout.

"Array, Thakor," Bapaiji said quietly as if to persuade him to reason, "if wishes were wings, elephants would fly. Think, no? Elephants would fly! But it is not so."

Thakor could think of nothing to say; he knew she couldn't do without him, but after thirty years working for her had become his life; she was no more able to do without him than he was able to leave her; besides, there were no jobs for an old man in Navsari; he needed her as much as she needed him; but she was being unfair and he remained stubbornly, silently, where he was.

"I will do one thing for you," Bapaiji said when she realized how he felt. "When I go to the cinema you can come with me – for free. Three times a week we can go to the cinema. Come, now, what do you say? That is fair or no?"

She knew she had won even before the big grin broke on his face. Bapaiji owned a second house on Station Road near the Navsari railway station, ideally situated for the three cinema houses to advertise their movies. She had struck a deal with the cinema houses: she allowed them to mount their posters on the walls of her compound; they allowed her and everyone accompanying her or coming as her guest, free admission at all times. Thakor realized the arrangement did nothing to help his daughters with their dowries, but he was too much of a cinemaphile to think beyond the next movie; besides, Bapaiji had said he could bring his family too – but most often he came alone and sat a few rows in front of Bapaiji in the balcony. On the occasions we accompanied Bapaiji to the movies we enjoyed his company even from the distance in the dark; his hyuh-hyuh-hyuh-hyuh laugh was more ubiquitous in the balcony than the movie.

The next day, if not for Mom, the wooden table in Bapaiji's dining room with the cracked dull dark tan leathern tablecloth, rolled in a stiff uneven scroll at the edges, would not even have been wiped of the spills of the day before – not that Bapaiji was a slovenly housekeeper; she had long accepted the humdrum in life; but as much as she enjoyed being feted by Maharajahs and Maharanis, her zeal for democracy required her to exhibit mostly her cussedness. The table was laid with the same old grainy dishes, with the faded swallows and tulips, that we had always used, the tall brass tumblers for water; the boi fish was served without the heads removed, and chapattis. Mom tried to persuade Bapaiji to remove the heads in the kitchen as in later days she would try to have them removed for Rusi and myself. "This is nothing to do with democracy, Bapaiji. This is only making things easier for your guest. At least put knives and forks on the table, no? In Bombay we always use knives and forks. That is how educated Indians eat now." But Bapaiji refused, and when the Maharani asked for a fork and to have the head removed from her boi, although Bapaiji complied without a word, she ate her own boi with a new relish, sucking repeatedly on its severed head and beady eyes. Later she grumbled to Mom: "Array, she thinks she's an English, saying What-phot and How do you do and all. Eating with hands is not good enough for her now."

Bapaiji didn't show me much of the ceremony that followed, I suspect, because Dad wasn't there and she didn't want to reveal how she felt about it, but she did show me a smiling picture of herself in the next day's *Jam-e-Jamshed*, standing in front of a pyramid of

The Memory of Elephants

pehlwans with a caption that read: "'Wah-wah,' says Bapaiji, 'look, no, everyone? What muscles!'"

The man in the dagla whom I had come to know as Bapaiji knelt on the grey stone floor of one of the bedrooms in the back of Hill Bungalow, winding up a toy chimpanzee wearing a red cap with a bell at the tip and cymbals attached to his hands. He put it on the floor and watched it hop around, clashing its cymbals, jingling its bell; a clockwork train ran around the chimpanzee, a bear lumbered by the tracks moving its head slowly from side to side, a frog leaped over the train. Other toys (I recognized them all) crawled and scurried and rang and tooted. Bapaiji had bought them during her trip to Japan and wound them up for us on special occasions. "I have simple pleasures now, Homi, as you can see. I did not think dying would be so complicated – I expected eternal unconsciousness, but it's not so. Actually, I had begun to change my mind about that even before, when your pappa died. Whatever our differences – and there were many, primarily about money – I was convinced that once I had died they would be resolved; but he died first, and he died with his resentment swollen to its fullest. How I regretted it at first, not what I had done but that he had died before me. If I had died first he would have forgiven me, he would have understood that I had saved the money for him, he would not have borne grudges against the dead – but he died first.

"He was too goodhearted to appreciate the value of money. In my time, Homi, prices remained the same over generations – but, to give you an example of how things have changed, the same kusti which cost ten annas when I was a girl costs one hundred rupees today! That is a hundred and sixty percent increase! I saw the first electric lights, the first engine trains, the first motor cars, but none of them astounded me as much as inflation.

"It wasn't until he died that I understood what it meant to be a mother, because he had died without love for me. I hated God then, I called him a trickster, but slowly I came to accept what I had known all along – that He could do no wrong. Everything was His will, and to challenge His will was to put myself above Him. Reason does not matter, nor does making sense; all that matters is courage, humility, compassion, virtue, faith; one must practise these and leave the rest to God.

"When we sent your pappa to the UK he was only seventeen; Hormusji said he was still young, but I said we must find the courage and send him. When he left I could not stop crying. I could not understand the shameful emotion, where the womanish tears came from. Hormusji said they were a mother's tears, but I was the mother, and the mother – not the father – had sent him away; I had wanted to reject the woman's – not the mother's – role, but I couldn't do one without the other and your pappa thought I was rejecting him. I should have had more humility; then I might have had the love of my son. I should have learned something from Hormusji; he had enough humility to fill the Indian Ocean. I don't know what to think; after Adi Gadiali gave me up for his sweet shop I never loved anyone the same way.

"But I like to think I exonerated myself at the time of your navjote. A hundred friends and relatives came to lunch and dinner for three days, and on the day of the navjote itself we had a thousand guests for dinner. My only regret was Hormusji couldn't be there – but I was glad to be able, finally, to do something for your pappa. Of course, I don't need to tell you about your own navjote; I only wanted to make the point that when it was necessary I spent like a fountain."

I remember the navjote well. Yes, we thought Bapaiji was stingy – a greased needle wouldn't make it through her purse strings, Dad would say – but it never affected my admiration for her, and the occasion of the navjote was grand for Rusi and myself.

The navjote is an investiture ceremony during which Parsis officially become Zoroastrians. The rituals were primarily embarrassing: first, indoors, we were to taste purefied (nevertheless rank) cow's urine (Rusi drank his entire portion because he hadn't learned yet to differentiate between tasting and drinking; I pushed mine away after just smelling it); then, to be bathed naked in milk, rose petals, and water by a fat woman with hairy arms who sang nasally what sounded like a single phrase, ohn-sa-ra, repeated endlessly, in the presence of a roomful of old women gathered by the open door of the bathroom; finally, to be brought to the front compound in lhegas and shawls around our shoulders, to the makeshift stage full of perhaps twenty white-robed priests seated around the centre, surrounded by the thousand guests on rickety chairs around the stage, where the officiating priests helped us don our sadras, tie our kustis, reciting the requisite prayers in Avestan (which we too had learned by rote), before seating us on low wooden platforms (still on stage, mine higher than Rusi's because of my leg) while reciting the Tandarosti (a health prayer) and showering us with rose petals, rice, and raisins.

But the personal embarrassment was greatly compensated by the festivities: a tent the size of a circus ring was erected in the compound in the back and eight large woodburning fireplaces were constructed to hold the huge smoke-darkened dekchis; for the main feast we had eggs fried with potatoes, patra ni macchhi (fish steamheated in banana leaves with a thick lemony white sauce and toy tomatoes), sali boti (lamb with finely grated deep-fried potatoes in a sweet spicy gravy), and chicken dhansak (a sweet brown rice with chicken in a lentil paste); there were also wafers, chapattis, chutneys, murrabba (a sweetener), kulfi (a thick creamy ice cream), and soft drinks; rows of tables with white tablecloths were arranged in the compound on the side for the guests and the food was served on banana leaves, to be eaten with one's hands, in three sittings; Rusi and I were free to roam the tent and sample whatever was available; when I was full I liked to hang around just to sniff the air – the Rander Takor Khana played Indian classical music on a sitar, sarod, sarangi, harmonium, and tablas instead of a band playing the regular Indian film music; I didn't care for the music, neither did Bapaiji nor Mom nor Dad nor Rusi, but the people who knew more about such things assured us it was sublime; it was certainly, as Bapaiji constantly reminded us, expensive; in Bombay we might have had the music we preferred, Goody or Nelly with their bands playing Western popular music, but Bapaiji had offered to undertake all the expenses only if the navjote were performed in Navsari so Dad didn't complain; there was even accommodation available for our closest friends from Bombay so that the celebration became more like a holiday than a religious event.

Between the Mosque
and the Temple

Bapaiji was awakened every morning by the crowing, ku-kre-ku, of the rooster. She was out of her four-poster bed almost as soon as she was awake. The dubri Pemmy was already sweeping the floors, and when Bapaiji got out of bed Pemmy folded the blankets and raised the mosquito net. As she got older Bapaiji became increasingly dependent on Pemmy, not only for the household chores but even for a companion and nurse. Mom, living in Bombay, could visit her only occasionally, but Pemmy, living with her husband in a single-room abode with walls of corrugated metal in Bapaiji's back compound, was always available. She had worked for the family for so long that when her son was born she brought him to Bapaiji saying not "I have got a son," but "Homi Seth's servant" (meaning my servant) "has been born." Bapaiji said her kusti prayers as the sun rose everyday and the other morning birds, koels, sparrows, bulbuls, announced their presence. One morning she said an extra Yatha Ahu Vairyo prayer because she was anxious about the outcome of the day. As Chairman of the Sanitation Committee Bapaiji had to settle a dispute between a Hindu and a Musalman faction about the placement of a rubbish bin; the Hindus said it was too close to their temple and wanted to move it further away, but the Musalmans said it was already too close to their mosque and wanted to move it closer to the temple. The Collector, who was responsible for the collection of revenue for the Seervais in the surrounding wadis, had warned her that a bloodbath might ensue if she were not careful, it was not safe for a man, leave alone a woman; but Bapaiji had said she was the chairman and set a day to examine the site.

After saying the extra prayer Bapaiji put on a plain cotton blouse, a plain sari with a plain border, and plain black walking shoes with plain brass buckles to look more businesslike. She never wore bangles and rings and tilas so she didn't even have to think about that. She breakfasted on one egg, one slice of bread, a cup of tea which she slurped from the saucer because it was too hot, while listening to the news on her Murphy radio. The Collector sent a car to pick her up, but she sent it back; she had chosen to walk because it wasn't far and she wanted to show the people she was just like them; but she was glad the two committee members who had come with the car stayed with her – they would have been little help in a riot but she was glad for their moral support.

The day became hotter as she set out and she held the sash of her sari over her eyes to shield them from the sun. Along the way a group of students from Hormusji's school recognized her and said, "Saebji, Bapaiji, how are you today?"

Bapaiji stopped. "I am good. But we have got some important work to do. We cannot wait around."

"Where are you going, Bapaiji?"

Bapaiji smiled suddenly as she thought how the students might help her. "Come, see yourselves. We are not going far. Everybody, come."

The students followed her and, as they walked, more people joined them, three women with baskets of vegetables on their heads on their way to the Mota Bajar, two men carrying a crate of tiffins between them on their heads on their way to the college, chanawallahs doing business as they walked, other hawkers, beggar children, animals, an acrobat, loafers. "Come, come," the students said as if they were on a picnic. "Come, see what is going to happen."

Soon the Collector's car approached them again and the Collector himself got out. "Why you didn't want the car, Bapaiji? It would have been better, don't you think?"

Bapaiji called him with her hand. "Come with us. See yourself."

The Collector understood. The retinue Bapaiji was building for herself was more impressive than even a Rolls Royce might have been; the populist was always more effective than the aristocratic approach. He took his place by her side.

Bapaiji led the parade, the men mostly in white, the women more gaily dressed, with dogs and goats and chickens, along the dusty wadis, the dirt paths, the cobbled streets, past the tiny huddled shops of the cobblers, tailors, potters, and other artisans, around phlegmatic cows swishing their tails at flies, past pyramids of drying dung, amidst the constant ringing of bicyclists' bells and honking of motor scooterists' hooters. When a white cow stood in their path, Bapaiji touched its flank and then her own forehead in obeisance and others did the same. She was enjoying herself immensely; if she could have somersaulted the others might well have followed suit.

When they got to the rubbish bin the Hindu and Musalman spokesmen and their followers stared with their mouths open, not just at the crowd but that the chairman was a woman. The Hindu, a fat man with a red handkerchief knotted at its four corners on his head, a long white shirt, a dhoti, and chappals, said, "Maiji, Maiji, you are the chairman? Maiji, you are the chairman?"

"Yes," Bapaiji said. "Why you are so surprised?"

"Nothing-nothing, but you are the chairman?"

The Musalman was much darker, wearing a red fez with a black tassel, a brown jacket buttoned to his neck even in the heat, and brown tailored pants which revealed red socks at his ankles over worn dusty brown shoes. He said nothing but his brow was wrinkled in puzzlement so that his eyebrows became one long ridge.

Bapaiji got straight to the point. "The solution is simple," she said, "but we have all got to be reasonable. We must find the place exactly between the mosque and the temple. I want you both to walk with me from the mosque to the temple and count my footsteps."

Bapaiji spoke with such assurance that a passer-by might have thought she had rehearsed for the event. The Musalman walked grudgingly, with a stiff back, a little to the side as if he were not with them, his brow still wrinkled as if he were thinking important thoughts, counting in his mind. The Hindu walked with Bapaiji, counting loudly in a singsong voice as if he were learning numbers in school. The crowd counted along just to add thunder to the proceedings.

They counted exactly two hundred and thirty-two steps to the temple. "Now," Bapaiji said, turning to the enthusiastic crowd. "What is half of two hundred and thirty-two?"

A number of cheerful voices replied, "One hundred and sixteen, Maiji. One hundred and sixteen."

She asked them to count with her again as she walked back toward the mosque and stopped at a hundred and sixteen. "This is the middle point," she said. "This is where you must put the bin." It meant moving the bin closer to the temple and further from the mosque. Bapaiji was relieved because she felt the Hindu would give in more easily than the Musalman. "This is the best place," she said. "This is the fair place. What do you think?" She looked at the Hindu.

The Hindu looked at his followers who nodded. "It is fair, Maiji. It is fair," he said, beaming. The Musalman did not smile, said nothing, but nodded his approval without even looking at his faction. Both of them thanked her, said it was a wise decision, that they were indebted to her, and if she ever needed them for anything to definitely call and they would come.

"Anyone could have provided the solution," Bapaiji said later, "but it helped that I was a Parsi, not a Hindu or Musalman, and it helped even more that I was a woman. That just surprised them too much to argue."

When George Bernard Shaw was fêted on one of his nonagenerian birthdays, he presented himself apologetically as just an old man instead of the legend some might have expected; the self-effacement was probably tongue-in-cheek, but his appearance was unmistakably frail, disbelieving, tentative, self conscious, even timid – in one word, humble. That was how Bapaiji appeared in her last days; she spoke of death with curiosity rather than resignation as if her readiness were everything; she had outlived her entire generation, even her son; those who remained admired her, wished her well, took care of her; Thakor, who now went to the cinema alone though still as her guest, still visited her in the mornings; Pemmy, with a family of her own in the compound behind the house, was always a bell-push away; Mom, who had doubled their salaries on the sly to allay Bapaiji's fear of inflation, visited her for a week every month; friends, associates, acquaintances, visited in the evenings; but of course none of them could give her back the world she had known. Like Shaw, she appeared unbowed but grateful, aware of her debts as much as her triumphs.

Bapaiji's last fascination was with a cassette player which Mom had bought her. She wanted to record the songs of her childhood which no one sang anymore, particularly the Bamdad Song, the Song of the Dawn, which the women had sung during their early morning chores. Pemmy learned how to operate the machine, but had to run from the room each time she pressed the Record button because she couldn't keep from laughing at Bapaiji's old froggy voice. Bapaiji didn't mind; she found Pemmy's amusement amusing herself, picturing the tiny pretty brown woman crouched behind the wall, her hands spread over her face like a child's, as if to muffle her laughter while hiding herself from view.

On Bapaiji's ninety-fifth birthday, the Collector organized a function in Seervai Wadi where speeches were made in her honour, a lifesize photograph was unveiled, and she was presented a purse of one thousand, one hundred, and eleven rupees. Bapaiji made a speech, but instead of recounting her public triumphs as was her custom she credited Hormusji with making the triumphs possible. She slept that night with my birthday card, received on the same day, in her bed. The next morning she was dead. Mom found an unfinished letter addressed to me on her writing desk:

My Dear American Grandson, Homi,

It has been a wonderful day, but more than anything else I am so happy that you remembered my birthday. I know you are a busy man with your experiments and college and life in America, but I am so happy that you did not forget an old woman's birthday. The Collector and some other people got together to make it a very memorable occasion. Your mamma was also there. But I am more tired than I thought and I have still to say my prayers. I will finish this letter tomorrow. . . .

The letter was the only indication that she had not anticipated death; otherwise, she had blotted the letter, capped the fountain pen, put the squat bottle of Quink ink in its box and into its corner in the drawer, arranged her thick lensed, full moon spectacles neatly on the page, said her prayers, turned out the light, left her slippers next to each other perpendicular to the bed as if they were on exhibition, and lying on her side, clutching my birthday card alongside her pillow, whispering God's will be done, with a smile on her face, passed directly into sleep.

Granny

Cambridge

I saw Bapaiji dead, fragile like an unwrapped mummy, lying on her side in her black wooden four-poster bed, with the green nightlight and switch embedded in its headboard, snug within the mosquito net, with my birthday card clutched like a pillow under her arm under the blanket – I had sent her the largest card I could find because of her eyesight – and the needles in my brain temporarily ceased their activity. The fantastic turned into the familiar; I recognized the bedroom of my childhood in Mayo House on Cooperage Road, as my eyes, now open, became slowly comfortable with the soft darkness enclosed by the drawn curtains and the cardboard to close the space over the air conditioner by the window. On the light green wall across from the bed (the other walls were lemon yellow) was my red wooden bookshelf still holding undisturbed the entire James Bond series in the Pan bindings I had loved because their spines were too flexible to crack, the thirty-five cent Perry Mason and Agatha Christie Pocket Books with their kangaroo emblems, the Four Square Tarzan series on the covers of which the sleek man in the loin cloth protected voluptuous women in harem wear from hostile tribes and sabre-toothed tigers in exotic locales, and the black rosewood elephant bookends with ivory tusks (before the books the shelf had held a colourful wooden train, perhaps four feet long – a black locomotive, a coal cart, two passenger cars, held together by tongue and groove couples); below the shelf stood the stylized wooden elephant lampshades on the desk (it was a long desk with drawers in the middle and kneeholes for Rusi and myself at each end); there were the same pin-ups of Brigitte Bardot and Sophia Loren on the adjacent wall alongside pictures of Einstein, Pasteur, Madame Curie, Isaac Newton, Alexander Hamilton, Edward Jenner,

Jonas Salk, and Albert Sabin; the next wall (behind me) had shelving holding the Telefunken stereo and speakers and the electric clock above them which we had brought back from Hong Kong with a miller and his dog hiking toward a windmill on the clockface (the vanes of the windmill spun to indicate the clock was working); the fourth wall held the window with the air conditioner and the door leading to the verandah.

The dark green, metal-framed bed, with its single flat mattress, was harder than I remembered, but not uncomfortable. I found strength enough to get up and walk slowly to my cupboard with the Elvis records which I had bought at two and three times their regular price from Ollie the smuggler, near the Strand cinema in Colaba, before RCA Victor had negotiated a contract with the Dum Dum Record Company to produce them in India. I browsed curiously through the records and my other artlessly variegated, newly meaningful, rosebuds: Dinky Toys, Matchbox cars, Rolleicord camera, coin collection, stamp collection, magnetic compass, chemistry set, biology set, Bayko set, Meccano set, skittles set, Odhams Encyclopedia, Collins Dictionary, Gray's Anatomy, Photoplay magazines, navy blue cotton school ties with the diagonal red and white band across the centre, hardcover prize books for my scholastic achievements (*David Copperfield*, *Robinson Crusoe*, *Swiss Family Robinson*, *Lamb's Tales from Shakespeare*, *The Three Musketeers*, and *Lorna Doone* among others), and the nipple of Bernadette Kell (I had cut it out of one of the men's magazines my father received from the public library, thinking he wouldn't miss just one nipple) among other things. The articles were the same, but time and distance had made them different, and the afterglow of the difference revived me as if I had unexpectedly recognized an old friend.

The cawing of crows – a harsh, nasal sound – distracted me from my foraging. There is a time in the evening before twilight when they call incessantly, ritualistically, to one another. I had seen them gather in their hundreds once in a maidan, flying and cawing over a dead rat, as if they were disputing a point of etiquette or conducting a court of law. It was frightening to think I might have underestimated the intelligence behind their cruel black faces. Their cawing more than the clock on the wall told me it would soon be dark and, feeling stronger, I opened the door to the verandah to catch as much of what was left of the evening as I could.

My first awareness was of the heat, then of the people; I never felt entirely alone in Bombay, even with no one else in the flat I was aware of the bustle of the city; one didn't walk but elbowed one's way through the streets of Bombay; at night people slept on charpoys on the streets; if wasn't until I arrived in Aquihana that I saw my first entirely deserted street.

I could feel the heat working against my enthusiasm, reminding me I was unwell, but I thought if I could make it to the railing of the verandah, just two yards or so from the threshold of the door, I would be all right. I walked around a low wooden bath stool; the ganga must have forgotten to return it to the bathroom after hanging the clothes on the line (she was too short otherwise); I limped a little because of my leg, a gesture toward my childhood more than my need, and ducked to avoid the clothes swaying in the slight warm breeze, secured by the clips, some wooden, some red or blue or yellow plastic; above the clotheslines my mother had encouraged mani plants to twine about a wire trellis she had rigged, so the ceiling of the verandah could barely be seen for the leaves..

I reached the railing safe but tired. Below me (we lived on the third floor) there was the same rubble gathered around the middle of the brick wall where it had collapsed five years ago; the wall separated the parking spaces of the adjacent buildings; the Fiats, Ambassadors, and Standard Heralds were parked on either side of the wall around the rubble as they had been five years ago, as if the accident had become a part of the overall design.

To my right, behind the house, were the Back Gardens, a large, right-angled triangle of space, occasionally grassy, occasionally sandy, with swings, a slide, a jungle jim at the narrow corner, two tennis courts at the middle corner, gulls (depressions no deeper than a tablespoon made by boys playing marbles) at the right-angled corner, and a great grandfather banyan tree at its fulcrum. The Back Gardens were the recess grounds for the Campion Boys' School (my high school, a tall, bright, imposing, red and white building) and the

Fort Convent School for Girls – but our recesses were staggered so there could be no mingling. It was also the ground for our assemblies in the mornings, our PT classes, and our scout meetings on Saturday mornings. The scouts would gather behind the banyan tree before the meetings hoping for a glimpse of Cecilia, the prostitute, who would sometimes appear in her black negligée at her third floor window with her lover of the night before, frequently a balding man, smoking a cigarette, wearing a sleeveless dirty-white vest, and they would smile and kiss each other for our benefit. I swore I would someday rescue Cecilia though she had never revealed signs of distress. No such compunction assailed me when, not much later, my father had taken me (to show me the world) to Lamington Road where the prostitutes solicited men from behind bars, inviting them into the rooms in the back. There was this difference: Cecilia could have passed for any of the Goanese Christians I had known among my teachers and ayahs, even among Mom's friends (she was younger and prettier than most), but the women in The Cages, some of whom might have been no more than thirteen years old, were too gaudy in their appeal to elicit my sympathy; besides, they called too loudly, too eagerly, to arouse desire, and their cages were not unlike those of the monkeys at the Victoria Gardens Zoo. It was easy to develop a fascination for the girls behind the bars, but just as difficult to act on the fascination as to act on the fascination of a serpent – each mesmerized too deeply for potency or desire – but Cecilia was different. Derek D'Souza, who had carried an FL, a flattened Trojan, in his wallet for three years before we finally, at one of the camps, filled it up with water until it burst, gave her his highest rating: ten jhing-jhangs, or ten pokes (if you poked a girl ten times and still wanted more you were being not only greedy but unfair to the girl), but the girls in The Cages rated only one jhing-jhang apiece, owing more to the kindness of the scouts than any merit of their own.

To my left, across Cooperage Road, behind the corrugated metal walls of the Cooperage Stadium, there was a function, the overflow of which spilled onto the narrow barren maidan outside the walls and onto the road. It was where Campion School had its annual Sports Meet. I couldn't tell by looking at the crowd what the function was today – perhaps a hockey match, or a football match, or something else, none of which held much interest for me. The game must either have been over or have reached its midway point. Crowds gathered around the bhelwallahs, the chanawallahs, the bhajiawallahs, the ice cream wallahs; men lit cigarettes and biris from slow burning ropes hanging beside the hawkers' stalls lit by hurricane lanterns and petromaxes; others chomped paan, spitting their reddened saliva around; the theme from "Come September", arguably the most popular of the Western hit records in Bombay alongside "Spanish Gypsy Dance" by Edmundo Ross and His Orchestra and "Walk, Don't Run" by the Ventures, was played over the loudspeakers.

"Come September" affected me like a cliché; it made me tired, it made me aware of the heat wrapping itself around me like a damp sticky blanket, of the flies, two of which boldly held their ground on the railing by my hand, one astride the other, while a third rubbed its forelegs as if it were washing, and a fourth, much larger, buzzed overhead like a bee. I looked for a flyswat, the wiremesh kind with the red cloth borders with which Rusi and I had spent Sunday afternoons at Granny's between chicken lunches at one o'clock and teas with pastries from Bombelli's at four, massacring flies by the dozen – but there wasn't one at hand. It wasn't unusual for us to tally more than a hundred flies each on the long oaken dining table with the linen tablecloth and slender, misty-blue vase with sunflowers from the garden, which seated sixteen on stiff-backed stately chairs upholstered in beige under crystal chandeliers with low wattage lightbulbs (the ceilings were so high that the corridors and rooms developed a cavernous appearance and the ceiling fans needed the longest spindles to be of any use). The flies tried camouflaging themselves against the speckled tiled floor, the dim lofty grey walls beside the prints of Watteaus, Fragonards, Constables, and Turners, even on the long, heavy, bluish-grey drapes which stood stiffly by the doorways and windows – but mostly in vain. When we were done with the flies I would lie in Soli Mama's beige, wooden armchair, adjusted to its most reclining position (Silo Mama, Mom's youngest sibling, had lived with Granny until he had married and moved from her flat on the first floor to his own on the ground; he took most of the furniture with him but left behind his armchair, bed, and cupboard, also beige, also wooden; when I had been very young we had lived on the ground floor, but the house belonged to Soli Mama – a part of his vast inheritance from the Camas – so my father had moved when the flat on Cooperage Road became available; but I still remember early days playing on the uneven mosaic floor of my bedroom, the sound of the sea at night across Warden Road at Scandalpoint, and the breezes from which the house derived its name, Zephyr), while Rusi jumped on Soli Mama's spring bed until Granny, awakened from her nap by the bouncing, would ask him to stop because he might break the springs. She hated to prohibit us from anything, and to compensate for the lack of our makeshift trampoline gave us three rupees for comics (*Superman*, *Spiderman*, *The Flash*) from Warden Book Store, Kamal Book Store, or Shemaroo, the circulating libraries near her house. In the mornings we might have started a game of Monopoly with Cyrus Mehta from the second floor and Anand Patel from the fourth; the game would be interrupted when we took the bus to Granny's for lunch, and resumed when we returned – though not until Cyrus and Anand had first digested the comics; we rarely completed a game of Monopoly.

Strange: I saw less of Bapaiji than of Granny but I knew her better, perhaps because during our two-week stays in Navsari I was swept entirely into Bapaiji's world, having none of my Bombay ties to distract me, but during our Sunday afternoons with Granny I was continually aware of the discontinued Monopoly game from the morning, and Cyrus and Anand awaiting our return with the comics. Granny's world was not as sweeping, she spent much time alone, she shunned physical contact, she was uncomfortable with small talk, she screamed too readily at her servants whom she preconceived to be duplicitous, toward the end she had kind words for only her children and grandchildren. Bapaiji's activities were never a secret (her early morning prayers sometimes awakened me, and her teeth in the tea cup by her bed were sometimes the last thing I saw before going to bed), but I could never imagine what Granny did with her time; I knew she read because she received *The Illustrated Weekly of India* (from which we ripped out "The Phantom" comic strip, always with her permission) and *Eve's Weekly* (from which we cut pictures of movie stars, again with her permission), but she was always finished with them by the time we arrived, so it was hard to imagine her actually reading them – did she read them lying in her wooden beige spring bed (the same as Soli Mama's), sitting on the soft, lime green couches custom-made to fit the curve of the sitting room wall before the glass-encased replica of the *Venus de Milo*, or at the long dining table where she played her games of patience in the dim light of the chandelier and the squeak of the low-reaching fan? I knew also that she took drives along Marine Drive, because I had seen her there once through the crowd of strollers in the back of her huge cream Studebaker (none of those tiny Fiats and Ambassadors for her even though she generally rode alone), with one of her card playing friends in the days when she had card playing friends, the back door open to let the sea air through, while her uniformed chauffeur in his Captain's hat squatted patiently on the sidewalk. I waved my cane from a distance (I was with Anand and Cyrus and Rusi and didn't want to hold them up), but she didn't respond; she might not have seen me (her eyesight was deteriorating), she might also have questioned the propriety of my gesture, hailing her so commonly through a crowd – but having seen her just once by the sea, I found it difficult to relate her to the person with whom we lunched on Sundays; it was too alien to my experience of her in the natural habitat of her own house; perhaps if she had responded to my wave she would have seemed less alien; but my image of her in the car parked on Marine Drive tied in more completely, sadly, with what I learned of her much later: she cruised Warden Road sometimes in the evenings looking for a ganga to sleep in the flat with her for the night because she was afraid to sleep alone; she couldn't pay the servants enough to stay with her because she screamed at them for the least thing; Soli Mama said there was nothing to fear because he lived downstairs from her and there was a chowkidar at the gates all night; but when she continued to solicit strange women to stay overnight with her for money Mom began sleeping over; then, when Dad objected, she sent me and Rusi over to spend the nights; then, when it interfered with our school schedules, Mom found a servant she trusted to stay with her nights; the servant did it as much as a favour to Mom as for the money (she was the servant of a friend of Mom's, had been on loan to Mom on the nights she needed extra help for parties, and her friend didn't need her nights).

"Come September" was followed by Indian film music. I recognized Lata Mangeshkar's familiar nasal voice easily; any Indian would have; she did the soundtracks for almost every Indian movie, and since the Bombay movie industry is larger even than Hollywood's, and since every Indian movie bar none is a musical, she has made more recordings than anyone else, a fact duly recorded in the Guinness book of records. The lipsynching in the movies is as laughable as the melodrama and filmcraft, but not to their vast, vastly entertained, audience – but for me Lata Mangeshkar's ubiquitous voice had become an even more soporific cliché than "Come September".

When I closed my eyes to rest a bit a renewed tug of voices in my head weakened me so that I had to leave the railing for the wooden bath stool and sit down with my face in my hands. Granny's voice was in ascendance. "Homi, this is Granny. Please listen carefully. I've been waiting a long time to talk, but you know how Banubai is. There is no stopping her when she has her mind set on finishing something." Granny insisted on calling Bapaiji by her real name. "She's not my bapaiji," she said, but that of course was beside the point. They were entirely different: Bapaiji preferred to eat with her hands scraping even fishheads clean with her teeth, Granny preferred an entire table setting whether or not she needed it; Bapaiji loved her cycle rickshaw, Granny had more use than affection for her Studebaker; Bapaiji wanted to make a difference, Granny wanted to maintain the status quo. Granny admired Bapaiji openly, even envied her, but she never understood her satisfactorily enough to be entirely comfortable with her; perhaps she insisted on calling her Banubai as much to maintain her own identity as to confuse Bapaiji's.

"I know how exhausted you are, Homi, I know how sick, but I have to say just one thing first; then, when you are rested, I will say the rest – but first, I love you, my Homi, my dearest, I love you. This will sound strange to you because I have never said it before, but I should have said it before, I should have said it often, because it is true, because it would have been good for me, and I think good for you too. I should have shown it more – but things happen, people settle like plaster, they become brittle, they're afraid to break. Disappointments make you brittle. It happened to me. It could happen to you. I shall do what I can to prevent it. Where shall I begin?"

Actually, Granny had once told me she loved me. It was at one of our big Papeti lunches at the sixteen-seater dining table with Mom, Dad, Rusi, Soli Mama, and Granny and myself of course. We had sweet buns with butter, patrel for the savoury, followed by mince patties, baked chicken with cherries, and a strawberry soufflé for dessert. Rusi and I were too young to follow the conversation, and too interested in the food to care – but I was hardly as invisible to Granny as she was to us. The cherries in the chicken dish had been pitted but I came upon one that was not. I slipped the pit back into the serving dish wishing not to clutter my plate, thinking no one would notice, but Granny did, although at first I couldn't be sure.

"Homi," she said, cutting through the conversation at the table (she was at the head, Mom to her right, then Dad, then Rusi, Soli Mama to her left, then myself), "you are a very good boy, my oldest grandchild, and I love you."

I had braced myself for a reprimand, but she had said she loved me; I didn't know what to expect next; I didn't have to wait long.

"When you were born I was so happy I didn't think it was possible. When you developed the polio I prayed for three hours every day for a month. It's better now but I still remember you in my prayers every day that someday you will be completely cured."

I was beginning to relax though I didn't understand what had precipitated her reminiscence. The others looked curiously between me and her. "Then we found you were a genius, not just intelligent, but a genius. I was so proud – and I'm still proud. There is almost nothing I wouldn't give you if you wanted it."

Even Rusi had stopped eating by this point and was staring between the two of us. I was so taken by her encomium I had forgotten about the pit. "But don't you think," she continued, "it was naughty of you to put that pit back in the serving dish?"

I wanted to crawl under the table. I reached to take the pit back, but Granny said, "You can leave it now. But don't do it again. It was not a nice thing to do." She explained what had happened to the others while I looked appropriately chastised and woebegone. I said "Sorry" when she was finished explaining and the matter was closed. What strikes me now more than my embarrassment at the time is the length to which Granny had gone to soften her reproach; she screamed so easily at the servants that I was always apprehensive that her tirades might just as easily be directed at me. I needn't have worried; she never shouted at any of her grandchildren; I don't think she could have lived with herself if she had.

Granny died painlessly, midsentence, seated in a chair, in her bedroom, talking with her three children: Mom, Jalu Masi who lived in Hong Kong, and Soli Mama; her head drooped before she could finish what she was saying. I felt no remorse when Bapaiji died; she had been in readiness, she had clutched my birthday card to herself for comfort in her death. Granny was the less responsive grandmother; she appeared to need less but she needed more; I wished I could have sent her off with a card or letter to hold in her lap, but when she stopped replying to my letters I stopped writing; if I had continued writing she would have died more happily and I would have received the news with more equanimity, with less of a feeling of desertion. There were times I had thought of her as Miss Havisham sternly directing Pip and Estelle to "Play," but now she and the other members of my family, dead and alive, seemed more like characters in set pieces constructed by the Ghost of Christmas Past, and I an ever unlikely, increasingly curious, increasingly penitent, Ebenezer Scrooge.

Granny sat at the head of her sixteen-seater dining table with the linen tablecloth folded a third of the way down exposing the oak finish, but she was not as I had ever seen her. She was still tiny, but she wore a dress with leg-of-mutton sleeves, not one of the saris to which I was accustomed, and her features, still as delicate as I remembered them, were porcelain-smooth, without the grandmotherly lines I knew. Her chin, cheeks, mouth and eyes were so tiny, so finely sculpted and tinted (except for her nose, too thin, too long, too shiny even in a dim light), that they brought to mind the sharp toylike elegance of tropical fish in pet stores. I couldn't see her legs, under the table, but her arms suggested they might be thin and supple with the spring of an antelope rather than thick and muscled with the kick of a pony. I recognized her by her expression (haunted, as if she were afraid that something or someone were always about to grab her from behind) and the cards she had spread out before her (the Royal Family decks she had bought during her stay in Cambridge, with a different monarch on the face of each card, and the Lion and Unicorn emblem on the back). I also recognized the upholstered wooden chairs at the table with the beige finish, the wood and glass showcases (also in beige), the crystal goblets, china dishes, cut-glass vases, papier-maché and porcelain figurines within them (ballet dancers, a sow nursing pink piglets, rosy bear cubs at cricket), and the splendid chandelier with the low wattage lightbulbs, but I was not prepared for the sight beyond the balcony at the far end of the room: elm trees, bare and bowed with snow, and the hind legs of a hare in midair, caught as if in a photograph, blurred against the shower of snow sprung behind by its feet. Snow! In Bombay! I looked for something to discredit my fantastic notion, but found instead something to verify it: a fireplace where the doorway should have been, which enhanced the cavernlike appearance of the room.

"Homi, no, you are making an understandable mistake. Yes, this is Zephyr, yes, my Bombay house, but, no, it is not in Bombay. I had my choice. I could put it anywhere I wanted. Banubai has already explained it to you so I don't want to go into it again, but it was unfair of her to make fun of me for wanting to stay in my house. Maybe there is more to life than chandeliers and paintings, but that is what I am accustomed to, that is what I want – but she is hardly in a position to criticize me, she should take a sharp look at herself before she says anything about anyone else. In those baggy white trousers with the thick cuffs so high at the ankles she looks like somebody's bearer. It was a good thing she had so many interests; a commotion of people and events keeps you from imagining things, it keeps you from going crazy – but it also keeps you committed to things instead of ideas, it also keeps you from seeing beyond what's obvious, and it can also be just another form of escape. Not that it matters, of course, once you're here; it's not as if you can change anything. So if she chooses to be a man, and I choose to resituate my house in Cambridge, why does she have to make an issue of it? Yes, that is snow outside, Cambridge snow – Cambridge, England – and the elms are Cambridge elms, the hare a Cambridge hare. The time I spent in Cambridge, chaperoning your Soli Mama while he was at King's College, was the happiest in my life. I resided at The Queen's Arms, not far from the Great Bridge over the Cam from which Cambridge got its name, where I met some of the staunchest bridge and bezique players – Muriel Fitzwilliams, Sarah Allsop, Agnes McGuiness, Nora Bomford, Iris Masters – most of them widows like myself, many of them had been married to armywallahs and spent some time in India – hence, our mutual affinity. They called me Mary. Meher was too difficult. They kept calling me May-her, accenting the first syllable so ponderously that I had to correct them every time. Finally, Agnes McGuiness said, "Why don't we just call you Mary, my dear, if it's all the same to you." Actually, I preferred it. It made me feel like one of them even though they always deferred to my opinion when we dined at the Koh-i-noor or the Taj Mahal despite their own vast experience with Indian cookery, and I continued to wear saris – I hadn't worn a dress in so long I would have felt uncomfortable in one; besides, it's true what Edith Sitwell said about Englishwomen, that they dress as if they had been mice in previous incarnations, or hoped to be in the next.

"But despite their appearance the English are the most splendid people. Their very rectitude is charming. Muriel Fitzwilliams never lost the opportunity to tell a new acquaintance the story of her friend who, going out to dine in Simla with, as she put it, a very exalted old dear, the wife of a very senior officer, what was known as a sakt burra mem, arrived to find the mem's bearer on his knees on the floor solemnly using a flitspray up her petticoats. She looked at Muriel's friend and said without a trace of embarrassment, 'Quite all right, my dear, quite all right. I find this very efficacious for the mosquitoes.'

"These were marvellous women and they made marvellous friends, whether we were taking a walk along the puntfilled river shaded by willows to Clare Bridge, by the exquisitely landscaped flowerbeds and trees – later, when I thought of Cambridge after returning to Bombay, I thought first of Clare Bridge, in a dim light, a fog, or late evening, how the arches of the bridge kissed their reflections in the water creating lovely orange shapes between them in the shadows – or shopping along the narrow, stall-lined lanes of Market Hill. I'm not much for walks myself; I prefer drives; but the English are the greatest people in the world for walks, and I obliged them mostly out of friendship. They looked out for me too. Being a foreigner, I took the utmost care not to give offence, but there were times I needed rescuing. I was shopping for flowers with Muriel once when one of the shopkeepers held an intimate garment with laces and stays in my face and barked, "'Ere yer are, lidy, jest whatcher want fer yer figger! Ten bob and its yers – it's a gift – who says ten bob?' I don't think he meant to thrust it in my face, he was just raising it and I just happened to turn around that minute, but all of a sudden there we were, frozen in that wretched situation, with everyone in Market Hill watching – at least that's how it felt to me. My embarrassment stemmed as much from the garment in my face as from my inability to follow his accent. I was caught between asking him to clarify himself, thereby showing an interest I did not feel, and ignoring him, which would have been rude. As he waited for my answer, my embarrassment embarrassed him. Fortunately, Muriel was quick to intercede. 'My dear man,' she said, taking the garment from him and putting it down, 'what this lady wants for her figure could be had for nothing, because it's nothing short of nothing she wants.'

"There was merriment; Muriel smiled cheerfully; I smiled grate-fully, humbly, and turned directly to a flower girl who'd been calling 'Vi'lets, lidy, fresh vi'lets,' and bought a dozen. Later, after I asked Muriel to explain what the man had said, we both laughed, I thanked her, and she said it was nothing.

"When they found out I had once played the sitar Nora Bomford got me one that her husband had brought back from India as a souvenir, and said I could keep it as long as I stayed in Cambridge. 'Much better to have it used, my dear,' she said, 'than lie there.' They lived on Magdalene Street, the Bomfords; the walk to their house – it was amidst a row of stately old homes with projecting stories, bay windows, and steep russet-tiled roofs – was quite lovely.

I hadn't played the sitar since I had been married because your grandfather, Rustamji Jamshedji, whom you unfortunately never met, said it was a servant's instrument – good Parsis played only the piano, or the violin. It was so silly, this pilgrimage toward all things Anglo, but that is the way many of us Parsis are – Jehangirji Kawasji Daboo named his daughter Bachubai Guinevere Daboo because he insisted that her great aunt, a few times removed, had been an Englishwoman; he was too obsessed with his notion to recognize how irrevocably the ridiculous juxtaposition of names had exposed his despair. Anyway, I was delighted to have the instrument and, in return, I played for them and even gave Nora some lessons, teaching her what little I knew about ragas and talas.

"Those were halcyon days. I chose the Gogmagog Hills, southeast of Cambridge, for the new site of Zephyr because between the east and west balconies of the house I can see King's College, the pinnacles and cupola of its gateway, the buttresses, and the wonderful Backs. If I use my telescope I can even see the heraldry, the woodwork, the window tracery, even the ducks by the river when the season is right. I can even see the awnings – green and white stripes, red and white stripes, blue and white stripes – of the stalls in Market Hill. Of course, I don't need a telescope to see all this, even with the Gogmagog Hills some fifteen miles from the town; here one can have what one wishes merely by wishing it – so long as it doesn't interfere with someone else's wishes – but I don't wish to leave the house, and the telescope adds to the reality of it all.

"Winter has become my favourite season. I keep it snowing most of the time and my fireplace crackling. I like the warmth of a fireplace in winter more than the warmth of summer. It's toastier, I don't feel the obligation of walks in the sun with friends, and, perhaps most importantly, I can turn the heat off if I wish unlike the heat of summer. Besides, I like the winter scenes better; the snow becomes a motif for the entire landscape: adults shovelling pathways to their doors, children throwing snowballs on their way to school, animals leaving deeper prints for naturalists to identify. And, of course, the fireplace in winter deepens the luxury of tea and hot buttered toast – or scones, or buns, or eclairs – or, if it's later in the day, of glasses of sherry, or olives, or cheese straws, or impaled dwarf sausages.

"Next to winter – and one must have variety to deepen one's appreciation, by contrast, for that which one loves the best – I like it when it rains. Its reassuring patter on a windowpane enhances the spell of the fireplace while enveloping the landscape in its own intrinsic personality: glistening streets, dripping elms, a rustle of mackintoshes, and, with the radiant arc of a rainbow, the crystalline song of a thrush.

"Unfortunately, the rainbow heralds the sun, and I have never liked the sun. At its best it is warm, but too often it is too bright, too hot, for comfort. The sun doesn't as much enhance life as expose it. It forces one to squint, adding lines to one's face, in order to view the landscape with the subtlety to which one is accustomed on less aggressive days. Of course, goggles are available for those so inclined, but goggles are for actors (who live on the words of others) and other such lesser luminaries who parade themselves for the attention they otherwise would lack. And, worst of all, the sun darkens the skin.

"Perhaps I should add that I recognize my affectation, I recognize my minority status as a cloud worshipper (both for obstructing the sun and heralding rain); even Muriel and my other friends wore goggles when the occasion warranted it (I didn't, not ever, not wishing to call attention to myself, no matter what they said); even Soli wore goggles on the sly, when he thought I wasn't watching, and he would prance in the sun in his corduroy slacks and tweed jacket with the leather elbows and cuffs like a sheep gone mad; but more than anything else I liked Cambridge, all of England for that matter, because it was a town, a country, that had found little favour with the sun."

Every one said Cambridge had changed Granny. She smiled more easily and there was a constant sheen in her eyes; Mom said it was as if she had fallen in love. I was nine years old the summer after she and Soli Mama returned from Cambridge and we all took a holiday in Darjeeling. Granny chose Darjeeling because she wanted a place, like Cambridge, with an air conditioner in the sky; also, she wanted to visit the home of the Darjeeling tea she had consumed in such quantities in Cambridge; besides, two of her bridge companions were going to be there too so she would have something to do (they could easily round up a fourth in the hotel). Dad had to work so there were just Granny, Soli Mama, Mom, Rusi, myself, and Julie, Rusi's ayah. My ayah, Mary, had been left behind to take care of Dad. She wanted to come instead of Julie, and would have prevailed on Mom until she'd gotten her way (she was twenty-five, selfish, stubborn; Julie was fifty, too kindly to fuss), but she was afraid to fly – we had to fly from Bombay to Calcutta, from Calcutta to Bagdogra, and then take a van up the foothills of the Himalayas to Darjeeling. I was so struck by the change in Granny during the Indian Airlines flight to Calcutta I even said something about it to Mom. "Why is Granny smiling so much?" It was right after the air hostess had passed around cotton wool for our ears and sweets on which to suck during the ascent and asked us to fasten our seatbelts. "It's because she's happy," Mom said, seated on my left. "Darjeeling is as close to Cambridge as she can get in India." Mom had said once that Granny had almost wished Soli Mama would fail his examinations so they would have an excuse to stay longer in Cambridge. "Now, hush – and remember to swallow." It helped alleviate the pressure to swallow I was told, so swallow I did, earnestly, frequently, clutching a second sweet in reserve in the event of an accident with the first. Soli Mama, seated across the aisle to my right, must have seen my nervousness. "Would you like another sweet?" he asked, offering me his. He smiled as if a laugh were everpresent in his mouth – something to do with Cambridge, too, I was sure, all this good nature – but he had other reasons as well to be jolly; owing to his inheritance, he was one of the most eligible bachelors in Bombay. "No, thanks, Soli Mama," I said, unclasping my hand for a moment to show him my reserve. "I already have an extra."

The most obvious difference between Bombay and Calcutta for me was the rickshaw-wallahs. There were none in Bombay. Bapaiji had a cycle rickshaw, but these were hand-drawn, like the ones I had seen in Hong Kong; these rickshaw-wallahs, as Soli Mama explained, couldn't afford bicycles. Otherwise, the gauntlet of the taxiwallahs, tongawallahs, hotelwallahs among others, and the brown spindly deformed beggar-children, was hardly unfamiliar. The double-decker buses were the same, the electric trams, and the congestion of people, cows, dogs, cats, and goats – but my pity was newly invoked for the beggar-children. I remembered that some parents deliberately broke their children's bones to give them a headstart in life as beggars. Being a visitor I felt I couldn't take the same things for granted that I had out of habit before. I wanted to give them money, but Soli Mama assured me that if we gave even one of them money we would never get away. I didn't argue; the air was fetid, fly infested; the ground was uneven, full of puddles; I was anxious to be settled for the night. We had to shout down the other arrivals for coolies, bargain for rates, beat our way through the crowd – Soli Mama did it well – to find a large taxi (with a meter; otherwise, we might have been cheated) to take us to the Great Eastern Hotel on Old Court House Street. Our flight for Bagdogra left early the next morning, leaving us without time to go sightseeing in Calcutta, but Granny made sure that we drove by the River Hooghli and the Howrah Bridge because I had studied them in Geography; the Hooghli is a tributary of the Ganges and empties itself, only forty miles from where we were, into the Bay of Bengal. There were dhobis on the ghats, and vendors and boatmen and bicyclists and cows, dogs, goats, etcetera, but they all seemed so much a part of the Hooghli and the Howrah that the landscape differed significantly from Bombay's only insofar as it seemed grimier and more congested. I was less impressed with the sight of the river and bridge itself than I was with the fact that they existed, rather like celebrities one has little regard for until one sees them; then, it is proximity that makes their stars rise, they gain currency not from their intrinsic worth which remains the same but because one has seen them oneself.

There was congestion and squalor everywhere; often a rickshaw, finding an opening too small for us, would weasel quickly past our taxi; the beggars were continually at the windows until Soli Mama shouted angrily at them to leave us alone (the taxi's window mechanisms were broken; they couldn't be shut). I understood he was right to do as he did, but I couldn't get them out of my mind until later when I was too overwhelmed by the automatic lifts of the hotel, the air-conditioned rooms, the giant glass doors manned by a smartly uniformed doorman leading to the Chinese restaurant full of guests in evening dress to think about them anymore, and the next morning it was still dark when we boarded the plane for Bagdogra.

It would not be too gross an exaggeration to say that the Bagdogra Airport was almost as large as the town itself. The town, of course, does not need the airport, but travellers to Darjeeling, Kalimpong, and Sikkim do. A van with three rows of seats took us from Bagdogra to Darjeeling. Along the way Soli Mama read from a guidebook. Darjeeling once belonged to the rajahs of Sikkim along with the rest of the land between the current borders of Sikkim and the plains of Bengal. During the 1700s, control of the land was wrested from the rajahs by the Bhutanese and the Gurkhas; by the end of the century, the British East India Company defeated the Gurkhas in a series of wars, restored power to the rajahs, and, recognizing the value of Darjeeling (then called Dorje Ling which meant Place of Thunderbolts) as a site for a sanatorium, a hill station, and access into Nepal and Tibet, pressured the rajah into renting them the site. It was mostly forested and uninhabited then, but the British were quick to build roads, houses, a sanatorium, and a hotel; they started the now renowned tea plantations; they also constructed a Toy Train to transport supplies and exports; the bullock carts, which had given Hill Cart Road its name (because even bullock carts could mount its shallow gradient), were much too slow to be of use anymore. The Toy Train now transported tourists along the steep mountainsides between New Jalpaiguri and Darjeeling. When our van reached the mountainsides we saw the train tracks. Granny said she would never get on such a train; the tracks reminded her of the train that gave children tours of the zoo in Baroda. Soli Mama said the train had been in use since 1881, there was nothing to be afraid of, it was called a Toy Train to make it appear picturesque, but it was actually a narrow gauge railway. We saw the train along the way, its little blue engine puffing smoke, tugging carriages through forests and tea gardens, reminding me of The Little Engine Who Could. Granny said she was glad they were in the van; even if the train were perfectly safe it was much too crowded for her; she liked her comfort.

Darjeeling is built in a series of steps cantilevered from the sides of the mountain, 7000 feet above sea level. As we went up I kept my eyes open for monkeys, leopards, jackals, bears, otters, hares, deer, even elephants, which, according to the guidebook, inhabited the area, but in vain, so I had to be content with watching the innumerable ponies and their riders along the way. It was raining when we entered the marketplace on our way up to the hotel, the Oberoi Mt Everest, and Granny stopped the van for a while to send Soli Mama to buy umbrellas for all of us, even for Julie. My mother thought one umbrella would be enough for Rusi and myself, but Granny insisted we were old enough to have one each.

There were no cars except for our van on the narrow street and a small blue Fiat which closed in alongside of us while we waited. "I thought that was Soli leaving the van just now," one of the passengers said from the Fiat, lowering her window. "How was the trip, Meher? We've been waiting for you."

They were Granny's friends. Everyone said hello politely, the trip was fine but we were all rather tired, we hadn't had a chance to rest really in Calcutta. Soli Mama returned with the umbrellas. Rusi's and mine had vanes of bright colours. "Array, man, Homi, look at this," Rusi said to me. "I thought all umbrellas were always black."

Granny's friend, sitting at the far window of the car, had hardly spoken. Now she said, "Is that how they teach you to speak in Campion School, Rusi? like a babu?"

Perhaps she meant it as a joke. I had seen her before at Granny's house playing bridge, but couldn't recall her name. Granny's friends all looked the same and none of them seemed comfortable without a set of cards in her hand. Whenever they visited they went straight to the verandah where Granny had the card table ready, and when the game was over they went straight home. While they played they caught up on their conversation and ate the confectionery and drank the sodas and Kalvert's Rose Syrup that Granny would have ordered for the game. They hardly looked at one another, and just as hardly at anyone else – so when her friend made the remark from the car I think she might have embarrassed herself as much as anyone else because now the attention was focused expectantly on her and Rusi when she might have meant merely to say something inconsequential. Granny's smile disappeared, her eyebrows narrowed in a way I had almost forgotten. She hated us to speak less than perfectly, but she must also have hated her friend for reproving her grandson in her presence. The rain seemed louder during the moment before Rusi answered. "No. I've just never seen such colourful umbrellas."

That might have put the issue to rest, but Rusi wasn't finished. Some days later, Granny and her friends had been at a game all morning in one of the hotel dens, when Rusi stopped me outside the den within earshot of the players, and said, "Array, Homi, man, this is a great hotel, no? What do you think, yaar?"

I understood what he was doing. "Array, man, of course. It is the absolute best, yaar. All red roofs and cream walls, just like in England, man." Without Rusi's instigation I might not have been so bold, but we were on holiday, and we were having a good time, and I didn't like the old lady anymore than Rusi did.

"It is just like in England, man, this carpet, and all these fireplaces, man."

"And the walls and the ceilings all so high, yaar. This was a chateau once, you know, man?"

"I know, yaar. Who would have thunk it?" (He smiled; even he didn't say "thunk" for "thought".) "Like a maharajah's palace."

I wasn't sure what to expect later when Granny called us to her side after lunch that day before going to her room for her nap. "I just want to say," she said, "that I think you are both very good boys, and you both speak very well." She gave us each two bars of Cadbury's Fruit and Nut Milk Chocolate and smiled as she went away. Darjeeling had worked even greater wonders on her than Cambridge. Rusi wasn't surprised. "Gran's not stupid, yaar. She knows what's going on."

Of course, our conversation outside the den had been exaggerated, but Rusi had never been as meticulous about his diction as I was. He had a breezier approach to everything. If he didn't get something one way he would get it another; if I didn't get something my way I didn't care if I got it at all. The way of the world was always his way, never mine. I lost everything looking for the right way; he found ways to make the wrong ways work for him. I am reminded of a joke my father used to tell that clarifies this difference between

Rusi and myself. A priest was warned that a flood was on its way and his parish was to be evacuated. Everyone left but the priest stood at the gateway of his church confident that God would save him. When a jeep offered him a ride he sent it away saying God would save him. When the water forced him up the steps of the church a boat came by offering to save him, but he sent it away saying again that God would save him. When the water forced him onto the roof of the church a helicopter came by but he sent it away saying once more that God would save him. When he began to drown he said, "God, God, I have been faithful. Why do you not save me?" And God said, "I sent you a jeep, I sent you a boat, I sent you a helicopter, but you sent them away. What do you want me to do?"

Beyond the punchline I recognized a second point: all too often I mistook pride for piety; it mattered less that I was unwilling to change my ways than that I was unwilling to accept their consequences with equanimity. In Darjeeling, for instance, Rusi picked up a disappearing walnut trick from the headwaiter in the hotel who showed him how to pop the walnuts surreptitiously into the sleeve of his coat. Rusi perfected a few flourishes and performed for Soli Mama, Granny, her friends, and even for strangers in the hotel. They were delighted and gave him four annas each for his efforts. I reacted with too much sensitivity, envious of the money he made, scornful of his acquisitiveness, angry with the adults for encouraging him. Too highminded to perform like a trained animal myself I tried instead to expose his sleight of hand by nudging his coat sleeve with my cane, but he only remonstrated patiently, in private with me later. "Array, Homi, you think they don't know? You think I don't know they know? I'm not a genius like you, yaar, but I'm not stupid. You should try it yourself, man, it's bloody fun." Unfortunately, "bloody fun" was not my style, but whereas I still took a dim view of the goings-on I kept myself from interfering.

But I couldn't stay disgruntled long; things were too idyllic. I was too young to appreciate the beauty myself – the snapdragons were the largest, the bluest I had seen, but I derived more pleasure from snapping than watching them – but the grownups were charmed, and that made things easier for Rusi and myself. The air was so clean it looked washed; the people never looked less than cheerful; Granny said it was the climate – cool enough for work, but warm enough for leisure. I remained for the most part tractable, but not easily impressed, not by the Lloyd Botanical Garden (flowers bored me), not by the Happy Valley Tea Estate (cultivation bored me), not by the Natural History Museum (old things bored me), not even by the Mountain Zoo (Bombay's Victoria Gardens Zoo was better), but even I appreciated the view from Tiger Hill despite my grumpiness at being awakened at four in the morning to be harried from my snug refuge under four blankets into a cold jeep for a forty minute ride to a two-storey concrete pavilion where we sat shivering under blankets, sipping tea and coffee, waiting for the sun.

A sunrise, always beautiful, is made even more memorable for what it reveals. Within ten minutes the panorama turned from black to gold; during the interim a rusty incandescence hung upon the clouds, the eastern sky turned brilliant with streaks of pink and red, the blue-grey mountains turning brighter reflected the brilliance so that the snowy peaks merged with the clouds and the horizon was lost. The sun rose, a translucent shimmering orange orb against a cerulean backdrop. To the northwest lay the Kanchenjunga range; in the distance Mount Everest was pointed out to me; it inspired a deep humility, unlike the pride I had felt on seeing the Howrah and the Hooghli in Calcutta: the Howrah and Hooghli were to be talked about later, but the Himalayas by sunrise were to be remembered; the former invited comment, the latter introspection.

Darjeeling may have sustained the spell of Cambridge for Granny, but what happened in Bagdogra during our return to Bombay broke it forever. She lost her smile, the sheen in her eyes, and resumed her conviction, forgotten when she had embarked for Cambridge, that there was a ubiquitous "they" perpetually involved in a conspiracy against her. The regression wasn't apparent immediately. When we first learned that our return flight to Calcutta was to be delayed by a day her brow wrinkled but she said nothing, but gradually, as the discomforts mounted – there were no quality restaurants in Bagdogra, there were no hotels, there were no private quarters in the airport, there were no baths, there was absolutely nothing to see or do, there were cockroaches, beetles, spiders among the assortment of bugs in the airport, there were rats, there were lizards, there were jackals that howled during the night in the wilderness beyond the runways – I could see the tension rising in her as clearly as the mercury in the thermometer with its bulb over a flame.

Mom and Soli Mama bought bread, butter, cheese, tomatoes (most of it either too hard or too soft) for sandwiches from the Bagdogra market which was a fifteen minute walk from the airport, hardboiled eggs for breakfast the next morning, and filled two thermoses with cold drinking water.

We were the only passengers at the airport that day, our flight was the only flight, and when the airport official, Mr Prasad, went home (which he did as soon as he had made the situation clear to us) the rest of the personnel followed and we were alone. Rusi and I were excited, particularly when the jackals started howling after nightfall, but Granny didn't like it at all. She made Soli Mama push a few couches around to form an enclave of furniture in the vast and otherwise empty waiting hall. She made us leave all the lights on all night.

The next day Mr Prasad didn't arrive until ten-thirty, but he called Dum Dum Airport in Calcutta on the radio right away (there were no telephones) and assured us that our plane would arrive at three-thirty that afternoon as promised.

Rusi and I spent much of the day on the runway, exploring the hangars, watching the mechanics at work, running and jumping (I, hobbling) up and down the stairs pretending to board planes with exotic destinations: Copenhagen, Kenya, California, Peru. We were warned not to go beyond the runways into the tall grass because Granny was afraid the jackals might be lying in wait there.

At three-fifteen Mr Prasad came out of his office, stood before Granny, and said the plane was to be delayed one more day. He was almost as tiny as she, appearing even tinier in a uniform much too large for him. He extracted something laboriously from his left nostril and studied it as if it might move on his thin delicate finger before flicking it away. We were still the only passengers at the airport. Granny stamped her tiny foot in its grey patent leather shoe. "I don't need the brains of a turnip to see what's going on here," she

said. "You're waiting for other passengers to make up the flight –
but we had tickets for yesterday!"

"Yes-yes," Mr Prasad said, smiling, eagerly agreeing, and "of
course-of course," but it was evident he must not have credited
Granny with even the brains of a turnip because he reversed himself
immediately. "But no-no. Even now they are repairing the aeroplane.
Even now they are working on it. Tomorrow it will be ready."

"Array, but that's what you told us yesterday." Soli Mama's
forehead was creased, his arms were crossed, but he spoke civilly.
"How do we know you're telling us the truth now?"

Mom, who hated confrontations of any kind, said, "Array, bawa,
now let it be. If we have to wait one more day we can wait one more
day."

Soli Mama, never one to slouch or stand on one leg or with his
hands in his pockets, uncrossed his arms and held them akimbo so
that with his feet widespread he looked like a five-pointed star. "And
if I *don't* have to wait another day, I *won't* wait another day. How
do we know he's telling us the truth now? This could go on
indefinitely."

Mom, embarrassed, smiled and looked away. "Well, of course, if
that's how you feel about it." I felt sorry for Mr Prasad, picking his
nose again, lost in his uniform, shrinking even further in the presence
of Soli Mama's indignation, even though it was evident he was lying.
Perhaps the plane had indeed been out of commission; perhaps they
had withdrawn the flight owing to cancellations; in either event it
seemed unlikely that Indian Airlines would schedule a special flight
for just the six of us; of course, they would give us the most
expedient of available answers, but the most plausible scenario
indicated that we would be staying at the airport until the next
scheduled flight which wasn't for another two days. Perhaps Mr
Prasad knew that, and knew that we knew it too, but he had to
follow orders, he had to maintain the integrity of the airline. "It is
the truth now," he said, still smiling to keep his dignity. "Tomorrow
you will see. Very good." He turned abruptly and walked stiffly
back into this office.

The next day he didn't even come out of his office; Soli Mama
had to go to him to learn that the flight had been delayed yet another

day. I could hear Soli Mama shouting at him but found it too depressing to stay and listen to him. When he returned I knew Granny would start so I hobbled onto the runway again with Rusi. When we returned Granny was still railing: "They're doing it to me again, the swines. They're always waiting-waiting, plotting-plotting. They pretend not to understand but they're sly, so sly. They're waiting to see how much she can take, the old woman, they're waiting to see me crack."

Soli Mama seemed as annoyed with her as with everything else. "Nothing of the sort," he said. "No one's doing anything to anyone. They just don't know how to organize anything. Just wait till I find out who's in charge of this operation."

The next day Mr Prasad didn't show up at all, but about eleven-thirty other passengers arrived bound as we were for Calcutta, preventing Soli Mama and Mom from making yet another trip to the Bagdogra market for more hard bread and cheese. We were sure the plane would arrive now, and it did, which was just as well because Granny had been awakened that morning by two geckos who had fallen from the rafters onto her outstretched hand. "Mare-re mua," she said, "the swine will never let me be." Her face became slowly distorted; from her brow to her eyes to her nose to her mouth to her chin her skin flattened, stretched, wrinkled, as if a demon were descending, scrambling, snaking his way down down down to settle in her heart. I felt sad, thinking that no number of shots of Cambridge could help her now. Bapaiji would not have been bothered by mere lizards. She had severed the tail of a gecko in her house for my edification once by beating it with a walking stick: the tail had wriggled around by itself for a while as if it had a life independent of the lizard; the lizard, Bapaiji explained, would soon grow another tail.

Rustamji Jamshedji Cama

"No, Homi, do not write me off like that. Things are never that simple. Stupid people think everyone else is corrupt and corrupt people think everyone else is stupid, but life is what it is supposed to be, not what you think it is supposed to be. I was stupid, thinking because people didn't do everything they were supposed to do that they were corrupt. I cut myself off from so many people because I found them corrupt – but I was not always like that. When I was in school, the same convent school to which your mother went later, my sister, Nawaz, and I always had friends coming and going, even English and Anglo-Indian girls. I was a big reader then, *Little Women*, *Black Beauty*, *Jane Eyre*, *Wuthering Heights*, *Oliver Twist*, *A Tale of Two Cities*, *The Count of Monte Cristo*, but it was mostly a backdrop for my other activities – dramatics, the choir, the sewing club; I was always in the middle of a book, but I was not always reading.

"I shared a room with Nawaz. It was a small room, but cozy. Our father was a jeweller – as you must know from his name, Motiwallah. You've seen the house many times, Dhun Abad, where Warden Road and Napean Sea Road meet. We lived in the flat on the ground on the left. I loved going to bed to the sound of the sea every night, feeling as if I were being rocked asleep. Sometimes, when I wanted a drink of water in the middle of the night, walking across the uneven floor, I felt as if I were on the deck of a ship. It was so silly, but everytime I did that I would be so scared of my own reflection in the full length mirrors of my cupboard and Nawaz's in the dark that I would wake Nawaz up and she would tell me not to be so upset, there was nothing to worry about, to go back to sleep. Nawaz was less than a year older then me; we were close like friends more than like sisters; she was always reassuring and I, as she was fond of saying, had too much imagination; I was more of a scaredy cat than her only because I had the imagination to see what she had not the imagination to see; she made it sound as if her courage were somehow a deficiency."

A montage appeared before me: a child Granny with clean skinny limbs skipping rope with her sister; playing tag with white-skinned, fair-haired friends; at a party playing London Bridge, Musical Chairs, Pin the Tail on the Donkey, a Tisket, a Tasket; in her grey and white convent uniform singing "All Things Bright and Beautiful" with the choir; before a school audience reciting "Out Damn Spot" with perhaps too much vivacity; sitting in a lime green dress with full length sleeves at a wooden table pasting pictures in a Queen Victoria scrapbook; wedged on the wide sill of a window opening from her bedroom into a porch, her back against one jamb, her feet against the other, lost in a clothbound, illustrated volume of *Alice's Adventures in Wonderland* which was so large that she almost dropped it everytime she turned a page.

In the last picture she looked about twelve years old: she sat in her bed in the dark, the sheet like a tent at her knees, her tiny hands holding it up to her mouth so that her shining nose could be seen over her bony white knuckles, her eyes fixed to what she saw reflected in the mirror. A patch of moonlight fell on the floor from the open window leading to the porch, illuminating a swirl of white and blue mosaic edging toward the bed. She prayed that the image she saw reflected in the mirror was only a nightmare from which she would wake; then she would wake Nawaz, tell her what she had dreamed, and the two of them would go to the kitchen, turn on the light, make themselves some Horlicks, and sip it slowly, talking in whispers until the sun came up.

Granny was too terrified to make any noise or movement, but her eyes flashed across the room. Her father was standing transfixed in the doorway in his sadra and pajama bottoms. Their eyes met and she knew his fear as clearly as she knew her own and she knew also his shame for his fear, but still he did nothing. A man was smothering her sister in her bed and they both behaved as if it were a movie and they were waiting for the horror to pass, he staring as if to punish himself for his fear, she looking away as if to deny what she had seen. Slowly her sister's struggles ceased, a white twitching foot became still in the moonlight in the corner of Granny's eye, but the man continued to press the pillow hard on her face. Then her mother came into the room in a long grey faded sleeping gown, with a rolling pin, and began beating the intruder on his back.

The man fell immediately on his knees, breathing heavily, shaking and crying and begging for mercy; she stopped beating him, she recognized his voice; she turned to Nawaz to see how she was, screamed, and continued beating the man until he lay unconscious on his side on the floor. Granny's father then turned on the light.

"Neither your mother nor Soli Mama knew this, but Nawaz was my half sister. My mother came from a wealthy family; her father, a doctor, had graduated from Oxford, a rarity in those days for an Indian; but she had fallen in love with a bounder who left her with child; no man with any prospects to speak of would marry her in that condition, of course, so she married my father, a nice man but with pronounced limitations. They had a good life despite the ostracism of her family, we had a happy childhood, but if she had married a bolder man Nawaz might have lived a natural life. The man who killed her was her natural father; why he did it, what he wanted, where he had been all those years, no one ever found out; by that time he was crazy.

"Of course, I learned all this much later from my mother who, after my father's death, had begun to show signs of slippage herself. Her family wanted her back after Nawaz died, but by then it was too late; she blamed them for everything, even for acknowledging her again only because her 'bastard offspring' was dead. Her last years were comfortable, but miserable.

"But before all this rot finally settled I got married to one of my father's customers, to your mamavaji, Rustamji Jamshedji Cama, after whom Rusi was named."

Child Granny stood on the rough grey stone floor in her grey long-skirted convent-school uniform and rang her doorbell. She switched her satchel of books from her left to her right shoulder, swung the narrow wooden flap marked letters back on its hinges on the door with her finger, and peered through the slot until she saw her mother's feet in the backless leather slippers with the velvet uppers approaching the door. When she had trouble with the latch Granny shouted impatiently, "Push with your knee, Mamma. Then open." Her mother did as she was told and the latch slid easily.

The flat consisted of a central hallway which held the ironing board, two cupboards, and suitcases, with the front door at one end and the bathroom at the other; the two bedrooms were adjacent to the bathroom, and the sitting room was across from the dining room and kitchen. If her father had friends Granny would try to slip by quietly so they would leave her alone, but on that day there had been too much noise. Much to her annoyance her father called her in and introduced her to his friend. "This is Mr Rustamji Cama. I am sure you must have heard of him."

Mr Rustamji Cama wore a white suit with a neatly knotted cream tie; a straw hat lay on the marble table over which they had been conducting business. He was the nephew of Jalbhai Phirozshah Cama, the industrialist, but that hardly interested her. "Yes, of course," she said. "Hello, Uncle." She held out her hand to shake his.

Mr Cama put aside a pearl handled cane, got up from his chair, and shook her hand. "No-no-no-no-no," he said. "What is this 'Uncle'? I am not an old man. My name is Rustam."

It was unprecedented for one of her father's friends to object to being called "Uncle"; she looked at him, still unsmilingly, but with interest. "Yes, Uncle – I mean, Rustamji." She couldn't call him just "Rustam" even then.

He was holding her hand. "She is such a pretty little girl," Mr Cama was saying, "but such a sad little face."

Her mother had entered the room and stood smiling behind a chair holding its back. When Granny returned to her room she looked at her face in the mirror. Mr Cama was right: it was a pretty face, but sad. After Nawaz had died she had lost interest in things, cultivated her sadness, proud of how it set her apart from others; she was flattered he had commented on it. He was not an old man, but he was closer to her father in age; she was only sixteen; but when she thought about him she found herself filling with hope.

I was not prepared for what I saw next: it looked like Big Ben – but with a row of swaying coconut trees in the foreground instead of Westminster Bridge and the Thames. I should not have been surprised – if Granny could move her house from Bombay to the Gogmagog Hills in Cambridgeshire, she could just as well move Big Ben to Bombay – but the scene had changed too rapidly – and, indeed, when I looked again I saw I had let myself be deceived. Big Ben was actually the Rajabhai Tower, the Big Ben of Bombay, which hardly seemed incongruous among coconut trees. I could hardly recognize the maidan – the Oval, where my classmates from Campion School had played cricket and football and kiddy-kiddy – beyond the Tower, because where I had been accustomed to seeing the Eros Theatre, the Churchgate Railway Station and Marine Drive, there was only water. I was looking at a Bombay before the ground on which these landmarks were built had been reclaimed from the sea. There was a function in the Oval, a celebration of the marriage of the then Prince of Wales, Prince Albert Edward, the future King Edward VII, the second child and eldest son of Queen Victoria and Prince Albert, to Princess Alexandra of Denmark. A crowd had gathered, Indians and English, for a display of fireworks. The rows of rickety wooden chairs had long been filled, but hundreds of Indians were content merely to squat at the perimeter of the official seating arrangements. Within the select enclosure of chairs an altercation was taking place: a tall, gangly, uniformed English official was trying to remove a chair "for one of the English ladies who just arrived" he explained, while a young Parsi in a dagla, white pants, and paghri was trying to restrain him. "I'm sorry," the Parsi said, "but this chair is reserved. My friend will be back in a moment." The Parsi was smaller, but with the thick density, the quick strength, of a dwarf in his body. He spoke politely, but his face was stern. "In fact, here he is now," he said without turning away, as his friend came up beside him.

"Let me go," the Englishman said, trying to get free.

"Put the chair down," said the Parsi.

The Englishman looked nervously from the Parsi to his friend and back. "Who are you to speak to me like this?"

"We know our rights," said the Parsi with the same politeness, the same unswerving gaze.

The Englishman might have backed off then if he could have saved face doing so, but it was too late. "I could have you confined for the night," he said.

"That is a risk I will have to take."

Fortunately for everyone, a second uniformed Englishman called from a distance, "It's all right, Roger. We've got all the chairs we need."

The first Englishman thumped the chair down without looking at the Parsis, and walked away immediately. The Parsi put the chair calmly back where it had been and said something to his friend with a confidential smile as the first rockets flashed into the darkening sky and fountains of flame erupted in the heart of the enclosure.

"Homi, that young man, to whom you so charitably granted the density of a dwarf, was Jalbhai Phirozshah Cama, your mamavaji's uncle, the first major industrialist of Modern India. Of course, you know who he is from the history books, but there are some things that bear repetition, especially when they concern the honour of one's family. Cama Enterprises was the first to institute an eight-hour working day and paid holidays when such things were unknown even in England and America. He also instituted the provident fund, accident compensation, medical aid, maternity benefits, and profit sharing long before they became required by the law. Grandfathers and fathers and sons and grandsons worked gratefully for the Camas as if they were working for their own families. Jalbhai himself said that without the human touch all work – composing a symphony or digging a ditch – became drudgery, and no amount of success could transmute that lead into gold. Fortunately, at least some of his successors understood that well enough to keep up the momentum he gave to Cama Enterprises. Unfortunately, our Rustamji Jamshedji Cama was not one of them. I should have known it on the night I saw the Bombay Players do *A Midsummer Night's Dream* at Cama Hall, but I was only a girl, still only eighteen, and my mother and father both liked Rustamji Jamshedji so much they thought I was a fool for not being as excited as they were. I was – but a girl has to keep her dignity – but I knew the way things were going and I didn't mind. Rustamji Jamshedji came at least once a week, ostensibly to see my father, to engage his services as a jeweller, but it was no secret that he was coming to see me. We didn't go out, it wasn't done; we were never without a chaperone even at home, but people talked about us so much – mostly because he was a Cama, very rich, and still an eligible bachelor – that my mother said he would have to make up his mind soon because people were talking, I wasn't growing any younger, and there was my reputation to consider. So he invited us all to the play. He thought it would be a good way for everyone to meet."

A Midsummer Night's Dream

Rustamji Jamshedji sent his carriage to pick up Granny and her parents on the day of the play. It was a pleasant fifteen-minute walk from their house along Napean Sea Road – first through a quiet residential street, then by the beach – to Cama Hall, but they had worn their best clothes and not only might they have gotten dusty by the time they arrived, but it would have been awkward arriving on foot after dressing up. Besides, it might have rained, they might not have felt like walking, so many things might have happened – and Rustamji Jamshedji wanted to be sure they would come. Her mother had wanted Granny to wear a sari; it seemed wanton for an eighteen year old to show her ankles and calves, but Granny insisted on wearing a dress and since she hadn't seen her so excited about anything in so long, she let her. Her mother, wearing all her jewels, her finest shimmering sari, was pleased enough herself to be riding in a carriage as if she were being vindicated for the misfortunes her family had heaped on her for her marriage; her father in a twice washed dagla and white pants, black paghri and shining creaky black shoes, was also pleased but nervous; these were not his people, but they had been his wife's and he wanted them to be his daughter's.

Rustamji Jamshedji did not live in Cama Hall. He was a Cama, but uninterested in commerce, preferring instead the life of a gentleman though some called him a dilettante – he painted portraits inspired by the work of Sir Joshua Reynolds, and had written two pedagogical novels about corruption in commerce and immorality in high places, creating a minor scandal in Bombay when his readers associated his characters with members of his family and circle of acquaintances; he was not popular among the Camas but they had established a generous trust fund for him because it would have been even more of a scandal for them to disinherit him; besides, otherwise they might only have provided him with fodder for a third novel. Granny and her parents had visited him occasionally on Sunday mornings in the past two years in his house, Cama Mansion, in a cul de sac near Kemp's Corner; they had been impressed (her mother less so than her father) with the least thing, but even his house, lavishly built and furnished though it was, could hardly compare with Cama Hall. As the carriage passed through the high iron gates and made its way up a winding hilly path to the high colonnaded entranceway with the marble steps leading into the mansion, her father became glazed with wonder, her mother smug as if indulging in a secret pleasure, and she herself so bright with excitement that everything around her faded as if it were colourless. Their feelings of privilege were heightened when a uniformed usher seated at a wooden desk by the steps found their names on a roster, issued them tickets, and directed them around the house to the back where the house projected from a living area onto a wide terrace like a proscenium, shaped like a crescent, with marble steps like ripples from the terrace and a curved marble balustrade issuing toward the lawn.

The terrace, easily accessible from both house and garden, was ideal for theatrical productions; if necessary, the lawn immediately before the terrace could even be used as a second stage. Wicker and rattan chairs had been arranged in rows for the guests. On either side of the clean green lawn were arbors with carefully landscaped beds of roses and smooth hedgerows enclosing picnic benches and tables, and coconut trees and mango trees strung with fairy lights so that, particularly as it got darker, one might have imagined Oberon and Titania and Puck and Peaseblossom and the rest even without the aid of the Bombay Players. Far to the back stood a gazebo with a domed top like a giant pearl, and behind the gazebo, past a narrow stretch of sand, lay the sea.

The skyscrapers of Malabar Hill have now sprung on the shoulders of these coconut trees, giving the landscape a majestic urban cast; but at the time it would have been impossible to tell from within the grounds that Cama Hall, so widely spread out like a country estate, had found so hospitable a space within the environs of a metropolis like Bombay.

They found their seats; they didn't speak to anyone but her father kept pointing out the luminaries he recognized in the Cama firmament; the brightest, Jalbhai himself, had been dead fifteen years, and his sons, Sir Kaikhushrau Jalbhai and Sir Dorabji Jalbhai, were in London and Beirut respectively on business, but there were dozens of nephews, nieces, in-laws, cousins, with some of whom her father had done business, others whom Rustamji Jamshedji had mentioned during their talks. The Parsi women wore mostly shimmering saris like her mother's, with necklaces, ear rings, bracelets, and brooches of diamonds, rubies, emeralds, sapphires, and pearls; their men wore mostly daglas and paghris. The Englishwomen wore mostly gowns or dresses with bare shoulders and less jewelry than the Parsis — many of the Englishmen wore uniforms with decorations almost as bright as their women's jewels. Her mother saw someone she knew and left to talk with her friend. Rustamji saw them seated by themselves and called them over to meet his company. Her father moved like a robot, but Granny could hardly stand still; she clutched her sequined handbag in one hand, brushed at her dress with the other as if to smooth the wrinkles, and swayed from side to side in a quick excited motion.

Rustamji introduced them to his friends: Teddy Wentworth, an Englishman of about thirty years, in a waistcoat and pinstripe trousers, with a narrow head of flat, striated, immaculately combed, dark brown hair, parted down the middle, which shone in the light; Helen Dastur, perhaps in her mid-twenties, in a long lime green dress with a discreet neck, her hair, so pale it was almost white in the light, held in a loose bun by a diamond barrette, the only piece of jewelry she appeared to be wearing; and Naju Cama, Rustamji's sister, perhaps in her thirties, one of the few Parsi women in a gown, with a diamond choker around her neck, diamond ear rings, and a diamond on her finger. Granny didn't like Naju Cama; she wore too much powder as if she were trying to appear more fairly complected than she was; her nose was as sharp and narrow as Granny's own, but her mouth was thin and long and flat, and her diamonds only made her appear aloof as if she slept in a bed of ice each night;

recalling that Naju's first husband, who had married her for her money (so the story went), had died mysteriously, Granny found it easy to believe (so, again, the story went) that she had poisoned him; but Helen she liked immediately – the simple gown, the single piece of jewelry, her undivided attention when someone spoke, made her appear so vulnerable that even Granny felt protective. She had heard about her before; her mother, of Norwegian and English parentage, had been a governess in the employ of her father, a Parsi – a married man. When her mother had become pregnant, her father had sacked her denying all complicity. Her mother had died when Helen was nineteen and she had lived since as a governess herself with all the sympathy and ostracism that the peculiarity of her position demanded: her features were tiny and delicate like a child's and her skin just as smooth. She had gentleman callers because she was attractive, educated, intelligent, and a finer conversationalist than most Parsi women of her time; she would have enjoyed the company of women equally, but unmarried women were too busy looking for husbands and married ones looking after them for them to consider what else might be done with their time; and mean minds speculated that her callers were after meaner satisfactions than the apparent ones of affection and camaraderie, though she lived much too humbly to support their speculations.

The women remained seated, Helen smiling with curiosity, Naju expressionlessly, when they were introduced, but Teddy Wentworth got to his feet. To her horror, Granny saw her father join his hands and bow his head ever so slightly as if he were about to say "Saebji" in his humble manner, the way he did when he felt overawed. It might have been all right to greet Rustamji that way but an Englishman would only think of him as so typically Indian. She thrust her hand forward immediately and spoke clearly. "How do you do?"

Teddy Wentworth snatched his glance from father to daughter, giving no other indication of surprise. "I say, so this is May-her," he said, shaking her hand. "Rustam is an old fox. He said nothing about how charming you were – how very charming."

Rustamji chuckled. "I do not like to boast."

"Stuff and nonsense. You have been trying to hide her from me.

You spoke of her as if she were a footnote. I find you guilty of keeping secrets from me, Rustam."

Again, Rustamji chuckled. Teddy continued to hold Granny's hand. She smiled broadly, amused that he had mispronounced her name. He spoke with no emphasis, but made his point unmistakably with the slowness of his speech, reminding her of the times she and Nawaz would "tawk such haw-haw English" for fun. Then her father put out his hand suddenly as if he didn't know what else to do, and spoke hurriedly, "How do you do?" and Teddy released her hand.

There were still a few minutes before the play so they all sat down together. "I was just saying," Teddy resumed, "that I really prefer Dickens to Shakespeare. How anyone can take fairies and love potions seriously in the twentieth century is beyond me. And his tragedies are all so bleak. But Dickens always leaves me entertained and edified."

Helen leaned forward. "But if it's realism you're after, you should really read Ibsen or Shaw. Dickens's characters are so flat you could pass them through the crack under a door." She spoke quietly, with assurance. Naju cut off the ensuing laughter abruptly. "I still say Shakespeare was the best. He had such a deep understanding of human nature. He must have been such an intelligent man."

She looked around the company as if she knew she had said the last word on the subject, but Rustamji replied with a chuckle. "I wish I had said that, Naju."

His irony wasn't lost on the company, but Helen turned to him for Naju's benefit. "But she's right, Rustam. He also understood how to fit his characters to his plays. If Hamlet had been in Othello's place there would have been no tragedy – he would not have smothered Desdemona so easily, and if Othello had been in Hamlet's place there would have been no play because he would have killed Claudius in the second act."

Before anyone could respond, Granny said, "Lord Melbourne told Queen Victoria not to read *Oliver Twist* because it dealt with paupers and pickpockets and other such things of which she should not be thinking." She had lost the track of the conversation because she had been searching for something intelligent with which to respond to Teddy's preference for Dickens.

"That's very interesting," Teddy said. "I didn't know that."

Granny was flushed with the excitement of having contributed to the conversation, but it was time to go back to their seats. "It's been a pleasure meeting you," Teddy said. "Perhaps we can resume our conversation during the interval."

Granny smiled, shook his hand, said "Perhaps," and followed her father back to their seats. Teddy was an unexpected bonus. No one had spoken to her that way before, certainly no man had, and she had never dreamed that someday an Englishman might. His hair was brown, he was well groomed, well spoken. She was relieved she had worn a dress after all instead of a sari as her mother had wanted; she felt she had impressed Teddy by appearing to be more of an Anglo than she was. She looked forward to the interval now as much as she had looked forward to the play itself before. When it came, Granny was disappointed to see Naju coming toward them alone, but her disappointment vanished when Naju invited her to a moonlight picnic on the beach after the play; Teddy would be there, and some of the other young folks. Granny and her mother were delighted, but her father, in deference to propriety, said it would be all right only if Rustamji would be responsible for her. Naju waved his objections aside. "With Rustam one can never be sure, but I will be there. It is settled, then." She spoke with a smile and an emphasis that made Granny think she might have misjudged her after all.

Toward the end of the evening Granny didn't know which was the more magical, the finery of the assorted fairies and lovers on stage or of the socialites in the garden of whom she felt herself increasingly a part, particularly when Naju came to her when the play was over. Naju's smile, still as flat as before, now seemed so generous that Granny felt ashamed for having disliked her before. "Rustam cannot come just now," she said to her parents, "but he said for you to take the carriage home. Meher can stay with me just now. Rustam will see her home later."

Her parents left with large smiles. After they had gone Naju said to Granny, "I'm afraid we can't go just yet. I must stay here until the guests start going home. I hope it won't be too much of a bother for you. Then we can go to the beach."

Granny was tired, but still too excited to care. "Not at all," she said as graciously as she could. "Not at all. Perfectly all right."

"Good. I knew you would understand."

Granny smiled, feeling she had said the right thing. She looked for Teddy and Rustamji and Helen then, but couldn't find them. Naju said they would meet them later at the beach; Rustamji couldn't be bothered with saying goodbye to anyone and had taken his friends with him for company; "but someone has got to do the dirty work." Naju smiled as if she had made a joke; Granny didn't find it funny but smiled back effortlessly as if no matter how tired she felt she had shifted into a higher gear than she had ever used before and, however different it felt, she knew she had done it correctly. It didn't matter that Rustamji would be the only person she knew at the picnic, that there would be Englishmen and Camas and their friends who might know one another more intimately than she knew any of them; she felt as if her strangeness itself made her special, as if the more of herself she withheld the more special she would appear; until she met the others she would content herself to cultivate her strangeness just saying goodnight to the guests who came to thank Naju for the entertainment; she was sure they must all be wondering who she was and why Naju had taken her under her wing.

"Shall I send for some port? or some sherry?"

Granny had never drunk wine, but she didn't want Naju to know it. "Some port would be nice," she said.

When the bearer brought her a glass, Granny sipped the port carefully as if it were hot like tea. Naju smiled knowingly, but not so Granny could see.

After an hour, the crowd had thinned and some of the lights had been turned off allowing the moon to grow in ascendancy, particularly by the gazebo whose pearly dome shone like a half moon itself. Granny and Naju had a moment to themselves for the first time since her parents had left. "I'm afraid this is going to take longer than I thought," Naju said. "Come along, my dear. Let me take you to the meeting place while we have a few seconds. The others should be waiting for us now. I'm sorry you had to wait so long. You must be so bored."

"Not at *all*," Granny said. "*Per*fectly all right, really." But she got up immediately from her chair.

They walked in silence, Naju a step ahead of Granny, until there was no one within earshot around them. "Teddy really likes you," Naju said then. "He's really looking forward to tonight. Don't tell him I said this, of course – he'd kill me if he found out" (she flashed a smile at Granny, adding a laugh as if at an afterthought) – "but he said 'A chap could get serious about a girl like her.' You should be flattered. He doesn't say that about every girl he meets. Also, he doesn't usually like Indian women in dresses – you and I are the exceptions that prove the rule, he said." Naju gave Granny another smile from over her shoulder. "He says they look so exotic in saris he can't understand why they would want to wear dresses at all. Personally, I think you impressed him with that thing about Dickens. He loves Dickens. How did you ever know that?"

Granny's smile was so broad it threatened to spring off her face. "It was in *Little Ladies* magazine. I get it from the library every month. I read it from cover to cover."

"That was fortunate," Naju said, turning face front again. "That really impressed him – and he's not easily impressed. He's not like so many of the English in India who are really paupers in England. They come to India because they would never get the same respect – the servants, the privileges, the salaries – that they would get in England. But Teddy is not like that. He is rich in his own right – he has a brother in the House of Lords. He was sent to India to be rounded out, sort of like a finishing school. He could have his pick of dozens of girls; that is why I say it is not to be taken lightly when I say he really likes you. I don't think you can even begin to realize what a compliment he's paid you."

Granny said, "I liked him too, I really did," but her smile had diminished considerably as if she knew that whatever she said would prove inadequate to her feeling, as if the matter were more serious than a smile might warrant.

"If I were you," Naju said, still facing front, "I wouldn't waste any time letting him know it. He's a busy man. If you waste this chance you might not get another. I only say this because I want what's best for you."

Granny didn't know what to say.

They reached the sand. Naju looked around as if surprised not to find anyone. "That's funny. They should have been here by now." They waited in silence for a few seconds. "I'm sorry, my dear, but I must be getting back. I'm sure they'll be here any minute. I hope you don't mind waiting a bit."

"Not at *all*," Granny said, but she cut herself short immediately. She had used that phrase altogether too often that evening. Besides, she wasn't sure that she didn't mind; something didn't seem right; but she didn't know what else to to do. "I'll be all right," she said with less enthusiasm.

"Are you sure?" Naju said, looking at her again, sensing her apprehension.

Granny was a bit lightheaded from the port, and afraid because she didn't know how it would make her feel next, but she nodded.

"They should be here any minute," Naju said. "Besides, it's a beautiful bright night. Nothing will happen."

Granny nodded again. "I'll be all right. Please don't worry."

"Bye-bye, then. I'll be joining you all a little later."

"Bye-bye."

Granny watched Naju until she was out of sight. She found the silvery shadows of the trees cast by the moonlight on the sand beautiful, and the spangles on the sea beyond, but she didn't like the brightness. Nawaz had been killed on a moonlit night; Granny could still recall the splash of moonlight on the blue mosaic floor and on Nawaz's pale motionless foot. She hid herself within the shadow of the thickest coconut tree and took off her shoes which had filled with sand. She stood for a few minutes in silence, listening to the waves, drawing deep breaths of the sea air to counter the effect of the port, following the stream of moonlight along the sea to the beach where it widened and got lost in the sand. She was about to step out of the shadows to go back to Cama Hall on her own when she saw a figure coming from the direction Naju had left and chose to remain where she was. It was a man; she couldn't see him clearly from behind the tree, even in the moonlight, but when he shouted, "Ahoy! Is anyone there?" she knew it was Teddy. "Is it Teddy?" she said, stepping into the light.

"Yes. Is it Mayher?"

"Yes. What's the matter? Where is everyone?"

"I'm afraid there's been a mistake, a misunderstanding, actually."

"Oh? What is it?"

He was still coming toward her; she remained where she stood.

"Naju was to bring you into the house. The picnic is at midnight. It's only eleven-thirty now. I'm afraid you've been waiting in the dark for nothing. I'm sorry."

They were standing next to each other by the time he was finished talking. He had brought with him a smell with which she was unfamiliar but guessed to be spirits. She felt suddenly awkward to be alone in the night with a man; her shoulders slumped, her gaze fell to a stone behind him, her body turned slightly away. "It's all right. Thank you for coming to get me. Let's go back."

But Teddy remained standing as firmly as before. "Actually, I thought we might stay here until the others came. It would only be time to leave again by the time we got back."

Granny felt it would be wrong to stay; Naju should have come back for her herself; surely she knew what being alone with a man, especially at night, especially in such exotic surroundings, could do to a young girl's reputation – but Teddy was an Englishman; she couldn't expect him to see anything wrong with his proposal; there was no way she could deter him from his argument except by exposing herself as the unsophisticated Parsi girl she was instead of the poised equivalent of the English girls to whom she knew he must be accustomed. "All right," she said. "We can stay."

"Good. I was hoping you would see it my way." There was a tremble in his voice which gave her the courage to look at him. His white face looked waxen and translucent in the moonlight as if it might reveal blood vessels and bones to a sharper scrutiny; it looked doughy as if it might be rearranged by kneading. He smiled, but his eyes appeared glazed. Granny wished the others were there already, but told herself that that was no way for a sophisticated young girl to behave.

Teddy put his hands on her waist and drew her to him. "Mayher," he said, and the smell of the spirits was stronger, "Naju said some things about you – very flattering things."

She turned her face from his, letting her hands holding her shoes hang loosely behind her, her handbag wedged under her arm. "What things?"

"She said you were a modern girl. She said you liked to have fun." He leaned over and kissed her temple.

His lips felt cold – and unclean. She brought up her hands with the shoes against his chest to push him away, but he only circled her with his arms and held her more tightly. Her handbag fell; the shoes between them hurt her chest; his unrelenting pressure panicked her; his face so close seemed like a giant's. She tried to hit his jaw with her shoe but couldn't get enough leverage; she tried kicking his shins but her bare feet had no effect; she struggled but he only held her more tightly as if she were a sparrow in a captor's hand. The smell of the spirits got worse. She thought to scream but that seemed uncivilized; she thought how ridiculously she was thinking. She relaxed momentarily as if in surrender; he leaned over to kiss her again; she butted her forehead against his nose. He dropped her with a shout; she dropped her shoes and ran the way she had come, screaming "Rustamji! Rustamji!" as if his shout had given her permission finally to break her silence, but he caught up with her easily, clamped a hand over her mouth, an arm around her waist, lifted her up, thumped her down, lifted her up and thumped her down again until she ceased to struggle, then whispered ferociously: "Do not – I repeat – do not make a scene. Naju told me some things. I'm sorry I believed her. I believe I owe you an apology. I'm sorry."

Granny shook in his arms; when he released her she fell to her knees crying. "I'm sorry," Teddy kept saying. "I'm afraid I've behaved like a cad. I thought you were something you're not."

She appeared not to hear him and continued crying. "I'm sorry," he said again. "Please don't make a scene. Nothing's going to happen. We can go back to the house as soon as you've tidied yourself up a bit."

She became more quiet then. "I'm sorry," he said again. "I'm going to get your shoes and your bag. Please wait for me."

By the time he returned Granny had adjusted her dress, wiped her tears, and was ready to go back. When they got to Cama Hall she pulled Rustamji aside. "Rustamji, I'm sorry, but I want to go home now."

Rustamji, surprised, argued. "But the picnic is only just beginning."

"Please, Rustamji, please."

There was a wild look in her eyes he had not seen before. Teddy intervened for her. "I say, Rustam, something happened. A misunderstanding, I'm afraid. A bit embarrassing, actually. Take her home. Let her explain it to you." He spoke in a low voice, but not surreptitiously. "Mayher, be sure to tell him everything. Do not leave anything out on my account."

Rustamji said nothing but sent for his carriage. Granny said nothing once she saw he was taking her home. She didn't even look at him, too immersed in her confusion. She didn't understand Teddy's pendulum swings of character. Was the prince who had proven himself a bounder proving himself still a prince by asking her not to spare him? She felt silly like Titania caught with Bottom, the weaver in the ass-head – but Teddy wasn't Bottom, and she couldn't tell if he was wilier or nobler; if wilier he might still make her appear a fool, but if nobler she might appear a fool in contrast. She thought of Lady Flora Hastings, one of Queen Victoria's ladies-in-waiting, who had suffered from a cancerous growth on her liver which made her appear pregnant; since she was unmarried a scandal had ensued, she was forced against her will to submit to a medical examination which proved she was a virgin, and a few months later she died of the cancer; even the Queen had suspected the worst because Lady Flora had been seen alone with Sir John Conroy on one occasion.

Once they were on their way home Rustamji asked her what had happened. It was a warm night but Granny shivered, pulled her shawl more tightly around her shoulders, and sat forward in her seat next to Rustamji clutching her handbag in her lap. "I think it might have been . . . I had a lot of . . . Naju gave me a lot of port to drink. . . ."

She told her story as if she could hardly believe it herself. "I'm sorry I've been such a silly goose. I'm sure Teddy didn't mean anything. It was just the port . . . if only Naju hadn't poured me so much port. . . ." As her voice trailed off she was afraid to look at him, afraid of what he might be thinking.

"If Naju hadn't poured you so much port she would have done something else." Rustamji's voice boomed more exultantly than it had all evening. Granny looked at him in surprise. He was smiling. "It is good this thing happened. She has shown us her cards and she has no trumps. She has already played her strongest suit."

Granny said nothing but continued to look at him in surprise. "Naju knows I am thinking of marrying you. This was the only way she could think of to stop it – by tarnishing your reputation. The old she-devil is running out of tricks if this is the best she can do."

Rustamji chuckled. "It is no big mystery, Meherbanu. Don't look so puzzled. It's a simple story, really. The old man, J.P., to make sure the name of Cama would continue, made it a condition that only male heirs would partake of his inheritance. If Naju had a son he could legally change his name to Cama, but she is not getting married again, and she is already too old to have children. She will always be well off, of course, but if I have sons it will mean she will have that much less." He chuckled again as if it were a good joke. "And, by God, I will have sons. If I had doubts before this has swept them away. I will talk to your father tomorrow morning. What do you think of that?"

Granny thought he should ask her first, but he seemed so pleased with himself, like a boy who has had the last laugh, that she didn't want to quibble. "I'm very happy, Rustam," she said, sinking back into the soft seat of the carriage; it was the first time she had called him Rustam as an equal instead of Rustamji in deference to his age; she was also crying and he put an arm around her shoulders and she hid her face in his chest, but she was thinking of that swine, Naju, and an image wafted in the air of a large pink sow with fat white udders floating in the sky like a balloon wearing Naju's blue gown reduced to a tutu around its waist, her diamond choker around its neck, diamond ear rings in its ears, and a diamond on its wiggly pink tail. It was at moments such as this that I knew my imagination was at least as responsible for what I "saw" as the directorial talents of my guides.

A Legitimate Heir

"Things went smoothly then for a while. The only difficulties were first when your mother was born – we needed a male heir – and then the next year when Jalu was born. We named them both for Jalbhai Phirozshah as you know, your mother Pheroza and her sister Jalu, but of course that was hardly the same thing. I hated the hypocrisy of it all; sometimes I think people only live for the misery of others; the important thing, they said, was that I had two healthy daughters, but their sympathy was always so sweet that I felt they were glad I had failed to bear a son as if my failure somehow either gave them more stature or reduced me to their level; there were some women who never forgave me for marrying Rustam as if I had spoiled their chances or their daughters' chances or even, sometimes, their granddaughters' chances; but less than a year after Jalu was born I was pregnant again."

Granny sat in the verandah of Zephyr, the house in which she was to live the rest of her life. She was sewing an intricate pattern of birds, butterflies, and flowers onto a baby's dress. The children were in the nursery with the ayahs. Between the stone balusters she could see the sea lapping at the Scandalpoint rocks. She could also see Naju's carriage as it came up her driveway, passed the coconut trees at the far end, and around the landscaped centre of roses and daisies and sunflowers. "Stanley," Granny called, and the Goanese Christian bearer, who had been seated on his haunches in the doorway to the sitting room by the verandah, appeared before her.

"Yes, Memsahib."

"Stanley, Najubai is here. Go, let her in. Bring her to the verandah."

"Yes, Memsahib."

Granny put her work down for a moment, stood up, and stretched. Rustamji was off so often on his business that she hardly saw him. She didn't know what he did except that he had given up writing and painting and rejoined Cama Enterprises as a board member as befitted his responsibilities as a husband and father. She had everything she needed; she was happy enough just to read, sew, organize the household, play with the children, and entertain her all too infrequent visitors. When Pheroza had been born, and then Jalu, Naju had sent them lavish gifts − clothes, toys, furniture, even jewelery − but Granny had wanted to send them all back; she wouldn't forget what had happened on the night of the play, but Rustamji had persuaded her to let bygones be bygones − after all, Naju was his sister, and had, however inadvertently, expedited the marriage with her machinations − and Granny was glad finally that she had allowed herself to be persuaded. Naju had helped Granny expand her social circle and become her most frequent visitor, sometimes bringing friends with her on her visits.

"There you are, Meher, my dear, hard at work as usual. How are you?"

"Quite well, thank you. How are you?"

Naju put down a brown paper bag she was holding. "Oh, my dear, at my age if you get up in the morning you can't complain." They embraced lightly, then Naju stepped back. "Let me look at you, my dear. I want to see how you're filling out."

Granny had on a loose green house dress. She turned around self-consciously. "I think I'm beginning to show already, even through this baggy old thing."

"That's a good sign, to show early, especially in your third pregnancy. It means the baby's healthy. I really didn't think you and the old man should have tried again. It's so unhealthy for old people, and the babies are so often born deformed."

Rustamji was almost fifty, but Granny was only twenty-two. She knew Naju didn't want them to have a son. After Jalu had been born she had said, "You two billy goats have made enough hay now, but you're getting much too old to be milking each other still." She had spoken as if she had meant to be charming, but Granny had been shocked to hear her talk, as she put it later, like a guttersnipe. Rustamji had only laughed, but in the privacy of their bedroom, curtained by the darkness, he had said, "Well, you old nanny goat, do you think Naju was right? or do you think we should try one more time?" Granny had held him tightly and spoken fiercely. "I think we should keep on trying until one of us is dead."

When Naju had learned that Granny was pregnant again she had said, "Well, best of luck, but it's going to be difficult." She had sent some sev. "It's a little bit sour," she had warned, "because I put something in it to help the pregnancy. My herbalist said it's guaranteed to give you a son. I put in more raisins to make up for the sourness. I'll send you the sev everyday. That way we'll be sure the baby will be all right."

The sev wasn't too sour, but Granny didn't want to eat it everyday; but Rustamji said if it made an old woman happy, especially her sister-in-law who had no children of her own, then she should, and maybe it would even actually help the pregnancy; so she did.

"Have you been eating the sev regularly?" Naju asked as she picked up her brown paper bag again. "We want to be sure of a healthy baby."

"Yes, don't worry, I have. Thank you."

"Good. Here, I brought you something I thought you could use. It's the purest 22-karat yarn you'll ever find." She pulled out a plump golden skein from the bag and held it up in her bony hand like an apple. Granny accepted it with thanks. "Don't thank me," Naju continued. "No one I know can weave a finer pattern than you, my dear. This is all I can do to help, just to bring you materials. I would go into the business if I were you."

Naju had brought her threads of silk and cloths of satin and velvet before. Granny felt ashamed again, as she always did when Naju did her a good turn, for all the resentment she had harboured – and, on occasion, continued to harbour – against her. She knew, of course, that Naju didn't mean what she said about going into the business; a Cama wouldn't work for money, but Granny often gave away pieces of her work – tapestries, carpets, shawls, stoles, handbags – and the appreciation she received enhanced the value of the time she spent on them. She asked if Naju would like some tea. They moved into the sitting room as Stanley brought the tea things on a tray – a porcelain kettle covered by an embroidered cosy, warm milk in a white porcelain jug covered by a doily, cubed white sugar in a pot with arms akimbo alongside a tiny pair of tongs, a strainer set in its rest, two cups, saucers, teaspoons, napkins, and a plate of assorted cream and fruit filled biscuits. Stanley put down the tea tray and retired to squat out of sight in the corridor outside the sitting room in case they needed anything else.

"In my fourth month things started going wrong; I felt as if something inside me was shrinking; my blood pressure rose, I had constant headaches, nausea, diarrhoea, I passed a lot of blood. After I lost the baby I didn't do anything for a long time. Then I read some books on miscarriages and found that all my symptoms could have been induced by arsenic or mercury poisoning in small doses. I was convinced then, and no one will ever convince me otherwise, that Naju had induced my miscarriage by doctoring the sev she had sent me every morning, but Rustamji refused to believe my story and told me not to repeat it because people would think I was crazy. Of course, she was his sister. How could he believe me? I said nothing, but I never stopped believing it. What I couldn't believe was how stupid I had been to trust Naju at all knowing what was at stake. Those years between my miscarriage and Soli's birth were the worst. My father died, followed two years later by my mother, but then Soli, a son, was born, and I felt I had finally done something right, I felt my purpose in life had been fulfilled, I had given the Camas a legitimate heir."

On the morning of the day Rustamji died, Granny had thought about the differences in her children and how evident they were so early in their lives. Pheroza played the piano slowly, cautiously, as if she might be punished for each wrong note; Jalu played at a furious pace as if she knew that however she played the applause would be the same, and she didn't want her playing to get in the way of the applause; Soli, on the other hand, had no interest in playing the piano at all, stating with unusual emphasis for a five-year-old that he would rather just sit and listen.

In the afternoon Rustamji had a fatal heart attack.

In the evening Naju came with a party of about ten friends and relatives to bear condolences and make the funeral arrangements. She also brought some malido and some bhakhras which her cook had made that morning, and which she had had blessed. Granny lost control: she ordered the bearer to bring the waste bucket from the kitchen and threw in all the sweets for Naju and her party to see; she screamed that she would not allow Naju to poison her family again, accused her of inducing her miscarriage with arsenic, and ordered her out of her house forever. Naju might normally have left quietly, considering the circumstances, but perhaps the dramatic note with which she chose to make her exit indicates the truth of what Granny said; she left immediately saying, "That's a strange accusation to be coming from someone who couldn't see the truth when it was right under her nose."

Naju knew Granny had always been sensitive about her sharp and shining nose, but her meaning became clearer still when Rustamji's will was declared. He had established a trust fund for Helen Dastur. Granny had enjoyed the company of the witty blond Anglo-Indian on several occasions after she had first met her on the night of the play; she knew Rustamji had sometimes visited her when he had time from work during the day, but she refused to believe (as the size of the fund persuaded so many others) that there was anything improper about the visits. She liked Helen, but she wished Rustamji had said something to her about it so that she might have been more prepared.

Word got around that the strain had been too much for Granny to bear, but Granny didn't care what anyone thought anymore; she tasted everything Soli Mama ate to reassure herself it was safe, sacked one of her servants when she learned that he had once worked for Naju, and didn't ease her vigilance again until both her daughters were married, Soli Mama was old enough to take care of himself, and she was ensconced in Cambridge chaperoning him during his academic years there. Then she looked, as my mother put it, as if she had fallen in love; Jalu Masi, had she not been married and living in Hong Kong, might have said that she had the strength of a survivor in her face; but the seeds of her paranoia must have been deeply sown indeed for a four day delay at the Bagdogra airport to undo a four year rest-cure in Cambridge.

The Episode of the Vase

Perhaps the last time Granny found the initiative to do anything was when Soli Mama got married. Among other things she sat at her dining table day after day for a month with the Bombay telephone book and went through it from A to Z by the dim light of her chandelier to make sure no one was left out; Naju, of course, was not invited. Fifteen hundred guests came to dinner, governors, chief ministers, and members of parliament among them. Granny sent out the invitations, planned the menu (ordering extra dishes including meringue for dessert in addition to the customary kulfi), and hired the band. It was also possibly the last time Granny got so lost in an endeavor that she entirely forgot the cost to herself: Soli Mama was the cornerstone of her existence; he had been with her for thirty years, she was not entirely glad of his choice, but she was glad that he was so sure of his choice himself, a vivacious girl of eighteen with the white skin and black hair one might have associated with Snow White. Of course, he would only be moving downstairs from her, but for a mother, particularly for one as jealous as Granny had been of Soli Mama, the distance was secondary to the weaning away process, the spur being to establish another generation of heirs for the House of Cama.

If there had been any doubt about Snow White's – or Farida Banker's, to give her her proper name – deservedness, they were put to rest by an incident which I remembered forever after as the Episode of the Vase. Turning the corner from her sitting room into her hallway Granny almost tripped over her bearer of six weeks who had been squatting there. She drew herself back immediately and launched into a tirade. "You swine! How many times have I told you not to sit in wait for me like that. But that's what you want, you

140

want me to fall – let the old woman hurt herself, let her fall and die, then we can rob her blind – this for all the money I pay you, all the food I give you, you who are not fit to eat lice – but I'm up to your tricks, you cunning, thieving sons of swine, so don't try anything with me."

Granny's outbursts always dismayed me, whether directed toward her servants, toward salesmen in long narrow dress shops for hiding the best cloths from her after they had cluttered their counters with reams of satins, cottons, rayons, toward maitre d's in quiet, dimly lit restaurants for hiding the choicest entrées on the menu, toward ticket agents in crowded places for hiding the best seats from her chauffeurs who would stand in line for her. More than embarrassment I felt sadness, particularly when, sometimes in the middle of a scene, she would turn to Rusi and me with a sudden sweet smile and apologize to us – to no one else – as if to exonerate us from all culpability in the affair. We would nod silently, awkward in the spotlight until she resumed her fury, while Mom or Soli Mama or whoever else might have been with us made entreaties to her rationality.

Of course, the servants didn't stay long no matter how well she paid them, and the current one was no exception. Sometimes, I felt they stayed because they recognized that she was harmless, that her imprecations said more about her than about them, that they were being paid for their endurance more than the work they did of which there was not very much; sometimes I felt they even pitied her but could only take so much abuse themselves. "Array, Memsahib," the bearer said, getting to his feet, "what is this talk? It is not so. I was only sitting."

"Swine! You dare to call me a liar! You think I cannot do without you? You are all like that, let us see how much the old woman will take. But you can get out. I will not have you here another day."

The bearer shuffled and asked for his pay. She said she would get it from the bedroom if he would wait right where he was – but then an unexpected thing happened. There was no reason for him to mistrust Granny, but he wanted to come to the bedroom with her; perhaps he meant her no harm, perhaps he meant to take more money than was owed him, perhaps he meant for once for his will to triumph over Granny's; no one would ever know the truth of the matter, perhaps not even the bearer himself, because at that point they had reached an impasse: she refused to go to the bedroom with him; he refused to let her go alone.

At this point Soli Mama walked in inquiring about the lunch Granny had promised to send downstairs for himself and Farida. When the situation was explained he told the bearer, as Granny had, to wait and they would get him his money, but the bearer, no longer even listening, chose to force the issue. He picked up a long-stemmed blue vase, threw out the sunflowers it had held, and, brandishing it like a weapon, tried to edge them toward the bedroom, but Soli Mama adroitly slipped the two of them into the dining room instead where the bearer followed them slowly, threateningly, around the sixteen-seater table.

It was during this slow stalk around the table that Farida came upstairs. When she understood what was going on she said to the bearer, "That is all? That is all that this is about? Then there is no problem. You come down with me, no? I will give you the money. You can come into the bedroom, you can come up to my cupboard. That is no problem at all." She spoke with a smile as if she couldn't understand what all the fuss was about.

Soli Mama and Granny were too amazed to speak. The bearer said, "This is a good memsahib. She will not cheat me. She does not shout and swear like the other memsahib." But Farida's Snow White appearance might well have been the most fundamental reason winning his trust. He put down the vase, she beckoned him with her hand, "Come," looking uncannily like one of the coy young girls the bearer must have seen so often in the Indian movies, and he followed her down the stairs. At the bottom of the stairs Farida looked up to see Soli Mama and Granny still speechless with disbelief. "Why are you two looking like two fishes?" she said. "Get inside, no? What is there for you to do now?" When Soli Mama and Granny had locked themselves into Granny's flat, Farida looked over her shoulder, past the entranceway to the house as if she saw someone she knew, and, when the bearer followed her gaze, slipped quickly into her flat, slammed the door shut, and bolted it.

This was an incident I had heard about, but not seen before. The scenes were becoming increasingly familiar as they caught up with the present. The bearer had rushed in a rage at Farida's brother who had walked right then into the driveway, who was, fortunately, stalwart enough to take care of himself. The bearer lost two teeth. He returned that evening with a knife when Farida's father paid him off enough never to come back.

Then came the painful scenes toward the end: Granny, off limits to Soli Mama's two sons because Farida worried about her influence; Granny, shouting at her bridge partners for cheating, reduced to playing incessant games of patience; Granny cruising Warden Road in her chauffeur-driven Studebaker for gangas to stay overnight because she was afraid to sleep alone even with Soli Mama downstairs from her and a chowkidar at the gate; Granny, dressed in rags, talking to herself, roaming aimlessly about her dusty cobwebby flat – on to the last, finally reassuring, scene of her death: Granny, seated in a chair, talking to all three of her children (even Jalu Masi, called from Hong Kong on a premonition by Mom) gathered around her, in a circle of trust, perhaps even a newly burgeoning love, her head dropping midsentence to her chest.

The image of Granny sitting on the chair, head slumped forward, faded into a silhouette with a bright glow around it. The shape was familiar, of a man, squat, dense, but I couldn't place it until what I can only describe as an aura revealed its identity; it was Jalbhai Pherozshah Cama, J.P. himself; when he spoke I recognized his voice from the time I had heard him speak, holding on to the chair he had reserved for his friend while the uniformed English official tried to take it away.

"Let me clear up a few things first, Homi. Everyone is always full of praise for me, but for all the wrong reasons. Bapaiji is cynical enough to think God is a trickster, Granny is bitter enough to think Him unjust, but they are both wrong; they think they're in heaven but they're not; they are at what might best be understood as a waystation. Bapaiji admired my industry, Granny my worldly goods, but they both admired the wrong things, the end product, not the means. Capitalism is fine, but without the human touch it is hardly removed from totalitarianism. Let me be more specific: I was on a sightseeing tour in Jerusalem once, staying at the Mediterranean Hotel. The city was full of history, of course, and there were groves of pomegranates, peaches, apricots, and oranges – I always bore in mind the possibilities of transplanting new fruits and plants in India – but more than anything else I was impressed by the sight of some nails, reputedly the nails with which Christ had been crucified, embedded in a stone some twelve inches thick. The nails did not make a Christian of me, but they deepened my respect for Christianity and, as a consequence, made me a better Zoroastrian. The month before I had attended a piano recital by Hans von Bulow in Boston where he had performed Beethoven's Diabelli Variations – one theme, thirty-three variations – but I had not been much impressed; I preferred the sonata form where a single theme is explored and developed to its fullest; but watching the nails I realized that variations are also a form of exploration and development; Christianity became relevant to me as a variation on the theme of Zoroastrianism; each of them was profound by itself, but their conjunction provided a breadth which neither possessed alone; the many religions of the world reveal the world in all its variety like the variations of a theme. Heaven is not a place as Bapaiji, Granny, and your pappa have imagined, creating it to suit their own needs, but a state of mind which encompasses all these possibilities."

Mom and Dad

Edinburgh

My head didn't hurt any more. The needles felt more like toy mallets. My temples throbbed with dull beats on the heels of my hands as they held up my head, where I continued to sit on the wooden bath stool in the verandah. The cawing of the crows outside had diminished, but the commotion of the traffic on Cooperage Road and the shuffle of the crowd and the hum of the conversation had increased. The sporting event, whatever it was, must have ended. The loudspeakers, mercifully, had been turned off. I must have been unconscious during Granny's revelations; otherwise, I would surely have heard *Jana Gana Mana*, the national anthem, as it marked the end of the program in the stadium.

A smell of frying potatoes wafted on the verandah from the second floor. I recognized the Mehtas' cooking oil. They made wafers, chips as I had learned to call them in the States, every evening for appetizers. Rusi and I had gotten into the habit of visiting them at that hour whenever we were free. No other wafers, not the OK wafers, not the Victory wafers, not the Coronation wafers, tasted as well as the Mehtas' wafers. The smell of the wafers more than anything else told me it had to be almost seven o'clock which was when the Mehtas had dinner, and sure enough a sweet curry smell followed shortly.

A door opened and someone entered my bedroom. I heard the light being switched on. "Baba? Where is Baba gone?" It was our ganga, Sunanda. She would doubtless call me "baba" even when I became a septuagenarian with a doddering step and a quaver in my voice. She had worked for the family (for everyone in Mayo House, in fact) ever since I could remember. She came for an hour every morning to dust and sweep and mop. She would have visited the

Patels on the fourth floor before us; she would go to the Mehtas on the second floor after us, then the Bannerjees on the first, and the Chibbers on the ground. She never aged. The work kept her fit. She hitched her sari between her legs, tied it in a knot, and stuffed it into her waist so she could squat comfortably as she traversed each of the rooms on her lightly muscled smooth brown haunches, first with a broom in hand, then a floor rag which she soaked periodically in a plastic water bucket; even her torso, exposed between the waist of her sari and the high rim of her choli, remained firm and trim. When Rusi and I had been young we'd been taken care of by the ayahs, but after they had left (Julie, Rusi's ayah, pensioned by the family, to live with her son and his family somewhere in Goa; my ayah, Mary, being much younger, to a subsequent position), Sunanda had helped Mom with the cooking, cleaning, light washing (the dhobi came once a week for the heavy wash), ironing, errands and the like on the days our regular help, Jairam the bearer, was off.

"Baba, where you are?" Sunanda couldn't see me where I sat in the verandah and I was too weak to say anything; I was only barely aware of her movements.

"Bai, Bai, come quick," she said then (she must have seen me). "Baba is got up from his bed." I heard her scurrying from the room. "He is sitting on stool in the verandah. He must be feeling better."

Suddenly, Sunanda and Mom and Jairam and Rusi were all around me. Mom put her hand on my back; I was still leaning forward and couldn't see her, but I knew her touch. "Homi, can you hear me?" Mom said, rubbing my back with a slow to-and-fro motion. "You don't have to talk. You don't have to open your eyes. Just nod your head if you can hear me."

I raised my head from my hands, wanting to answer her, wanting to see them around me, wanting to stand up, but my head felt too heavy and I would have toppled forward onto my hands and knees if Rusi hadn't caught me and, along with everyone else, helped me back to the bed.

"The heat must have made him weak, Mom," Rusi said, closing the doors to the verandah. "We don't know how long he's been sitting there. He'll be better when the room cools down again."

148

"Yes. Maybe." Mom was tucking me in again.

"Bai," Jairam was saying, "Bai, Baba is better?"

"Array, Jairam," Mom said, "what can I tell you? He got up. That is a good sign." She spoke conversationally, but with an edge as if she were afraid to hope for too much.

"Baba is better, hey-hey! Teep-Taap! Yes-very good-hurray! I will make him soup like you showed me, Bai, chicken soup. Baba will like."

I could just imagine him then, the tiny man with the large head, the embarrassed but pleased smile, wanting to help but afraid to get in the way, skinny wiry limbs emerging from his striped bush shirt and white shorts. He had joined our service less than two years before I had left, which was a shorter time than any of our other servants, but he had been with Mom during the time Dad had died which had led to a mutual trust between them that time alone might never have established. We provided his board and lodging; he kept his things in our godown, sleeping there on a thin mattress on the floor, and visited his wife and two daughters in Bandra on his day off every week. He wished his wife would move even further so he would have an excuse not to visit her at all – I understood she was a large woman, and though he gave her all his earnings she continually badgered him for more; he didn't care how infrequently he saw her. At first we had a bearer, a ganga, two ayahs, and a cook; but when Rusi and I became too old for the ayahs, Mom found it easier to retire the cook with the ayahs and teach Jairam a few things in the kitchen than to manage so many of them at once. Jairam could not have been better pleased; he loved to show off his newly acquired skills. "I will cook curry-rice, Bai," he said. "I will cook lemon soufflé for Baba. He will like my cooking."

"Wait, Jairam," Mom said. "Wait. If Baba wants soup I will tell you."

"Also curry-rice, Bai, also curry-rice I have made. You said, no, my curry-rice is good?"

"Yes, Jairam, but first Baba must drink. If he cannot drink soup, how will he eat your good curry-rice?"

"Yes-yes. Bai is right. Bai is right."

"Now go to the kitchen. If I want the soup I will tell you. Sunanda, there is nothing more for you to do now today. Come back tomorrow."

After the two of them had left I heard Mom pull one of the wooden folding chairs to the bed and sigh as she sat down. "He looks better, Mom," Rusi said, "not so white like before. He's going to be okay. He just had a relapse after the long trip – the doc said he might, I told you, no? He must have been conscious to go to the verandah like that, no? I'm telling you, he's going to be okay."

I sensed he was standing beside her, both of them looking at me. "I hope so, Rusi, I hope so. Ssh!" The hum of the air conditioner worked to ease the throbbing in my temples. Mom put her hand under the covers and squeezed my hand. "Homi," she said, "if you can hear me, if I make any impression on you at all, give me a sign – nod your head, open your eyes, move your hand, anything."

I opened my eyes. Only the bedside lamp was lit. Rusi put his hand on my shoulder. "Can you say something?" Mom said. "Can I get you something? anything?"

How can I explain the sensations? She could not see that my eyes were open. I was in limbo with access to eternal secrets; she was on a one way thoroughfare from which death is the only escape. I couldn't hear her as much as read her thoughts – not even read her thoughts (which implies a conscious effort) as much as think them with her, or perhaps a nanosecond later, as if I were hearing her thoughts. I opened my mouth to speak but no sound issued; I needed someone to hear my thoughts as I imagined I was hearing hers – but however bizarre the situation felt, I no longer thought I was going crazy; I understood that I had somehow stumbled upon a different mode of communication. "Would you like something to eat?" Mom said, "some chicken soup? Jairam's made some. It's quite good. There's also some sali boti."

I still couldn't see her lips move with the words but they twitched as if something else were on her mind, her eyes darted as if to avoid mine, and around her the entire panorama shifted. We were at our four foot square, wooden dining table with the glass top in our regular formation, Rusi on her left, myself on her right, and Dad across from her. The bearer had filled our water glasses, left a second bottle of refrigerated water on the table, and cleared away the empty blue soup plates. "Did you like the chicken soup?" she was speaking to Dad; her lips twitched and she avoided his eyes; she had prepared frog legs for the main course; she liked experimenting with exotic foods, Dad hated her experiments, but she persisted and was invariably stalemated in her attempts to make a gourmet of Dad.

The bearer brought in the katchoubar and the breaded frog legs on a large blue dish. "What is this?" Dad said immediately, looking suspiciously at Mom.

"It's only chicken," Mom said, pretending to have difficulty spooning the katchoubar into her plate. "Try it."

Perhaps if she had said simply "Chicken" or "Chicken. Why?" he might have believed her, but Mom was a lousy liar; she had to say "It's only chicken," as if it might have been something else; she had to say "Try it," as if he'd never tried chicken in his life. Dad saw through her right away. "It's frog legs," he said. "Do not lie to me. How many times have I told you not to do this to me?"

Mom's eyes were wide like those of a child who can't believe her ruse has been discovered. "It's chicken! Try it. I'm telling you it's just like chicken."

Well, it had to be either chicken or just like chicken; it couldn't be both. Dad swallowed his glass of cold water in a single gulp, dumped his napkin next to the wooden owl napkin ring (Mom's was a duck, Rusi's a penguin, mine an elephant), noisily pushed back the wooden cane chair, and shouted at Mom. "I wish you would not do this to me. Now, because of you, I will have to go hungry." Without waiting for her response he stamped out of the room.

Mom's eyes filled with tears. "I wish he would try it. I wish he would at least try it. How can he know he doesn't like it if he doesn't even try it."

Rusi and I were silent, not entirely convinced of the edibility of frog legs ourselves. "Mom," I said, "where's the rest of the frog?"

"I don't know," she said distractedly, touching at her eyes with her tiny lace handkerchief. "I think it might be too small to eat."

I picked at my frog legs, fantasizing that perhaps they didn't kill the frogs but merely amputated them, popping them back among the lily pads in their ponds and swamps with tiny crutches and wheelchairs.

"If he stays hungry it's his own fault," Mom was saying. "It's not my fault if he won't even try something new. You like the frog legs, don't you, Homi-Rusi? They're not so bad. They're just like chicken, aren't they?"

Rusi, nodding, was eating the frog legs happily enough – but he, of course, had drunk cow piss just as willingly during our navjote; but for me eating the frog legs meant more than merely eating an exotic food – I felt I was betraying Dad by eating the frog legs just because Mom had applied a lace handkerchief to her eyes; if it tasted just like chicken then why the hell didn't she just serve chicken and save everyone all this bother, particularly when she knew how Dad felt about it all? It was a way Mom had of straitjacketing Dad. When I broke the slender blue vase they had brought back from Japan with my tennis ball in the sitting room, Mom said I was not to tell Dad because he would get mad (he didn't even notice the vase was gone); when I lost a friend's schoolbag of textbooks Mom said I was not to tell Dad because he would get mad; when he was home we were not to make a noise because he worked hard to make money for us and needed his rest; all this made him something of an interloper in his own home, and through these incidents Dad became more of a stranger, and the more he became a stranger the more I felt I betrayed him. He was most visible to us at breakfast before he left for the office and at dinner after he returned. At the table he was Dad, which meant he didn't have to eat porridge, he could have two fried eggs to our one each, sometimes he got an omelette (with however many eggs it took to make one), he got two cups of tea to our one each, the choicest fruit (bananas, papayas, mangoes, chee-koos, apples, oranges, mosambis, figs, pomegranates, leechees, custard apples), the first, the largest servings of everything, the refrigerated water (when we were very young we only drank water from the matka which was cool, but not so icy that it might give us colds) – but even then Mom was the civilizing influence, telling him to eat more slowly, to keep his mouth closed, to use his napkin, not to talk with his mouth full, and, when he farted audibly, saying, "Adi! Not at the table!" more to fill the silence which followed than anything else; when he farted away from the table, in company or even just among the family, she would say simply, "Adi!" like the sternest of Victorian parents. Dad would smile then, say it was a natural thing he did, and fart again as often as he found necessary.

Sometimes, if I were hungry, I would fix myself a snack in the evening after dinner, generally six slices of buttered toast. The process was more intricate than it sounds because I wanted the butter to melt directly on the toast, which meant I had to take it out of the refrigerator about half an hour before I applied it so it would be soft, and I had to butter the toast as soon as it popped – otherwise, the toast would cool and the butter would lie thick and yellow and pasty and cold instead of bright and fluid and warm. Since we had a two-slice toaster one slice would necessarily be cooler than the other when it was buttered; I toyed with the idea of toasting just one slice at a time so I could butter each to perfection while the next was being toasted, but gave it up because it seemed a waste to use a two-slice toaster for just one toast at a time; I learned instead to butter quickly and to ignore all distractions. On the night of the frog legs dinner I had just buttered six slices when Dad came into the kitchen. "Did you make those for me, Homi?"

He was grinning as if he'd made a joke, but I couldn't smile; I knew I was about to be done out of my toast as I had been before; what annoyed me even more than losing the toast was his manner, as if I were being entirely too humourless. "No," I said, "I made them for myself."

"Do you mind if I have some then? I didn't have any dinner, you know."

Of course I minded, but I couldn't tell him that; he was Dad, and everything we had in the house we had because of him. "No, I don't mind. You can have them."

"I'll only take two. Then you can have four. Will that be all right?"

My rage made me stubborn; I had to have all of them or none. "No, you can have them all," I said solemnly, without looking at him. "I'll just finish off the left-over frog legs."

But I didn't want the frog legs; I wanted the toast; I told Mom about it and she must have said something to him because he never asked for my toast again – he even stayed out of the kitchen when I made the toast – but that was not what I wanted either; I had pushed Mom between the two of us again; what I wanted was to be able to say No to him myself, but that was an understanding which was a long time coming.

Dad's temper was quick (his frustrations were many); I learned to be surprised not when he lost but when he controlled his temper – surprised and relieved because I hated to hear him shout; I hated to hear anyone shout; it made me rigid with helplessness, and resentful. The following incident stuck in my memory like a needle to a groove because his control was in ascendance. I was learning to drive; Dad was standing to the right front of the car (the 1948 Ford, which Rusi called the Humpty-Dumpty Ford because of its shape and because we had had it so long he expected it to break – the first car in Navsari, which had been presented so spectacularly, draped in marigolds, to Mom and Dad on the occasioin of their fifth wedding anniversary by Hormusji and Bapaiji). He was directing me out of a parking spot and keeping a lookout down the road; Rusi was in the back seat; a young American with a nimbus of cauliflower hair, blue jean bell bottoms, beads, beard, flowers, and sandals, stopped by the car and asked Rusi the way to the Taj Mahal Hotel; Rusi invited him to join us since we were going that way; it wasn't until we were well on our way that Dad became aware of the silent smiling addition to the backseat; his double take was worthy of Chaplin or Laurel and Hardy or The Three Stooges, each of whom he revered; I steeled myself for his anger at the cheap thrill we had provided ourselves, but instead there was a choking sound in his throat and a momentary look of pain, even panic, on his face, as if we had betrayed him by not saying anything; I felt my complicity as if worms had suddenly erupted on my face, but the new presence was swiftly explained and Dad was just as swift to pretend for all of us that the moment of shame had not existed; I felt the exercise of his control as if it were something physical between us. "This might be your last chance, Homi," he said when he learned the hippie was from California, "ask him everything about America. You must take advantage of your chances." I asked questions about universities and scholarships, questions I had already asked, at Dad's prodding, of every American I met and everyone who had been to America, the point being that a diversity of opinion would give me a jump on the culture shock I was bound to experience.

Dad couldn't prepare me enough for America. "Americans are great kidders – that is what they call jokesters. You should read this book" (handing me a jokebook); "it will make you a hit at all the parties." There was also another way to be a hit at all the parties. "Read history. Read about old things. Americans love old things. If you don't know something, make it up; if something is a myth, pretend it's true. When I was in Edinburgh I told them that after Shah Jahan built the Taj Mahal he cut off the hands of the hundreds of labourers so they could never duplicate the feat. When the Taj Mahal Hotel was built in Bombay, I told them the plans were read upside down so it faces a back street instead of the sea. It doesn't matter what is true; it only matters what they believe." If he could have had his way he would have sent us to the University of Edinburgh where he was an alumnus, but the tuition was three times as much for overseas students and only the American schools had scholarships.

The tableau of the happy hairy hippie in the rear view mirror as I drove was removed like the past month of a calendar to be replaced by the tableau of Mom seated by my bedside again – I felt the tug to the present like a muscle spasm in my head – but a Mom as if I were seeing her for the first time, or rather more like an unexpected variation on a theme I had taken for granted. Her lips, always small, sometimes gaily painted, were more pinched; her cheeks, always high, were heavier; her hair, stiff because of her permanent and black, appeared soft and white; her skin, customarily well creamed, reflecting all light brilliantly, reflected only grey; the wells under her eyes, customarily well powdered, were deeper, darker, glistening with tears. She spoke again, but again her lips appeared not to move. "Homi, please don't go. I need you. Please don't go."

She appeared to be concentrating so intensely, as if to heal me by telepathy, that I assumed Rusi had left the room. I thought my eyes were closed but I could see her. I tried to return the pressure of her hand under the sheets, but I couldn't be sure that I did.

"I have lost too many already, Homi." Her hand gripped mine more tightly. "When your dad died – he was the first – I said I needed time, everyone said I needed time, time and prayer, time and prayer. I thought it would heal me if I repeated it to myself – Time

and Prayer, Time and Prayer, Timeandprayerandtimeandprayerand-
timeandprayerandtimeandprayerandtime — as if it were a prayer in
itself. But then Mummy died and Bapaiji less than a month after her,
and all three in less than one year — and then this horrible, horrible
thing . . . this horrible . . . Oh, God!"

Ah, this mother of mine, always a little girl in the body of a
woman, now the body of an old woman, always lovely to the world,
even to Mr Grouse, my curmudgeonly Physics teacher in high school
who once remarked, "That's quite a mother you've got there,
Homi," watching her walk away, his mouth open, his eyes glazed,
barely aware he'd spoken to me. I thought he looked silly but I
didn't know why; I knew it had something to do with my mother
but I didn't know what. When I told her about it she smiled like a
six year old with a new doll. "Everybody says that," she said,
refusing with a coy smile to elucidate further. She thought the world
was her oyster and couldn't understand why her openhearted appeals
were occasionally resisted. There we were, on the upper deck of a
red lumbering BEST (Bombay Electric State Transport) bus, returning
from a visit to the doctor (Great News! I might soon dispense with
my cane altogether) and a shopping spree (bags on our laps, in our
hands, at our feet); we would normally have taken a taxi but perhaps
Mom felt she had been profligate enough with her purchases (Dad,
who took the car to work everyday, despaired of ever convincing
her that she was no longer a Cama). A young man in a white shirt
and shorts revealing dark sinewy bonehard workman's limbs sat in
front of us with a transistor radio set to its loudest pitch, tuned to a
station playing Indian film music. Mom's request was hardly
overbearing: "Array, baba, turn that down a little bit, no? please?"
There was an almost obsequious cajole in her voice, in her expression, as if to obviate the possibility of offensiveness, but the young
man turned and said, "Array, wah-wah, Memsahib. You think
everyone is your servant, to tell them what to do — but this is not
your private motor with your private driver. This is a public
convenience, for all the people."

The man faced front again. For a moment Mom said nothing;
then, with more dismay than anger, she said, "What a horrible,
horrible man! Come along, Homi. We're getting off." We picked up

our bags and descended the stairs. The man didn't even look at us. "We can stay downstairs, Mom," I said. "We can't hear him so loudly from here," but Mom wanted to get off the bus altogether. We took a taxi the rest of the way home. Mom couldn't stop talking in the taxi about the "horrible" man; she just couldn't understand him; she had done "nothing wrong". I understood that Mom was "right", but I also understood that there had been more at stake than a loud transistor radio; perhaps she worked it out for herself subsequently, but I cannot understand, even at this remove, how she had kept herself so ignorant for so long.

"Wait, wait, Homi, you are not being fair to your mummy." Dad was talking now; I was not surprised; I had been expecting him after Granny had finished. "It is you who fail to understand. You cannot discredit her anymore than you can discredit the system that made her – the world makes us in its own image. First her family shielded her, then I shielded her. If she is ignorant it is our fault more than hers. Everywhere there is a balance. You might think she had nothing to worry about, but she paid for her security in ways that you do not understand. Bear with me, Homi. I have the advantage of hindsight over you, and your misfortune with your machine, your memoscan, has made it possible for me to reveal this to you. Bear with me."

The face of the young man in front of me so resembled that of the young man in the pictures I had taken on my arrival in Aquihana in a photo machine in a Woolworth's on Main Street, that just for a moment I thought it was mine: handsome, yes, quite handsome, though I say it myself, and so glabrous it might have been carved from marble, a big confident adolescent grin with perfect teeth, hair swept back with no part and flat as if he'd just taken off a cap (my hair in the photographs, though, with trim sideburns reaching below my ears, had a part on the left, and was swept in a puff from my forehead) and eyes wide with adolescent curiosity (just like mine except that I had inherited wells under my eyes from Mom which Dad did not have).

Dad's face shrank away then as if a camera were panning away from it revealing a torso draped in a tartan mantle secured on the left shoulder by a brooch, a tartan kilt with a leather pouch hanging in front, tartan breeches barely visible beneath the kilt, brown knee stockings, green flashes hanging from his garters, and black buckled shoes. In his hand Dad held a boat-shaped cap with two ribbons hanging behind it, and as I watched he put it on his head completing a picture we had of him in the family photograph album. "This mantle, Homi," he said, touching it lightly, "as you call it, is a plaid. It is part of the Highland dress. At one time it was five feet wide and twelve to fifteen feet long. A Highlander could pleat it around his waist and throw the loose end over his shoulder just like a sari, he could draw it over his head in the rain and roll himself in it to sleep at night. This leather pouch is a sporran; the French called it a cache-sexe, but it is just a purse; that's the French for you. These breeches are trews; if Bapaiji had looked carefully she would have seen that the Highlanders are not always naked under their kilts – when King George IV paid a state visit to Edinburgh in 1822 he wore pink silk tights under his kilt – but Bapaiji was more interested in making fun than anything else; in retrospect, though, I think it might just have been part of her strategy to get me back to India – she was so afraid I might like Edinburgh too much to ever return.

"This boat-shaped cap as you call it is a glengarry; sometimes a balmoral is worn with the Highland dress, but the glengarry looks more authentically Scottish; the balmoral looks too much like a beret, too French. These stockings are hose and these shoes are brogues." Dad acknowledged me with a professorial nod. "Look, now, Homi. I want to show you something."

The room, revealed as Dad was panned on his way to a Grundig radiogram (the same that he had had in his bedroom in Bombay) against a paneled wall, was spartanly furnished: the large compartmentalized wooden cupboard, L-shaped desk, rotary chair on wheels, green spring couch, unmade spring bed, which were all duplicates of the furniture in Bombay; there was a fireplace against the wall adjacent to the radiogram. Dad flicked a switch, a record dropped, and bagpipe music filled the room. "Now, Homi, be patient," he said. "It seems you have to be Scotch to like bagpipe music – Bapaiji called it that snake-charming music – but it didn't take me long to acquire the taste. Actually, it is sinuous music;

Bapaiji was right but not in the derisive sense she meant; two of the notes in the scale of the bagpipe are quarter tones – that is why it cannot be used in a symphony orchestra; that is why it has an oriental tone; that is why it sounds like a snake-charmer's pipe which also has quarter tones like so many Indian instruments. I knew better than to take Bapaiji's remarks seriously, of course – or perhaps I should say personally; she was seriously trying to get me to return with her to India; she wanted to show all her friends for sure that I had not married a 'muddum' which was what they called all occidental women; they were all so afraid that their well educated sons might be trapped into marriages with waitresses and landladies' daughters.

"Anyway, let me get back to what I was showing you. Watch me now." He stood with one arm curved by his head, listening intently to the music. I watched his bare knees enviously; however much I resembled him my left knee would never be as healthy as his. He broke suddenly into a series of intricate steps executed on the same spot; it was a vigorous performance but also exceedingly delicate, particularly when he hopped on one foot while moving the other in front of and behind the calf. "This is the fling," he said, executing another loop with his foot, "and the dance is called the Highland Fling. It's something I never mastered while I was in Edinburgh. There is an irony here, Homi. This is a victory dance; I wanted to dance it when my exams were over, when your mother said she would marry me, whenever I received a promotion at work, but I had to die before I could do it well, when I had no victory to celebrate – well, maybe one; I died before Bapaiji; that was perhaps my only victory over her – but what good is a victory with no one to share the celebration, and what a cruel reason anyway for a celebration; it is spiteful of me, I know, but I can't help myself; I know she always resented me; I always blamed myself and tried to make it up by being whatever she wanted, but that is not the way; people hate you if you go against their wishes, but they despise you if you don't; and a man may be hated but only a coward is despised.

"Perhaps there is no irony after all. I thought my greatest satisfaction when I died would be her dissatisfaction, but I was wrong; I felt only loss. I want to reconcile the loss, and yet I have chosen to be here in Edinburgh, where I was farthest from her – but that is not the only reason, that is hardly the only reason, no! Edinburgh is beautiful – beautiful! I love Edinburgh. In this respect I suppose I am just like your Granny – her Cambridge is my Edinburgh, her Englishmen are my Scotsmen. Perhaps for you, though, never having lived in the United Kingdom, there is no difference between the English and the Scots; of course, there is no reason for you to have given it any thought, but let me just clear up some things.

"The English are too blasé to care what you think, but the Scots, with a more tenuous hold on their identity, are less so; they still bridle when their sovereign is called Elizabeth II because, as they rightly object, Elizabeth I was never queen of Scotland; it is impossible to be like the English because the English never want to be like anyone else, but the Scots find such adulation flattering; the English have a dry sense of humour, but the Scots, as they say, require a surgical operation to get a joke into their brains; but it is this vulnerability that makes the Scots lovable – like the Loch Ness Monster is lovable; they call her Nessie as if she were a pet; her danger is secondary to her charm; common sense, you see, is not highly prized by Scotsmen.

"Actually, the one time that comes to mind of the Scots aping the English proved disastrous for the Scots. In 1698, there was talk of merging the Scottish and English parliaments at Westminster; Scotland's standard of living was decidedly lower than England's, there was always the fear that without unification hostilities would break out, but the Scots hesitated to hack yet another notch into their sense of nationhood; they decided instead to found the colony of Darien on the Isthmus of Panama so they could reap the same benefits in raw materials and trade with the American natives and their Spanish conquerors as the English with their growing empire overseas; unfortunately, most of the Scottish fleet was shipwrecked, the surviving colonists found only disease, starvation, and hostile natives in Darien, and the economic debilitation resulting from the Darien Expedition did much to hasten the union with England. I think you get my point. King James founded the University of Edinburgh in 1582, but omitted to endow it with any money so that for two hundred years this mighty institution was accommodated in a dingy cluster of buildings; the City Observatory was built in 1792, but there was no money for a telescope; a civic war memorial to commemorate Wellington's peninsula campaign was begun in 1822, designed to resemble the Parthenon, but it was left unfinished because once again funding ran short.

"Do not laugh, Homi. We Indians are the same. We spend hundreds of thousands of rupees on weddings and ceremonies and celebrations and live the rest of our lives like mendicants. Maybe that is why we got along so well for so long with the British. We were like children; they were our mothers and fathers – but how meagre the common sense of the English appears contrasted with the wall-to-wall hearts of the Scots – and, to be fair to the Scots, an American professor discovered that next to the Jews the Scots exhibit the highest incidence of genius per head of population than any other race on earth: David Hume, Dugald Stewart, James Boswell, John Knox, Sir John Napier, Sir Walter Scott, Sir Arthur Conan Doyle, Robert Lewis Stevenson, Thomas Carlyle, Alexander Graham Bell, J. M. Barrie, Charles Rennie Mackintosh, James Craig, Robert Burns, Robert Adam, Adam Ferguson, Adam Smith. . . .

"But instead of talking so much, all this buk-buk as Bapaiji would say, let me just show you what it was about Edinburgh that got me so excited in the first place."

Dad led me to a tall narrow diamond-paned window which he opened with a flourish. "Look," he said. The pride in his voice, in his smile, rivaled that of any mother with her newborn. "Take a deep breath and look on the face of paradise."

I took a step forward, a deep breath, and looked, hoping I wouldn't have to fake my appreciation because I didn't want to hurt his feelings, but the sight filled me immediately with wonder. I saw first a castle like a crown atop a rugged rise of hill with a dry moat, a drawbridge, bronze statues in niches on either side of the gateway, towers, turrets, ramparts, a wide esplanade with a cannon, and a flag fluttering vigorously in the bright cloudless sky. "That," said Dad in a new deep rich voice, "is Castle Rock. You might have heard of the cannon on the esplanade, Mons Meg; it weighs five tons, it's known all over the world." He spoke as if he had discovered

Castle Rock himself. I found his joy infectious and listened attentively.

"There is a new and an old Edinburgh," he said. "First there was only the Edinburgh on the rock – the town sprang up around the Castle because it was best fortified that way. The houses were built, one squatting on top of the other, the first form of flats in a skyscraper, what you call highrises in America, because the only possible expansion was upward; the Edinburghers preferred to huddle on the slope of the Castle Rock despite the lack of sanitation (tunneled drainage was difficult in rock; citizens poured buckets of excrement and waste from the windows each night, at the sound of the ten o'clock bell of the church of St Giles, with perfunctory cries of 'Gardyloo' for 'Gardez l'eau' meaning 'Watch out for the water' upon unsuspecting passersby, to be picked up by cleaning men next morning) because the base of the slope was covered by the unassailable Nor' Loch, a fetid marsh; but in the early nineteenth century, when the threat of invasions became less imminent, the loch was drained and the Princes Street Gardens you now see before you was created in its place."

Dad couldn't tell me enough about the gardens: the flowers were set in beds which were changed ten to twelve times a year; the floral clock which embowered a quarter hour cuckoo was the first in the world and had some 24,000 plants within its 36 foot circumference; the recreational areas included a bandstand and an outdoor dance-floor; of the numerous memorials, the Scott Monument with a statue of Sir Walter and characters from his works, so tall, so slender, appearing from the distance like a coronet carved in stone, was the finest. A fantail of railway lines threaded the gardens and converged at Waverley Station, the second largest in Britain. The gardens reached the thoroughfare directly below me.

"This thoroughfare," Dad continued, "is Princes Street. As you can see the buildings are all on one side so the view isn't lost. To my mind it is the loveliest street in the world – and I'm not alone in my pronouncement. But come, I want to show you more."

I felt as if he lifted me by the seat of my pants for I was suddenly airborne. Spires, steeples, pinnacles, rows of chimneys lodged in rows of tiled roofs, rows of streets, hills, gardens, always the sea at the periphery, came at me in kaleidoscopic forms, at breathtaking speeds, always as if each perspective had been planned just so, but the civilized splendour was juxtaposed with perspectives of a valley with upthrusting crags and sombre craters much like a moonscape. "The ordered spaces," Dad explained, "are from the New Town which was planned after the Nor' Loch had been drained, and the crags and craters are from the Old Town, behind the Palace of Holyroodhouse where the royal family resided and still does when it visits Edinburgh; there are five extinct volcanoes within the city limits. This is what I find so irresistible, this mix of elegance and savagery; Edinburgh is so manly, so noble.

"But I was impressed even more by the people than by the city or the country. They were so fairminded I couldn't believe it.

"But I'm talking too much again. Your Bapaiji and even your Granny are better story tellers than I am. Let me just shut up and show you what happened."

Dad, young and lanky in a blazer and trousers as baggy as a sack, stepped into a cobbled mews from Mrs Dowds's boarding house. Mrs Dowds thought he must be very clever to be studying engineering at the university and had fixed him a breakfast of tea and bread and butter, haddock and eggs, allowing him as many servings as he wished and even adding Dundee cake which she knew he loved because she knew he had a very difficult examination that Monday for which he had been studying all weekend; also because she felt a little sorry for these poor handsome young men who journeyed so many thousands of miles from their homes for the sake of an education; she admired their determination and mothered them as best she could.

Dad walked with the spring of a grasshopper; he had stayed indoors all weekend studying applied mechanics and it felt good to be out again, particularly on such a sunny and bracing morning. I envied him his exuberant step; however much I had recovered I would always walk with a cautious step. He looked at his watch and chose to take the long walk to the tram stop because he wanted to enjoy the magnolia trees, the rhododendrons, poppies and primulas. Edinburgh, like Rome, is situated on seven hills, and Dad caught unexpected glimpses of the sea and distant countryside along the way – but I could see something that he could not: his tram had left by the time he got to the stop; he had been so busy studying the previous weekend that he had forgotten to wind his watch; the next tram wasn't due for half an hour. By the time he realized his mistake it was too late, of course; he asked two bicyclists in balmorals and kilts with the reddest knees he could remember what time it was.

The wonders of the country no longer entranced him; he closed his eyes instead, praying for the next tram to arrive soon, when it arrived he prayed for it to hurry; when he got off he dashed headlong to the examination hall as witlessly as the most arrant schoolboy. He was afraid he would not be allowed to sit for the examination at all. When he tried, full of consternation, to explain to Professor Macauley, the invigilator, about the weekend, the watch, the weather, the old man with the luxuriant white goatee shushed him. "Mr Seervai," he said. "You are already half an hour late. Why do you wish to make it later with your explanations. Take your seat. Begin."

Dad thanked him, thanked God, prayed for speed, and started his paper. When Professor Macauley said, "Gentlemen, please put your pens down," Dad put down his pen, but the old man continued in the same deadpan voice, "except Mr Seervai. Mr Seervai was half an hour late. Mr Seervai may have another half hour."

Dad looked at the old man in the tweed jacket and tie as if he were God; in Navsari, even at the university in Bombay, he might have been punished by having to take the examination again, or by losing the half hour, or even by a caning from Hormusji since he was the headmaster's son and had to set a good example – and yet what purpose did the punishments serve? It wasn't as if he had been purposely recalcitrant. He was full of admiration for the wisdom of the Scots, particularly for that of Professor Macauley.

I Was His
Mother and Father

"I had never liked the authoritarian streak in Bapaiji and Pappa, but I had never imagined it questionable; they were my parents; it was their duty, not their privilege, to treat me as they saw fit – and it was my duty to respect them for it. Nevertheless, one occasion arose when I knew they were wrong, but I kept quiet; it was not my place, however contrary the evidence, to say anything. I spent much of my childhood playing with the dubro, Ratilal; we would chase stray goats attempting to ride them, or catch squirrels in a mousetrap cage the size of a shoebox – but they always escaped when we tried to domesticate them; Ratilal was the only person my age that I could play with because our house was so far away from everyone else's, so Bapaiji let me play with him but she told me never to go inside his hut – I might catch a disease or, at the very least, that servant odour they carried around with them. It was a mud hut, and I entered it anyway out of curiosity, but only once because it was so dark I felt as if the walls were closing in on me. There were no windows and a cloth covered the doorway; two sheets were laid on the earth floor of the inner of the two tiny rooms for beds. In the front room was a hurricane lantern, a wooden chest of drawers, a coal brazier, and rudimentary articles of cookware. On the wall was a picture of Hanuman ripping open his chest to show that his devotion to his rulers Ram and Sita was so great he had enshrined them where his heart should have been – but you have been in the dubra huts yourself; they have not changed in all the years.

"Ratilal dressed mostly in my hand-me-downs: shirts like parachutes on his twiglike frame, pants like brown paper bags falling to his knees. Most of the time we just fooled around together. He would imitate a clown he had seen once by crooking his knees (the clown had been a dwarf), walking bowlegged in circles, holding out his arms stiffly to the sides, clapping his hands periodically, shrieking meaningless phrases, 'Aar-phaar! Aaiee-oh-vaaieek! Vairy vairy good!' to an imaginary audience. I would parade behind him, imitating his motions and sounds, acknowledging the cheers of the same imaginary crowd. His most hilarious antic, however, was wrestling cockroaches.

"The cockroaches were two to three inches in length sometimes with long antennae waving as if they might have been drunk. We stepped on them without thinking when we saw them, but Ratilal made a production out of it. He would bend over the cockroach, stalking it as if it were a wild animal, calling, 'Hey, cutulut! Ho, cutulut! Vairy vairy good!' blocking its avenues of escape with a strategically placed foot or hand without actually touching the cockroach until it was scurrying to and fro within the arena of a square foot or so. Then he would pick up the cockroach, fall on his back and hold it over him, writhing as if it were holding him down. Finally, grunting as if with a renewed effort, he would roll over on the cockroach and place it on its back on the ground. If the cockroach righted itself and ran he would hold it in place with a sure finger over its feelers before stepping on it with his bare foot and raising his arms in victory, again for an imaginary audience, as if he were a pehlwan. I would applaud, and he would smile and parade around like a conqueror before cleaning up the mess.

"I was so entertained by his performance that everytime I saw a cockroach, instead of stepping on it I would block off all its escape routes and call Ratilal to wrestle with it. At first he came willingly but after a while he tired of it and finally he said he didn't want to do it anymore.

"I was too stubborn to let him off easily – besides, he was my servant – and I continued to demand that he come and wrestle with the cockroach until, sulkily, he came – but instead of wrestling the cockroach he stepped on it, killing it outright.

"I flew at him in a rage. I was stronger than him but he was too scared to retaliate against his master anyhow. I held him with my head against his chest, my hands pulling his waist toward mine in a bear hug. He felt pitiful in my hands; I was surprised to feel the thin sticks of his ribs against my forearms, the frantic thudding of his heartbeat against my forehead, to hear his breath in such shallow gasps, as if being a servant he could not also be human. It wasn't until he shrieked, startling me (we'd both been silent until then), that I dropped him. He fell on his knees with a sharp intake of breath and a groan, his face twisted with terror as if I were a demon.

"Suddenly, aware of my power over him, I was frightened myself. He had felt so fragile; I could have broken him so easily. I got on my knees in front of him and hugged him, carefully, telling him how sorry I was.

"Years later, after I had been ensconced in Mrs Dowds's cozy boarding house in Edinburgh, I felt I understood something that Bapaiji and Pappa had never understood, that Ratilal and all the other dubras and also all the shopkeepers and tradesmen and other sundry workers looked upon us as their mothers and fathers in much the way that India looked upon England as her mother and father; nothing could be said, of course, but everyone knew it; some accepted it with benevolence and respect, others with hatred."

Dad's itinerant memory sparked one of my own from my days in high school when, in the wake of my recovery from polio, I had agonized continually over the meaning of life. I had not always resented the polio; I had once thought that everyone was like me, but when I saw others play cricket and hockey, run relays, bicycle, even after I got well, I continued to resent that I had not always been well; the illness had prohibited me from too much; Einstein was wrong when he said that God did not play with dice; order was a fallacy, chaos the rule. The moon was full on the night in question. I was returning home from a movie, *From Russia with Love*, at the Regal Theatre, which I had seen with my friend Erach; we might have had a cup of tea at Chiquita's, but it was getting late – it was only ten o'clock, but whereas I lived around the corner Erach had a forty-five minute bus ride ahead of him to his home in Vasundhara, by the Cadbury Fry building at the junction of Pedder Road and Warden Road across from the Mahalaxmi Mandir. I saw him off at the bus stop, but instead of going home I decided to drop in on Vijay who lived a little further away in Colaba to see if he was up for some tea. I took a shortcut through a lane along the way to save time. The lane was deserted, narrow, dirty; it stank of fish because it was the path taken by the fishermen to bring their catches to the shops, and was littered with fishheads, scales, and bones; it was a mudpath full of puddles, rubbish, dung. There were no streetlamps, but the sharp black silhouette of a palm tree against the full moon and the residue of gall deposited in my stomach by the James Bond movie filled me with adventure.

Unfortunately, three bends into the lane the moon passed behind a cloud and everything became blacker than the face of a monkey. I refused to panic, telling myself that the moon would soon reappear, that my eyes would get accustomed to the dark; I walked more slowly, afraid that I might step into something or trip over something. The stench covered me like a shroud; when something crumbled under my foot I cringed imagining it was a fishhead; when something scurried over my sandaled foot I froze – I had forgotten about the rats. I walked a few more steps in the dark before I bumped into a low branch and came to a halt. While I waited, jumping at the least sound – the nasal cawing of a solitary crow, the crackle of paper under rats' feet – I felt, uncannily, as if someone were watching me.

When the moonlight returned I breathed more easily watching the shadows recede to the sides of the alley. I took a deep breath and stepped carefully forward when something touched me from behind. I jumped as if it might have been a snake. Behind me were two upturned palms, hands without fingers, raised in a supplicatory attitude. A strangely familiar voice intoned, "Baksheesh, seth, baksheesh." A black head with patches of wormy hair, ears reduced to rubberbands of flesh, a nose pushed so far back it looked like a gaping mouth, looked up at me through eyes as narrow as wire. It appeared to be grinning. The skin of the torso shone in the moonlight as if it were covered with scales. The body was seated, crosslegged, on a square wooden platform on wheels. The legs appeared to be moving because bugs were crawling heedlessly over them. A fly the size of a bee whirred into the nasal cavity. The figure made no attempt to brush anything away but continued to hold up its decaying hands, to say in its hollow voice, "Baksheesh, seth, baksheesh."

I turned and fled the way I had come, crying with the fear that I might have caught his disease, down the middle of the road when I tripped over one of the charpoys on the footpath. Back home I went straight to the bathroom, turned on the red light for the geezer, and filled a bucket with scalding hot water. As I sat on the tiny wooden bathing stool, pouring water over myself from a brass tumbler, soaping myself over and over, scraping my skin raw with the pumice stone, particularly where he had touched my thigh through my jeans, I recalled I had seen the leper and others like him innumerable times before, ragged cloths on their faces against the sun, swollen reptilian skin threatening to burst and spill pus. I had even dropped baksheesh in their cups, though always with an inward shudder of disgust – they were lepers, as distinct from me as mongrels, lizards, and vultures, even more so since they were diseased – but what did anyone do to deserve that?

Rusi was still out somewhere, but Mom and Dad knocked on the bathroom door curious about my late night bath. When I came out I told them my story calmly; I didn't want to cry because I knew Dad wouldn't like it, but I couldn't help myself as I reached the end and my fear of the disease overwhelmed me.

Mom tried to hug me but I pushed her away. Her eyes were narrow with anxiety but Dad's were wide with amusement. "It is not so easy a disease," he said, "that you can catch it just like that in a jiffy. Remember Father Damien? on the island of Molokai? It took him years to finally catch the disease. There is nothing to cry about. Be a man."

During the days that followed I found more opportunities to drop baksheesh in the leper's cup, actually a grimy soup tin. It was as much as I could do; I felt – as Dad had felt with Ratilal – that I was his mother and father; the felt relation said more about order in the universe than I could understand, but more than understanding I thought perhaps it was acceptance that determined one's peace of mind, one's relations with God.

The Two Girls Huddled
Together Like Monkeys

"A wag once said that Yes, the Scots are intelligent; they leave Scotland the first chance they get. He was being facetious, of course, but it's true that the Scottish winters have the chilliest fingers and the standard of living has always been higher in England. My problem was not that I had left Scotland for England – my first job was assistant to the Chief Engineer of the Great Western Railway in England – but that I allowed Bapaiji to persuade me back to India. I had wanted to be an aeronautical engineer – it was a new field then, there were many opportunities – but Bapaiji wanted me to be a railway engineer; she said I was her only son, that I would die up in the sky, she refused to acknowledge that I would not even need to fly, but I knew what it was – she wanted to ride in the deluxe cars of the Indian railways, and she wanted the preferential treatment accorded railway employees in India; it didn't matter that much to me, so I humoured her. I loved working with the English; they had the same sense of rectitude, fair play, decency as the Scots; if something wasn't cricket it was beneath contempt – but Bapaiji crushed all my arguments as implacably as a steamroller. She had the craziest stories about Englishmen in India: there was the colonel who kept a live cobra on his office desk to test the mettle of his visitors, the general whose wife divorced him because he slept in his uniform including his boots, the governor's daughter who slept with a handsome second class steward on board a ship and said to him when he approached her the next morning, 'In the circle in which I move, sleeping with a woman does not constitute an introduction.'

"I didn't take her seriously at first; I wanted her to enjoy her visit; I didn't want to fight; but everything I showed her compelled a slighting comparison with India. When we travelled on The Flying

Scotsman, the first locomotive to do 100 mph, she said the locomotives in India were just as fast; when I showed her the equestrian statue of Earl Haig erected by Sir Dhunjibhai Bomanji, a Bombay Parsi, on the Castle Esplanade she said the Parsis might be the tiniest community in the whole world, but they were everywhere; when I introduced her to Mrs Dowds she called her Mrs Dowdy and was critical of her meals (she ignored Mrs Dowds's daughter's proffered hand when I introduced them) – the Dowdses, nevertheless, were charmed by her bluntness (an eccentricity), her saris, and her Gujarati; when I took her to Mother India, an Indian restaurant, she said she could cook better food in her own kitchen.

"Of course, in many respects, particularly concerning food, she was right. All those game birds, grouse and woodcock and snipe, considered such delicacies, are so dry; and brain cutlets and boiled turkey and lamb chops and roast mutton have as much spice as grey has colour; and their haggis, a pudding made of the heart, lungs, and liver of a sheep, chopped up with oatmeal, suet, onions, and seasonings, and boiled in the sheep's stomach, tastes as bad as it sounds; nothing, of course, as rich and deeply satisfying as a dhansak or a sali boti.

"There was no one thing that convinced me to return with Bapaiji, no single moment of truth – I showed her Edinburgh, London, Paris, Frankfurt – but slowly I realized that outside of India I would always be a stranger; even with my superior education I felt inferior to Mrs Dowds's daughter because she spoke better English than I did even though she was just a landlady's daughter. That was one thing that impressed me so much about your mummy; she had had a convent school education, the same as your Granny, the same school in fact, and she spoke English as if she had been born to it even though she was a Parsi. One of the things I asked for when I got to this place was the ability to speak the King's English, the irony is, of course, there is no one with whom I might speak – and even if there were, the medium of communication here is thought, not language, and you would understand me clearly even if, as Bapaiji said, I spoke Zulu."

Rusi removed the pressure of his hand from my shoulder with a final reassuring squeeze. "Mom, I have to go. I'm meeting Paresh for dinner at Chiquita's if you need me for anything, but don't wait up. I might be late. I don't know what we'll do after dinner."

Mom nodded without looking away from me. "I wish he would just open his eyes. I know he's all right – he even looks more peaceful today – but I wish I could establish some kind of communication."

"He got up by himself today, Mom. That's a good sign. He's gonna be okay."

Mom nodded again. "I know. You go have your dinner. I'll be all right."

"Attchha. Bye, then."

"Bye-bye."

As soon as the door clicked shut behind Rusi, Mom renewed her litany of "time and prayer". I tried again to return the pressure of her hand, to catch her eye, but even when I looked directly at her I must have appeared asleep, – but as I looked she shrank as I imagine Alice in Wonderland might have when she obeyed the command, Drink Me. Her hair grew longer, curling into ringlets which fell to her waist, her face turned fresh and smooth, and her expression changed from anxiety to a more restrained seriousness. She was sitting at one end of the side of a long table, her ankles locked and dangling from the chair, a notebook open in front of her, a pencil held laboriously in her hand as she struggled to transcribe some lines in Gujarati. Across the table from her sat Jalu Masi, younger than Mom, her hair cut so short she might have been a boy, but I recognized her eyes: bright as an early morning light with eyebrows perpetually arched in curiosity; Mom's eyes, by contrast, were sleepier, reflecting more of a late afternoon light. Jalu Masi also had a notebook open in front of her, but her pencil lay untouched to the side, her feet swung to and fro, and her attention was fixed on the man seated between them at the head of the table. "But Popatlal-Master," she said. "Why were you gone so long? Mummy says we will never learn any Gujarati if you keep on disappearing like this."

Dad spoke again. "Homi, do not be alarmed. I am in charge. I will be directing these sequences relating to your mummy since she is still alive and has no control over these things. Just put your trust in me."

Dad need not have worried. I was beyond alarm. The collective unconscious was not the realm of the dead alone; it included the living; but I was glad to have Dad for my guide.

Mr Popatlal, who taught the girls Gujarati, was a tiny man with a thick black moustache against a wheat complexion; his hair shone with grease, and his upper arms, revealed by his white short-sleeved bush shirt, were inclined to sag. "I have been away so long," he said in a singsong voice, "because I have been in jail. The British put me in jail for nonviolently disturbing the peace."

"You were in jail?" Jalu Masi's eyebrows shot even higher. "But Mummy says only bad people go to jail. Are you a bad people?" She sounded anxious as if she wished to be proven wrong. Mom said nothing, but she stopped writing in her notebook and her face wrinkled with disapproval.

Mr Popatlal leaned back with a shout of laughter. "No, no, little Jalu, not to be so worried. I am not a bad people."

Mom spoke up seriously. "But Mummy says the British are good, and all my friends at school – Edwina Keegan and Pamela Wright and Abigail Barlow and Charlotte Colchester – are good. So if the British put you in jail, then you must have done something bad."

Mr Popatlal raised his hands as if to calm them both down. "Yes, yes, your mummy is quite right. The British are good, your friends are all good, but sometimes good people can have a bad system. You girls are lucky to go to a good school, a convent school, where you can learn good English and British History and all, but you have to hire a tutor like me to learn Gujarati, our own native language, and you learn nothing about our own Indian History except what the British are teaching you. Do you think this is good? that another country should tell us what to do?"

Mom looked scared as if she were defending something she didn't understand, but she replied stubbornly. "But they don't tell us what to do! We can do anything we want! If I don't want to take piano lessons at school, I don't have to. Many girls don't. But I want to!"

"That is good," Mr Popatlal said, smiling to put her at ease. "That is very good that you want to take piano lessons. But the piano is a

Western instrument. What I am saying is if you wanted to take sitar lessons the school should also have a teacher for you. Do you get what I am saying?"

"I get! I get!" Jalu Masi was kneeling on her chair leaning across the table toward Mom. "Popatlal-Master is right, Pheroza. Mummy was playing the sitar, but Daddy said not to play it because it was too Indian. I heard him, I heard him. It's true."

Mr Popatlal raised his hands for quiet again. "Quiet, please, quiet." When Jalu Masi had settled down again, he continued. "I am not saying the British are bad, I am not saying our friends are bad" (looking at Mom, who appeared mollified by his solicitude), "but even the best people can have a bad system. It is a bad system for one nation to rule another. The British have ruled us for too long now and, with Gandhiji to lead us, we will gain our independence again."

"Have you met Gandhiji?" Mom seemed for the first time to be interested in what Mr Popatlal had to say. "Daddy says he is a great man."

"Yes-yes," Mr Popatlal said. "For him only I went to jail. And for him I will go to jail as many times as he wants. He is the greatest man in the world today."

Jalu Masi's eyebrows arched again. "Greater than God even?"

Mr Popatlal smiled. "No man is greater than God. Ghandhiji is a saint, but he is still a man."

"Greater than Zoroaster?"

"I cannot say greater than Zoroaster. Zoroaster is, after all, your prophet."

Mom spoke again. "Greater than the King of England?"

Mr Popatlal nodded his head. "Yes, I think we can safely say that Gandhiji is greater than the King of England."

Jalu Masi stood up on her chair. "The King of England is a bad man because he put you in jail."

Mr Popatlal twirled his moustache with amusement. "No-no, little Jalu, this has been going on before he was born. He does not know how wrong it is because he takes us for granted. We have to show him – with nonviolence – how wrong he is. That is why I wear khadi always. That is my way of supporting home industries."

Mom's expression had turned, slowly, more forgiving. "What is khadi?" she asked, her eyes widening.

"Khadi is cloth that is woven in India only, with Indian materials only, by Indians only. It is one way to show our independence."

Jalu Masi had exhausted her interest in the subject but she didn't want to get back to the Gujarati lesson. She jumped down from her chair. "I am going to bring our baby brother. He is so big now. You must see him."

"Array, Jalu," Mr Popatlal said. "How we will teach you any Gujarati if you are always running? See, no, Pheroza has done two pages already. Come, sit, I can see your brother after the lesson, no?"

Mom recognized what Jalu Masi was up to. "Jalu, we have got to work first. Popatlal-Master can see Soli afterwards."

"But he is so cute, soo cute!" Jalu Masi said. "And afterwards he might go out." She dashed from the room before anyone could stop her. "Oh, Soaa-leee, Soaa-leee!"

Mr Popatlal shook his head with exasperation, but he smiled. Mom got out of her chair. "I will get her back," she said, but Mr Popatlal shook his head again. "No, no, it is all right. She will be back. No need to interrupt your lesson also."

Mom glowered as she sat down again. She didn't like the lessons anymore than Jalu Masi, but she lacked Jalu Masi's knack for getting out of these things.

During subsequent lessons Mr Popatlal related the great Indian epics to the girls, *The Ramayana* which chronicled Prince Rama of Ayodhya's rescue of his wife Sita from the demon king Ravana of Lanka with the help of the monkey god Hanuman, and *The Mahabharata* which chronicled the dynastic struggle between the five Pandava brothers and their cousins the hundred Kaurava brothers; he related stories about the great kings Chandrasekhar, Asoka, and Akbar; he related fables from the *Panchatantra*; they did not learn much more Gujarati until Mr Popatlal was put in jail again and replaced by a new tutor. There was a corollary to Mr Popatlal's departure: Jalu Masi said to Rustamji, "Daddy, can I wear ka-di?"

Rustamji was seated in a rocking chair reading a newspaper; Mom was practising Bach's "Minuet in G" in the next room;

Granny was not to be seen. Rustamji laughed but he spoke patiently. "Why do you want a khadi dress, my dear, when you already have so many prettier dresses?"

Jalu Masi answered just as patiently. "Because, Daddy, Popatlal-Master wear ka-di."

"Popatlal-Master wears khadi because he is a nationalist, my dear. You are only a little girl, a very pretty little girl."

Jalu Masi ran behind Rustamji's rocker and stood on the rails, holding on with her hands, rocking him gently. "I want to be a nashulist, Daddy. Can I be a nashulist?"

Rustamji turned back to his newspaper. "No. You are a little girl. Why do you want to be a nationalist?"

She rocked him more vigorously, watching the reflection of the ceiling light on his bald pate move to and fro. "Because, Daddy, I want ka-di."

He was alarmed at the amplitude she had set for the rocker. "Jalu, get off the chair at once. You will get hurt." But he was too late. Pushing with her legs, pulling with her hands, Jalu Masi pulled the rocker over its edge and on to herself. Rustamji lay on his back with his heels over his head, afraid to move for fear of crushing her under him. "Pheroza, Pheroza," he called, but Mom was already in the room. "See if you can get Jalu out without hurting her," he said, but Jalu Masi had already crawled out by herself.

As soon as Rustamji had extricated himself from the chair he called Jalu Masi and held her tenderly. "Oh, my dear, are you hurt?"

Jalu Masi, her eyebrows still high from the excitement and fear of her fall, said, "Daddy, ka-di, please?"

Years later, when the Chinese amassed their troops along the Eastern Himalayan border, threatening to invade India, I enacted a variation on the theme of Jalu Masi's protest: prior to the news about the Chinese, Mom and Dad had bought me two new pairs of shoes from a Chinese shop; against their wishes I threw both pairs of Chinese shoes onto a rubbish heap far enough from our home not to be easily found.

Jalu always got her way. Mom was furious. Rustamji had bought Jalu a khadi dress which she didn't even wear, but he wouldn't buy one for Mom. He said Jalu had paid the dues for her dress with her fall. Jalu had been grounded (the bark of a dog, Jalu Masi barking back, Mom telling her to leave the dog alone, Jalu Masi kicking Mom leaving a white splash of powder from her tennis shoe on Mom's grey convent school uniform, Mom preserving and presenting the spot like an exhibit to Rustamji), but Rustamji was taking Jalu with them on their excursion to the aerodrome that day. It wasn't fair!

Sunlight streaming through the window on to Mom's mattress on the sitting room floor had awakened her before anyone else. During the hot season the ayahs dragged the mattresses to the sitting room every night where hurdles of dried straw called khas-khas tatties were put across the open doors to the verandah within reach of the chowkidar in the compound who would fling water periodically during the night on the tatties to cool the air that passed through it into the house; a bucket of water was also kept near the tatties in the house for the early morning when the chowkidar was gone; Mom had even gotten to like the mildewy smell of the water on the tatties. Her features wrinkled with resentment as she leaned on one elbow to look at Jalu Masi still asleep on the mattress beside her; she had no right to join them on their excursion when she had been grounded. Mom got up from her mattress and went to the window from where she could see Gopal bring freshly cut grass and oats in a bucket to Toby, their carriage horse, in a stable.

I recognized, not the stable, but the site (later the stable became a two car garage for Granny's steel blue 1955 Studebaker and Soli Mama's cream 1961 Chevrolet); despite the lack of familiar buildings which had been subsequently constructed I recognized the arrangement of the palm trees with coconuts and targollas.

Mom heard sounds of stirring in the house from where she sat with her face cupped in tiny fists by the window. She saw Jalu Masi move lightly and dashed into action thinking she might never have such a perfect chance again. Dipping her hands into the bucket of water saved for the khas-khas tatties she flicked her fingers at Jalu Masi. Within minutes, Rustamji, in blue pajamas, awakened by screaming, was striding into the sitting room wiping sleep from his eyes; Jalu Masi was standing on the sofa pulling Mom's ringlets;

their pink and blue night dresses were soaked; "Girls, girls," Rustamji said, "stop it, stop it this instant! What is going on?" – "She started it! She started it!" Jalu Masi said. "She splashed me!" – "It was an accident!" Mom screamed. "I was splashing the *tatti*!"

"All right, all right, all right," Rustamji said, wiping his forehead wearily with his hand. "I don't want to hear anymore about it, not a word. If you don't stop, then no one is going to the aerodrome today."

"Daddy! She started it!"

"Daddy! It was an accident!"

"I said, NOT A WORD!"

The girls were quiet immediately; Rustamji rarely shouted at them and they didn't want to risk cancelling their trip; however dangerous Rustamji said it was they both hoped someone would give them a joyride in one of the two-seater planes even if it were for just five minutes; but the antagonism remained between them until Granny smoothed it away explaining to Jalu Masi that Mom had wet her accidentally and to Mom that she should be more careful.

The aerodrome canteen was crowded but Rustamji found a table with a good view of arriving and departing planes. The cups, saucers, and plates on which they received their tea and toast were old and chipped; the square wooden table was rickety and covered by a cracked sheet of glass secured by a single hinge on each side; the wooden chairs, just as rickety, had seats woven with cane. Granny took Jalu Masi to the bathroom. Mom stared enviously at a family on the tarmac waving goodbye to friends boarding the stairs to their plane. She knew there was no chance of her getting a joyride but she wished Rustamji would at least let them go closer to the planes. "Daddy, why can't I go where that family is? They are not in danger. Can't I even go as far as they are?"

Rustamji spoke gravely. "No, Pheroza. What they are doing is very dangerous. We are in the best place for watching the aeroplanes."

As if to bear out his words the family – two men and a woman with a baby in her arms – disappeared (all except the baby which fell to the ground) in a brilliant stippled arc of blood in the sunlight, sliced by the propellers under the wing of an incoming plane.

Rustamji held Mom immediately telling her not to look. Mom had registered only the colour and the brilliance; she might have found the arc beautiful if not for the screaming that followed; instead, her faith in Rustamji's infallibility soared.

A crowd gathered blocking their view. Jalu Masi and Granny returned while Rustamji was still holding Mom. "What happened?" Granny asked, her forehead wrinkled with fear. "What was all the screaming?" Jalu Masi's eyebrows were high on her tiny white forehead.

"An accident," Rustamji said. "I will tell you about it, but I think we should go. Let me get the bill first."

But the silence among themselves while they waited for the bill while everyone else made so much noise was too much for Jalu Masi. "But what has happened? Tell me no, what has happened?"

"An accident," Mom said, in a new voice that was calmer than she felt. "Don't look. I will tell you about it later." She held Jalu Masi tightly, feeling as if her horrific vision had conferred upon her a responsibility to shield her baby sister from things of which she had no understanding. There was a sweetness about the two girls huddling together like monkeys, but Rustamji was too concerned with getting the waiter's attention to notice and Granny still too uncertain of the situation to smile.

The two girls huddled together like monkeys became separated; Jalu Masi disappeared along with Rustamji, Granny, and the panorama of the people in the airport canteen into a swirl of dust on all sides of Mom; Mom grew larger, older, until she appeared seated by my bedside again, and the dust swirl unwound itself slowly to reveal the familiar enclosure of my bedroom walls – but Mom looked more animated; the grey in her cheeks was rosy; the anxious wrinkled eyes were wide with hope. I thought she must have seen my eyes open, felt the pressure I returned with my hand, but when she spoke I understood her delight correctly. "Is it really you, Adi? Adi, are you there? Are you all right?"

She had sensed Dad's communication through me, and when he spoke she sensed it again. "Yes, it is really me, Philly, darling. I am all right – never better, in fact, except that you are not with me. But enough about me. I might not see you again for a long time and to carry on this exchange might harm you in the long run; it will unquestionably harm Homi; he was not meant to prove a medium between us. I am well; Homi will be well; be happy."

The mallets in my head began pounding more thunderously even as he spoke. Mom stood up still holding my hand, her face turned heavenward. "I love you, Adi. I love you, my darling. Take me with you. Please take me with you."

"Not yet, Philly. Your time is not yet."

My hand slipped from her grasp, her face turned white, and she fainted, falling across me in the bed. As she fell I felt her consciousness slip as if it were something tangible and spatter around me splashing and shivering like globules of mercury. One such globule opened revealing Mom and Dad thrashing fiercely against each other under a shining white silk bedsheet, but I pushed the image away; another revealed her in labour in a bed in the Saint Elizabeth Nursing Home on Napean Sea Road in Bombay about to give me birth, but I pushed that image away as well; yet another revealed a fantasy so bizarre, involving feathers and dead fish, that it could only have sprung from a well too deep for even Mom to fathom with her consciousness – but this image from the collective unconscious made me too squeamish, as if it might have revealed the exact moment of my death, to explore it further. I scanned the other globules feverishly until I found an image with which I was comfortable.

First Class! Absolutely
A-Number One-First Class!

Dad first saw Mom across the drawing room of the King George V Hotel in Karachi, seated alongside Jalu Masi at the grand piano. A man with what might best be described as a patient face – confident, interested, implacable – stood by them in grey pants and a grey sleeveless sweater over a white long-sleeved cotton shirt. He made requests each time one or the other of them finished playing and they complied, sometimes in turn, sometimes together playing duets. At one point they asked him to sing. Dad trembled to hear him sing "Santa Lucia" in a deep voice which vibrated with the strength of a thousand double basses. He had no such talent himself to allow him entry into their circle. He noted with relief, however, that the man had his eye conspicuously on Jalu Masi.

"You like her, no?" said Mr Gupta, the owner of the hotel, with whom Dad was sharing tea. "That is Pheroza Cama, the granddaughter of our J. P. Cama. She is here on holiday with her sister and her mother and her brother." Dad had assumed Jalu Masi was the sister because of the resemblance. Now he followed Mr Gupta's expression and saw Granny on a couch along the side of the room, working on what appeared to be some rather fine embroidery, silk on gauze with beads; Soli Mama sat obediently beside her in short pants, shirt, sweater, and tie, obliviously reading *The Hound of the Baskervilles*. "I know them well," Mr Gupta continued. "They come here every summer for a week. Come, I will introduce you."

"Who is that man with them?" Dad took a sip of his tea to cover his consternation.

"That is Sohrab Cama of the Shanghai Camas. J. P. opened branches everywhere as you know, even in Shanghai. But when the communists came the branch was moved to Hong Kong. Our Sohrab is here just now looking for a Parsi wife – not too many Parsis in Hong Kong, you know. But I think he is mostly interested in the sister." I had recognized Sohrab Uncle the moment I heard him sing. I had only met him on two visits, but "Santa Lucia" had remained his signature tune and his voice was unmistakable. "Come, no?" Mr Gupta invited Dad again. "I will introduce you."

But Dad shook his head. He would feel more comfortable approaching her alone. "No. I will do it myself. I will find the right time."

"Okay, but do not wait too long. They are only here a few days. You are leaving even before them."

Dad's smile looked plastic as if it had been glued on. Not only was Mom lovely – she still had the ringlets from her girlhood but the rest of her had grown into a willowy young woman – but she reminded him of Honoria who had also worn her dark hair in ringlets, and treated him with such disdain when he had worked for the Chief Engineer of the Great Western Railway in England. Mom was also dressed in a pleated grey skirt with a sweater much as Honoria had often dressed. It panicked him to think they might be alike in other ways. He was shaken from his reverie when the girls rose from the piano bench and joined Granny and Soli Mama with Sohrab Uncle. Wanting to make his presence known before they retired he clapped loudly. "Bravo! First Class!" he said, ignoring all the other guests in the drawing room, giving Mom the tiptop sign with his thumb and forefinger. "First Class! Absolutely A-Number-One First Class!"

Mom ignored him after a single astonished glance, but Jalu Masi waved and Sohrab Uncle smiled and said "Thank you" in his deep voice. When they sat down Mom said "What a silly man!" but she smiled as if she were pleased, and though she didn't look at Dad she didn't try to hide her smile. She had noticed him before following her around with his eyes, but looking away the moment she turned in his direction. She would never have been so bold as to stare directly at him, but she was flattered by the power she felt when he scuttled so easily – she was used to being stared at; it was nice to create a bit of a stir upon entering a room; but she hated the men who kept their eyes on her mercilessly, disregarding her discomfort.

Mom usually went to breakfast earlier than the others. She liked sitting in the alcove with the rattan chairs and glass-topped tables, adjacent to the dining room, from which she could watch the white-uniformed waiters setting the tables with the china tea things, the teapots nestled in their cosies, linen napkins folded in origami patterns; she liked watching the tennis games from the tall narrow windows of the alcove, listening to the chirruping of the squirrels and doves and koels while she sipped her tea and leafed through the pages of a book she might bring with her. Later, the hum of the cheery wishes of the first morning guests would swell and the sweet smell of her tea would be enlarged by the smells of porridge, eggs, bacon, and fruit served expertly from steaming spotless metallic containers with racks of toast, pats of butter in dishes with buttons of ice, and cut-glass containers of jam and marmalade.

She rarely got much reading done but she didn't mind. She had brought with her *Pride and Prejudice* which she had read before. She liked Jane Austen, but she had read *Lady Chatterley's Lover* the month before and Jane Austen had receded into a hinterland of a child's world which she wanted to leave behind. She didn't understand Lawrence but he filled her with a sense of daring; even his titles – *Sons and Lovers, Women in Love, The Virgin and the Gypsy* – challenged her; but of course she couldn't read the books in public – she could hardly even read them in private! What confounded her most was the mystery; some things were forbidden but she didn't know what and she didn't know why, and she couldn't get their mystery out of her head. The man who had so riotously expressed his appreciation the night before seemed inexplicably related to the mystery; she thought he might have the key; but when she saw him coming she pretended not to notice, appearing to concentrate on her book while she remained intensely aware of his presence.

Dad had prepared nothing to say and felt as if someone had stuffed a pillow into his lungs making it difficult to breathe, but he imagined if he thrust himself deeply enough into the situation initially, it would resolve itself and reveal what needed to be done. "What are you doing?"

His voice was high, his question so innocuous that it composed her again. "Reading." Her smile was big and confident, her tone teasingly sardonic; she knew he was interested but he didn't know she was.

"What do you like to do?"

"I like to read."

"What do you like to read?"

She showed him her book.

"I haven't read it. I like adventure stories – like Kipling."

"This is the second time I'm reading it."

"What else do you like to do?"

"I like to play the piano."

"What else do you like to do?"

"I don't know. I like to read. I like to play the piano."

"What else do you like to do?"

He seemed unable to say anything else, but a huge grin remained on his face reminding her of the Cheshire Cat illustration by Sir John Tenniel. She didn't know his name but felt it was up to him to volunteer the information. She still found him silly but she liked the way he looked: his straight wet hair combed back without a part from his smooth white wide forehead with the black encroaching claw of a widow's peak in evidence already; his cheekbones high, his cheeks pink with the continual nip of the season; his face inclined to roundness particularly with the wide fixed grin; his long-sleeved grey pullover pulled back slightly to reveal the fine hairs on his wrists tinted brown in the sunlight beginning to stream into the alcove. Besides, she was enjoying herself. It was the first time she had talked alone with a strange young man. At nineteen she had already received proposals of marriage from at least a dozen eligible bachelors but had never spoken with any of them in this manner; the proposals were always sent to her parents. However silly Dad appeared his approach was decidely more stimulating. "I've already told you what I like to do," she said, grinning in return. "What do you like to do?"

Dad pulled a four anna coin from his pocket. "Do you know how to play Up, Jenkins, Raise Your Hand?"

'Of course I know. Even a child knows that."

Dad flipped the coin. "You go first," he said, clapping his hands over the coin.

"I say Heads. Up, Jenkins, raise your hand."

It was tails. Dad looked gleeful as if he had staged a coup. "Let's do it again," he said as if it were generous of him to give her another chance.

She lost again. "This is a silly game," she said, losing patience after she had lost twice more in a row. "Don't you know anything else?"

Dad slipped the coin back into his pocket. "What would you like to play?"

"I don't like games," she said. "I think all games are silly."

His grin lost strength and his eyes fell to the floor. She felt he needed help. "What's your name?"

He looked up again immediately. The relief in his eyes gladdened her. His grin was replaced by a chastened hopeful smile. "I am Adi, Captain Seervai. I'm on leave from my posting."

An army man! He seemed suddenly more exotic. "Where is your posting?"

"In Ledo, in Assam, near the border. The Americans are going to help us build the Ledo Road which will give us direct access to the Burma Road. They are afraid the Japanese will have too much advantage if they capture the Burma Road, so we're trying to build a new access for our own advantage."

Mom's eyes widened. "Have you been in the fighting?"

"No, no, not like that. I am an engineer in the army, a civilian, building roads and bridges and other construction – but I saw some fighting once, an air battle. It was very interesting." He had heard the sounds of airfire and had imagined puffs of smoke behind the clouds, but he left that up to her imagination, knowing she would find it more interesting that way.

"My name is Pheroza," she said when she saw he was going to be silent again. "We're here on holiday from Bombay."

"Yes, yes, I know all that." His grin returned, blindly self-assured as before, as if he had staged another coup.

"How do you know?"

"Mr Gupta told me. He is a friend of mine."

"Oh, yes, of course. You were with him last night. He's a good friend of Daddy's."

When Granny and the rest of them came to breakfast they found Mom and Dad chatting so comfortably that Jalu Masi, her eyebrows ascending again, said later, 'Pheroza was sitting there, so cosmopolitan, as if she had known him all her life and she had only met him that morning!" Mom introduced him to everyone and Granny, on hearing he had a degree from Edinburgh, invited him to join them for breakfast. Dad didn't understand Sohrab Uncle's connection with the family – he wasn't related closely enough to appear so intimate a friend – but it didn't bother him, particularly when he realized that his attentions were focused primarily on Jalu Masi.

A thick grey monsoon rain fell on Scandalpoint. The sea across Warden Road from Granny's house had engulfed the rocks along what passed for the beach where Rusi and I had scooped on occasion the tiny grey fish that swam in the pools among the rocks into our nets and brought them home to display in jars. The monsoon meant sweating constantly under heavy pastel plastic raincoats with hoods, and socks that slid insistently off one's feet and lodged uncomfortably in the toes of the tall heavy black rubber gumboots in which we lumbered like elephants all day at school; on schooldays we were always either barely dry, wet, or about to get wet – but the first rains, coming on the heels of the hot season, were always a relief and a joy, as was the sudden profuse greenery with frogs and toads hopping about the paths and snails the size of golf balls in the shrubbery.

Scandalpoint wasn't quite as I remembered it – Ben Nevis and the other tall buildings along the sea were missing; so were many of the bungalows of Oomer Park behind Zephyr which was almost the only house and certainly the largest, appearing, with its red tiled roofs, red brick corners, pale stucco exteriors, large bay windows, and columned entranceway, like a mansion in a wilderness. The chowkidar in his khaki uniform sat with his danda hanging from his belt on a wooden stool in the foyer barely out of the rain, moving his stool from one place to another depending on the direction of the wind.

A carriage came along Warden Road, turned into Granny's gate, and stopped in front of the foyer. The chowkidar stood to attention immediately. A footman descended with an umbrella from the front of the carriage. He opened the carriage door, telling the chowkidar to ring the door bell. A tall white-haired woman emerged from the carriage; the rain appeared to lessen as she stepped out with a gracious smile for her footman who held the umbrella over her; she was young, perhaps in her thirties, her white hair imparting dignity more than age. Her sari, bright with the colours and forms of spring, swirled around her like a spiral. She held it up slightly to keep it from dragging on the wet muddy ground, revealing slender white ankles in slender green open-toed shoes encased in plastic guards, and walked with a light sway to the front door. When the servant answered the chowkidar's ring the lady said, "Tell Bai and Seth that Mrs Perin Cama is here to see them."

The servant led Perin Cama into the sitting room. Seth wasn't home, she explained, but Bai was. She turned on the light (the monsoon filled all homes with a continual gloom) and the fan and asked her to wait. Perin Cama settled comfortably, confidently, in an armchair. Someone was playing a Chopin waltz on the piano in another room; there was a smell of roses. The piano playing stopped and Jalu Masi popped her head around the sitting room door, disappearing immediately she realized their visitor was looking at her; Perin Cama had no time to say anything but she smiled broadly and was still smiling when Granny came into the room.

That was when they first heard of Sohrab Cama who was in Bombay from Hong Kong for six months, looking for a Parsi wife. Perin Cama had a letter from Sohrab Cama requesting permission from Granny and Rustamji for him to see Mom "with a view to matrimony". Mom was seventeen then and in no hurry to get married; besides, no one, she least of all, relished the idea of her moving to Hong Kong. Granny was in awe of Perin Cama's appearance; "she was so tall and lovely," she said, "and so perfectly dressed and made up even coming in from that awful rain"; but she turned down Sohrab Uncle's request — "he might be a nice man," she said, "but what is this going to Hong Kong?" — inviting Perin Cama to stay instead for a respite from the rain with tea and biscuits.

Six months later Sohrab Uncle still hadn't found a wife but the

Japanese had taken Hong Kong, forcing him to stay in Bombay. A year later Perin Cama returned with a request for him to see Jalu Masi for the same purpose; there were more biscuits and tea and Granny laughed after Perin Cama left the second time; "that Chinaman must have the brains of a turnip," she said, "to think I would send one of my daughters to Hong Kong and not the other," but Jalu Masi defended him; "He's not a Chinaman. He's a Parsi just like us. And what's wrong with going to Hong Kong? Who wants to stay in stinky old India their whole lives?"

"Jalu, you must not talk like that."

"But I don't care, Mummy. I mean it."

"Jalu!"

Many parents acceded to Sohrab Uncle's requests to "see" their daughters, even allowing him the unheard of luxury (for the time) of spending time alone with them, but he found no one to make him happy. He stayed in Bombay for six years, until the British had retaken Hong Kong, and during that time, although he never got to "see" Jalu Masi the way he wanted, he met her at innumerable parties, and after a while it became customary for him to single her out for his attentions, and even Granny didn't mind because his attentions seemed harmless in the midst of so many people, she had already clarified that neither of her daughters was going to Hong Kong, and she felt sorry for him alone and so far removed from his home. Besides, he came from a rich and reputable family, she liked his company even on their holidays, she loved his deep songful voice, and the girls loved to accompany him on the piano.

A small crowd was emerging from a school building on to a road I did not recognize. When I spotted Granny with Soli Mama, Jalu Masi, Mom, Sohrab Uncle, Dad, and Mr Gupta I knew it must still have been in Karachi. There were posters on the side of the school building and I could tell even in the dark blue night that they were advertising a gramophone recital for Lehar's *The Merry Widow*. Granny was in front with Soli Mama and Jalu Masi, Mom and Sohrab Uncle close behind, with Dad and Mr Gupta leisurely bringing up the rear. "But Mummy," Jalu Masi was saying, "it's such a nice night. You take the carriage if you want. We'll walk. The hotel isn't that far."

Mom held her purse in front of her as if she were about to jump up and down like a kangaroo. "Yes, Mummy, really. You take the carriage, but I'm not at all tired. The walk will make me nice and tired."

Sohrab Uncle didn't want to get in the way, but when Jalu Masi nudged him hard in his ribs he said in his deep voice, in as responsible and manly a manner as he could simulate, "Yes, yes, do not worry so much, Aunty. They will be all right. We men will see to it, won't we, Adi?"

Dad and Mr Gupta had been talking between themselves, apparently oblivious to the conversation in front of them. When Mr Gupta had found the Camas were going to the recital he had persuaded Granny that it would be a good idea to take Dad as well; it hadn't taken much persuasion since Granny was impressed with Dad's credentials: his family (even she had heard of Bapaiji), his education, his employment; but she had insisted that Mr Gupta come along as well. "Of course, of course," Dad said. "We men will see to everything."

They had reached their carriage. "Well, okay," Granny said cautiously, "but only if Mr Gupta walks with you."

"Oh, he will, he will, of course he will," Jalu Masi almost shouted. "Won't you walk with us, Mr Gupta?"

Mr Gupta smiled and said he would, so Granny got in the carriage with Soli Mama and was driven away. The crowd got thinner as more carriages drove away and more people went different ways. Jalu Masi was ahead of the group, not walking so much as swaying forward to a waltz rhythm. "The sky is such a midnight blue," she said. "Just as I imagined it in *The Merry Widow*. Isn't it lovely?"

Mom was more restrained in her movements, but she walked languidly, playing with her ringlets, humming the main theme of *The Merry Widow*, "Dum, de-dum dum / Dum, de-dum dum / Dum, dum, dum," over and over.

The road along which they walked had only a few people left; there were hardly any buildings; there was a park nearby; the crescent of the moon was sharply focused against the dark blue sky.

"Everything was so beautiful and so decadent," Jalu Masi said, "so beautifully decadent – the music, the story, the people. I could watch *The Merry Widow* forever."

Mr Gupta found it prudent to inject a cautionary note. "Yes, yes, but nothing happened, remember? Absolutely nothing happened."

"Of course, of course, if something happened that would ruin everything. I always want a happy ending – but the feeling is nice, such a feeling of danger without any real danger. Ah, such bliss!"

She waltzed with herself, humming the melody along with Mom. Sohrab Uncle who had watched her in silence until then, began to sing the words. "Lippen schweigen/'s flustern Geigen/hab' mich lieb!/ All die Schritte/sagen bitte/hab' mich lieb!"

"Oh, isn't he amazing?" Mom said twirling in a circle. "He even knows the German."

Sohrab Uncle tapped Jalu Masi's shoulder and joined her in her waltz when she turned while continuing to sing. "Jeder Druck der Hande/deutlich mir's beschreib/Er sagt klar, 's ist wahr, 's ist wahr/ ich hab' dich lieb."

Mr Gupta nudged Dad toward Mom with a wink. "Go, dance with her."

Mom was whirling on her axis, counting breathlessly, "*One*-two-three, *one*-two-three," her arms and ringlets wide and free. "You are like a helicopter," Dad said. "Would you like to go on an aeroplane?"

"On a joy ride?" Her eyes were wide. "Oh, yes, yes. Will you take me?"

Dad drew her to himself for an answer, lifted her off her feet, and continued to spin in the circle she had begun maintaining the one-two-three one-two-three rhythm of Sohrab Uncle's singing.

Mom liked the pressure of her chest against Dad's as he spun her around – danger without danger; she didn't know Dad but she was among friends.

Mr Gupta smiled, watching the billowing parabolas of the girls' skirts as they flew through the air. When Sohrab Uncle finally completed the song and Dad put Mom down she was laughing and dizzy. "You look so lovely," he said, whispering for fear of embarrassing her. He had to hold her to steady her but her face appeared to grow brighter and she put a hand on his arm as if for support. "You really think so?" she said, also whispering. "Really?"

"I know it. I know it. You are lovely. That is all there is to it."

She smiled, pretending to stumble with dizziness, leaning against him the rest of the way back.

The hotel was quiet when they returned. Dad wanted to kiss Mom goodnight but hadn't the courage so he just said he'd had a wonderful time. The girls went off to their room; Sohrab Uncle, Dad, and Mr Gupta went to theirs, but no sooner had Dad entered his room than he heard screaming and came dashing back to the drawing room. "There's a monkey in our room," Mom shouted. Jalu Masi screamed. "He has a big black face!" Dad grabbed a nearby vase and dashed to their room. The monkey was howling, more scared than anyone else as he dashed panicstricken around the room, upsetting clothes, lamps, toiletries, looking for the window. He found it just as Dad entered the room. Dad slammed the window shut behind the monkey, turning victoriously as the others came in. "He's gone," he said, laughing. "It was only a black-face monkey. We have so many of them in Navsari. The way you were screaming I thought it was a gorilla."

"It was the shock," Mom said, shamefaced at the commotion she had caused. "We turned on the light and he was sitting on Jalu's bed."

"I went chhoo-chhoo to him," Jalu Masi said, "but he made a face like he was spitting. We're not all like you, Adi, growing up with monkeys in Navsari, like Tarzan or something."

Dad just laughed again. "Anyway, he is gone now and I have shut the window."

After the noise had been explained to Granny and the other hotel guests and they had all retired again Mom found a moment to thank Dad for coming so quickly to her rescue. "If there is another monkey, or a snake or an elephant, just scream and I will come again," he said.

She looked uncertainly at him as if she were afraid he was making fun of her, but he put an arm reassuringly around her shoulders and quickly kissed her cheek. "I am serious," he said, and he wasn't smiling anymore. He felt like a hero. "You can call me any time and I will come."

But there was no need for heroics for the rest of their stay in Karachi and as his leave drew to an end Dad still didn't know if he would be seeing Mom again. "May I write to you?" he said. "Maybe if I am in Bombay I can see you again."

They were seated in the drawing room again round the piano with Granny and Soli Mama to the side. Mom could still feel his lips like feathers on her cheek. It had all been too sudden for her and she had rationalized his boldness thinking she would only be seeing him for a few more days — but she didn't know how to say No to him. "I suppose so," she said. "I'd have to ask Mummy."

"Oh, come on, Pheroza," Jalu Masi said, slapping her sister's arm impatiently. "Don't be such a nervous Nellie. He's not asking you to elope."

"If he were asking me to elope it would be stupid of me to ask Mummy," Mom shot back triumphantly.

Dad grinned as if he couldn't believe how smart he was. "Will you elope with me?"

Mom struck a pianissimo chord abstractedly with her left hand playing a motif with her right. Jalu Masi spoke instead. "Oh, where would you take her?"

"Casablanca, Samarkand, Damascus, Istanbul, Baghdad, Kilimanjaro, anywhere she wants."

"Oh," Jalu Masi moaned. "Take me! Take me! I'm so tired of India."

Sohrab Uncle spoke as if on cue. "Are you really? Really?"

Jalu Masi gave him a look with narrowed eyes. Mom spoke up instead. "Adi, have you got a pencil and paper? I could give you our address right now."

On the train from Karachi Dad wrote letters. Mom heard from him from Delhi, Lucknow, Calcutta, and finally Assam. Mom could tell when his train had reached a station because the handwriting got steadier. He wrote about some of his escapades in England: to save money he had stuffed his pant bottoms into his socks to simulate plus fours; thinking Benedictine to be a kind of sacrament he had emptied a glass in a single gulp and fallen to his knees with the shock; expecting a tent and acrobats and animals he had asked a policeman at Piccadilly where the circus was. He did not tell her about Honoria of whom she had reminded him – though, he realized subsequently with relief, aside from the ringlets and the pleated skirts they had little in common. When he had complimented Honoria on her loveliness in much the same way he had Mom, she had spoken as if he had unwittingly entertained her. "How very lovely of you to say that," she had said, adding with a thin smile, "and how very quaint." Dad felt he would rather have been a murderer than quaint – but she was English; he could alter the rhythms of his speech to sound more English to facilitate communication, but he couldn't alter other people's rhythms to sound more Indian; he would never follow an English as easily as an Indian cadence, his assimilation would always be slower and it made him feel stupid. He neither expected Honoria to understand, nor himself to feel less wretched with time. How much sweeter Mom's response had been. He had purged himself of Honoria with a Soho prostitute in a tiny room with a naked lightbulb, an unmade bed, a cracked washbasin, a single hanger in the cupboard, and a bathroom down the corridor. The incident replenished his self esteem (he didn't care if he never saw Honoria again), but he never needed to repeat it.

Dad wanted to know all the details of Mom's life, what she ate, what she did, what she wore; if she had written as often as he wished she would have done nothing but write to him saying that she did nothing but write to him; he wanted souvenirs, photographs, x's, constant reassurances that she thought of him. Mom found him just a little importunate but she was enthralled nevertheless. "Do you know what he went and did?" she said to Jalu Masi on one occasion, her voice quick with excitement.

"No. What?"

"Well, it appears he's in charge of some Naga tribespeople and he asked one of the Naga men to show his overseer some track which was about a two day hike from where they were. The next morning he found all the Naga men had gone with the overseer, even the village chief, every single one of them – so he was left alone with all their women. So do you know what he did?"

"What? What?"

"He had a snap taken of himself with all the Naga women. Look, he sent a copy."

Dad, grinning so you could see all his perfect teeth, was surrounded by sturdy dumpy women with pale round faces and coarse black hair knotted loosely on their necks, dressed in calico and silk with dark cotton sashes around their waists over which some wore girdles of bell-metal discs; their necks were laden with beads, their legs spotted as if with insect bites, and their calves constricted so tightly by bands of woven cane that flesh bulged over the edges.

The girls laughed over the photograph. "So what does he say?" Jalu Masi wanted to know.

"He says I am not to be jealous of all his women. He says there's no need." Mom laughed. "He's such a silly — as if I could be jealous of them. He's always joking like that." But she didn't let Jalu Masi read the letter herself because Dad had addressed her as his dearest darling and he had filled the bottom half of the last page with x's.

It Has Got to Be
Now or Never

"In my life, Homi, I had three great loves. First, as you know, there was Edinburgh. I would have been happy to stay, at least in the UK, but I gave that up for Bapaiji. Bapaiji got me a cushy job working for the Maharajah of Baroda; I was working for the state so I had a bungalow and servants and a high salary – but there were not very many Englishmen or Parsis around, mostly just vegetarian types, so my social life was hardly the best. With all the benefits I still didn't like working for the Maharajah; I preferred working with people with whom I shared more interests; but Bapaiji loved all the privileges, especially travelling in the luxury compartments of the Indian Railways at the state's expense, so when the war broke out and there was a chance for me to join the army on loan from Baroda (I could come back when the war was over) I joined without saying anything to Bapaiji. She was furious but there was nothing she could do.

"My second love was the army; not only did I have the same privileges that I had had in Baroda – because I was a construction engineer, not an enlisted man – but I met Americans and Englishmen, and even the Indians in the army were more worldly than the ones I had met in the Maharajah's employ. I stayed in the army even after the war was over because I didn't want to go back to Baroda, but I left finally because your mummy wanted me to – she wanted to settle in one place with a family, not roam from one posting to another, like gypsies she said.

"Your mummy was my third and greatest love. You might even say that I gave up my first two loves for her – I would have taken her back to the UK with me to stay; I became so sick of the constant chaos of India that even Bapaiji couldn't have kept me – but you know your mummy, she is not the adventurous type; if she had wanted to leave India, she said, she would have married your Sohrab Uncle in the first place. But do not misunderstand; I had no complaints; I wanted to be with her, wherever she wanted to be, much more than I wanted to be in either the UK or the army. I would have married her the first day I saw her. Bapaiji had already shown me enough women for me to know exactly what I wanted. An education abroad is a desirable advantage jobwise in India, but it makes all Indian girls seem so provincial. But your mummy spoke English as well as any English girl; her class in Sofia College was the first class of women graduates in Bombay; and her degree, as you know, was in English Literature. Your Jalu Masi got her degree in Commerce which made her just perfect for your Sohrab Uncle who, as you know, is in business. He had the same problem I had – he had even grown up in a foreign country – but that only made us that much surer of the kind of girl we wanted.

"I wrote to Bapaiji immediately telling her I had found the girl I was going to marry. She did not discourage me – in fact, she was very impressed that your mummy was a Cama – but she said not to do anything until she had seen the girl. I was in no mood to wait myself, but fortunately the war conspired to bring your mummy and Bapaiji together. There was a bomb scare that year. Everyone was afraid the Japanese would bomb all the major cities in India and all the people who had places to stay outside the city moved. J. P. Cama, as you know, was born in Navsari and had two houses there. Your mummy and her family moved there for almost a year so that she and Bapaiji had many opportunities to meet. Bapaiji was happy with my choice so after that it was mostly a question of setting the day – or at least that was what I thought."

Dad could not leave a new piece of work alone. He enjoyed merely visiting sites to see what he had accomplished. It was still early in the evening; he had already written Mom a long letter that day; he didn't feel like playing darts or bridge with the others; the weather looked promising; so he packed three chapattis with cheese, two bars of Cadbury's Milk Chocolate and a water bottle, and set off in the army jeep for one more look at the airstrip he had planned and supervised the week before. The Army dak bungalow was soon behind him. On either side of the military bridle-road were miles of clay banks enclosing irrigated fields of rice. The rice crops gave way to millet as the road got higher and as he approached the foothills the vegetation grew denser with pussy willow, violets, peach trees, pear trees, cherry trees, black stemmed banana trees, and on the rim of the woods tree rhododendrons. Far to his right on the slope of a hill lay a village on stilts, huts built on platforms, the inner edge of each platform touching the ground, the outer edge ten to fifteen feet above, the stilts pointing in all directions as if the huts had been propped and underpinned many times without removing any of the worn out timbers. The earth beneath was inches thick with refuse in which chickens scratched and big black hairy pigs rooted. Dad had watched the inhabitants through field glasses; they wore cane helmets with folded cloths around their necks for protection against arrows, wrapped cloaks around their middles like cummerbunds, and carried shields made of hides stretched on oblong frames, bows, arrows, and long bamboo lances. It was like a scene from the movies and Dad revelled in its wildness; his favourite stretch of the drive was through an upcoming gorge where the pine trees made a bower overhead and the road narrowed to a barely perceptible path. A river, about fifty yards at its widest, flowed alongside the path, green as the forest under the sun, and black patterned with foam in the shadows of the tall cliffs on the other side. Dad stopped the jeep. He liked watching the big grey kingfishers and the multicoloured butterflies in the sunlight while he ate – but first he anointed himself generously with insect repellent from a bottle he kept in the jeep; the biting dimdam flies were most prevalent in the early mornings but he was taking no chances.

He sat on a flat rock overlooking the river for fifteen minutes, thinking how much better food tasted in the open, wishing Mom could have been with him. When he was finished eating he took out the photograph she had sent, which he had not been without since, and kissed it. Love at first sight was not just for the young; he was thirty-four; it was for anyone who wanted it. He put the photograph back in his pocket, cleaned up, and got back into the jeep humming The Merry Widow waltz. It wasn't until the first time the ignition failed him that he realized he should have checked the petrol tank before he had left the base.

If he pushed the jeep a little he thought he might get it to go for at least a little way. He didn't care whether he got to the site or whether he got back home that night but he wanted to be out of the forest before dark; but moving forward he had to push uphill, turning around was even more difficult, and he knew he would never make it on foot in time. He kept trying to start the jeep up with a push, but by the time the night shadows began to descend he had moved the jeep barely forty feet from where it had stopped. A harsh anguished cry, like that of a baby, sounded overhead, but he recognized it, even muffled by the fog, for that of the greyish white cranes he had sometimes observed through his field glasses standing four feet tall on their long twiglike legs. The desolation in their cries seemed an omen, but as it got darker even the most innocent sounds – the splash of a kingfisher in the water, the rustle of the wind in the trees – became ominous. He understood he would have to prepare himself for the night because no one would miss him until the morning. He left the jeep to look for a thick branch he might use as a weapon; he didn't know what to expect, he couldn't calculate his chances of survival through a night in the jungle, but he wanted to prepare himself for the worst. He found a branch of substantial girth and swung it through the air striking a tree with a satisfying thwack, but as he turned to return to the jeep the sun disappeared and he couldn't see his hand in front of his face. He walked slowly, certain he would reach the jeep if he only walked in a straight line, but after five minutes which felt more like thirty he recognized that it was a hopeless task. At first he thought the blinking lights around him were fireflies but soon he realized they were eyes. If his vision had been comparable he might have stood a chance but suddenly the branch in his hand felt as reassuring as a toothpick.

There was nothing to do but settle for the night. He found a wide tree and wedged himself as comfortably as possible between its roots, his right hand holding the branch, his left the penknife he used to cut his nails. Something scurried across his ankles, something furry brushed his cheek, something wet fell on his fist clutching the knife, but he didn't move, afraid to set another, less manageable force in motion. He recited all the prayers he could remember under his breath, grateful that he was at least warmly dressed; he thanked God he was not married (Mom was too young to be a widow), but if he survived the night he vowed he would marry her immediately. He thought of Bapaiji and Pappa and his own bapaiji and bapavaji and all the others living in the house in which he had grown up who had called him their Lion of the Jungle. "Well, Bapavaji," he thought, amused by the irony himself, "what do you think of your Lion of the Jungle now?" It was his last thought before falling asleep.

When he awoke he wasn't sure at once that he was awake because his sleep was as black as anything he could see, but there was no mistaking the heat and the fetid smell of meat rotted for days in the sun, and the unnerving vibration of a low purr, not unlike that of a cat's but magnified perhaps a hundredfold. The purr became a growl and Dad saw for the first time two narrow yellow eyes like candleflames in the dark. A black panther was standing before him its mouth hanging open in his face, its head appearing the size of an elephant's, and its growl (it might have been just a cough) as if it were the sound of concrete cracking in an earthquake. Dad felt a chill in his head as if someone had driven a razor along his hairline and rolled his scalp open. His branch and penknife would have been of no use even if he'd held on to them in his sleep. The panther put a paw on his chest; there was a cracking sound; Dad lost consciousness.

The next morning he was awakened by the sound of his bearer calling him. He answered weakly, unable to believe that his party had found him so quickly. He was less than twenty feet from his jeep; he had a broken rib, gouges in his chest from where the panther had stood; he was still shaken but excited about the story he had to tell. He liked to brag later that after even three days of continual scrubbing he had still found leeches and lice that had attached themselves to him during his ordeal.

Either Dad's sense of direction improved or else he had had an off night when he got lost in the jungle; I recall a moonlight picnic on Government Beach when our entire party might have drowned but for his infallible instinct. Mom and Dad liked dinner parties, bridge parties, movies, concerts, Sunday morning social calls, and musical evenings at which some of their guests would perform music that they had prepared, but perhaps the most fun of all their social activities was provided by the moonlight picnics. Mom knew someone who knew the Governor who could occasionally get us passes to the private Government Beach. During the hot season the night was the best time for picnics and the nights of the full moon were the best of the nights. About six carloads of us would arrive at nine o'clock on the beach with sandwiches of lettuce and tomato, sugar and butter, chutney, mutton, chicken and mayonnaise, chocolate biscuits, cheese straws, samosas, patrel, chicken patties, and lemonade, park the cars at the edge of the sand, and talk, hopping from car to car while the moon highlighted streaks of silver on the waves. Sometimes we would walk along the shore, the children playing catching cook like satellites around the grownups. On one such occasion we walked a longer distance than usual, found ourselves in a cove, and stopped to sit and chat on the rocks. It was midnight when Minoo Sanjana said, "I think we had better be getting back. The tide is coming in."

Almost as soon as we set off there were doubts raised about whether we were walking in the right direction. "This beach looks much narrower than when we came," Mitha Shroff said. "I think maybe we should have gone the other way."

"I think you're right," said Jalu Daruvala. "I don't see our footprints. We must have made so many footprints coming, no?"

Dad took charge. "This is the way. Our footprints were washed away by the tide. That is why the beach is narrower."

"Are you sure, Adi?" Mukund Agtey looked doubtful. "I think we should at least try the other way. I think we might have got mixed up at the cove when we sat down."

"Yes, yes," said his wife, Madhavi, "this looks completely different."

On one side of us were unscalable cliffs, on the other was the sea coming in. Perhaps the cliffs had been there on our way to the cove, but as the beach narrowed their significance became more grave.

"No, no, I am sure, I'm telling you," Dad said. "We don't have time to go any other way. Come on, let us hurry."

Everyone followed him, but grudgingly, as if they remained unconvinced. Mom kept asking, "But are you absolutely sure, Adi? How can you be so sure?"

After a while he stopped answering her. I thought it was because he was unsure of his direction, but as I realized later it was because he was afraid we might not reach the cars in time. We had removed sandals, shoes, socks; the water came to our feet, to our knees. "If I find myself in heaven tonight," Zarine Jairazbhoy joked, holding on to her husband Ashraf's arm with one hand, her sari up to her knees with the other, as she waded through the surf, "I'll get you if it kills me, Adi." Dad just smiled, wading ahead of everyone with the cuffs of his pants rolled up. There were some in the party who still thought we had a chance, but only if we turned back immediately. He wanted to reach the cars before the consensus turned against him.

Dad's instinct had not failed him – or us. Some of the party had lagged far behind, but when Dad shouted that he could see the cars they redoubled their efforts. Everyone complained about how soaked they were as if that were the important thing; perhaps they didn't want to think about what might have happened but no one argued with Keki Paymaster when he said, "Better wet than dead."

Mom was still in Navsari, in evacuation from the bomb scare, when she received Dad's letter about the panther. She read it sitting by the pond in the front compound of Cama House in Navsari, considerably less impressed than Dad might have wished. Soli Mama was perched in a nearby banyan reading *The Sign of the Four*; Jalu Masi rode a bicycle around the house looking for the densest thickets through which to plough. Granny appeared at the front verandah calling, "Pheroza, will you come inside for a minute? Daddy and I would like to talk to you."

"Coming, Mummy," Mom said, folding the letter and putting it in the pocket of her dress, too distracted even to imagine what Granny and Rustamji might have to say; she had met and liked Bapaiji, but the repeated visits were beginning to stifle her as if Dad had become a context for everything she said and did; there was an undertext to his story about the panther as if the story itself weren't as important as the impression he wished to create, as if he might have been importunate enough to make up the entire story to create his impression. "Yes, Mummy, what is it?" she said, entering the sitting room.

Granny stood by the door; Rustamji sat upright in one of the reclining chairs. "Sit down, Pheroza," he said. "We want to have a word with you."

She sat on a wooden stool facing them both, wondering for the first time why she had been called; Rustamji looked so solemn. "Yes, Daddy?"

"Tell me, my dear," Rustamji said, his eyes on the intricate pattern of the Persian on the floor. "Do you know where babies come from?"

Mom didn't understand why she was embarrassed but she felt he wouldn't have asked her if not for the letters she'd received from Dad. "Why," she said, gesticulating with her hands like a magician to cover her consternation, "everyone knows that. You get married and then God sends you babies."

Granny and Rustamji looked at each other as if for cues on how to proceed. "Have you read this book?" Granny said finally, showing Mom *Lady Chatterley's Lover*, which she had been holding behind her all along.

Mom's head felt hot; she knew there was something wrong with the book, she knew she should have thrown it away instead of hiding it in her cupboard behind the old petticoats she no longer wore – but then she couldn't have returned to the illicit feeling of reading it when she pleased even though she had never unravelled its mystery; again she felt sure her predicament would not have arisen if not for her letters from Dad. "Yes," she said, "but it's not such a good book, Mummy. If you're looking for a book then read *Jane Eyre*. That's a lovely book."

Rustamji cleared his throat. "My dear, did you understand what you were reading?"

Mom's customarily dreamy eyes flashed. "Of course I understood. What's there to understand? It's not Einstein's theory of relativity."

Rustamji and Granny looked at each other again. They might

have expected such defiance from Jalu Masi; Mom would have been apologetic. Rustamji nodded understandingly. "I told you, Meher-banu. It's the expurgated version."

Granny gave Mom another book to read. "If you're going to get married," she said, "you should know what married people do."

Mom read the book but it made her sick. "It's so unladylike," she said to Jalu Masi. "I can't believe ladies have to do that."

"Oh, my God," Jalu Masi said, "but that's like going to the bathroom together. What a thing to get married for! Much better not to get married at all."

"But it's got to be done," Mom said seriously. "Otherwise, how will the human race survive?"

"Well," said Jalu Masi, "if it's got to be done, it's got to be done – but still . . . what a thing to do."

Mom was glad later that she had learned about it the way she had instead of the way Dad had, from the goondas who loafed around the atash behram in Navsari, but what upset her more than anything was that everyone took her marriage for granted, taking her choice away from her, and Dad had not even proposed. Besides, she had met him on only the one occasion in Karachi and already he expected her to write to him everyday, to send him photographs, to bob her hair like an English girl's, to wear frocks and pants – or, if she had to wear a sari, not to show her tummy – not to wear tilas, not to wear bangles, to take piano lessons not to teach but to perform. When she saw him again in Navsari on his leave he kept touching her and kissing her as if they were already engaged, when all she wanted was to be left alone. She was glad for the custom which dictated that they had to be chaperoned by a grownup everywhere they went until they were engaged, but on his second visit, this time in Bombay, he said, "I am fed up with all these old people trailing us everywhere. You may be young but I have no time to waste. I made up my mind a long time ago, when we first met, but you have not given me an answer."

They were seated on the wide stone steps leading to the wooden swing gate of the hexagonal back verandah of Zephyr with its rows of balusters along the open walls; Granny sat in a rattan chair embroidering a stole, barely out of earshot.

"You never asked me," Mom said, "so what answer can I give you?"

"In every way except words I have asked you," Dad said. "I think we could have a nice life together. What do you think?"

"I don't know what to think. This is all nothing like I thought it would be."

He shook his head impatiently. "What do you want? If you want a formal proposal, like in the eighteenth century, I will get down on one knee and bow my head and kiss your hand like a cavalier. Is that what you want? Just tell me and I will do it."

She was terrified that he might make just such a spectacle of himself before Granny; it would have been the crowning humiliation to what she had thought would be the most beautiful day of her life. "No, no, no," she said. "I do not want anything like that. Now that I know what you want I have to think about it."

"Then think about it," he said, "but I have to go in a fortnight. I must have your answer by then."

Everyone had said she should marry Dad; Granny had said she was a very pretty young girl but she would not be for long; but Mom hated the pressure, and after the fortnight could only say that she still wasn't sure, but Dad said he couldn't wait another year for her to make up her mind. "I have had a very difficult year in Assam," he said, "and I want something more definite. It has got to be now or never."

She couldn't believe he was being so demanding. "If it's got to be now or never," she said, "I can only tell you it's certainly not going to be now. I need more time."

When he saw how firm she could be Dad panicked, became suddenly contrite, blamed his impatience on the way he had felt after the panther had broken his rib, told her to take as much time as she needed to be sure, such matters were not to be rushed.

After he left for Assam again Mom felt she had more power, and liked the feeling of equality; her parents still got proposals for her from young men or their parents who had seen her and knew who she was, but she recognized that her chances of getting to know them the way she had come to know Dad were slender. When she wrote to ask how he could be so sure about the two of them he wrote back, "The dogs may bark. The caravan goes on." It was hardly what she wanted to hear, but they continued their correspondence and the next time they saw each other neither of them doubted that they were going to be married.

"Homi, are you there? I feel you tugging at me. There is no need to pull so hard. I'm not hiding anything."

Mom still lay across me on the bed where she had fallen, but I didn't question the nature of her communication. Of course, she was hiding things, but only unawares; she was unaware of the image I had glimpsed of her fantasy with the feathers and dead fish; monsters lurk in all the recesses of the subconscious; consciousness is a mechanism to keep them at bay, at least enough to get us from one day to the next with the requisite control; if I dug deeply enough I would unearth not only her monsters, but mine, yours, everyone's; I would find that all our monsters are the same where the subconscious gives way to the collective unconscious; I have neither the stomach nor the appetite for such revelations at present, but perhaps after the crisis. . . .

"On the day of the wedding I was as unsure as I had ever been about the whole thing, and your Dad didn't make it any easier. First of all, he was late. Actually, he was just in time, but he had circulated rumours that he thought the wedding was at Albless Baug instead of Cama Baug – his pappa, Hormusji, was furious that he could have made such a stupid mistake; but it wasn't a mistake, he had done it on purpose, for a lark. I was so scared; I felt I was marrying a stranger – and he was, indeed, a stranger; it had been three years since I had met him, but we had spent only forty-two days together (he had been counting), the rest of it had all been letters.

"I had to be there before him because I had to go through the ritual bath; he was exempted from that because he was a navar – you know what a navar is, I'm sure, even though we didn't have the ceremony performed for you and Rusi; essentially, it means you have to learn more prayers and it qualifies you for the priesthood; Bapaiji was more exacting about our Zoroastrian customs than either your dad or myself, but as much as she wanted us to perform the ceremonies for you and Rusi we couldn't see the point, particularly since it didn't make you any more or less a Zoroastrian the way your navjote did; and since only boys can have navars there had never been even a question of it for Jalu and myself.

"Anyway, he didn't have to take a bath but I had to be bathed by the dasturji – but, of course, for the sake of modesty, I bathed myself, leaving the door slightly ajar while the dasturji waited in the adjacent room. I put on my wedding clothes, a white sari with gold embroidery, and the diamond necklace and earrings Bapaiji had given me for the occasion. By the time I came out Granny had already done the achu michu for your dad – you know, that's when they bless you by circling your face clockwise seven times with symbols of good will, an egg for life, saakar for sweetness, a dried date for resilience, rose petals for joy, and so on and so forth. He was already seated on one of the chairs on the stage, hidden from me by a white cotton sheet held vertically between our chairs. Bapaiji did the achu michu for me, I was led to my chair, given a handful of rice to hold in my left hand, his hand to hold in my right. According to the ritual, when the cloth was pulled from between us, the first one to throw the rice at the other would be the more loving partner in the marriage. Our clasped hands were bound by a cotton thread, the priests recited their prayers while the same cotton thread was wound clockwise seven times around our chairs, the sheet between us was removed – and, of course, he was the first to throw the rice, but I felt if he had really loved me he would have let me throw the rice first.

"But he was saving the worst for the last – when he was asked by the dasturji whether he had agreed to take this maiden, me, for his wife he didn't say anything. When the dasturji said, 'Come on, Adi, what are you waiting for?' he said, 'I'm thinking about it.' Even the dasturji got angry. 'Thinking about it?' he said. 'Is this the time to be thinking about it?' I couldn't even look up from my lap but your dad answered as if he were enjoying himself. 'If not now, then when?' The dasturji knew he was joking then and said, 'Come on now, Adi. Be serious.'

"I was scared and he didn't seem to care; he was like a hunter who had bagged his quarry; but later he explained it to me: he was so happy that it made him cocky. I understood more than that: I think he might just as well have been cocky from relief. Gustave Flaubert said in every kiss there is always one cheek and one pair of lips; and both of us knew, at least in the beginning, that my contribution to our kisses had always been the cheek; in that light it all seemed quite funny, even to me – but even in the literal sense I was not a kissing person, at least not in public; and sometimes I felt he was just trying to show everyone how westernized he was, but I was afraid that if I let him get away with a kiss he wouldn't know where to stop."

Sum Mare Luccica

"After all that trepidation I still have to say marriage is great, there is nothing like it, I cannot even imagine not having married; even our Zoroaster has said that the married man is closer to God than the unmarried; those Catholics have it all wrong: maybe monks who live in monasteries are martyrs for God, but priests and prelates and popes are martyrs only to vanity; if they want to help people they should be happy and secure themselves, and nothing makes you happy and secure like a good marriage. Take it from me; I know; the one thing I did best was marriage. Sometimes I think I could have been a better mother, but I don't think I could have been a better wife. Oh, of course, someone else might have been able to do more for your dad, but he did everything he could for me and I did everything I could for him; we didn't expect miracles from each other, only a mutual respect through the good times and the bad, and we got pretty much what we expected.

"Anyway, then it was Jalu's turn. Everyone was glad the war was over, of course, but this meant Sohrab would finally be going back to Hong Kong. He still spent all his time with us; he hadn't requested to 'see' anyone in more than a year; of course, he had been 'seeing' Jalu all the time anyway, but he hadn't proposed to her yet. Your dad said Jalu should pretend to have lost something dear to her – like an earring or a brooch or something – and then cry about it to Sohrab; then, when he came to dry her tears with his handkerchief she could put her head on his shoulder or chest and he would understand – but I thought that was silly; I just took the bull by the horns and asked him about it myself."

A panorama accompanied Mom as she spoke, sneaking behind her voice like a backdrop, the same white stone steps with wide treads, leading to the same hexagonal verandah with the wooden swing gate and rows of balusters, on which Dad had threatened to get down on his knees to propose to Mom — but this time Granny and Dad were nowhere to be seen, and Mom had told Jalu Masi to stay away. Sohrab Uncle, in a sweater and white pants, sat on the top step; Mom in a frock with a floral print and a shawl around her shoulders, her ringlets replaced by a wild black mane around her neck, sat beside him with a secretive smile. She didn't look at him as she spoke but she kept the smile. "Sohrab, do you want to marry my sister?"

Sohrab Uncle looked sharply at Mom. His thin, curly hair had already begun to recede, his eyes seemed to grow larger behind his spectacles. "Of course. I thought she knew that."

Mom still didn't look at him. "How could she know? Have you asked her?"

"She said No when I asked her. I didn't ask her again because I was afraid she would say No again."

"That was five years ago. And you didn't ask to marry her, you asked for permission to see her. Well, you've seen her now. Are you going to ask her to marry you?"

Sohrab Uncle's eyes still seemed large behind his spectacles. "I was going to ask her before I left. She is the only girl I have wanted to marry of all the girls I have seen. If she said No again I was going to go back by myself. But I thought she didn't want to go to Hong Kong."

"That was Mummy. Jalu will go wherever you want."

"But I couldn't take her if Mummy didn't want her to go."

Mom was enjoying herself. She continued smiling as if she knew something he didn't. "Array, but you men are all so stupid. That was five years ago. You can call my mother Mummy as if you were already married to Jalu but you're still too afraid to ask her to marry you. Mummy used to call you That Chinaman then, but she doesn't anymore. She likes you."

Sohrab Uncle's eyes resumed their normal proportions. His grin stretched like a crescent moon across his face. "If what you say is true, then I am the happiest man in the world."

"It's true," Mom said, looking at him for the first time. Of course, she was happy for him, but later she teased him constantly for taking her sister so far away just as Jalu Masi constantly teased Dad for taking Mom away.

Bravo! Well done! I wanted to cheer, applaud, bounce, float, fly; Mom had played a fine Cupid for the finest of men, my Sohrab Uncle, what can I say? I had met him on only two occasions, when I visited Hong Kong, when he visited Bombay; he didn't like travel, I was too young to travel as I pleased; but I remember him well – generous, kind, considerate, steady, balanced, centred – that is, if you can trust the impressions of first a five then an eight year-old boy; there were also the less profound but all too important attributes of money and status; and, of course, always, the ocean-deep voice. Well, yes, he had thinning hair, a bulbous nose, and swarthy complexion, but even Granny, a stickler for pale European complexions, didn't hold that against him – but let me cut the blather, let me get specific.

First, I was five years old, in Hong Kong, on the mainland peninsula of Kowloon, where Sohrab Uncle, Jalu Masi, and my four year old cousin Zarine lived – with Mom; Dad was to join us later; Rusi was too young and had been left behind with Bapaiji. We lived on the fourth (the top) floor of a residential building; there were two flats on each floor; the Chinese women, in Mandarin collars and pants, with pigtails and wide smiling faces, did their ironing every morning on the landings; Sohrab Uncle wanted Zarine and myself to wish everyone we met a good morning on our way down; he would converse with them at a leisurely pace in fluent Chinese, perhaps about the weather, perhaps about their health, perhaps about their relatives – I didn't understand, I didn't want to understand, I wanted to be away, particularly if they were discussing my limp and I couldn't understand them, but I hobbled dutifully along at Sohrab Uncle's pace despite the cloud of self-consciousness through which I struggled.

Once, seeing my chance (Sohrab Uncle was still packing his briefcase, Zarine finishing a glass of milk), I shouted, "I'll meet you down the stairs," waving my cane as if for balance, ignoring all the ironers as if I were in too much of a hurry to acknowledge them. I waited almost ten minutes on the narrow street lined on both sides with shops and advertisements in the pictographic Mandarin script, rows of laundry perched in unseemly juxtaposition with rows of ferns on hastily improvised scaffolding fronting the faded facades of the teeming residences over the shops, watching coolies hefting bamboos on their shoulders with cargo weighted at both ends, and rickshaw-wallahs with shallow conical hats and wiry calves, before Sohrab Uncle came down with Zarine. He looked amused but he spoke sternly. "Did you say Good Morning to everyone coming down?"

I mumbled something noncommittally.

"That is not good enough, Homi. Now, I want you to go back up the stairs and wish everyone Good Morning. Take your time. There is no hurry. We will be right here waiting for you."

Dad would not have made me do it. Dad would not have made me do it. He would have said good-humouredly, "If the boy got around it let him go," but Sohrab Uncle was not Dad; he grew suddenly more honourable and just – not that Dad was dishonourable, but he was less inclined to push unless he were pressed himself; he was prone to let things slide; and he might have lost my respect for letting me so wilfully have my way.

Second, Jalu Masi and Mom sat side by side on Jalu Masi's long upholstered seat in front of her dressing table, Jalu Masi in a sky blue silk sari on which voluptuous blossoms had been handpainted, and a darker blue satin blouse, Mom in a plain shimmering sari of gold and a gold satin blouse, each putting the finishing touches to their makeup in the glare of fluorescent lights over the three way mirror in front of them. Sohrab Uncle sat on the bed pulling on his socks and shoes. "The Rachmaninoff Second is my favourite," Mom said. "I can hardly wait."

"It's everyone's favourite," Jalu Masi said good naturedly, waving her hand impatiently. "I prefer the fourth. I like all those clumps of notes."

"Yes, but the second is so irresistible." She began to hum the theme, "Da de/Da de/Da da/Da da dum. . . ."

"We all know how it goes," Jalu Masi said, interrupting her. "It's so easy to follow, but the fourth is more avant-garde."

Mom's eyes opened wide; she had forgotten that Jalu Masi liked to be contrary sometimes just to be provocative, but Sohrab Uncle knew what she was up to and came to Mom's rescue. "Sum mare luccica," he sang in his deep voice, "L'astro d'argento."

"Here we go again," Jalu Masi said grinning. She knew what he was doing. "Quiet, Sohrab," she said. "We're having a discussion."

"When I hear you having a discussion," Sohrab Uncle said, looking up from his shoes, "I will be quiet." He turned back to his shoes, singing loudly, "Placida e l'onda/Prospero e il vento."

Jalu Masi raised her eyebrows, staring at his head bent over as if she might smack him, but Mom interrupted, not understanding that they were playing. "Oh, let him sing, let him sing. I never get tired of listening."

"I just wish he'd learn some new songs," Jalu Masi said. "That one's had it."

She sounded exasperated but Mom noticed with relief that she was grinning. She wished she could pick up on what was going on more quickly; sometimes she just felt so silly.

Sohrab Uncle had barely finished his verse before I saw myself in pajamas, limping into the room without my cane, up to Mom at the dressing table, squinting in the light. "Goodnight, Mom. I just came to say Goodnight."

Mom stared as if she couldn't understand why I was there. It was the fourth time I had appeared to wish her Goodnight. "Yes-yes," she said. "Goodnight. Goodnight."

I sat by her while Sohrab Uncle put on his tie. "Don't you think you should be going to sleep, Homi?" Mom said. "It's way past your bedtime."

I felt strange in the apartment in Hong Kong without her; I didn't want to sleep with her bed empty next to mine in the dark bedroom we shared with Zarine; I wanted to stay with her in Jalu Masi and Sohrab Uncle's bedroom; I wanted to leave with her when she left; but I said, "Yes, of course. Goodnight."

"Goodnight."

I sighed deeply. "Goodnight, Jalu Masi. Goodnight, Sohrab Uncle."

They said Goodnight. Sohrab Uncle looked thoughtful. "I don't think he wants you to go, Pheroza," he said after I had left the room.

"Oh, but I do so want to go!" Mom looked alarmed as if she were afraid he might order her to stay. "He'll be all right. He likes the amah. He'll be all right."

As if on cue I re-entered the room and sat by her again. "Goodnight, Mom. I just wanted to say Goodnight."

"Homi, what is the matter?"

"Nothing. Why?"

"Maybe you should stay, Pheroza." Sohrab Uncle spoke kindly. "I think the boy wants you to stay."

Mom's voice was high with uncertainty. "But I can't stay. I have a ticket."

"We can get another ticket another time. I think the boy needs you tonight."

Mom seemed caught between desire and maternal duty. "There's nothing to be afraid of," she said to me. "We've left you and Rusi with Mary and Julie so many times in Bombay. The amah is right there in the next room if you need anything. She's very nice. There's nothing to be afraid of."

I remained silent. "He's still new here," Sohrab Uncle said. "I'm sure if this were Bombay he would be asleep by now."

Mom's eyes relaxed first; then her shoulders slumped. "I suppose you're right. I suppose I should stay." I hugged her then and our embrace and expressions provided a tableau sentimental enough for a Mother's Day greeting card – but I knew she would not have stayed if not for Sohrab Uncle. I remember watching the harbour tilted at a crazy angle from the train to Victoria Peak, I remember the dense floating fishing village of Aberdeen where everyone lived on junks with red sails and white shaped like batwings and the smaller flat-bottomed sampans, I remember the ferry onto which Sohrab Uncle drove his Fiat every morning to cross the mile of harbour from Kowloon where he lived to Hong Kong Island where he worked – but best of all I remember Sohrab Uncle looking grave, compassionate, determined, saying, "I think the boy wants you to stay. I think you should stay."

Third, I was at my desk with the elephant lamp struggling over some long division homework I had been set by Miss Sandra Rodricks, my fifth standard high school teacher, a thin olive-complexioned young woman of Portuguese descent from Goa, with whom I was infatuated. I had convinced myself that she had shown the class that a thousand divided by ten was ten and, consequently, I continued to get the wrong answer to the problem. I hated to ask Dad's help for anything because he shouted at me if I didn't understand everything he said the very first time. Sohrab Uncle spent an hour trying to shake me from my delusion, going over the multiplication tables, laws of arithmetic, calculations from first principles; I understood him perfectly but I couldn't understand that Miss Rodricks could be wrong; "But, Sohrab Uncle, she is the teacher! How can the teacher be wrong?"

"Ask her again tomorrow," he said patiently. "You will see that there has been a misunderstanding."

"But there is no misunderstanding. Maybe you are both correct."

"If we are both correct then ten would equal one hundred, and that is impossible."

"But maybe not."

"Just ask her tomorrow."

It wasn't the first time my infatuation had ruled my good sense, and it wasn't to be the last. Sohrab Uncle was right, of course; I had misunderstood Miss Rodricks; the legacy of the circumstance was not mastery of long division, certainly not of infatuation, but a consolidation of my image of Sohrab Uncle as solid, patient, dependable.

Nehru
and Lady Mountbatten
Had an Affair

"During the early years of our marriage your dad and I did a lot of travelling, mostly because the army gave him a number of postings, some for only four months depending on what needed to be done – but we also visited all the towns and cities near the postings, so I got to see Calcutta, Darjeeling, Kashmir, Ladakh, Nagpur, Kanpur, Lucknow, Delhi, Lahore, Poona, Madras, Bangalore, Mysore, Ooty, Conoor, Cochin, and I'm sure I've left out dozens of places yet. There were coffee parties, swim parties, garden parties, dances, clubs, concerts, pictures, shows; we had a gala time all the year round. When we were in Calcutta I took piano lessons from the conductor of the Calcutta Symphony Orchestra, Professor Jacques Sandre, a graduate from the French School of Music in Paris; he was impressed enough with my technique to ask me to play with the orchestra, he wanted me to practise the Grieg Piano Concerto – and I would have, but your Soli Mama became seriously ill with typhoid and both your Jalu Masi and I flew to Bombay, she all the way from Hong Kong, to be with him and Granny.

"Those were idyllic years; your Dad couldn't pamper me enough. When he first gave me the housekeeping allowance I misunderstood and spent all the money on a new sari; when he found out what I had done he just laughed and gave me an even bigger allowance. I could do no wrong in his eyes; at the dances I hardly got to dance with him at all because the other officers kept cutting in on us saying, "You are privileged to be the husband. Let us do the dancing," and when we left he would say to me, "You know what, Mrs Seervai? My wife was the loveliest girl at the ball." He was so gallant – everyone was so gallant – and charming; there were GIs in Calcutta at the time and wolf whistles came my way all the time. I was so happy, always so happy, year after year after year, and it showed; someone came up to me once in a restaurant and said, 'I don't know you, ma'am, and we may never meet again, but I just had to tell you that you've made my day, just looking as you do: not only lovely, but also happy – an unbeatable combination.'

"But of course I was still very young and didn't know how to do very much besides sit and look beautiful for your dad. The first cocktail party he gave was a revelation to me. He organized the drinks, the snacks, everything, with the cook and bearer because he knew how inexperienced I was in these matters. The party was by a swimming pool, there were about fifty people, it cost five hundred rupees, the snacks kept coming, the bottles kept popping, your dad kept circulating, and I kept sitting! Every now and again a guest would turn to your dad with a fresh drink, glance in my direction, and toast me saying, 'To your charming wife, Major.' Toward the end some of them got so drunk – even the ladies! – that they jumped, fully dressed, into the pool, and had to be fetched out. A brigadier whom we knew very well must have seen my expression. 'Don't look so disapproving, Mrs Seervai,' he said. 'They are just having fun. You should join them.' I wasn't disapproving as much as shocked; I took consolation in the fact that at least your dad wasn't making a fool of himself.

"I'm afraid, though, that I was something of a Marie Antoinette because, unfortunately, these were not the best of times for our country. We were in Calcutta at the time of Mr Jinnah's Direct Action Day; there was blood on the streets – literally; people were being killed outside our living quarters; your dad went to work with an armed escort; I could even hear the wails of the dying, but I lived in such a self-absorbed world that what happened outside seemed to have nothing to do with me; it was not that I didn't care but there was nothing I could do, nothing any of us could do; but it was such a relief when Gandhiji's fast saved the situation and Calcutta gradually returned to normal; I remembered my old Gujarati teacher then, Popatlal-Master, and I understood why he had been willing to go to jail so many times for Gandhiji; I felt I would have gone to jail for Gandhiji myself; he was more than a man, a saint, the most Christlike figure in the modern world.

"We were in Nagpur when we finally got Independence; it was a great occasion, of course, but the difference between the British and Indian governors was nevertheless ludicrous. We were invited to Government House at midnight of August 14, 1947, to attend the inauguration of the new governor. The Durbar Hall was floodlit; all the British officers, civilian and military, wore their medals, decorations, tailcoats, etcetera, etcetera; their ladies wore ankle-length gowns and jewelry; there was a band in attendance; everyone was set for the oath-taking ceremony – but Mr Pakvasa, the first Indian Governor-to-be, was late, an unheard of occurrence during the British Raj. Finally, some sadhus, wearing dhotis and smeared with saffron from the waist up, took their places onstage and performed puja, preparing the way for Mr Pakvasa, who made his appearance shortly in a kurta, dhoti, and Nehru cap. To you this might seem commonplace, but to us, accustomed to the British ways, this had all the magnificence of a comic strip. But then we stepped out on the perfect lawns, the Union Jack was lowered, the National Flag was raised, the National Anthem was sung for the first time in public, Nehru held his tryst with destiny in Delhi, Mountbatten became our first Governor-General, and I cried and cried and cried, I was so proud."

Dad had begun to put on weight even before his wedding. When I saw him shake hands with Dr Mistri, our dentist, also a friend, he was already heavier than my earliest memory of him, his widow's peak more prominent. He smiled stiffly as he shook hands with Dr Mistri, but as he left the office, walked down the corridor past the frosted glass windows, past the wooden shingles bearing various names and degrees in white block letters, past the plaster walls covered with red expectorations of paan to the lift, his smile dropped abruptly and his eyes glazed over with disappointment. He looked like a child who had been cheated. Philly was right. She had told him not to give away his services so freely; they needed the money, particularly after he had quit the army to freelance; but Mistri was a friend he had said, he would do the same for him – but he hadn't. Dad had drawn up blueprints for a bar for Mistri's sitting room without charging him, supervised the construction, found the materials; Mistri had fixed him the first drink at the bar. "Anytime you want a drink, come on up," he had said. Dad wasn't a drinking man but he had needed a filling for a tooth. The filling wasn't expensive but he was damned if he was going back to Mistri; the man had no sense of honour.

But he had done this before; he had done work for the Desais and the Vazifdars without charging them but they had charged him for work done in return. He did not mind losing their friendship, but he was beginning to think he had missed the big picture; perhaps honour had nothing to do with it, perhaps it never had, perhaps it was a fiction which had been perpetrated to take advantage of those who believed the fiction, perhaps men of the world understood this and he would never be such a man; was it honour that kept him apart? pride? foolishness? was there a difference?

It was a hot day. His bush shirt clung to his back, heartshaped with sweat, as he got into the Ford and drove to Napean Sea Road where he was to pick Mom up. She was visiting Mr Gokhale, the Chairman of the Reserve Bank; when the chairman had learned that she planned to visit Kashmir that summer with Rusi and myself he had insisted that she visit him first so that he could inform her, looking at the latest reports (the Defence Minister was his good friend), if it were safe (he had heard that the Chinese might be making advances at the border). Dad had been surprised at Mr Gokhale's concern; he had warned Mom to be careful; she had pooh-poohed him as she usually did; "He's the Chairman of the Reserve Bank. What's he going to do with me? He's just being nice." Perhaps she was right; she had been right about Mistri; he hated to tell her what had happened. He hoped she would be on time; he had never been able to convince her that it was rudeness, not the privilege of a lady, to keep others waiting; she had never been able to convince him that a lady lost respect if she treated a social engagement as if it were a military detail.

Mom was heavier too, but she spread her weight evenly unlike Dad who concentrated his in his stomach; whereas Dad looked simply heavier Mom looked more womanly. Her hair was short and waved like Debbie Reynolds's, and her light blue, short-sleeved, cotton dress was dark at the armpits. She waited for Dad at the gates of Mr Gokhale's mansion. Adi had been right. Men were all the same. There had been a British brigadier at their hotel in Calcutta who had flattered her with conversations of Keats and Shelley and Byron every morning at breakfast for a month, attempted to force his way into her suite when Dad had been at work, and left as soon as she had started screaming; there had been Mr Rao who had invited her to meet his family who spoke no English, from whom she had accepted two glasses of wine and almost passed out before she had torn herself from his embrace and hailed a taxi home (she should have known better; any woman who drank wine in the daytime, particularly in the absence of her husband, might just as well have branded herself promiscuous); there had been others; Adi had warned her but she had assumed, always erroneously, that if she felt nothing but friendship for a man he couldn't possibly feel anything more for her; the British brigadier had been thirty years older, Mr Rao of an entirely different class, the chairman was, well, the chairman – but in this one respect they were all the same. He had told her she was lovely, he had kissed her hand, he had told her to think about it, he was a powerful man, he could help her in many ways, he could help her husband! He had shown her a private bedroom behind his office! She couldn't believe he had propositioned her after she had spent such delightful evenings with his wife and children who lived on the other side of the mansion, but she had held on to her indignation because she was afraid of what he might do, and had left his office immediately. He had offered to have her driven home, but she had told him her husband was coming and she preferred to wait at the gate. She wished he would come soon but she hated to tell him what had happened.

Dad was surprised to see Mom at the gate with the guards instead of in one of the wicker chairs in the garden or on the porch by the driveway, but he was too obsessed with what he had to say himself to notice her distress until she spoke. "You'll never believe what happened," she said, getting into the car.

Dad didn't say anything.

"I can hardly believe it myself. I still can't believe it."

The wonder in her voice, almost shock, caught Dad's attention more than what she had said. "What? What happened?"

"Just drive. I'll tell you."

Dad's fist tightened on the wheel as he listened to her story.

"He said we were all grown-ups now. He said his wife knew. He said he could help you. He even has a bedroom behind his office — with a bed! I still can't believe it."

Dad stopped the car. "The swine! The bloody swine!"

Mom, more in a state of bewilderment now than indignation, looked at Dad as if she were seeing him for the first time. "Adi! I will not have you swearing like that!"

Dad stared at her so piercingly that she was afraid. "Are you crazy?" he shouted. "The man has defiled my wife, and you are telling me not to swear at him?"

The way he said "my wife" made her feel as if he were talking about a third person. Usually, when she told him about the passes other men made, he was angry with her for being so trusting; sometimes he had laughed; she had never come to harm and made the stories amusing; she had grown less trusting and she could barely remember when the last incident had occurred; but she didn't know what she found more surprising, Mr Gokhale's behaviour or the violence of Adi's reaction. "You can swear if you like," she said, unsure what to say, embarrassed by her uncertainty, "but no one was defiled and no one was hurt. I just never want to see the man again."

Dad turned the car around. Mom looked alarmed. "What are you doing, Adi? Why are you turning around?"

"I am going to give that swine a piece of my mind. Chairman or no, I am going to tell him exactly what I think."

"Adi! No! Don't do anything foolish now. He's a powerful man. He could hurt the business."

Dad shouted without looking at her. "Damn! Woman! Whose side are you on?"

Mom remained silent while Dad drove back the way he had come, through the gates of the mansion, and up the driveway. Later, when he told her about Mistri, she understood that her story had stoked long-burning coals, but at the time she had feared his mood as much as the possible repercussions of his actions. The guards and servants knew him from previous visits so they let him through; Dad knew his way around so he strode directly to Mr Gokhale's office and pushed the door open violently. Mom followed, hesitantly at first as if she wished to slow Dad down, but, when that didn't work, as if she couldn't resist the vacuum in his wake.

Mr Gokhale was alone at his desk. Dad didn't stop until he had picked up a paperweight from the desk and slammed it down. "I say, Mr Gokhale," he shouted. "I want to know who the hell you think you are treating my wife like a bloody tart."

Mr Gokhale rose from his desk. I recognized him immediately, his trim long torso in the dark brown Nehru jacket, his thin angular handsome brown face, his greasy grey hair combed flat and straight back on his head. I had exchanged comics with his son at school; I had wondered why Rusi and I had suddenly been forbidden to talk to his son.

"Now, now, Mr Seervai," Mr Gokhale said in his soft voice, "we are civilized educated men, is it not? I do not know what you are talking about, but let us discuss it calmly. Otherwise, nothing will come of it. Why don't you sit down? Mrs Seervai, won't you come in?"

Mom was standing at the door as if she were on guard. She looked at Dad for a cue but he ignored her. "I will not sit down," he said, still shouting, "and you know exactly what the hell I'm talking about."

Guards came rushing to the door, looking at Mr Gokhale for instructions; he held up his hand and they waited at the door. "Mr Seervai," he said sternly, "if you do not lower your voice I will have to have you ejected. Please sit down."

Dad sat on the chair that was indicated. Mr Gokhale dismissed the guards with a wave of his hand. "Mrs Seervai," he said, indicating a chair, "please?"

"What about the door?" Mom said, not sure what to do.

"You may shut it." Mom shut the door and found herself a chair next to Dad's. Mr Gokhale continued. "Now, what can I do for you?"

Dad spoke with less fury, but no less urgency. "I want to know what the hell you mean behaving like a bloody swine with my wife."

"I do not know what you mean. I have always treated your enchanting wife with the utmost civility."

Mom felt nervous; Mr Gokhale appeared so sure of himself; perhaps she had misunderstood his intentions – but then she remembered. "There's the door to the bedroom, Adi – with the bed," she said. "He showed me the bed."

"It is a room to which I retire when I am tired," Mr Gokhale said. "I was just showing Mrs Seervai around. Nothing unusual in that."

Mom appeared so nervous, Mr Gokhale so self-assured, that Dad began to doubt Mom. He did not look like a man with anything to hide.

"I think there has been a misunderstanding," Mr Gokhale said. "Perhaps that is all, is it not, Mrs Seervai?"

"There was no misunderstanding," Mom said, panicking. "He tried to kiss me. He said his wife did not mind. He said he could help you."

Dad's moment of doubt vanished; he couldn't believe the effrontery of the man, to be so clearly wrong and so clearly conscienceless; the wild look came back into his eyes. "Now, now, Mr Seervai," Mr Gokhale said. "We are men of the world, is it not? Our Nehru and Lady Mountbatten had an affair" (pointing to a portrait of Nehru on the wall garlanded by lilies). "Are you thinking Lord Mountbatten did not know? He was looking at the big picture. This is happening all the time – and, after all, what does it signify? two bodies rubbing? I can get you big commissions, Government contracts, the Brindavan Buildings."

Dad's mind went blank again. There were those phrases again: "men of the world", "the big picture", "happening all the time"; were they just excuses for behaving shabbily or was that the way of a sophisticated civilization? "If I have offended Mrs Seervai," Mr Gokhale said quickly, "I apologize. I never meant to offend her, only to flatter her. I am sorry if I did otherwise."

Mom shuffled uncomfortably in her chair; Dad could see that she was ready to go, but if he left feeling bested, as he did, then everything he believed in would remain continually at stake. He got up. "Your Nehru had the affair," he said. "My Nehru won us independence." He picked up a lamp from the desk and threw it on the floor. The shade flew, the bulb smashed, the door opened, the guards came in. Dad took Mom firmly by the arm and led her out; behind them they heard Mr Gokhale say, "Nothing to worry – an accident, that is all."

Back in the car, as soon as they were outside the gate, Mom kissed Dad quickly on the cheek. "You were wonderful, just wonderful – especially when you said that about his Nehru having the affair and your Nehru winning us independence."

Dad grinned, feeling better than he had in a long time. "Someone had to teach the swine a lesson."

"Maybe that Sigmund Freud knew something: your dad was always so patient with me, but I saw how impatient he was with you and Rusi when he helped you with your homework when I could no longer do so, all that Physics and Chemistry and Biology and Ad Math; whenever we were apart I knew he missed me more than I missed him; it was painfully obvious from the length and frequency and ardency of his letters; he could hardly wait until we were together again, whereas I found little difference between my single and my married days when he was away; but with the years I came to love him deeply and I can honestly say that not even once – never – did I have amorous thoughts about any other man although I had multiple opportunities; whatever our differences he was always the only man for me, but while he never needed to be reassured about other men he constantly begrudged the attention I lavished on my sons – his sons as well, of course, but that seemed almost incidental even to him. We did so much travelling – England, Scotland, France, Japan, Africa – but after we took you to Hong Kong that one time he never wanted to take either you or Rusi anywhere; he said you were too young to appreciate it but, of course, that wasn't it. Bapaiji had always treated him so aloofly that he thought I made too much of a fuss over my children; he wanted the mothering from me that he should have got from her; of course, he would never have admitted this even if someone had suggested it to him, but it was too late for Bapaiji to change, and there was nothing that I myself could do about it.

"But one thing I did I wish I had not done, I wish I had not made him leave the army; I thought it would be better for you and Rusi to be settled – Rusi was born on his last day in the service – but he was never as happy again as in the first glow of our marriage; he worked longer hours for less money, he missed the military life, the free housing, the constant travel, the privileged accommodation; and, additionally, he was now responsible for a family. I was wrong; it was more important for him to be happy than for us to be settled; if he had been happy everything else would have been resolved more easily.

"You know what happened after that – money became more of a problem than it ever had before; of course, everything worked out, you and Rusi got scholarships to go to the States, but he worked so hard he was usually too tired for his sons – what time he had he liked to spend alone with me – and finally the years took their toll; in the end he had ulcers, high blood pressure, diabetes, two strokes, a weak heart – and he was only sixty years old."

Mom appeared grey and lost, walking along a hospital corridor, her hands clasped in an attitude of prayer before her; she looked as if she didn't know where she was. A nurse touched her arm, speaking in a kind voice. "Mrs Seervai, you must make an effort to look more cheerful. He depends on you, you know."

Mom seemed surprised to see her there. "I know – but I just can't help it."

The nurse spoke firmly. "You must. He notices nothing, he appears unconscious all the time until you come into the room. Then his eyes follow you everywhere. Last night I held his hand because he was reaching out and I didn't think he would know the difference, especially in his state and half asleep in the dark – but he threw my hand away with so much force I couldn't believe it. You've got to be strong for him, don't you see?"

"Yes, yes, I suppose I do." She spoke gazing blankly ahead of her. "I'll try. I'll do my best."

The nurse smiled, giving her arm an encouraging squeeze.

Dad was asleep; he had not been shaved recently; his head looked scraggly on the pillow because his hair was longer and whiter than I had ever seen it. Mom sat quietly by his bedside in the artificial afternoon darkness created by the curtains. Less than a minute later he raised his hand toward hers; she took his hand, smiling as soon as she realized he was awake, surprised to see his eyes still closed. "Hello, Adi," she said in a level voice.

He opened his eyes.

She leaned forward. "You know what I was thinking, my darling?" she said. "I will be fifty years old this year. Now we can both grow old together."

His head moved slightly to one side as if to deny what she had said. She leaned closer still to hear what he had to say. He spoke slowly as if each word were a hurdle for which he had to prepare himself. "You will never grow old, my darling. You will always be nineteen, always like when we first met."

She nodded, losing her smile, not knowing what to say.

"You have one bad habit," Dad whispered. "You have always made me wait; and I know you will make me wait even longer after I am gone."

Mom shook her head, dropping her gaze, drawing a deep breath to keep from choking.

"I do not mind waiting," Dad continued, "but you must not let yourself go; otherwise, I will not recognize you and I will have to settle for one of the other angels fluttering around me there."

Mom shook as if invisible hands had grabbed her. She withdrew her hand to find her handkerchief and dabbed at her tears. Dad appeared bewildered. "What is all this, Philly? I have told you you must be the merry widow when I am gone." She wished he would stop telling her. She hated it when he reminded her of the old days. When he had hummed the theme once she had cut him off with a kiss. "You must marry again if you wish, Philly," he said. "You have been well taken care of. There is nothing to cry about."

That was how he talked, as if the important thing were that she was taken care of; she was the sole beneficiary of life insurance payments, stocks, the Seervai properties in Navsari, various other assets and savings that had accumulated over the years; I was already in Aquihana on a scholarship; Rusi was the only unsettled element in her life; she understood, of course, that he spoke breezily of the things that mattered so little because he had relinquished all the other controls to God. When the moment came his eyes were already closed; she felt his hand go limp in hers, stood up to see if he were asleep, and murmured, "OhmyGodmyGodmyGodmyGodmyGod!" continuously until she felt her knees buckle and fell across him in a faint on the bed.

My first memory of the Tower of Silence, the dakhma, is of vultures hidden within palm trees over the rocky cliff alongside Gibbs Road leading from Kemp's Corner to the Hanging Gardens and Kamala Nehru Park on Malabar Hill. Julie was taking me and Rusi, who was still small enough to be carried, to the park. The panorama of Marine Drive from the Naaz restaurant on the hill, arcing alongside the sea, was breathtaking, people and cars and buildings the size of matchboxes by day, and bejewelled by lights at night, giving rise to Marine Drive's best-known sobriquet, the Queen's Necklace. The vultures surprised me because I couldn't see their bodies and from where I stood their bare skinny s-shaped necks growing into flat heads and hard hooked beaks resembled nothing so much as snakes. Julie explained they were vultures because the Tower of Silence was nearby; snakes didn't stick out that way from trees.

Zoroastrians feed their dead to eaters of carrion, earth, fire, and water being held too sacred to be polluted by putrefying flesh. Within the stone walls of the tower, open to the sky, are three concentric slabs of stone; the outermost, the widest, holds hollows scooped in the stone for men; the middle, narrower, is for women; and the innermost, the narrowest, for children. A drainage system allows liquids to seep into a central pit. The bodies are picked to the bone in less than thirty minutes. The birds have grown so tame through the centuries that they wait for the priests to administer the last rites before they descend. More to the point, whereas a claim can still be made for arcana in this verdurous enclave in the heart of industrial Bombay, it can no longer be made for privacy; sights which are restricted by religious edict only to Zoroastrians, some only to Zoroastrian males, are now available to anyone who can secure a vantage point in one of the multistoreyed residential buildings that so profusely dot Malabar Hill, and complaints continue to mount against the presence of the Tower when some of the less than considerate vultures litter the balconies of Mr Kumar, Mr Kapur, or Mr Srinivasan, with disembodied fingers, ears, and other such appendages.

Rusi

Maybe If I Had Been a Quadriplegic

With the night came silence, disturbed only by the infrequent whirr of a car passing along Cooperage Road outside, the even less frequent cawing of a solitary crow, and the twang of a weaver's instrument for softening flax, hefted on his shoulder as he made his way home. Normally, it would not have been possible to hear these sounds over the hum of the air conditioner, but I understood that I was tapping into ultra-sensory apparatus of which I had been unaware before. I heard next scrunching footsteps along the gravel driveway of Mayo House. I thought it might be Rusi returning from his dinner with Paresh at Chiquita's, and knew I was right when I heard the lift ascend and its outer door (also the front door to our flat) unlatched. I had just heard the cuckoo sound ten times (Mom must have brought the clock to Bombay after Bapaiji died) and waited in vain for the German boy fiddler, but Mom must have detached the weight that set his mechanism in motion; the fiddler's tune had become white noise for Bapaiji, but Mom still tired of hearing it; she could only enjoy it if it were reserved for special occasions. The door to the bedroom opened. "Array, Mom, are you feeling okay?"

Mom was still sprawled across my stomach where she had fallen on the bed just as she had fallen across Dad when he had died. Rusi shook her gently by the shoulder. She jumped as if she had been tripped into wakefulness. "Adi! OhmyGodmyGod! No!"

Rusi shook her more firmly. "Mom, it's not Dad. It's Homi. Are you feeling okay?"

She stared at him, her eyes wide as if she were afraid of him. "It is Adi, it is!" She pulled her shoulder away from his hand. "Leave me alone. Why are you shaking me like that? What have I done?"

Rusi backed away with an openhanded gesture. "Mom, it's me, Rusi. I just got back from dinner. You were fallen on the bed. You must have been dreaming."

Mom sat slowly on the chair as if she were trying to absorb what he said. "I was, you know. I was dreaming, I must have been — everything about Adi, until he died."

"Yes, a dream, that is all."

"But no, Rusi, I talked with him. I could swear I actually talked with him." Her voice was soft with thought, with puzzlement. "He said he was all right. He said Homi was going to be all right, but if we kept talking Homi might get worse, so we stopped. I don't know what to think. Maybe Homi became a medium for us. It's so strange."

Maybe I had been a medium, but maybe, also, I had tapped into my own genetic memory, a subdivision of my collective memory; for the first time since I had succumbed to the memoscan I wanted to be well and back in Aquihana continuing my experiments once more. Rusi spoke stoically. "Go to bed, Mom. You must be tired. I will stay with Homi for a while."

"Yes, maybe you're right. It's all so strange." She touched my forehead softly and walked as if she were in a daze from the room. At the door she turned. "If something strange happens, Rusi, come and get me. You will know what I mean."

"Yes, yes, of course — but nothing's going to happen."

"Yes, that's what your Dad said."

"Dad's gone. Dad is not here. I told you no, the doc said he might have a relapse after the trip? But he's going to be okay."

Mom just nodded, shut the door behind her; Rusi leaned over to look at me; I thought my eyes were open but he sat on the chair Mom had recently vacated as if I were asleep, leaned back, clasped his hand in his lap, and shut his eyes. I was immediately barraged by what I can only describe as emanations of his thoughts — array?/ again?/what is . . . /some things never change/I'm telling you/always . . ./hell!/man!/you only/bloody hell!/always you . . . /I swear! — the barrage was more annoying than painful, like a tune that will not be placed, or, if placed, will not be put out.

"Come, come, Homi. Don't be so stubborn. I can place the tune,

I can put it out, whatever you want, but first you must let me help you."

Dad was back. "Help me with what? I don't need any help."

"Yes, you do, like you did with Mummy. You are not an island, whatever you think. I can unscramble Rusi's thoughts for you like I unscrambled Mummy's. You can order your own thoughts, we can order ours for you, but you need help ordering those of other sentient beings. It's a little bit like unscrambling a language – and, like Bapaiji said, we can make you understand even Zulu. So just relax. Let me do the work."

I was feeling much better; I was enjoying the show; I shrugged and gave myself into his care. The emanations continued to stream from Rusi.

"I swear, Homi, this is too much. What does a bugger have to do in this family to get a little attention? I mean, you're my brother and I love you and all that, but it was no bloody joke being your brother. Maybe if I had been a quadriplegic, or had leprosy or cancer or something I might have stood a better chance, but maybe not even then. You had not only polio but all that light brown hair like a European when you were born – how could I compete? It wasn't enough I had an IQ of 140 because you were a certifiable genius; your IQ couldn't even be properly measured, two hundred and something it was. Bapaiji never even taught me Gujarati because you didn't want to learn it – and then she got mad because I couldn't speak it. Let's face it, yaar, you were one maha spoiled bugger, spoiled rotten. You were always the favourite; I was always left out from concerts and things because I was too young – they took you to Hong Kong but they left me in Navsari with Bapaiji – but even when I grew older I was always too young. You got all the new clothes, and I had to wear them when you outgrew them, never mind that our tastes were different. Everyone said of course you were going to America and they made a big fuss at the aerodrome and everything, but I had to do all my own correspondence and even Mom didn't come to the aerodrome when I left, just my own friends; of course, Dad was dead by then and she was going a little cracked herself, but still she could have come.

"And now I'm making a life with Jan, finally someone who gives a damn about me first – I mean, hell, we're having a baby – and what happens? Homi has an accident with his machine, Homi has to be brought back to Bombay, Homi is back where he belongs – centre-stage – and who cares about Rusi or his wife or his baby"

Yes, yes, yes, yes, yes, it's easy for Rusi to complain. It was no bloody joke having polio either. I was four years old; we lived at Scandalpoint then in Zephyr, Granny's house, on the ground floor; it was two weeks after my first tonsillectomy; my throat still felt sore when I awakened that morning, I had a headache, I got up to go to the bathroom and fell down with the first step; my left leg hurt too much to stand on, as if someone were bending it the wrong way at the knee; when I tried to call for Mom I vomited all over myself.

I got used to the braces and the cane; I got used to resting month after month through the school year without being detained a single term because I was still able to pass the examinations; I even got used to the painful bending exercises with which Mom and (more frequently) Mary helped me; I understood that I was lucky to have been less severely affected than possible (some polio victims had to live in iron lungs); I understood that poliomyelitis was derived from the Greek words "polios" meaning "grey" and "Myelos" meaning "marrow" and the Latin suffix "itis" meaning "inflammation of" (inflammation of the grey marrow of the brain and spinal cord), as if understanding that I understood why I had been struck rather than a million other kids; but I didn't understand that I had been rendered fundamentally different until three years later by which time we had moved to the house on Cooperage Road. We were playing French cricket rather than cricket in the Back Gardens as a concession to me, because in Frenchie the batsman does not have to run; runs are made by swinging the bat (cricket bat or hockey stick) around oneself rather than running to and from the bowler; the batsman stands with his feet together and is counted out if he either moves his feet or allows the ball (rubber or tennis) to hit him below the knees, or if the ball is caught on the fly. At such times polio seemed a boon to me because I got to bat for both teams without having to field for either. Someone had left a bicycle with a tiffin carrier in the back standing by the banyan tree, and a resoundingly hit but unfortunately placed ball spilled an unknown luncher's repast (rice, dal, sliced onions, curds) at my feet, and all the erstwhile players fled, bounding over the old and easily negotiated enclosing wall.

I hobbled panic-stricken toward the gate, which appeared to move as quickly away from me as I moved toward it, when Rusi hissed me toward the wall and helped me hand and foot over it. No one was caught; someone lost a tennis ball; someone else lost a lunch; but while the misadventure was recalled with glee by the others for days my left leg appeared to get ever skinnier; I laughed as if I had been an equal partner in the mischief but I wished I could have flown with their ease, their fat muscular sausagy legs like balloons, heedlessly scampering, scrambling over the wall.

"Let's face it, yaar, Homi, you were a maha spoiled bugger and a maha sore loser on top of it. Everybody treated you like a prince and you only took it for granted. I swear it, yaar, you took too much for granted.

"I mean, we played chess every day of the summer hols – because only you wanted, not me – and one game out of maybe sixty I beat you and you went thup-thup, and slapped me twice, and never wanted to play again – talk about a sore loser. Who would play with you then? But you yourself lost interest then, even in your kite fighting – which was a pity because you were the best bloody kite fighter on Cooperage Road. You just stood by the balcony all day and one by one, sometimes even two by three, cut off every bloody kite that came near; you had a too-good wrist action for anybody."

I had forgotten my kite fighting days, how proud I had been of my hands, callused by the bright taut glass-encrusted twine, manja, used to bear kites aloft, how I had enjoyed crossing the manja of a kite already in the wind with mine and sawing it until it snapped and the erstwhile sovereign kite, its authority usurped, drifted on its torn plumage to a rooftop, or fell like a tarred arrow spinning to the ground. My too-good technique consisted primarily of keeping my kite on a short twine, below the stratospheric arena, until I had tested the wind and established my control; however unpredictable the wind, the best kite fighters learn to use it to their advantage; during the finest moments the two kites tangled, spiraling furiously around each other, circling like cobras joined at the neck.

I remembered precisely when I had lost my interest in kite fighting. I had been ten, rooting wildly for the Loyola House team against the Xavier and Britto Houses in the 1500 metres relay at the Annual Campion School Sports Meet, when my cane had slipped and I had fallen between the wooden tiers, ten feet to the ground. I had fallen on my side and lain, unmoving, suddenly aware that there were two spectacles being enacted, suddenly watching (at a second remove) the spectacle of which I had just been a part. I might have broken my bones, or, had I fallen from the highest tier, been killed, and no one would have noticed or cared till the end of the race. I was unhurt aside from a few bruises; I was shocked less by my fall than by the ferocity of my friends urging on their respective champions, a ferocity I had shared just moments earlier. Their passion was like a drug. I didn't care who won the race after all; the victory was too small a compensation for the narrow self-absorption it demanded; there were finer uses for such concentration and angst – but recalling the thrill of the kite fights I wanted once more to leave my bed, head back to Aquihana, and continue my experiments; I had disengaged myself too long from the challenges of life; but I was still too weak to do more than absorb what Rusi was showing me.

"Okay Homi, so I got your drift about the sports meet, but who could undertand the words? angst? self-absorption? second remove? Mom said you were a genius so we let it go; Mom said you had polio so we let everything else go; maybe if we had had it out more you would have learned something more about people – but the worst thing, what I felt most sorry for, was not the genius or the polio but how Mary used to really give it to you. If you did something wrong, dhaar, she'd give you one, and if you tried to explain, dhaar, she'd give you another; she just kept going dhaar-dhaar until you shut up or somehow got away – and there, for whatever reason, Mom always took Mary's word over yours."

Rusi was right about Mary. She was too clever to let Mom catch her. She scarcely needed an occasion to smack me, rap me, thump me, ostensibly to discipline me, but the occasions seemed prompted more by her whims than my fractiousness, and it was difficult for Mom to accept the word of a highstrung imaginative boy against that of a responsible indispensable housekeeper, especially since one night when she and Dad were attending a concert, Mary had persuaded Jeckie, our bearer, with whom we later learned she had been conducting a liaison, to hide in the godown in the dark and sing Goanese songs in a spooky voice to scare me into finishing a dinner of prawn curry with rice (I hated prawns). Mom smiled when I told her there was a bogeyman in the godown, but she did stop serving me prawn curry on the assumption that it affected my imagination. I uncovered the deception a while later when I heard Jeckie sing to himself as he dusted the sitting room – he had a naturally spooky voice, tuneless and sibilant – but I could not prove a thing. Later, after Dad had given Jeckie the sack (something to do with Mary), I found a way to get back at her. I told her Jeckie wanted to meet her at the gate downstairs, and to wait for him if she didn't see him right away because he was going to buy cigarettes. She didn't believe me (it was April Fool's Day; we had been playing pranks all morning), but the possibility was too enticing for her to resist; she was gone an hour before Mom realized she was missing. When I told her what I had done she smiled but she said it was a naughty joke even for April Fool's and Mary had waited long enough, so I called to her from the window, "Mary! April *Fool*!" so that everyone would hear. Mary stormed back, her single long black plait wagging furiously with her gait, her black rectangular face as cold as that of a praying mantis; she ignored me until Mom and Dad had gone out for the evening; then she twisted my arm behind me, called me a liar, threw me on my stomach, and beat me across the back and shoulders with my own cane until Julie stopped her. I did not report the instances to Mom anymore (Mary had ingratiated herself too well for her to believe my stories; Mom would tell Dad who believed that sparing the rod spoiled the child and that I was already too spoiled for my own good), but I never tired of devising schemes to embarrass Mary – until the occasion of my ninth birthday.

It was my turn to retaliate in our continual feud; the latch on the bathroom door was broken and Mary had warned me not to come in while she was taking a bath; I gathered my guests by the door and pushed it wide open with my cane; Mary sat, naked, on the low wooden stool, a brass tumbler in her hand with which she poured water over herself from the brass bucket in front of her. She screamed at the congregation tittering before her (gauzy party dresses, starched shirts and shorts), threw the tumbler at me narrowly missing my knee, and slammed the door shut again – but not before I had noted the shame in her eyes (unfocused as if by rendering her audience invisible she became invisible herself), and the blackness of her torso (of course, she had black arms and legs, but I had imagined her torso as pale as my own, as pale as the palms of her own hands, the soles of her feet); I coupled her shame and her blackness and associated them with Disney's Goofy who had the only other black torso with which I was familiar; the world divided into people with pale and goofy torsos, and I felt sorry for her as if her blackness, her goofiness, were a secret I had unfairly exposed. When she paid me back later for her embarrassment I felt I deserved her blows, and responded more diffusively than before, striking at Rusi instead because he had beaten me at chess, at Julie because I knew she would not hit me back, and at my cousin Zarine when she visited from Hong Kong because she was a girl, enhancing Rusi's estimation of me as one maha spoiled bugger. It was a stupid stupid cycle: Mary struck me, I struck someone else, she struck me again for striking someone else, I struck someone else again for being struck by Mary for having struck someone else, ad nauseam.

Yes, I was a maha spoiled bugger, but I was surprised that it still affected Rusi. I had always envied him: being the favourite I fettered myself with standards to uphold of which he was always free; his ayah was Julie, not Mary – kindly, grey, soft, round, wrinkled Julie who unrolled her bedding alongside his bed every night so that she might cushion him with her body just in case he fell out of bed in his sleep (he was four years old before he realized that Julie wasn't his mother; he went into a sulk for weeks, upset with both Julie and Mom; Julie's face wizened as if she had lost a son); and best of all his friends constantly dropped in, not infrequently bearing gifts – a battered guitar, a barely audible transistor radio, a cassette player with a damaged rewind mechanism, old records, psychedelic shirts. I had often wished for the elan with which he carried off his escapades. He was only six at the earliest such occurrence I can recall. Mom had planned one of her musical evenings; she had even typed copies of the program for everyone. I introduced the evening, playing under duress, "The Anniversary Waltz", on the harmonica (I hated the harmonica lessons – not least because they meant sacrificing an hour of sleep before school every Tuesday morning – but it was one of the things I did to set a good example). A punch was served, Havovie Sanjana sang Schubert's "Die Forelle" to a piano accompaniment, Khorshed Bhagat played The Goldberg Variations, an interval followed with cheese wafers, patrel, bhajias, sandwiches (egg, chutney, mutton), the Paymasters played The Kreutzer Sonata, Gool Paymaster played Liszt's Hungarian Rhapsody, No. 2, and Mom wound up the proceedings with Chopin's Ballade in G Minor. "Array, Rusi," Adi Joshi said when Mom had ducked into the kitchen to see about the coffee, "and what about you? What are you going to do for us today?" – "Yes, yes," said Nergesh, his wife, "it's your turn now, Rusi. What have you prepared for us today?"

Rusi had recited nursery rhymes in the past, turned somersaults; perhaps everyone's favourite of his antics had been when he'd sung "How Much Is That Doggie in the Window" supplying the barks, the parrot squawks, even humming for the "bowl of little fi-shies"; he had drawn more applause than Beethoven that evening. "Yes, yes, Rusi," Aloo Chibber said. "What are you going to do for us this evening?"

Rusi surprised everyone by jumping from his chair, falling to his knees on the blue and red rug Mom unrolled for special occasions, holding up his hands, and chanting loudly, "Array, Ram-Ram-Ram, Ho Ram-Ram-Ram, Ho-hai Ram-Ram-Ram-Ram, Ho Ram, Hai Ram, Array Ram-Ram-Ram." His eyes were shut and he swayed from the waist. Everyone stared in silence not knowing what to make of him; Dad said, "Get up, Rusi. What are you doing? You mustn't be so silly," but Mom, coming in from the kitchen, understood what was going on. "Array, the Mehtas hired professional mourners yesterday. Someone died in the family. I was explaining it to him just this morning." The guests encouraged him to continue his caterwauling over Dad's remonstrance. Rusi was canny enough to wait until Dad left the room before he went up to Adi Joshi and said, "Mom said the mourners got money for their mourning." He collected a rupee and five annas in one and two and four anna bits. I sat rigidly thinking how he had cheapened himself, wishing I could have done the same myself.

You Think This Is Communist Russia You Can Just Walk into My Room?

I didn't know how long it had been since Rusi and I had left Aquihana for Bombay, but Rusi must have been tireder than he had thought because he had slumped in his chair by my bed, his mouth a little open, his hands trailing the floor. I had not known him with his beard which grew wildly, apparently at its own will, giving his face a grimy cast, but his thick curly black hair, the hollows under his eyes, the tiny upturned bump of his nose, and the full sensuous lips unhidden even by his beard, were comfortingly familiar. I wanted to touch him, to say I was sorry for all the trouble I had continually caused him, but there was no time for recriminations; his beard disappeared and as the dark turned to light around him my room turned into his (the room adjacent to mine with which I shared the verandah). The wall was covered with posters of Joplin, Hendrix, The Doors, The Beatles, Dylan, Gracie Slick, and (just for the hell of it) Frank Sinatra. *Sgt Pepper's* was on the record player; Rusi sat on the bed strumming chords on his guitar and singing softly along with "Lovely Rita"; he wore flared blue jeans that almost hid his feet, a white kurta almost to his knees, and his hair was bunched untidily into a pony tail. There was a knock on his door but he ignored it. The knock sounded again but he continued strumming and singing to himself. The door opened and Shiv Chowdhari – Solo, as he was known in Rusi's band, Just Us Folks, because of his prowess with the lead guitar during jams – came in, wearing a plain bush shirt and pants. A flap of his straight black hair fell constantly over the left lens of his spectacles but he was never so unhip as to push it aside. "Array, Rusi, what is this? You heard me knocking or no?"

Rusi continued to ignore him.

"Array, listen, no? This is important, yaar – about the amplifier."

Rusi scowled at him, still strumming; Solo picked up one of *The Beatles Books* lying on the desk and began leafing through it; he was the largest member of the group, but Rusi was the boss.

When the song ended and the cock crowed to introduce "Good Morning, Good Morning," Rusi looked up. "Did I say you could come in? Where you learned your manners?"

Solo put down *The Beatles Book*. "Array, Rusi, don't be like this, yaar, this is bloody important."

"Ask me if I bloody care. You think this is bloody communist Russia you can just walk into my room?"

"Array, sorry, yaar, Rusi, but Bunny bloody says he's going to sell the amp to bloody Chitku if we don't come up with the bread by Friday. What are we bloody going to do?"

Rusi turned back to his guitar, strumming and singing to "Good Morning, Good Morning," – "Nothing to do, it's up to you/I've got nothing to say, but it's okay."

"Don't be so bloody cool, yaar, Rusi. What are we bloody going to do?" Solo's voice was getting shrill.

Rusi put the guitar aside. "Don't get so shook, yaar. We'll get the bloody cash is what we'll bloody do."

"Five hundred bucks? From where? I bet you haven't even got a bloody ten chip note on you."

"It's so bloody hot, yaar, Solo. Get me a coke from the fridge. Get yourself also. It's too bloody hot even to talk."

"Damn the bloody coke! Don't be so bloody cool, yaar, Rusi. What are we bloody going to do, no?"

"I'm going to get a coke. You want a coke?"

Solo shrugged helplessly. "Yeah. Sure. I'll take a bloody coke."

"Go get it then. Get me one also while you're there."

Solo went to the kitchen for the cokes. When he got back "A Day in the Life" had just started and Rusi was strumming and singing again. He put Rusi's coke down next to him, sat at the desk with *The Beatles Book* again, and drank his coke; even after the last heavy percussive chord had sounded and faded away he said nothing.

"Attchha, I'll tell you what," Rusi said. "Make sure Bunny keeps the amp till Friday," Rusi said. "Tell him I'll have the cash for him then for sure."

Rusi peered around the door into Mom's bedroom. "Mom, you got a minute?"

Mom was at her dressing table with the three-way mirror, rows of lipsticks, perfumes, sprays, powders, and other cosmetics; the fluorescent light atop the middle mirror was lit; she was wearing a grey satin petticoat, a grey satin blouse, painting her fingernails red with the tiny brush adjoining the nail polish cap with a swab of cotton wool ready by the bottle just in case her hand slipped. "Yes, Rusi, what is it?"

Rusi sat on the bed. "Mom, you know how much Gran gave Homi on his birthday?"

Mom looked up from her nails. "You know perfectly well how much he got, Rusi. Why are you asking me?"

"Just answer, no? How much did he get?"

"A hundred and one rupees, like he always gets."

"And how much did I get?"

"Fifty-one."

He appealed to her rationality with an openhanded gesture. "So, you only tell me, Mom. Is that fair?"

Mom went back to her nails. "It's because you're younger, Rusi. You know that."

"But is it fair?"

"But, Rusi, I always give you both the same. I don't play favourites."

"But, Mom, just answer my question, no? Is it fair what Gran does?"

"Array, bawa, if you must have your answer, then no, of course it isn't fair – but what can I do? It's your gran's money. I can't tell her what to do with it. If you feel so strongly about it, then you tell her."

Rusi picked at the nap of the beige candlewick bedspread. "Mom, I can't talk to Gran. You know how she gets. She might start shouting like a madwoman. Even Bapaiji only gives me fifty-one rupees."

Mom's hand slipped and she used the cotton wool; she didn't like it when Dad or anyone else called her mother names, but though her attitude became defiant she never said anything. "I told you, Rusi, it's because you're younger. That's the tradition. It's not anything personal."

"But it's not fair."

"Then ask Bapaiji, no? At least she won't shout at you like a madwoman."

"Bapaiji's too stingy. If it wasn't tradition she wouldn't give me even fifty-one rupees."

"Oh, very nice. So one grandmother is a madwoman and the other one is stingy. Well, it's no wonder, if that's how you feel about them, that they don't give you any more — but I really don't see what I can do about it."

"I thought you could make it up. That would only be fair." He continued to pick at the nap.

Mom looked up from her nails. "Rusi, I wish you would stop doing that. You've ruined one bedspread already."

Rusi stopped. "It's not bloody fair."

"What did you say?"

"It's not fair."

"That's better." Mom replaced the cap on her bottle of nail polish and waved her hands to dry her nails. She knew he was right but she didn't know what to do about it. "Get my purse from the cabinet in the cupboard," she said finally. "I'll give you a hundred rupees. Then I don't want to hear anymore about it."

"Mom, a hundred rupees? You owe me at least a thousand rupees to make it up."

"Array, and then what am I going to do for money?"

"You can get more from the bank, no?"

"Array, but I also have a budget to maintain. I can't just go to the bank every time I need some money. We'd all be flat broke."

"Then at least five hundred, Mom. I need five hundred for an amp by Friday."

"Rusi, I am not going to bargain with you. If you keep this up you won't even get the hundred."

"It's not fair."

"If you don't think it's fair then I'm sorry, but that's the way it is. The way I see it I'm giving you a hundred rupees that I don't even owe you. Is that fair to me?"

Rusi took the key from its hiding place under the wrapped bundle of clothes on one of the shelves of the cupboard, unlocked the cabinet above the shelf, took the money, and replaced the key. "Can I have some rum?" he said, referring to the bottles of cooking sherry and rum which Mom kept on the bottom shelf of her cupboard to use in desserts.

"Only a little."

Rusi took a long draught drinking straight from the bottle. "Thanks," he said with a grin, replacing the bottle.

There was Rusi, the hundred rupee note in his pocket, poking through books with lurid covers at the Empire Book Stall, *The Temptress*, *The Hellcat*, *The Things Men Do*, until he found what he was looking for, *The Kama Sutra of Vatsyayana*, which he bought along with the latest issue of *Playboy*; there was Rusi cutting pictures out of the *Playboy* and phrases out of the book – "The Long-Suppressed Oriental Manual", "The Art and Techniques of Love", "The Ancient Arts of Love", "Kama Sutra", "The Hindu Ritual of Love", "Complete and Unexpurgated", "The Arts and Rites of Love" – and pasting both pictures and phrases onto the cases of blank cassettes, also recent acquisitions; there was Rusi, walking from the Gateway of India with its hidden beehives behind the high gothic arches, along Apollo Road with the Arabian Sea on one side and the solid grey and white stone Taj Mahal Hotel on the other, to the Radio Club where Dad had designed and supervised the construction of an L-shaped swimming pool, and back, soliciting American tourists, Bill and Jeanne, Fred and Bev, Steve and Sandi, Bob and Joan, with the tapes, saying "Heavy shit, I'm telling you" to the men and "very instructive, very educational" to the women, "very hot, only one hundred and twenty-five rupees each," handing each of them flowers that he wore in a garland around his neck; there was Rusi showing Solo five hundred rupees, two new shirts with floral prints, a new pair of felt pants, and a hat with a brass buckle in front and a blue feather sticking out from the side.

Look at His Hair
Like a Gollywog

Mom wore a smart pleated blue skirt with a white blouse, Dad a white bush shirt and grey pants, as they walked from the Ford through Breach Candy (what I now call Americatown because of the American consulate, the club and swimming pool in which Indians were not allowed except as guests of American or European members, and the kindergarten school where Rusi and I had been enrolled, attended also by the children of foreign diplomats), past Bombelli's restaurant and pastry shop (famous for its kobe steak, its German chocolate cake), past Chimalker's (a dream shop for children, where we had purchased our Monopoly and carom sets – and Enid Blyton books beyond number, courtesy of Granny, on New Yearses, Christmases, and birthdays), and Readers Paradise (where I had bought the first of my adult books, Erle Stanley Gardner's *The Case of the Duplicate Daughters*, Agatha Christie's *Hickory Dickory Death*, and Ian Fleming's *Moonraker*), into a lane and into the foyer of Aquamarina, one of the new skyscrapers (sixteen storeys), up the automatic lift to a door bearing the plaque Dr Armaiti (Amy) Bhatia, where they rang the doorbell and were admitted into a sitting room; it was obviously a home but also, evidently, an office. The doctor, a thin Parsi woman, dressed in a sari, her hair in a bun, smiled and asked them to "Please sit down," speaking with a distinct American accent. "I noticed you have both your names on the door," Mom said, "Armaiti and Amy. Do you have a preference?"

"Well," the doctor said, sitting on a straight-backed chair across a coffee table from the couch holding Mom and Dad, "they called me Amy when I was at the University of Chicago. It's easier for them, of course, than Armaiti; then it was picked up by some of my friends here; but my clients usually call me Dr Bhatia, or just Doctor. Your Rusi calls me Doc."

"My, my!" Mom said, raising her eyebrows, "it certainly didn't take him long to make himself familiar."

"No, no, not at all," the doctor said. "He was very refreshing, a joy to talk to."

Dad, sunk low in the upholstery of the couch, stared at the embroidered carpet under the coffee table, smiling weakly.

"Well," said Mom, her eyebrows still high, "that's certainly nice to hear, but hardly what we expected."

"Well, then, tell me. What were you expecting?"

The doctor leaned forward. Mom sank back into the upholstery, her surprise turning to consternation; she looked helplessly at Dad. Dad struggled to lean forward in the couch, to put himself on an equal footing with the doctor. "Well, Doc – you do not mind if I call you Doc also?"

"Not at all, Mr Seervai."

"Well, it's like this. Rusi has been behaving very strangely and we were at our wits ends what to do with him. I was sure that someone like you, with your foreign degree from America, would see what was wrong from the start."

He smiled knowingly at the doctor as if there were nothing more to say, but she said, "Well, that's why I wanted to talk with you and your wife. I've had two sessions now with Rusi, and I find absolutely nothing wrong with him. He's quite your normal teenager. In fact, I found him quite entertaining. Clients like him make me feel I should be paying them for the session."

Dad's face dropped, as if he had been betrayed, but he said nothing.

"So, tell me, Mr Seervai, what do you find so strange about his behaviour?"

Dad sank back into the couch, staring at the wall. "What is so strange? Look at his hair, like a gollywog, never combed, always dirty. When I tell him – nicely, not shouting – to cut his hair, he just combs it a little. What am I supposed to do? He's too big to spank now. And look at his clothes, even a girl would be ashamed to wear his clothes."

"He's young. It's how youngsters express themselves today. Self expression is healthy."

Dad shook his head. "I don't know what you mean. I never self-expressed like that."

Mom bounded into the conversation as if she'd had a sudden insight. "That's not true, Adi. You were the same. I've seen pictures of you with the walking stick in the bowler and tails. You looked quite silly yourself then."

Dad looked sharply at her as if he couldn't understand why she was there. "I did not look silly. I was in UK. Everybody dressed like that there."

"But that is precisely my point," the doctor said. "It doesn't matter where you are. Styles may change, but clothes always remain a form of self expression. You carried a walking stick, Rusi grows his hair. What's the difference?"

"What's the difference? I'll tell you what's the difference. He gives away flowers on street corners like a jaripuranawallah. Don't give me What's the difference."

"But this is the Beatles generation. Flower power is in. Everyone is like that."

"Our other son was not like that. He was interested only in studies – and look where he is now – in America! But who will take Rusi, looking like that?"

"Adi, Homi was a special case. You have to admit that."

"Of course he was a special case. Why do you think they took him? But who is going to take Rusi?"

"Lots of universities will be happy to take him, Mr Seervai. They don't care how he looks, only about his scores."

"He's not doing badly in school, Adi. His marks are not all that bad."

"They take everything into account. I'm telling you, they take everything into account."

Mom looked at the doctor; the doctor looked at Dad; Dad looked at the carpet. "Let us go," he said finally. "I have wasted my money."

Mom smiled apologetically, getting up. "Thank you, Doctor, for your time. I hope we haven't been too much trouble."

"Not at all. If I can be of any more help, please give me a ring." She held out her hand; Mom shook it gingerly, but Dad ignored it;

he did not even look at her. When they were outside again Dad said, "We should not have sent him to a woman doctor; they are too emotional, especially where boys are concerned."

Dad appeared in his kilt once more, carrying bagpipes. "I envy you, Homi. If you remember these things when you have children you will be better off than I was; I was getting old, I was already sick, I wanted my sons settled happily before I died, so I panicked when things didn't go as I wanted, I tried to rush things because I didn't know what else to do – but I only made things worse. I died soon after the talk with Dr Bhatia, but in that time I had stopped talking to Rusi; we didn't have anything to say to each other; when I died we were worse than strangers (strangers, at least, have no obligations to each other). I am not complaining; do not get me wrong; I meant well but what counts is what I did; this is poetic justice – I never forgave Bapaiji, Rusi never forgave me – but I want to thank God for giving me a second chance. Your sickness was a boon; otherwise, I could not have shown you these things; I am sorry; I love you; I wish I could have done more; let us go on from there."

"Homi, what is this? What is going on? Mom was right. Something maha strange is going on that I am talking to you like this, but it is a good thing. This all needs to come out in the open. Actually, I tell you, Homi, it was lucky Dad sent me to the psychiatrist. After he died she not only told me how to apply for admission to the US universities, what to do about SATs and ACTs and all that – she even gave me a recommendation; it was a solid help.

"But before that, before Dad died, things got maha bad for a while. I mean, I don't know exactly what happened when he saw the doc, but after he came back he just stopped talking to me. Mom said I should apologize but I said For what; she said For your dad's health, but I said What about my health? She even gave the doc a ring again to set up another appointment for me, but the doc said she could not help me because I did not have a problem – Dad had the problem. Mom told me all that only to butter me up so I would speak to Dad, but I told her that was not going to solve the problem, so then she just let it go.

"In the meantime I concentrated on developing the group, Just Us Folks. We got pretty good, actually, and we got quite well known in Bombay before I left. The trouble was, when Dad died, the day of the funeral, I was committed to a concert. Mom went crazy, I tell you, telling me to cancel the concert and how could I sing when Dad had just died and all – but I had booked the hall myself, the sponsors were counting on us, the advertisements had been paid for, the tickets were all sold out, the group was counting on me, how could I let them all down? I told her I would be at the funeral but I would have to leave early – and that's what I did. It was touch and go, yaar. I changed clothes in the cab going to the auditorium. The driver got a maha shock, I tell you – I was wearing my dagla from the funeral when I got in the cab and my Davy Crockett shirt when I got out, like Clark Kent and Superman or something.

"Anyway, the next day, in the papers they wrote, 'Dad Dies, But Son Carries On' – 'The Show Goes On' – 'The Biggest Trooper' [sic] 'of them All' – 'Rusi Seervai Sings Through His Tears'; I don't know where they got all that from, like it was a maha big thing, like I was a bloody hero or something – but at least it made Mom feel better. The thing is, after Dad died, something changed, you know. I started thinking about my future and all, I started thinking about coming to America."

Chicago

Rusi arrived at O'Hare Airport carrying a shoulder bag and a guitar in its case. He was met by a friend of Dr Bhatia's who was to drive him to the campus, a brisk bright bony woman who pumped his hand vigorously. "Hi! I'm Chris Hahn, Amy's friend. You must be Rusi Seervai. Did I pronounce that right? You said you'd be wearing a brown corduroy jacket."

"Oh, hi, yes."

"Good. Let's get your bags. Sorry for the rush, but the flight's over an hour late and I have to drive all the way back to Kankakee – that's where I'm from – after I drop you off. I thought you were never getting here."

Rusi liked her smile, but he was tired and felt himself overpowered as if she were blaming him for the late flight. "Turbulence," he said.

"What? You'll have to shout, I'm afraid. It's so noisy in here."

"I said *Turbulence*."

She only nodded then, taking the shoulder bag from his hand before he could protest, and turning sharply to cut a swathe through the crowd heading for the baggage terminals; Rusi was a head taller than her but he almost had to run to keep up, one arm wrapped around his guitar case. He wanted to make a good impression, but he had already committed his first faux pas on the flight when he'd asked the air hostess for a cup of tea. Instead of a kettle brewing tea under a cosy and a strainer she had brought him a pot of hot water and a tiny bag of tissuelike paper containing tea leaves. Not wishing to trouble the hostess again for the strainer he had ripped open the bag, brewed the leaves in the pot, and decanted the tea into his cup; he had done it with a flourish, a cosmopolitan young man aboard a transatlantic flight, but wished immediately that he had kept a lower

251

profile when he saw a young lady across the aisle from him soak her tea bag in the pot before pouring it.

Rusi remained silent most of the way to the campus, not just because he was tired but because Chris pointed out the sights as she drove and it was all he could do to absorb them. He marvelled at the plush interior of her Datsun, the automatic shift, the air conditioning, the perfect reception on the radio, "Bridge Over Troubled Waters" – "Instant Karma" – "Mama Told Me (Not to Come)" – "Band of Gold" – "Hey There Lonely Girl". When they came to Lake Shore Drive he wanted to say it was like Bombay's Marine Drive, but caught himself; Lake Shore Drive could hold six cars abreast, it had an inner drive that could hold four more, Marine Drive could only hold four altogther; Chris drove at over seventy miles per hour, Dad had never driven over forty on Marine Drive; Bombay might have had more people but they seemed always to be going in circles, Chicago had more cars and they all seemed to know exactly where they were going; Bombaymen spoke with a lilt, Chicagoans with command; God might have been everywhere in Bombay, but Chicago appeared to be God Himself; besides, there was nothing in Bombay to compare in size to the black steel and glass John Hancock Tower, big black Xs buttressing its facades, antennae like horns on its head in the sky, resembling, eerily, what might have passed for a post post post post contemporary – a 21st century – Dracula's Castle in the twilight.

Rusi was relieved when they got to the campus, but the dormitories hadn't opened yet for the semester, so Chris drove him to a YMCA on the south side of the loop, the downtown area, put down six dollars to get him a room for the night, wished him good luck, and left. Rusi was tired – he had been flying for almost a day – but he was too thrilled with the newness of everything, the idea that he was in America, in Chicago, to rest. There was a rumble outside his window and raising the shade he saw an approaching train, like a giant worm in the night light, negotiate a bend in a track on an elevated structure that passed directly by him. The tall flat massive ratty façade of a dark brick building faced him across the tracks with regular yellow rectangles of windows and a fire escape crawling up one side. The sight depressed him, the floor of his room creaked, he could hear the couple in the next room quarrelling, he did not understand the mechanism that locked his door so he latched it instead and secured the chain because he didn't want to appear stupid by asking, it was not what he had expected of America; he thought of Dick Whittington who had arrived in London expecting the streets to be paved with gold; but he reminded himself that things had looked better on campus. He was still too excited to sleep, so he thought he would find something to eat. The concrete pavements were as wide as the roads in Bombay, but they were cracked and dotted with shrubs and shards of hard green grass. Neon signs flashed, advertising parking, x-rated movies, burlesque shows, hotels, restaurants; he entered Dawg Lovers, drawn to its logo (Pluto, with a long frankfurter torso), wanting to sample a real American hot dog, sat at a corner table by a greasy window, and tried to get the attention of the cashier to serve him – but the cashier, a young muscular black (negro, as Rusi thought of him), only scowled at him. Rusi was aware in the garish light of the naked yellow bulbs that the other customers were all blacks, but they seemed so bold, unlike the Uncle Toms he had anticipated from what little he knew of them; he wondered what he would do if they refused to serve him until he saw someone place an order at the counter and followed his example; he hardly tasted his dog; he felt he had entered America through a warp, that his expectations were continually to be twisted.

The light of the morning emboldened him again; he brought down his bags and guitar case and asked the concierge to get him a cab; anxious to be away from the Y, to be on the campus again, he waited with his bags in front of the building; it was no less depressing outside than it had been the night before, but at least the sun was shining. He felt hot and conspicuous wearing his corduroy jacket but it was easier than carrying it along with everything else. He watched so intently for his cab that he did not notice a figure shuffling up to him until the figure spoke. "Would you like to hear some po-try?"

The voice was almost indecipherably guttural; the man had not shaved in a few days and smelled of garbage; his forehead and cheeks were red and cracked with dirt; he carried a creased leather shoe in one hand and appeared to limp on his unshod foot – but that was what Rusi expected of poets. Besides, he felt like a guest, and if his host, however unsavoury his appearance, chose to be hospitable, he didn't want to appear ungracious – and he had time until his cab arrived. "Sure," he said.

The wino (it didn't take Rusi long to recognize him for what he was) pulled out a sheaf of papers from his coat and started to read. Rusi could not understand a word he said, his cab arrived, the meter started ticking, but he couldn't cut the wino off politely. Finally, he interrupted him by patting his shoulder, picked up his bags, said "Thanks, but I have to go," and got into the cab.

The wino spoke through the window. "What did you think of the po-try?"

Rusi looked straight ahead as if he had forgotten the recitation already. "It was okay."

The wino gripped the window with his hands as if to prevent Rusi from raising it. "I think that's better than anything Shakespeare ever wrote."

Still, Rusi looked ahead. "Everyone has got his own opinion."

The wino thrust his head forward. "I want a quarter for my reading."

Rusi looked at the wino again. "I asked you to read? Why should I give you a quarter?" He told the cab driver where to go, but the wino put his elbow over the window. "You give me a fucking quarter or I'm gonna break this fucking window."

Rusi looked helplessly at the cabbie who jumped out immediately with a baseball bat. "You break that fucking window and I'll break your fucking head."

It was not the kind of help Rusi wanted. "Here," he said, giving the wino the quarter he had so desperately earned. "I don't want any trouble."

As they drove away the cabbie said, "You shouldna done that. He wouldna done nothin. He was too drunk."

"It's okay," Rusi said. "I don't want any trouble. This is my first day in America."

During his first week on campus Rusi understood why American girls had a reputation with Bombay cab drivers for being easy. There were twenty times as many men as women on campus, but during orientation week, when the fraternities scouted the incoming fresh-men for pledges, girls (sisters, cousins, friends, girlfriends, and their friends) came from all over Chicago for the parties. Rusi was unimpressed with the fraternities; they were too alike, like toy houses, shoe boxes of brick and glass; their inmates were like children, streaking with car tyres around their necks to be initiated, having food fights, water fights, belching and farting competitions (when they learned he was from India some of them walked quietly away); their food was the same, sloppy joes, burgers, dogs; but he made the rounds of each of the nine fraternities each week, initially to satisfy his curiosity, then for the extra food, the music, once a movie, but finally, most of all, for the girls. He saw them everywhere, strong, desirable, and seemingly so available; there were couples in clinches in dens and basements and living rooms and hallways and stairways and bathrooms; Creedence, Zeppelin, Chicago, Santana, and Joplin played at one hundred decibels; red lights and blue lights and green lights and strobe lights bathed them, but they appeared so unselfconscious that Rusi was afraid to watch, feeling out place as if they knew something he didn't – but he knew they couldn't all know one another as well as they appeared to, and toward the end of the week he thought he might see if after all he might know them better himself than he had imagined.

Rusi had had some experience with girls – particularly as Just Us Folks had become better known – but it had remained limited; either the girls had proven too unsophisticated at the crucial moment, or he had proven too prudent himself, perhaps even (though he hated to admit it) too bound by tradition; but in America the rules were different, he had to rethink everything. He usually attended the fraternities with Faisal Ahmed from Karachi and Rajiv Dua from Delhi, both freshmen he had met on his first day, but on this occasion he chose to go alone. Actually, with the unnatural lighting it was hard to tell what anyone looked like, and with the loud music it was impossible to talk, but Rusi didn't care; how they looked and what was said were minor details in his scheme of events for the evening. He sat silently in a corner of the Tep (Tau Epsilon Phi) House watching the single girls; they were all lovely, in miniskirts, in halter tops, in breeches, in culottes, in shorts, in jeans, but he hesitated to make his move because he felt sure his difference would make a difference to them – but perhaps if he moved fast enough they wouldn't notice the difference. He deliberated for more than an hour, accumulating courage from draft after draft of beer, fixing on one, finding her too muscular, too cheerful, too smug, too American, fixing on another, before rising suddenly, walking in a trance directly to a newcomer in the doorway, and forcing himself to speak before he could find her in any way too excessive. "Hi. How're you doing? I'm Rusi Seervai – from Bombay, in India. What's your name? Can I get you a drink?" He had learned early that How're you doing was an American variation on Hello or How are you; it did not mean they cared about his health; by the time he'd thought about how he was doing they appeared to have lost interest. He mentioned he was from Bombay to waive questions about his name and anything else that might get in the way of the serious work of the evening.

The girl jerked her head back so suddenly that her pony tail snapped in front of her. "Oh, hi. No."

"No, what? You don't want a drink?"

"No. No, thanks."

"What's your name?"

"Diane La Fontaine."

"La Fontaine? Like the chap who wrote the fables, like Aesop? I know him. When is your birthday?'

Her eyes, which had been widening, narrowed as she regrouped. "October 2nd."

"What year?"

"1952"

He circled her waist with his arm. "Oh, yeah, a Virgo – or is it a Libra?"

She moved firmly away from him and spoke clearly. "I can stand very well by myself, thank you."

He mumbled, "Oh? Yah, of course," leaving the Tep House immediately. He found her too loud; he had moved too fast; he ducked into the Tee-Eck (Theta Xi) House, the adjacent fraternity.

He had to slow down, he had to slow down, he had to adjust his pace to theirs, he had to allow the conversation to carry itself, not shoulder it all himself. He took a deep breath, a draft of his beer, and scouted the room at leisure, focusing at length on a girl to the side of the room in a black top and tight blue jeans; she stood out from the rest because of a black satin neckband which made her appear nightclubby. He approached her more nonchalantly. "Would you like to dance?"

She looked at him coolly, soft hair waved at the tips lightly brushing her shoulders as she swayed to the music. "No."

She was smiling. She hadn't turned him down completely. "Why not?"

"The music isn't right."

Mary Magdalene was singing "Everything's Alright" from *Jesus Christ Superstar*. "What's wrong with the music?"

"It's in 5/4 time. You can't dance to 5/4 time – at least, not a slow dance – at least, not unless you're very good."

"Why not? They're doing it."

She smiled again. "If you can call that dancing."

If she hadn't smiled he might have found her too superior. "You have studied music, yes?"

"No."

"But you know something about it, yes?"

She looked down at her hands, still smiling. "I'm a singer."

Rusi chortled as if she had said something prophetic. "What? Really? No kidding? Me too!" When she looked at him he continued. "No, really! I am a singer. I had a band, Just Us Folks, in Bombay. I'm from Bombay, India. No kidding, you are a singer?" Her eyes grew softer as if she were amused. "So, tell me," he continued. "What's your name?"

"Maureen."

"Mau-reen." He spoke her name thoughtfully, as if he were developing a taste for it. "It is a good name, Mau-reen. You are the first Maureen I have met. Hello, Maureen."

She said nothing but continued to smile.

"I say, Maureen. I got an idea. Why don't we go to my room. I have a guitar. I could sing for you."

She looked at him cautiously.

"Only sing, nothing else. You can also sing. What do you say?"

She nodded her head. "Okay."

Walking back to the dormitory he couldn't stop talking, about his band, about Solo, about how "maha" the Beatles were, "too bad, yaar, that they broke up."

She stopped him once. "What is Yaar?"

He had thought all slang was universal; he would have to adjust his way of speaking. "It's just a way of talking, like Man. It doesn't mean anything."

She didn't understand everything he said, but listened without interrupting him then, watching him as if for a fitting, smiling all the while.

When they got to his room, number 313 in East Hall, he locked the door behind him, praying his roommate, Tim Joseph from Alaska, would not be back for a while. One bed lined each of the long walls, a desk at its head, a dresser at its foot, a closet by the dresser, the door by the short wall between the closets, windows across from the door. He lit Tim's reading lamp (the dimmest light in the room), turned it toward the wall, took his guitar from the closet, sat on the desk chair, and invited her to make herself comfortable on the bed. He started with the last song he had written; "I always like the last song best," he said; but as he finished he realized she hadn't been listening. She had slipped off her shoes, sat crosslegged on the bed leaning against the wall, and played with the zipper of her jeans. She continued to zip herself up and down when he was done. The sound was ominous in the near dark, as if he were being tested. "Is something wrong?" he said, scared as if he might wake himself up from the best dream of his life.

She was watching him closely. "I think my zipper's stuck."

He didn't understand how it could be stuck if she kept zipping herself up and down, but he said, "You want me to fix it?" glad that the light was behind them.

"Do you think you could?"

"I could try."

He knelt in front of her, zipping her jeans up and down. When he was sure there was nothing wrong with her zipper he unclasped the hook at her waist. "You fixed it all right," she said with a giggle, wriggling out of her jeans as he pulled them down.

He had to sneak her out later because it was long past visitation time; he made plans to see her again the next day as they walked to her car, a plush lime green Ford Falcon, by the el stop on 35th Street. "We also have a Ford," he said, "a 1948, a Humpty Dumpty I call it. This is your own? not your dad's? I can't believe it."

She smiled. "This one's an oldie. Dad was going to trade it in, but I convinced him to let me have it. It's no big deal – not like you. You have servants."

"Everyone there has servants."

"Everyone here has a car."

"Still, I can't believe it."

"Can I give you a ride back to the dorm?"

"Sure, sure."

He didn't want to stop kissing her goodnight; when she left he didn't want to go to bed; he roamed the campus, marvelling at the wide streets, the large flashy cars, and Maureen, most of all Maureen. "This is America," he repeated over and over as if he couldn't believe it. His grin was as large and curved as a cradle. "This is America. I am in America. I am in America. Rusi Seervai is in America."

He was ten minutes early for his rendezvous with Maureen in the dormitory lounge with the Miesian furniture and Yamaha baby grand the next evening, but after forty-five minutes she still had not shown. He wished he had taken her phone number; she might have had an accident; she might have misunderstood their arrangement; maybe she had thought he had meant the following day, Sunday, not Saturday, because Friday night had slid so imperceptibly into early Saturday when he had asked her – but she was leaving for Valparaiso University in Indiana on Sunday; she could not have misunderstood. She had a brother at the Tee-Eck House where he had met her, but he hesitated to approach him about his sister because some of the frat rats (as they were known in the dormitories) resented his presence – but after he had made a round of all the fraternities in vain he went back to the Tee-Eck House and asked a group of members congregated in the doorway if John were there.

The group got suddenly quiet looking at him. "John who?" one of them asked loudly as if he were addressing a child.

"John, Maureen's brother. Maureen was here yesterday. She said her brother is a member here."

"John Kemp, he means. He's in the basement. I'll go get him."

"It's okay. I can go."

"I said, I'll get him."

"Attchha – I mean, okay."

Rusi waited by the narrow gravel border that circled the house, someone went to get John Kemp, the rest continued in the doorway as if he weren't there. He thought he recognized someone coming out of the house, an ROTC (rotsy, as it was called) haircut, a T-shirt at least one size too small. "Hi, Nick. How're you doing?" he said, holding out his hand.

Nick ignored his hand. "I'm John Kemp. What do you want?"

Rusi swore under his breath. They all looked so alike. It was not the first time he had made such a mistake. "Sorry."

"What do you want?"

"Is Maureen here?"

"Who wants to know?"

"I had a date with her for tonight. She never came. I thought there might have been an accident."

"Maybe she didn't want to come."

"Then she would have called, no?"

"No. If she did not want to call she would not have called, no?"

Rusi felt embarrassed, wondering what Maureen might have told him. "Would you please give her this when you see her," he said, holding out a folded sheet of notepaper. "It's just my address and phone number."

John Kemp took the note, tore it three times in half, and let the pieces fall to the ground. "I said she didn't want to come."

Rusi turned and left, muttering "Bastard" under his breath when he was sure he could not be heard, as angry with Maureen as with her brother – she could have called him if she wasn't going to come; the dormitory number was available through the exchange.

Jan Schultz

As Rusi turned into the hallway from the stairs on the third floor of East Hall he took a deep breath – someone was fixing a sign to his door with scotch tape, her face hidden by a drop of dark glossy hair that fell forward in line with her jaw; his breath was taken by her long naked brown legs. He was learning to say "french fries" for "potato chips", "bag of chips" for "packet of wafers", "wafers" for "crackers", "crackers" or "cookies" for "biscuits", "biscuits" for "rolls", "rolls" for "buns", but he still couldn't hide his awe of the big beautiful American girls who swore so cheerfully, defied authority so wilfully, and slept so readily with their sweethearts. He tried not to think of Maureen, immersing himself instead in his books, but there were some occasions such as this when he couldn't help himself. "Hi. How're you doing? You looking for me?"

The girl looked up. "Are you Russy Seervai?"

Her forehead was so wrinkled with concentration, visible even from the distance in the dim light of the hallway, that he was sure she hated him. The cut of her hair shaped her face like a diamond, her head was perhaps too small for the thick sturdy trunk of her body, but he marked her expression with regret because the size of her breasts and her sleek complexion, brown from the sun, filled him with admiration. "Roo-si Seervai, yes. Something is the matter?"

"If you're Russy Seervai, there is."

He looked at the sign she had posted on his door:

RUSI SERVAI

is

a SCAB!!

Send Him Back
Where He Came From!
J.S.

Rusi felt a chill but he didn't know what he had done. "What is J.S.?" he asked.

She stood by with her arms crossed, as tall as him even in sneakers. "Jan Schultz. That's me."

"What is a scab?"

"You are a scab."

"Why am I a scab?"

"Because you take jobs from people who need them."

Rusi washed dishes with Manolo Carillo from the Philippines and Roman Hudec from Czechoslovakia in the cafeteria for a dollar an hour because the job had been advertised on the dormitory bulletin board; he needed the money and had not even realized that they had displaced other workers until Manolo had said that he hoped they would stay on strike until he had added enough to his savings for an engagement ring for his girlfriend, May. "If they need the job they can have it back," Rusi said to Jan. "I'm only keeping it for them until they come back."

He had spoken sincerely; he wanted her to like him; but he must have said the wrong thing. "Ha. Ha. Very funny." She turned and walked away.

Rusi took the sign down and stood it up on his desk in his room. The encounter had shaken him because he did not wish to offend anyone. He felt more vulnerable in Chicago than in Bombay. When his roommate came back Rusi pointed to the sign and asked, "Is it bad to be a scab?"

Tim, who was so meticulous he took his clothes folded to the washing machines in the basement insisting they kept the crease better that way, said, "It's a word, like cat or dog. You can't help it if you're a scab."

Tim was no comfort. Rusi despaired of understanding Americans. They appeared to use a kind of shorthand among themselves; even when he understood the words something was lost in the reverberations. He hesitated to speak too directly because he felt himself too easily misunderstood, too easily drawn into explanations that would have been unnecessary in Bombay. He developed a phrase for the way he felt – ethnic anxiety.

Rusi didn't like dishwashing, particularly when some bored tech-hawk might have squeezed a whole orange into a water glass or glued five plates together with mash potatoes and gravy, and he would have to pry out the orange and unglue the plates; besides, he didn't like to think he was a scab – it made him feel even more unclean than the work, unworthy even to talk to someone like Jan Schultz who looked at him as if he were a lizard whenever their paths crossed. He found himself another job, cashier at the campus drugstore on weekends, and the next time he saw Jan he burst into a broad grin. She was across 33rd Street from him, heading for the women's dormitory; "Jan, I say, Jan," he shouted, jumping up and down, waving his arms like a windmill in a gale; when she failed to respond he glanced quickly to his right down the road and dashed headlong in front of a car (he was to have several such brushes before getting accustomed to the American left-hand-drives), but not even the avalanche of honking and screeching and swearing and apologizing that followed prompted Jan to turn her head. "I say, Jan, wait up a bit, will you? I have good news," he said, catching up with her on the tarmac in front of the dormitory. "I swear," he said, grinning, running backward beside her, "a chap could get killed and you wouldn't bloody care."

She didn't look at him, but she said, "I care about the things worth caring about."

"I say, but listen, no?" Rusi, still running in reverse, stumbled over a curb, and fell heavily backward. "Oof!" Jan had her keys ready and would have left him without another word but she couldn't resist a smile and a shake of her head. "I have good news," he said without getting up, raising his hand as if he were making a point in a debate. "Wait up, no? Niagara Falls will still be there tomorrow."

She waited. "What is it?"

He crossed his elbows over his knees, still seated on the ground. "Let's go to The Bog for a coffee and I will tell you." The Bog was a dimly lit coffee room with a jukebox in the basement of the Hub (the Grover M. Herman Hall) which also enclosed the campus auditorium and was a centre for cultural events.

"I don't think so. I don't have the time." She fitted her key to the door.

"Wait, wait. Let us just go to the side then, out of the way of the people traffic."

He got up and led her over to one of the linden trees by the entrance. "What is it?" she said again. "I really have to go."

She seemed so uninterested that his news seemed anticlimactic even to him, but he managed to keep smiling and said, "I'm not a scab anymore. I thought you would like to know."

Her brow wrinkled, the skin on her face flattened as if someone had tightened it a notch. "Why would you think a thing like that?"

"Array, when I was a scab you made a sign for my door. Now, when I'm not a scab anymore, you don't even care?"

"Look, Rusty . . ."

"My name is Rusi."

"Sorry. Rusi. Look, this is nothing personal. I just don't like foreigners coming here and interfering with the American process. If workers go on strike you can be damn sure it's because they're getting ripped off by some fat cat complex or the other, and people like you don't make it any easier for them."

She started to walk away but Rusi caught her arm. "Yes, yes, yes, and how am I supposed to know this? For you I am just a foreigner, something to occupy your free time to make you feel important, something to talk about when you go back to your own kind. For me, what a country this is – everybody is a foreigner! Even their names are like from novels, Maureen and Tim and Diane and Jan – but the true American, the first American, was the Indian, no? And I am an Indian, no? So, you only tell me, who is the American and who is the foreigner?"

He smiled, his eyes on the ground as if he were embarrassed by his own feeble joke, but hoping she would at least acknowledge his effort; she ignored it altogether. "Let go my arm," she said.

"Go, go," he said, letting go. "No one is holding you."

Rusi appeared in a sequence of images: seated before a terminal with a Fortran manual, composing a flowchart diagram; before a microphone with his guitar, his beard fuller and a peace symbol hanging from a cord around his neck, performing for a small group amidst the plumbing in the basement of the graduate dormitory; shooting pins with Tim and Rajiv and Faisal and their roommates Bryce and Chuck in the pink and orange bowling alley in the Hub basement, his thick curly black hair kept out of his face with a leather headband; skipping like a fool in a long coat and top hat (which he had appropriated during Halloween) through a car park at night during the first snowfall of his life; standing in line for tickets for a showing of *Butch Cassidy and the Sundance Kid* in the Hub auditorium with a pretty Chinese girl, her hair long and thick and glowing and straight and black and soft to her waist, his bound in a pony tail; ordering pizza with everything from Connie's and fried rice and egg rolls and egg foo young from Shanghai's late at night with Rajiv and Faisal and others in the dormitory; crossing Jan's path without saying a word, keeping his eyes on her all the way while she looked in the opposite direction; finally, seated in the Hub auditorium filled to capacity (900 seats), overflowing into the aisles, with strategically placed microphones throughout the hall through which the student body at large was to confront the president of the university, Dr John T. Rettaliata, standing behind a lectern on the stage, ostensibly about university politics but, as became evident with the first questions, more pointedly about defining a position for the university regarding the Vietnam war.

Rusi couldn't understand how students who owned stereos, tape decks, bicycles, even cars, could still be so discontented as to stage antigovernment rallies, call the campus cops Pigs to their faces, and give them the finger; he couldn't believe that a president of the United States who had promised to initiate the peace process in Vietnam, as Nixon had promised, would escalate the war, as Nixon had done adventuring into Cambodia; he was willing to give Nixon the benefit of the doubt – the government was privy to information which influenced decisions incomprehensible to others – but the Kent State killings had bewildered him; tensions had run so high on campus that Rusi had almost expected a hooded figure in place of

Dr Rettaliata on the podium – the Tech News had dubbed him The Phantom, portraying him as a shadowy figure in its cartoons and pamphlets, owing to the low profile he had maintained during negotiations between his administration and the student body; Rusi did not know what to expect when he entered the hall but wanted to keep his preconceptions at an ebb; the students posed their questions, mostly deferentially, but he was amazed that the questions were being posed at all, as if the president were on trial; he understood that it had something to do with the meaning of America.

Rusi couldn't always follow the questions – he still found the accent occasionally problematic – but he understood that Rettaliata was answering the questions relating to academics and his administration, but avoiding those relating to national politics. "I cannot answer that," Rusi understood him to say, "because my politics are my own business and I cannot saddle my administration with the burden of my personal point of view." Fair enough, but the students wanted him to issue a statement for the national record for the university against the war. "I cannot speak for all the students; I cannot speak for all the staff; they cannot all be of one accord. I can speak only for myself, but that is no one's business except my own." His response deflected the question for a while, allowing once more for parleys about academic and administration policy, until someone repeated the question again, and someone else again, and someone else, and again. Finally, the embattled Dr Rettaliata issued a heated rejoinder: "I cannot speak for anyone else, but as for myself, I think President Nixon is doing a damn good job and has my full support in everything!"

Almost three quarters of the audience rose en masse and left the hall; Rusi would have stayed to see what happened next but he saw Jan pass him along the aisle and followed her out. He said nothing until he saw she was headed back to the women's dormitory. "I say, Jan," he said. "Wait up a bit, I say."

She said, "Oh, hi, Rusty," as if she were surprised, but he knew from the casual way she looked at him that she had known he'd been following her.

"My name is Rusi," he said, catching up with her.

"Sorry. Rusi."

"But you can call me Rusty if you like. I like it."

She smiled. He felt as if they knew each other well, as if she had ignored him so determinedly for two semesters that they had become a part of each other's lives.

"That was quite something, no? what happened in the Hub?"

She stopped smiling. "Yes, wasn't it? Now I have to think about changing schools."

"I say, no – not seriously."

"You heard what Rettaliata said. That's as good as a statement for the school."

"Yes, but you can't do that."

"Why not?"

"He's not worth it."

She said nothing, but looked at him closely as if she had expected him to say something else.

He shrugged as if she had backed him into a corner. "I would miss you."

She did not look at him. "But you don't even know me."

"I would miss seeing you on the campus. I would miss getting to know you. I would miss being ignored by you."

She remained silent but smiled again; her face appeared to recede into a soft focus; he stepped closer, squeezing her shoulder. "You're very pretty."

She pulled away, grinning broadly. "That doesn't mean you can mash me."

His eyes grew wide. He had made such an effort to keep from looking at her breasts. "Who was mashing? I was only saying what I think."

She laughed. "Just kidding."

He took a deep breath. "Oh, yes, my dad said Americans are great kidders. It's true."

"Tell me about your dad."

"He's dead. He died before I came here."

"Oh, I'm sorry."

"It's okay – but would you like to get a coffee in The Bog. We can talk better there."

"Seriously?"

He knew from the way she was grinning that she was kidding him again. "Seriously, you betcha your bottom dollar."

She had a funny laugh, as if she were choking, but he found it charming.

"Let me get a sweater," she said. "It's getting chilly."

"I won't budge. I'll be right here." His heart was beating, budda-budda-budda, like a machine gun; he was cold himself but didn't even think of getting a sweater, afraid he might never see her again if he missed her this time; when she returned she had brought an extra sweater for him.

"After that, Homi, I swear, things moved so fast I still can't believe it. We spent nights just talking, having coffees. Her grandparents, German Jews, were killed by Nazis; her father got lost in New York when they came; her mother lives with her older brother and his family near Gary in Indiana; he's a financial analyst which means – she said this – he gets paid even when he loses money for his clients; she doesn't like to go home, she said, because they are all so bourgeois; array, I said, he's making money, no? he's feeding his wife and kids, no? (also the mother, she said) then what is the argument? She is in liberal arts – what is she going to do for her mother? When she has no answer she turns the subject to me – why am I in computers? Array, but that is what I want. Array, she says, but I am only asking. I swear, when she uses our Indian slang like that I feel that I would do anything for her. I cannot tell her enough about India. She says biculturalism is the best thing because it armours you from the abuses of patriotism: nationalism, insularity, myopia. She is not a liberal arts major for nothing.

"She got pregnant almost right away – you know how it is, yaar, no stopping these Seervai hormones. I said we could get married or have an abortion or give the baby for adoption, whatever she wanted. She wanted to get married. I said, Are you sure? She was sure; someone in the dormitory had said 'Now she's going with Indians, soon it's gonna be blacks'; it was an asshole thing to say, but she said it had concentrated her mind beautifully; she did not want to sleep with anyone else again, not blacks, not whites, only me! I said some people wore their Americanism like a badge, but she slipped into it as easily as into a pair of blue jeans; she said some of her liberal arts was rubbing off on me.

"One development I thought was funny, actually – for a child to be born Jewish the mother must be Jewish, but with us it is the father who must be a Zoroastrian. We talked about it – no bar mitzvah for the child and no navjote, only love and a good education, and the rest will take care of itself.

"She wanted to come with me to Aquihana when we heard about you but I did not think it would be a good time. Besides, she is taking a summer class – but she can't wait to meet you my genius brother who is such a faltu chess player – and Mom. I think you'll like her; I think she might even beat you at chess – but if you slap her I swear I don't know what I will do. That was always your trouble, no resilience; you had trouble with some girl they said; you kept calling out her name, Candace; you should have written to me what you were up to; but that's all over now – you are going to be an uncle! Think about it. Why do you want to throw it away?"

I did not want to throw it away. I wanted to meet Jan. I wanted to be an uncle. I wanted to hug my beautiful brother as he sat slumped in the chair, exhaling the occasional buzzing breath of sleep – but I couldn't shake the mass of clay I had become. I shut my eyes instead, matching the rhythm of his sleep with mine, making a bridge of our breaths.

Homi

Penny

I had synchronized my breath just once before as I synchronized it now with Rusi's, on the only night I had spent with Candace – on the only night I have spent with any woman – fitted to her back, preparing to sleep; I could think of nothing more precious after the hundred and more butterfly kisses I had spent on her hair and shoulders (the first had made her giggle as if we were adolescents again after the adult business of sex, but the next had put her into a quicker sleep than I had thought possible, while I remained with unblinking eyes unwilling to sacrifice even a few of such magical moments, holding a lovely naked woman, so trustingly asleep, in my arms, until my eyes felt reptilian with the strain and I found a new comfort, tracing her breaths with mine, falling instantaneously asleep; but though I traced Rusi's breath with the same assiduity I could not get to sleep. I thought instead about Candace, about what my friend Dale Schweppenheiser might have told Rusi about her, and the room dissolved once more, focusing its new configuration on her face, her thick wavy ocherous hair spreading like the rays of the sun as I remembered it on her pillow at the Come Back Motel between Aquihana and Tunkhannock, her eyes shut so tightly that creases multiplied in their corners and her pale brows vanished amidst the furrows that etched her forehead, giving her face the selfish wanton aspect for the endless repetition of which ineffable sight I had so finely tuned the memoscan; this, then, was the moment for which I had been willing to sacrifice science, life, wisdom, on the altar of a feckless woman's vanity – but the moment was glorious and I wanted to enjoy it at least one more time, from her eyes closed but not in sleep, past the sugar and spice bump of her nose, the dark open cavern of her mouth sheltering the thick red undulating wedge

273

of her tongue, the soft round jut of her chin, the long narrow tunnel of her throat, the hard ridge of her clavicle converging over her wide flat heaving breastbone, the pale flesh and pink swollen tips of her breasts – but as I manoeuvered for a wider angle two brawny hairy arms (not mine) flanked her shoulders, two brawny hairy thighs (again, not mine) straddled hers, and her long tawny arms garlanded a thick narrow neck (as they never had mine) knotting themselves at the wrists.

A horrible sight: another man in my place, a ridge of thick black hair crawling like a giant worm from the dome of his back and shoulders, spreading like a delta over the small of his back and the paler globes of his buttocks, beneath which . . . the hard brutal work of pistons and valves, sweat running like grease, the wet slap of his heavy dark hairy balls against the soft white pads of her buttocks – but it could not be, it could not be, not only because I did not want it so but because I had no memory of such voyeurism, and without memory there is no recollection. I should have noted the differences from the start: the pillowcovers at the motel had portrayed bouquets of roses, now the covers were white; the motel had offered a bed as wide as a desert, now the bed was a thin mattress on the floor; the motel room had smelled of a lemon deodorant, now the room smelled of armpit and groin. The throbbing returned to my temples, the needles resumed their weave in my head; I had to do something to counteract the effect; I imagined the tuft of hair at the base of the intruder's spine growing fleecier, becoming a wagging wedge of tail, becoming the coarse grimy flanks of a black and white goat with spindly forelegs on her ribcage, its horned head, its yellow slitted eyes – but I couldn't shut out the rising swell of her moans, his grunts, until I found the bathroom across the untidy clothes-strewn floor, entered, locked myself in, turned on shower, taps, ventilator, and repeatedly flushed the toilet.

How could it be? An issue of *Cosmopolitan* on the bathroom floor, dated September 1971, weeks *after* I had been taken to the hospital in Aquihana, provided the answer; I was not only *not* recollecting any more, but projecting into the future – or at least into a present which, viewed from the distance of my coma, appeared to be the future. I was watching her in her bed in Aquihana from

mine in Bombay despite the separation of thousands of miles and a
time difference of ten hours (afternoon light played on her blinds;
night blacked out my windows); over the white noise provided by
the running water and air I pieced it all together. "For us," Einstein
had said, "the distinction between past, present, and future is only
an illusion, albeit a stubborn one." How can I be more specific? A
chair becomes visible when it reflects light from a source (sunlight,
electric, candle) onto the retina of an eye; if the eye could follow the
rays of light reflected from the chair faster than the speed of light it
would see the chair *before* it appeared, it would see the chair in time
as if time were a fourth dimension – but this is nonsense because the
speed of light is absolute, impossible to exceed, barely possible to
approach; the traveller, approaching this velocity, 186,000 miles per
second, finds space contracted, time expanded, and achieving this
velocity (a hypothetical situation at best), space and time collapsed
into one, no more the geography of here and there, the history of
now and then; the traveller is everywhere, always; ironically, one
achieves this velocity only to find there is nowhere to go; one is
constantly wherever one wants to be. This absolute state might be
compared to the ocean of which Bapaiji had spoken in which a drop
of water becomes not lost in the ocean but the ocean itself – or to
the collective unconscious, the repository for the record of the
universe, resident in all sentient beings, adjunct of individual
memory, into which I had unwittingly tapped when I had probed
the vault of my own memory, stranding myself in limbo between the
absolute and the commonplace, the metaphysical and the physical,
in which diffuse state I could drop in at will on the unsuspecting
universe.

Her moans were becoming perceptible again, rising gradually,
rhythmically, to a crescendo, until she was screaming how much she
loved it (it, not him), and he was shouting so that all Aquihana
might hear, calling her a slut, a cunt, the best goddam fuck in the
world, as if he were complimenting her. How pallid my feathery I
Love Yous must have sounded in contrast. The weave tightened in
my head, I climbed into the shower, drew the curtain, and turned
the water to cold.

How long I waited I cannot say, but it seemed no more than a few minutes before she, still naked, came smiling into the bathroom, stoppered the bathtub, and started the water. None of my machinations (the closed bathroom door, the running air and water, the drawn shower curtain) was evident to her; we were together but our distances from each other were relative – I was halfway around the world from her, she was halfway across the room from me. I withdrew the shower curtain, stepped out of the tub, turned off the taps. The goat who had been her lover had left, hurriedly it seemed (a large dirty white crumpled handkerchief still lay on the floor), as if he were sure enough of his plumbing not to indulge in the softer, less lubricious kisses of afterlove (my afterlovemaking had taken even longer than my lovemaking, even excluding the time she had fallen asleep), as if anything more than the stark brutal friction he had provided were pretentious, apologetic, unmanly, and she, so summarily accommodating his churlishness, appeared to be rebuking the ardour I had shown in my time. An additional, less subtle rebuke awaited me yet: next to her bath oil in the medicine cabinet stood the sandalwood elephant I had given her, faded from its wash in an Aquihana University washing machine when I had forgotten to remove it from my pants, given to me by Adi Ghadiali, Bapaiji's sweetshop sweetheart for whom Dad had been named, when our rickshaw had developed a flat in the Mota Bajar and he had plied Rusi and myself with plates and boxes of sweets which we had subsequently given to the rickshaw-wallah for his family; a white cloud appeared above her head linked to her by smaller rounder clouds like smoke signals as she picked up the elephant, revealing as if in a thought balloon in a comic strip a caricature of myself standing naked, face chagrined, left leg like a hockey stick; she laughed, threw the elephant in a waste basket under the sink, sprinkled bath oil in the water, and settled herself comfortably in the tub.

Some things remain inexplicable; where physic stops metaphysic steps in; an act of faith accomplishes what an act of will cannot. I did not think I could have concretely raised her shower lift and turned the water to hot in my phantom state, but I did, provoking a shriek from a suddenly standing Candace scrambling to turn off the water; I did not think I could have retrieved the elephant from the waste basket and tossed it on her suddenly flame-red shoulders, but I did, provoking a sonata of screams which promised delightfully never to end. I might have left her satisfactorily on that sweet cacophonous note (notes, actually), but a framed mother and daughter photograph on a worn wooden dresser, standing apart from lotions and lipsticks, caught my eye: a skinny smiling pretty girl Candace, blond curls to her shoulders, waist high to a skinny smiling plain woman in a plain calf-long dress, her hand on Candace's shoulder. Candace's head began to bob as if she were in a rowboat on the sea; her mother faded behind her into the flat wide panorama of the Breach Candy nursery school littered with the colourful baggage of preschoolers – a jungle gym cluttered with children, a pedal-powered car driven by a five-year-old, a stuffed elephant large enough to sit on, and, behind it all, the seventh class in which I was the youngest pupil by nine months (the consequence of two double promotions). Candace's bobbing head appeared to get larger, closer, laughing more loudly by the moment. "Are you scared?" she shouted. "You look scared."

It wasn't Candace, of course, but Penny Miller, whose face I remembered primarily from the photographs of my early birthday parties in which our hands were invariably linked, the daughter of an American diplomat stationed in Bombay, and a dead ringer for the girl Candace in the photograph. She was a tall girl, a year older than me; we were seated at opposite ends of a green rocking boat, she rocking it with all the strength of her plush pink limbs, I with my leg stretched forward in its brace, my knuckles white where they gripped the sides of the boat, more than a little seasick but stubbornly refusing to acknowledge my panic to my peers; according to the game we had invented whoever panicked first had to cede his seat to the next challenger; I had entered the boat with Penny because I liked her and because I didn't think any girl could outrock me even with my leg, but she was rocking the boat to an amplitude I had not believed possible, springing to her toes with each crest and slamming herself down toward each trough; I knew I would be all right as long as I kept pace with her rhythm, but she kept changing it and I was afraid she would soon either tire me out or catch me by surprise; Fatso Kapoor, who also liked Penny and wanted to get in the boat with her, edged himself in front of the crowd, shouting, "Scaredy Cat! Scaredy Cat! Homi is a scaredy cat! Homi is a cowardy custard." I bristled; Penny held the trough down a moment longer than I had anticipated; I flew like a javelin in an arc and landed on my hands. Fatso chanted, "*De-fea-ted*! *De-fea-ted*! Homi is a *wea*-kling, de*feat*ed by a *girl*." I was unhurt (compensating for my leg I sometimes showed off by falling directly forward on to my hands, braced by stretched arms stiffened at the elbows, hitting the floor with a sharp slap of my palms) but I was too dazed to retaliate – but Penny wasn't. Jumping from the boat she clenched her tiny hands and drummed her soft fists indiscriminately on Fatso's head, back, shoulders, arms, whatever he presented to defend himself, until he ran away; then, making mewling noises, she came to where I still lay on the floor and cradled me clumsily in her arms.

So it began, my first, my only love affair before I came to America; I was five, she six; we became so inseparable that by the time we graduated to the first standard in the grey-domed Walsingham House Girls School (boys under seven were admitted), originally Cutch Castle, Fatso Kapoor had perpetrated the rumour that we were married under the mistaken assumption that I would be embarrassed into relinquishing Penny. Felicitations followed: Penny, tying my shoelaces in the vast entrance hall to the school for anyone to see, while I leaned against the glass showcase which displayed an immense stuffed Bengal tiger; Penny, fighting boys, monitors, prefects, teachers, so we could sit next to each other in music class, striking instruments (her tambourine, my triangle), accompanying Mrs Somack playing "The Merry Peasant" and "The British Grenadiers" on the piano; Penny and myself, licking each other's faces on Saturday afternoons in her bedroom at the Millers' residence on Napean Sea Road (where I had my first apple pies, my first peanut butter sandwiches) because that was how Fofo, her golden cocker spaniel, showed affection... Penny, descending the schoolbus, flaxen hair flying as she turned her head for a final (too prophetic) goodbye, flashing her last big happy sweet last lover's smile before the rush across the street to meet Erica, her English speaking ayah whom she called Nanny; a screech, a thud, a scream, Miss Bean (responsible for the children on the bus) shouting, "Do not look. Nobody is to look out of the window."

How does a five year old cope with the loss of his sweetheart? He puts himself in quarantine, he lowers his resistance, he searches out toxins as if they were grail, he dreams of a reunitement (pupal angels in a Hansel and Gretel heaven). In the two years that followed I contracted mumps, jaundice, chicken pox, typhoid, two kinds of measles, three kinds of flu; I underwent a second tonsillectomy, an appendectomy; I had yet to run through cholera, smallpox, tuberculosis, and whooping cough, but something I read and someone I met so exposed the self-indulgence of my quarantine that even the most benighted eyes (mine) began to see.

I had resigned myself to a bedridden life, a diet of rice, chicken stock, and water, when I read an article, "Explorer of the Human Brain," in the July 1958 issue of *The Reader's Digest* (I remember the date because I kept the issue and took it with me to Aquihana where it must be even now among my other effects), about Dr Wilder Graves Penfield who used an electrode to probe the brains of epileptics to determine the root of their affliction. The patients were administered local anaesthetics so they could immediately report the effects of each probe. Dr Penfield successfully located the ridge of tissue which, when removed, cured or greatly improved the condition of the epileptic in seventy-five percent of the cases – more importantly (from my perspective), not only was he able to identify the areas of the brain cortex controlling toes, elbows, eyelids, etcetera, in this way, but he also established a link with memory which he postulated was stored in the temporal lobes. During one of the probes, a middleaged housewife from New Jersey exclaimed that she seemed to be giving birth to her child all over again; she proceeded to report, vividly, the sights and sounds of the delivery room as if the events were taking place again before her eyes – a young South African suddenly found himself back in a family gathering, the piano playing, his cousin telling a joke; he insisted it was happening all over again even though he knew he was with Dr Penfield in Montreal – a young woman found herself in the living room of a house in which she had lived with her family more than fifteen years ago; the march from *Aida* was playing on the phonograph; when Dr Penfield removed his probe the music stopped, when he applied it again it started again. What I understood better than anything else was that Penny was not as irrevocably lost as I had imagined; she was trapped – retrievably! – in my brain; but by that time I had already contracted a case of hydrocele, a seepage of fluid into one of my testicles until it was more than twice as large as the other, making it impossible for me to sit or walk comfortably. It was not serious, essentially a question of draining the testicle with a syringe, a stay of no more than a week in the hospital, but I had had enough of hospitals and so had Mom and Dad, so when Mary suggested a healer of whom she had heard miraculous things we chose to visit him instead.

Dad drove us out on a Sunday morning in the Ford, Mom in the front seat, Mary and myself in the back, through the city, past Byculla, Dadar, Bandra, Thana, Borivli, the most distant suburbs, until we were alone on the road (actually, a dusty cow path). Dad parked the car to one side because Mary said cars weren't allowed beyond that point. We still had about half a mile to go, but we had come prepared with a wheelbarrow since I could hardly have walked the distance on my own (my leg, my testicle); Mom, Dad, and Mary took turns pushing. It was a pleasant walk – a beach on our left, coconut trees, cool salty air (we had made an early start) – but I felt foolish sitting in the wheelbarrow and was relieved when Mary pointed to the healer's hut in the distance.

The hut was of mud, cone-shaped, thatched with palm leaves, built on a step, unicellular with two windows facing each other, a writing table with drawers in which herbs and powders were kept, a wooden chair with a cane seat to go with the table. The healer sat in a lotus position with his eyes closed in the middle of the room, ash on his face, necklaces of beads of many colours and the kernels of fruits around his neck, naked except for his dhoti, praying; his ribs showed clearly (like those of fakirs who appear too weightless to be harmed when they lie on beds of nails), but the long black hair coiled on his head, the perfect posture perfectly still, and the detached expression on his face made him appear the healthiest person in the room; we learned later he was only twenty-seven years old. He spoke with us through an intermediary.

He never opened his eyes, but when he learned of my medical history he said he couldn't help me because I did not want to be helped, I wanted to be sick; when Gautama Siddhartha, the Buddha, had witnessed old age, disease, and death, he had renounced earthly pleasures to better understand the will of God, but confronted with the death of a small girl I had sought only to escape from life. Amazed at his clairvoyance I acknowledged what had once been true, but (without going into the story of Dr Penfield's experiments) submitted it was true no longer.

The healer nodded as if he believed me, said I had gifts it would be a shame to waste, prayed for about five minutes to vanquish my demons, gave me dry leaves (everything through the intermediary; he himself barely moved) to wrap around my testicles, and told me to come back in a week.

The leaves were prickly on my testicles but I wore them stoically for the week; we returned to the hut every week for a month for more prayers and leaves by the end of which time the fluid in my testicle was vaporized and I could conduct myself normally again. When Dad broached the subject of his fee he said he would lose his powers if he accepted money for his services, but he gave Dad a list of charities to which he might donate if he felt so inclined.

One of the side benefits of my plethora of illnesses was that I lost a year of school, so that when I finally entered the Campion Boys High School I was no longer the youngest student in my class.

Corollary: Granny had a friend who lived in one of the tall buildings that had sprung up in the sixties from which we could look into the sprawling shapeless Breach Candy swimming pool, so large it had islands built into it for those who couldn't traverse its bulk in a single lap, so that it appeared more like a lake than a pool; it was always full of golden-skinned American and European women in bikinis whenever we visited Granny's friend, each of whom might have been Penny had she lived – each of whom, I sometimes imagined, *was* Penny, who had broken with me the only way she knew how, by faking her death (for a while I had even convinced myself that Hayley Mills, whom I had seen in the *The Parent Trap*, though she was some years older, was really Penny in a new life she had invented for herself).

Of course, I did not reveal my hypotheses to anyone, but I did ask Mom to find someone who might take me swimming in the pool (membership was restricted to Americans and Europeans, but Indians were allowed as guests). She suggested the CCI (Cricket Club of India) pool where we were members, but I insisted on the Breach Candy pool and she didn't argue because the doctors had said, at all costs, to encourage me for the sake of my leg, to be more physical; she asked Mr Hartley, an English business friend of Dad's, who had become a social friend after a picnic (the Seervais and the Hartleys, Arthur and Rae, their kids, Heather and Warren, both younger than Rusi and myself) at the Elephanta Caves, an island about an hour away in a boat from the Gateway of India. Mom didn't come ("I can't swim!" but actually she had a horror of appearing in a bathing costume); neither did Dad ("I do not much care to swim," but actually he was uncomfortable with Rusi and me without Mom).

The occasion was an embarrassment for everyone concerned. Indians were allowed as guests, but only in the small, rectangular, indoor pool. The Hartleys argued for us in vain, Heather and Warren complained continually about being confined to the indoor pool, Rusi refused to enter the pool (he might have been piqued but all he said, complacently enough, was "I don't feel much like swimming any more") and sat in his costume on a bench by the pool while the rest of us had our fun as determinedly as if we were executing a plan of battle. I entered the pool feeling vaguely unclean, vaguely compromised, wishing I could have been like Rusi, but feeling also vaguely responsible for the fiasco.

Penny cast a longer shadow than I had imagined, hardly peripheral, but subterranean, invisible; I was only beginning to distinguish its murky penumbral outline because it had barely appeared to touch me in the wake of my self-imposed quarantine – it had not touched me when Rusi and I raced snails named after knights of the round table (we kept snails, abundant during the monsoon, with bits of verdure in our pencil boxes), not when the Seervais holidayed at the Happy Valley Hotel perched on the brink of a deep canyon in the

Panchgani hill station and played "Swedish Rhapsody" continually on the wind-up gramophone because it was the only record available and seemed to enhance the view, not when Mom and Dad took Rusi and myself to cottages they had rented for weekends alongside Juhu Beach with their bridge partners, the Jairazbhoys, their daughter Nishat, their son Quasamali (the winnings went into a common pot until they became substantial enough, perhaps once or twice a year), not when the surprise earthquake of 1960 threw me out of bed and made me dance on the floor, but inflicted more inconvenience than damage on its victims (Bapaiji's commode was broken), not when the air raid siren sounded during a Geometry examination during the Indo-Pakistan miniwar of 1965 and Mr Brown warned us not to rush to the basement shelters as we had previously been instructed, but to continue with the examination, not when the 43rd East Bombay Scouts camped annually at Madh Island, each of its three troops ranged in a semicircle of tents for ten days at a time, not when my best friend Vijay and I took long walks or faked our way with deep voices and phony moustaches into adult movies (*Girl Happy* and *Goldfinger*) – but appeared to affect me increasingly, though always subtly, after I arrived in Aquihana, Pennsylvania.

Aquihana

Dad praised me because my hair was never freaky like Rusi's, my clothes never psychedelic, my friends never loud, my teachers always glowing, my behaviour always exemplary, my appearance always immaculate. My differences with Dad were more subtle than Rusi's, manifesting themselves in ways I could not explain: I resented the resemblance I bore him – particularly in the early photographs taken in Edinburgh and London, the handsome, glabrous, smiling face in glengarry, balmoral, top hat, trilby, derby, and deerstalker, the wide jaw (Bapaiji's legacy) with the narrower chin which, before it inclined toward flab, might have been shaped by the bottom of a tea cup – as if I couldn't help being his son, but he had usurped my father's place; he took credit for my scholastic accolades as if I were a prize tomato he had cultivated, as if he robbed from the meaning of my life to give meaning to his, as if I were first his trophy and only incidentally his son, as if he had chosen finally to forgive me for the sickly boy I had been instead of the son he had deserved. He wanted me to attend the University of Edinburgh where he was an alumnus, but the university provided no scholarships for foreign students who were required to pay triple the regular tuition fee. His next choice was Harvard; modesty counsels against full disclosure, but I was offered a full scholarship, a grant to cover all expenses, and eighty hours of credit on the strength of my college boards and the Bachelor of Science degree from Bombay's St Xavier's College (Princeton and Yale among others offered variations of the same enticements) – but for the first and only time (he died shortly after I left) my resentment became concrete. I went through the College Handbook from A to Z looking for universities with high accreditation, higher ratios of women to men, of which Dad had never heard;

284

Aquihana University, among the As, was the first to accept me, the one I accepted.

Aquihana University was an institution on the make; I would have been admitted with a muddier record than the one I presented – though, to be fair to the institution, this says more about me than about its requirements; the administration wanted to develop an international reputation and amply compensated for its lack of prestige with its excess of attention to foreign students, trying to accommodate them into the homes of Pennsylvanian students, particularly during holidays, so they might feel less like strangers. I was met at JFK Airport in New York by Dale Schweppenheiser who had volunteered to be my official big brother. I had been afraid he might have found me too unhip for America but his hair (uncombed, but short), his clothes (not like Rusi's), and his grin reassured me from the beginning. "Hi, Hommy," he said, as if we had met before. "You look just like your photograph."

I had sent him a photograph but I was sensitive enough, even then, to think he had recognized me by my barely perceptible limp. "Hello," I said, extending my hand. "How do you do? Are you Dale?"

"At your service, Brother Hommy. How was the flight?" He took my hand in both of his.

Later I understood he called me "Brother" because he was a Jesus freak and I was his brother in Christ, but at the time I thought he was speaking as a member of the university's Big Brother program. "A little long," I said, "but comfortable – except for that delay at the end. I think we must have circled the airport for almost three hours."

"I know, Brother Hommy. I've been waiting while you've been circling."

There was no reproach in his tone, not even impatience; he looked so glad to see me I felt suddenly unworthy. "My name is Homi," I said, "like in Hoe-Me – Homey."

"I'm sorry. Homey, Homey. I won't forget. I couldn't tell from the way it was written."

"It's okay."

"We should get moving. There's going to be a lot of traffic getting out."

He insisted on carrying both my suitcases, leaving me with only the overnight bag I had carried on to the plane. "You've come a long way," he said when I protested, "all the way from India. Let me take over. You're my guest now."

There was a disturbance ahead of us. A large man took a wild swing at a considerably smaller man and hit him in the face. The smaller man fell, scampering feverishly from his attacker, and ran toward us. I heard him blubbering, muttering obscenities, threats, holding a dirty white handkerchief to soak the blood from his mouth as he passed by us. I was too shocked to move, never having seen a grown man actually hit another so hard at such close quarters, until Dale nudged me. "I'm sorry you had to see that, Brother Homi," he said. "New York is an ugly place, hardly the best introduction to America. I hope you will suspend your judgment until we reach Pennsylvania. I know you're going to love ol' Ow."

"Ow? What is Ow?"

"A-U, Aquihana University, better known as Ow."

It was after three o'clock in the morning; for the next thirty minutes we found ourselves in lanes which moved as if the cars had locked bumpers. I was still excited about seeing New York as the traffic thinned when a cabbie cut in front of us, shaking his fist at Dale, threatening to knock his head off. Dale slowed down, waved him on, flashed a peace symbol, and said, "Sorry, Brother." There was a sticker on the cabbie's bumper: God Loves Single People. "What is the matter with everybody?" I said. "Why are they all so angry?"

Dale shrugged. "It's just New Yorkers. They don't mean any harm."

"Array? Not mean any harm? That fellow hit the other fellow at the airport. He was bleeding. I saw him. What do you mean they don't mean any harm?"

Dale kept his eyes on the road; whatever I thought of New Yorkers, I liked him; he seemed solid; I was glad to be with him. "It's the overcrowding," he said. "People get touchy when their space is invaded. They're very jealous of their space here."

"Array? Bombay is overcrowded. There are not people like this in Bombay."

He shrugged again, as if in apology, as if to say for some questions there were no answers – then, to change the subject, he said, "What was that you said earlier? a word, you used it twice."

"What word?"

"A-ray – something like that."

"Array – you mean Array?" I laughed, remembering a time when Mr Hartley, Mom and Dad's friend who had taken us to the Breach Candy swimming pool, had remarked at a party that sometimes he felt as if the conversations in the room went into a tunnel, when the speakers lapsed momentarily, even midsentence, into Gujarati or Hindi.

Dale smiled, no doubt amused by my amusement. "Yes, that's the one. What is A-ray?"

I told him about Mr Hartley's observation first so he wouldn't think I had been laughing at him. "It's a portmanteau word," I explained then. "It can mean you are surprised or disappointed or impatient, even angry, depending on the context – a little bit like saying Well, or Good God, or No Kidding, or something like that."

"Ah!" After a brief silence he said, "You can sleep if you want. We have a long drive ahead."

"No, no, no. I want to see everything. Who knows when I will come back to New York."

"We can come back sometime for a weekend if you like. You must be tired. You can lean your seat back if you want."

"Thanks – but still."

I gazed at everything indiscriminately, spinning my head like a top, hardly daring to blink, afraid I might miss something. Dale apologized for not being a better guide, but he was a country boy and avoided cities, New York particularly, as far as he could help it. 'I feel unsafe here," he said, "as if everyone is a doberman pulling on a leash and I never know when it's going to snap."

I understood his feeling; phrases such as "asphalt desert" and "concrete jungle" came readily to mind. "There are no trees," I said as we passed through Manhattan. "It would help if there were trees."

"Right on, Brother Homi. Right on! Just wait till we get to the country."

I tried to imagine the banyan tree from the Back Gardens behind Mayo House on Cooperage Road in Bombay, its peeling bark, its leathery vines, its welcoming niches, its network of intertwined roots fanning away from it into the earth, rerooted at one of the New York City intersections when we stopped for a light, but the scale was so overpoweringly disproportionate that the great old banyan appeared to shrink into the shining black macadam; I could more easily imagine King Kong atop the Empire State, even (ghastly sight) squads of Tyrannoasauri Rex marching down the avenue around the corner and squadrons of pterodactyls swooping down on us from behind.

I must have been tireder than I thought because the next thing I knew we were on a mountain road by a valley carpeted (so it seemed in the distance) with trees and tiny creeks and waterfalls glittering in the sun. I was too astonished to do anything but stare until Dale spoke. "Good morning, Brother Homi. Welcome to Pennsylvania."

Nothing seemed real; my life in Bombay culminating with the festive sendoff at Santa Cruz Airport (a party of thirty, a coconut broken for good luck, garlands of marigolds), seemed like a dream, my brief passage through New York a nightmare, the alternating alpine vistas from the car, as if veils were being removed with each bend in the road, like shimmering visions – but this, finally, was America! I had not thought I would ever actually get there. "Good morning," I said, feeling a flush as if I might have been beaming.

Dale kept his eyes on the road. "For someone who wanted to see everything you sure slept a lot," he said.

I thought I might have offended him but he was grinning. I shrugged in explanation. "This looks like Daniel Boone country," I said, "all these trees like big Christmas trees."

He held his head high as if he might have created the trees himself. "Actually, you're not far wrong. Daniel Boone was born around here, near Reading, but then he moved on to Kentucky and Missouri."

Dale named some of the trees – walnuts, cedars, chestnuts, poplars, pines, oaks, elms – as we passed them; I identified Indian trees by their characteristics for him, mangoes by their long narrow leaves and pulpy fruit, peepuls by their heartshaped leaves, banyans by their roots and vines, tamarinds by their pods; the most evident difference between his trees and mine was size – everything in America was larger, even the squirrels were fatter, bushier, as large as rabbits in India.

A blue Volkswagen appeared ahead of us, puttering so slowly that we had barely seen it than Dale had caught up with it. I didn't understand why Dale began honking (there was room enough to pass the Volkswagen with ease) until he told me to read its bumper sticker: Honk If You Love Jesus. I became newly aware of the white cloudshaped sticker on Dale's dashboard which said Jesus Saves in red toy letters. "Jesus loves you, Brother," Dale shouted as he passed the Volkswagen. The man in the car, with a beard like a leprechaun's, removed a pipe from his mouth. "He loves you, too, Brother," he said in a deep voice.

"That was nice," I said as we pulled away from the Volkswagen, "much nicer than New York."

Dale laughed. "This is Pennsylvania, Brother Homi," he said, "the land of universal brotherhood."

I nodded slowly, smiling.

"Tell me, Brother Homi," Dale said, his eyes narrowing on the road ahead. "Are you saved?"

I gave him a blank look. "Saved? from what?"

"Have you accepted Jesus? Have you given yourself to Jesus?"

"You mean, like a Christian?"

"Yes, like all true Christians."

"No, no, no, I am not a Christian – true or false. I was born a Parsi. My religion is Zoroastrianism – but I am not devout. I believe in God, but not too much in any one religion."

Dale's eyes grew brighter as if I had suddenly opened a window. He had heard of Zoroaster, older than all the prophets (so some theologians argued) of the Old Testament, and of his religion which (so the same theologians argued) had influenced Judaism, and, consequently, Christianity, and, indirectly, even Islam. I wasn't surprised that Dale had heard of Zoroastrianism, but I should have been; when the subject arose on subsequent occasions; most Americans thought only of a black hatted, black caped, black garbed figure from a previous century in California who had brandished a sword and whip, but Dale wanted to be a theologian and was able to tell me things even I didn't know, that the Wise Men who came from the East were Magians (Zoroastrian priests), that they had come in accordance with one of Zoroaster's prophecies, that Nietzsche had chosen Zarathustra (the prophet's true name, later westernized by the Greeks to Zoroaster) to expound his own philosophy in *Thus Spake Zarathustra* because (so Nietzsche argued) only Zarathustra, being the first prophet to enumerate the laws of good and evil, had the right to revise them with impunity (and revise them Nietzsche did until they bore no resemblance to the originals), that the Jews had been influenced by the Zoroastrians for over two hundred years (from 597 to 331 BC, first as exiles in Persia during the Babylonian occupation, then as subjects of the Persians after Cyrus the Great vanquished the Babylonians and allowed the Jews to return to their homeland) to incorporate such concepts as Satan, a Saviour, heaven and hell, the host of heaven, the last judgment, the resurrection, free choice, and the immortal soul – concepts absent from the texts of the pre-exilic Jews.

My contribution to our conversation was more literary (Mom's influence): Fedallah, Ahab's harpooner in *Moby Dick*, is a Parsi, though Melville, interested more in exotics than Parsis, might as easily have chosen a Bantu or a fakir for all his knowledge of Parsis (Joyce was more scholarly in his reference to the Towers of Silence in *Ulysses*); and social: Zubin Mehta, the conductor, and Persis Khambata, the model and actress (Dale had heard of neither), were Parsis.

A voice sounded, as if from Rusi, as he continued to lie slumped in the chair by my bedside, but it was no longer his voice; it was deeper, more resonant than any of the voices I had yet heard – but even that is not strictly true since I wasn't hearing voices in the conventional sense as much as sensing them. I was too distracted at first by the intonation to listen to the words, but I soon recognized the Yatha Ahu Vairyo prayer:

Yatha ahu vairyo atha ratush, ashatchit hacha, vangheush dazda manangho shyaothananam angheush mazdai. Khshathremcha Ahurai a yim drigubyo dadat vastarem.

They are blessed who follow the Truth for they are loved by Ahura Mazda. They are blessed who work not for themselves because they work for Ahura Mazda. They are blessed who give to the poor because they know the will of Ahura Mazda.

It was the prayer with which Ahura Mazda, also known as Ormazd, the Wise Lord, had hurled Angra Mainyu, also known as Ahriman, the Demon of the Lie, back into the darkness from which he had emerged at the end of the first of the four periods of three thousand years each, of the twelve thousand years which spanned the history of the world. Bapaiji had recounted the cosmogony to me. It was not until the end of the first quarter that Angra Mainyu had discovered the light, and rushed to annihilate it only to be repulsed himself. During the second quarter Ahura Mazda had created the sky, the water, the earth, the plants, the primal beast, and the primal man in that order. During the third quarter, Angra Mainyu, recovering from his confusion, had sprung like a snake through the vault of heaven, shattered the order of the planets, polluted the water, filled the earth with serpents, scorpions, lizards, and toads, poisoned the plants, and brought illness unto death to the primal beast (a bull) and to the primal man (named Gayomard) – but plants grew once more by Ahura Mazda's decree from the marrow of the bull, from its semen appeared more fish, birds, and animals, from Gayomard's members came the metals of the earth, and from his semen, Mashya and Mashyoi, the parents of humankind. The battle was joined between the two forces until the end of the third quarter when Zarathustra was born.

I tried to visualize the events more fully, but all I could see was a brilliant white ball of light, yellowing and reddening toward the edges like the sun, with a play of flashing figures within, accompanying the narrative which I gradually realized was Bapaiji's (I was still not accustomed to her new deep intonation). "Do not ask too much, Homi," she said as she became aware of my frustration with the indistinct images. "Some things even the dead cannot show you. Maybe my next death will make things clearer. Maybe after you perfect your memo-machine you will find out the truth for all of us. We cannot even be sure of the date of Zarathustra's birth. Scholars have said it might have been any time between 6000 and 600 BC — but if one is to believe the story of the four periods of three thousand years then he could not have been born much before 1000 BC because at the end of the fourth three thousand years Ahura Mazda is to triumph irrefutably over Angra Mainyu, and that has not happened yet. We know that he was born in western Iran, perhaps in Azerbaijan, perhaps Rayy, perhaps Shiz, perhaps somewhere else, to Porushaspa and Dughdova; we know of his miracles, of his ten year pilgrimage in the Elburz Mountains during which he was tempted by Angra Mainyu with palaces of gold and the kingdom of the world, and of his struggles to bring the revealed word of Ahura Mazda to the world — but perhaps the more relevant of these details, apart from his teachings, relates to his posthumous sons. Zarathustra had taken a wife, Hvovi, and fathered three sons and three daughters, but on three other occasions his seed had been sown through Hvovi and into the ground, to bear three sons through three virgins at thousand year intervals during the fourth and last period of three thousand years, Ukhshyat-ereta, Ukhshyat-nemangh, and the last, Astvat-ereta, the Saoshyant, the final Saviour, to be born fifty-seven years before the end of the twelve thousand years."

Dale's brother Broderick worked nights cleaning up at a cannery. He usually drove to work, but since Dale had needed the car to pick me up he was going to pick Broderick up that morning after driving me home to their farm in Watsonburg. When he realized how late my flight was going to be he had called home to say he would pick up Broderick before coming home. "I hope you don't mind," he said. "I know how tired you must be."

"Not at all," I said. "I'm enjoying the drive. Besides, I am in America. You who have always lived in America do not know what that means."

"What does it mean?"

"It is everybody's dream to come to America. I cannot explain it. Your daily life is my dream come true."

"Well," he said, grinning. "I'm very happy to be here too."

I felt comfortable enough with Dale already just to remain silent. "Sugar, Sugar" was on the radio, and "Honky Tonk Women", "Get Back", "In the Year 2525", "Bad Moon Rising", "Aquarius", all of which I continue to associate with my arrival in America. The road became less mountainous; covered wooden bridges spanned (not rivers, not brooks, not springs, Dale insisted, but) creeks; we passed fields of corn, pumpkins, strawberries, rows of crysanthemums by Joe Steiner's Flower Farm, cows, orchards, bee hives, log houses, stone houses, barns larger than the houses with stone ends and overhangs and dutch doors, post and rail fences neatly lining their roads, hickories, gumwoods, ashes, beeches, and more, purple fox-grapes with asters and goldenrod (Dale appeared to know every tree, every flower; it came from growing up on the farm), a grouse drumming in sunlight on a log in shades of brown and yellow and grey; right off the wood path there would be deer, wild cat, sable, weasel, mink, raccoon (I looked, but in vain), and, less than a hundred miles away in the Poconos, bear and beaver; I followed Dale's road map noting names I might otherwise have found too strange for America (King of Prussia, Bird in Hand, State College), and others, beautiful (Susquehana, Shenandoah, Catawissa), known (Philadelphia, Pittsburgh, Bethlehem), conventional (Danville, Bloomsburg, Sunberry) and, of course, Watsonburg, where Dale lived, which we bypassed on our way to pick up Broderick from the Hanover Cannery.

Broderick was waiting for us by an open door in the side of the factory. "What took you so long?" he yelled when he saw us. He was taller than Dale, stouter, his hair much longer, more tousled, his arms more corded with muscle.

"The flight was late," Dale yelled back. "I called Ma to say we'd pick you up first. Come on. Get in."

Broderick didn't act as impatiently as he spoke. He looked unhurriedly into the window from Dale's side. "So this is Hommy – finally. How's it going, Hommy? I'm Broderick."

He extended his hand through the window so that Dale had to lean back. I shook it lightly because he was still shouting and because

I didn't want to discomfort Dale longer than I could help. "Okay," I said. "How do you do? Hello. I'm fine."

"His name's *Homey*, not Hommy," Dale said. "We got it wrong. Brother Homi, this is Brother Broderick – Bro Brod, as we call him in these parts."

They were still shouting. It was the American way, as I was soon to realize, to shout, to be direct, the consequence perhaps of the spaciousness of America compared to India, the sparsity of its population, but at the time it made me uneasy. "Hello," I said again. "I'm very pleased to meet you."

"*Homey*," Broderick said as if he'd just thought of something. "That's much better. Hommy made me think of hominy." He shuddered making a face. "They were canning hominy – that's corn – yesterday. I've been hosing down those machines all night. You have to reach into the machinery sometimes to pull out the husks and kernels that don't get flushed out. They're warm and wet and soft – like dead rats. Ugh!"

"We call it maize," I said, unsure whether he wanted to provoke sympathy of shock, "what you call corn."

"Let's go, Bro," Dale said. "We can talk along the way."

Broderick got in the back. "Today it's potatoes. That's not so bad. They don't have husks and kernels, just skin."

I saw a large grey woman through the side door sitting on a low grey stool with a knife in her hand gazing expressionlessly at a hill of potatoes as if she herself, her doughy grey head and body, were no more than a large potato. The image she presented was anomalous, nothing like the Rockwell interiors I had anticipated, particularly in the wake of the Pennsylvania I had witnessed that morning, but I soon forgot about it. "Excuse the smell," Broderick was saying. "We have to wear these rubber hats, boots, everything in rubber, so we don't get wet hosing down the machines, but then we sweat like pigs all night."

"And smell like pigs all day," Dale shot back, ducking and chuckling as Broderick clouted him from behind. I had noticed the smell but had not wanted to say anything about it. "It's quite all right," I said. "It doesn't bother me."

My formality was unnecessary, but unfamiliar with Americanisms it was the only way I knew to respond, particularly since the slang with which I was so comfortable had recently been rendered irrevocably meaningless. Broderick smelled, even after he had showered, but it didn't bother me; there was a smell of dried dung from the distance in the house, but that only reminded me of Bapaiji's house; my room was the third floor landing, with a draft and a noticeable incline from the back to the front, but the floor tilted just enough to invite a tumble into the bed, and the bed was so neatly made alongside the far wall, with barely enough room to sit without bumping into the low sloping roof beams, and the low dresser so neatly laden with towels, that even the musty space looked cozy and I wanted only to ingratiate myself with my hosts. Mrs Schweppenheiser hovered like a hen; I might sleep if I wished, I might shower, or I might partake of the breakfast she had prepared. Neither she nor Mr Schweppenheiser could keep from smiling but he remained laconic through the introductions merely nodding his head when he shook my hand. "I think I'd like a bath first," I said, "and then breakfast sounds wonderful."

The breakfast table, covered by a gay table cloth, filled the entire kitchen. I lost track of the number of cats and dogs that slunk continually from room to room. The farm was actually on the outskirts of Watsonburg and the wide kitchen window revealed trees and rolling meadows (no houses) lit by the sun and birds unlike any I had seen before. "It appears so wild around here," I said, spotting what I later learned was a goshawk, "so . . . like a frontier."

"Thet it is," Mr Schweppenheiser said. "We're always on the lookout fer weasels and possums in the henhouse. If they git in there they just bite their heads off, the hens' heads. Whut d'you think o' thet?"

It was the first thing he had said to me and he looked expectant as if he were afraid his effort might have been wasted. "My goodness," I said, and then, wishing I had not been so feeble, "No kidding."

He made a sound deep in his throat as if he might have been laughing. "No kiddin, nossir. Jes las month I surprised a possum early in the mornin in the henhouse. He got away but I had to pick up them chickens, no heads and blood all around. Whut d'you think o' thet?"

"Sounds pretty wild," I said, uncomfortable with his attention.

"Now, then," Mrs Schweppenheiser said, "not at the table, Father. Let the boy eat." She smiled, staring at a plate of bacon.

"Jus lettin him know, Mother. Jus lettin him know. He asked."

There were eggs, milk, pancakes, waffles, toast, butter, jelly, bacon, pork chops, potatoes, tomatoes, onions, corn on the cob, strawberry shortcake, two kinds of pie (apple and peach), and cream. "Everythin you see," Mr Schweppenheiser said, "was grown on the farm. You name it, I grown it – milk's from the cow, the Missus made the butter, and the pork's whut it is cause it's cornfed. I bled the pig myself, strung 'im up and slit 'is throat, and grew the corn that fattened 'im too. Whut d'you think o' thet?"

I was impressed but Mr Schweppenheiser continued to look at me so expectantly that I couldn't think of anything to say. "They have servants, Pa," Dale said. "Why should he think anything of this?"

"Servants!" He made the sound in his throat again as if he might have been laughing. "Whut good are servants? They only make you idle and you know whut they say about an idle mind, don' you?"

"He's right," I said, cutting into Dale's response. "If we didn't have servants we'd learn to do a lot more for ourselves."

Mr Schweppenheiser had never stopped smiling, but now his eyes lit up as if he had scored a victory and he made the sound in his throat again. After that he said nothing again but continued smiling as if he'd made a point.

Mrs Schweppenheiser said nothing except to urge me to more helpings of everything. "You're a growing lad," she said, beaming into the shortcake she passed me once more. "You've got to eat. That's real shortcake – not your shortbread or your sodabread, not your sponge cake neither. It's richer. I put in three more egg yolks, and a half cup more sugar and milk."

"It's delicious," I said, taking everything she offered me as much for the food as for the pleasure I derived from watching her pleasure.

After breakfast I slept away my jet lag for the rest of the day, not even getting up when Mrs Schweppenheiser rang the bell for dinner.

On Sunday afternoon Mr Schweppenheiser took me to the fire station to show me off. "He got polio – an' he's from Hindia, Bhombhay, land of the Zorroers. Whut d'you think o' thet?"

There were no regular firemen but the men of Watsonburg rotated shifts voluntarily for fire duty; no one was on duty more than three times a year, but the fire station had become a kind of men's club; there was always a group at cards or billiards (pool, as I learnt to call it) or draughts (checkers). I entertained them by writing their names in Hindi, and, when someone produced a mouth organ, by playing "Your Cheatin' Heart", "Sixteen Tons", "Swannee River", "Spanish Eyes", "Beautiful Dreamer", "Danny Boy", and "De Camptown Racetrack" among others. All those years of getting up early for my Tuesday morning lessons, of practising for Mom's interminable musical evenings, finally paid off. "Even in Hindia," Mr Schweppenheiser said, "whut you got? American culture."

I spent ten days with the Schweppenheisers before leaving, with Dale and Broderick, for Aquihana, hardly enough time to exhaust the resources of the Pennsylvania backroads, but I was too impatient to get on with my life in America; besides, a city boy, even one from Bombay, can only drive down so many country roads, visit so many fast food stops, make so many late night spam sandwiches (Dale's favourite: Wonderbread, Miracle Whip, spam sliced and fried in a sugar solution till the water boiled away leaving the spam sweet and crisp), before he misses the urban life; I helped milk cows, mend fences, collect eggs in the hen house (just once; the smell was too much). I wasn't sorry to leave the Schweppenheisers because I would be seeing them again in less than three months for Thanksgiving.

The panorama didn't change from Watsonburg to Aquihana; even the towns were much alike, each with a Main Street, barber shop, movie house, United States Post Office (flag over the entrance), library, hardware store, grocery store, Woolworth's, and stuccoed office buildings; the side streets were wide with elms and double-storeyed frame houses with great cool awning-shaded porches; each had also a schoolhouse, clinic, court house, and fire station; Aquihana had a longer Main Street than Watsonburg (fifteen blocks to six) and, additionally, a hospital with a research laboratory and, of course, the university.

It was a four-hour drive to Aquihana; Dale drove since Broderick would be taking the car home by himself. He pointed to the university's administration building, Carter Hall, where the president had his office, as soon as it was visible, at the top of the hill leading from Main Street, a structure of rose-coloured brick with a four-columned portico and clock tower, shadowed by elms. Behind the hill the rest of the university sprang into view, but before we got there Dale stopped the car and honked. "Yo, Candy!"

He was looking at a blond girl walking along the sidewalk across the street from us toward Main Street. Broderick nudged me from the back seat. "It's the slut," he said, but he wasn't even looking at me; his eyes were like flames and he was grinning, leering actually, at the girl.

What registered? A blond girl, a woman actually (she was older than Dale) but I was too inexperienced myself to think of her as a woman – besides, her face was fat like a child's when she smiled, and her eyes shy and roving when she talked. Did I see vestiges of my own lost child darling Penny in her even then? Was unconscious memory so much a master of one's will? All I knew for certain was the hush I felt as when one enters a place of worship or recognizes a moment of destiny.

What else? A white dress, the miniest of miniskirts, the most golden limbs, a bright tender mouth cleft with a hint of cruelty, a foreshadowing perhaps of madness behind the hallowed façade, or, more simply, a defence against the world.

"Oh," she said, stopping momentarily, waving, "Hi, Schwep," before walking on.

Dale got out of the car. "Wait, yo, Candy. I want you to meet some folks."

Inside the car, still leering, Broderick spoke sibilantly. "Yess, yess, yess, yess, yess."

I didn't think Candace would turn around, but when Dale began running after her she chose to meet him halfway and walked back to the car with him.

"This is my brother, Broderick, Bro-Brod. I told you about him" (she nodded; Broderick remained crouched, leering, openmouthed, speechless in the back seat) "and this is Homi. He's from Bombay, in India. He speaks Hindi, plays the mouth organ, and he's a bona fide genius. I'm to be his big brother. Folks," (looking at us), "this is Candace Kirchner."

Candace seemed to affect everyone's balance. I might have found Dale patronizing but I found myself wanting to impress Candace myself and was happy to let Dale do it for me. "Hullo," I said, and, unable to choose among the greetings I had brought with me and the new ones I had learned, "How do you do? How is it going? I'm fine. How are you doing?"

She smiled – it seemed especially for me. "Nice meeting everyone," she said, "but I have to be going."

"Ciao," Dale said. I nodded, wishing I had grown the moustache that Mom had talked me out of the year before. Broderick remained frozen in his stance like a lizard. No one said anything until Dale got in the car again and revved the throttle. Broderick spoke then as if the sound of the throttle had broken a spell. "Va-va-va-Voom! All right, Dale babay, brother mine, All Right! She can work my mojo anay-time!"

Dale responded sheepishly, keeping his eyes determinedly on the road. "She's a charming girl – a little lost, but quite charming."

"Charming! Yes, charming!" Broderick hooted. "If she was any more charming she'd be the whore of Babylon. Tell him about the celebration, Brother Dale. Tell Brother Home about the celebration."

There was a ministry on campus called the Community of the Spirit which held celebrations (informal services) every Tuesday evening in the minister's living room where the communicants sat in a circle on the floor, passed around bread and wine, and sang hymns and songs some of which had been written by the minister, Jay Rochelle, himself, who also strummed a guitar accompaniment. On the one occasion when Dale had persuaded Candace to attend she had passed around a joint after the bread and wine; Jay had either pretended not to notice or let it pass good naturedly as something that would not recur. "She was just having fun," Dale said. "We were all just having some fun."

The long ride seemed to have gotten to Broderick. He was rocking gleefully in the back seat. "She was just having fun," he said, mimicking Dale. "Come on, Brother Dale. She's a slut. She puts out. Tell Brother Home what she does for a living."

I did not expect Dale to answer but he seemed as fascinated with Candace's life as Broderick. "She's a bar maid at the Inn Different. She's real popular down there."

"Yeah! Real popular! What else? What else?" Broderick shook Dale's shoulder from behind.

"She's a model. She poses for the art classes on campus sometimes."

"Without a stitch! Without a goddam stitch! In front of the whole goddam class! In broad daylight! Oo-Whee! Tell him, Brother Dale. Tell Brother Home what else."

"What else? What else is there to tell?"

"About how she lives with her boyfriend, about how she sleeps around, about how he always takes her back."

"Well, Bro-Brod, I don't know about that. That's all hearsay."

"Where there's smoke there's fire, Brother Dale. Where there's smoke there's fire."

Dale seemed to be getting tired of the exchange. "You know what it says in the Good Book, Bro-Brod. Let he who is without sin . . ."

"Cast the first stone. Come *on*, Brother Dale. I don't want to cast stones. I want to be her acolyte."

Neither Dale nor I responded, not to his words, not to the thunderous laugh that followed, and Broderick soon subsided, as silent as he had been noisy before. His girlfriend of two years had married a virtual stranger just that spring. He had decided to drop out of school and work until he was more sure of what he wanted to do. Dale said he was actually better off without the Wagner Girl but Broderick, whatever he said, was yet to be convinced himself.

"Would you like to come to our Community of the Spirit sometime?" Dale asked. "I think you might like it."

"You don't have to be a Christian?"

"Everyone is welcome."

"Yes, maybe, if you don't have to be a Christian."

Manasni, Gavasni, Kunasni

It was the privilege of foreign students (all six of us) to be treated like dignitaries at Ow. During my first summer the administration even scheduled a class just for my convenience so that I might graduate at the end of my second year — not preferential treatment, they said, merely their way of expressing appreciation for their finest student ever, confirming my notion that I had chosen the right university after all (would Harvard have been so accommodating? even to Einstein? and I was hardly that). On Tuesday evenings I attended celebrations at the Community of the Spirit, on Thursdays folk dances organized by the philosophy department, and on Saturdays either a dance or a movie or something else (body painting, folk singing, poetry reading) at the Onion (the Student Union). I was too self-conscious to ask anyone (girls) to any of the occasions, but I got my message across to Julie Clooney, at the Community of the Spirit, by losing count of the number of times I hugged her, ostensibly to celebrate the Kiss of Peace during the service, less ostensibly because the pressure of her large soft chest against mine filled me with a more profound peace than the service was otherwise able to provide. She felt sorry for me (Dad had died), took me to a Carroll's outside Aquihana for dinner (she had her own car), and gave me my first goodnight kiss, a barren brushing of lips, which nevertheless awakened the sleeping monster of my flesh.

What is there to say about Julie? She was tall, sensitive about it, wore flat shoes, walked with a crouch, liked me, leaned against me a lot, had the chest, a receding chin, long wavy chestnut hair, wanted to be a teacher, was a devout Christian, had a car, liked me, let me kiss her, let me touch her breasts (never uncovered), took me home to meet her parents for Christmas, they liked me, I liked them, they were devout Christians too but asked me questions about Zoroastrianism.

What about me? I wanted Candace but could never think of anything to say to her besides "Hullo. How are you? How do you do? I am fine. How is it going?" She never offered conversation herself, and after a while I felt so awkward in her presence that I avoided her when I saw her coming and, if I were too late to avoid her, ignored her as if I hadn't seen her. Candace lured me like an open sky but Julie was my safety net; she talked when I had nothing to say because it made us both more comfortable even when she knew I wasn't listening. Candace never ceased to affect me when I saw her but she ceased to be important; she even became a catalyst once between Julie and myself when we passed by her on Willow Street on our way to Angus (known for the best steak and service in Aquihana) where Julie was taking me to dinner for my birthday. I went through my customary barrage of greetings; Candace barely smiled; Julie looked at me curiously. "I didn't know you knew her."

"I don't, not really, only hardly, a little bit." I told her how Dale had introduced us.

"Leave her alone," Julie said. "She's no good."

I was surprised that she was so presumptuous. "Dale said she was a little lost. He wanted to help her. I thought I should be friendly."

Julie had attended the celebration to which Dale had brought Candace. "If Dale thinks he can help her he's a little lost himself. She's a . . . she's not good, and he knows it."

It was the hour following twilight; the dim distant street lamps cast lush conflicting shadows behind the elms; there was no sound but the champ-champ-champ of our footsteps in relief against the rustle of the trees; Candace had faded in the semidarkness behind us but I was afraid she might yet be within earshot. Julie was looking at me as if being "not good" were the saddest thing. "That's hearsay," I protested. "Besides, Christians should show a little charity."

Julie gave me a sharp look, as surprised as myself that I had invoked charity as a specifically Christian virtue. Perhaps she understood immediately, as I did much later, that it was my indirect way of piercing her hypocrisy, because although she deflected what I had said, she spoke with a gentler tone. "I think you meant chastity, didn't you, Home, Dear?"

"Maybe," I said, disinclined to argue, thinking about the imminent dinner and the many other kindnesses she had shown me.

I spent my first Thanksgiving with the Schweppenheisers and my first Christmas, but I spent my first Easter with the Clooneys in Allentown, and the next Thanksgiving, Christmas, and Easter. I heard from Rusi in Chicago during my second year at Ow but was too involved with my research to do more than acknowledge his letter. When I had told the Dean of Students of my interest in Dr Penfield's research on memory (I had shown him the *Reader's Digest* article I had brought with me from Bombay) he had introduced me to Dr Edward Horvath, a lecturer on campus and also head of research at the Aquihana Hospital, who had worked with Penfield himself at McGill University in Montreal, whom I impressed sufficiently over the course of my first year to grant me access to the research facilities. According to the Dean, Dr Horvath had said that I worked intuitively, that sometimes he didn't think I knew what I was doing until I had done it, but he wanted to take the risk of giving me a free rein. "We'd be burying our heads in the sand," the Dean told me later when I couldn't stop thanking him, "if we did anything else." He was almost as excited as I was. I could only beam and repeat endlessly, mindlessly, "Thanks. Thanks. No kidding. You will not be sorry. Nosirree. No kidding."

I soon justified their enthusiasm and mine with a crude working model of the memoscan, with which I was able to electrically stimulate the brain of a rabbit, using a non-invasive technique, an x-ray instead of the electrode which Dr Penfield had applied directly to the brains of his patients during his research on epilepsy. I was able to bob the rabbit's tail, cock either of its ears, or twitch any of its legs by making appropriate adjustments; I was able to explore, localize, and record the functions of its brain (a question of developing a series of cross-sectional graphs of its brain using a mathematical model I developed which I hoped to computerize when I had the resources). I was able to produce gross movements only; finer movements required finer tuning of the x-ray itself, a finer wavelength which I hoped to induce using a diffraction grating or a laser. My primary interest lay, of course, with the invisible rather than the visible consequences of the stimulation, the retrieval of memory rather than the vulgar display of twitching limbs. To this end, with Dr Horvath's help, I explored and recorded a series of graphs of my own brain. The graphs were necessarily rough, the memories predictably unclear (I couldn't see what I remembered so much as feel the attendant emotions as I tracked the imprint of my life on my brain); I could confidently pinpoint only two occasions on the graphs even though they had remained a jumble of images – Penny's death, and my arrival in America. It struck me even then that Candace, despite her minimal role in my life, haunted the convolutions of my brain as frequently as did Julie, but not that her influence might have been yoked with that of Penny, certainly not that I should let her influence interfere with my plans to marry Julie.

Marriage: I thought I knew what it meant. What did I know? I had my degree. I had a research scholarship. I always received all the grants and scholarships for which I applied (the Dean saw to it personally). I had known Julie for almost two years. I knew her family. Everyone liked everyone else. I thought I understood Julie's needs. I thought she understood mine. What did we understand? I don't think it would be presumptuous of me to speak for her. Neither of us could think of anything that might have interfered with our plans. We took each other for granted – mistakenly so. Where shall I start? These are painful recollections.

It was a moonlit night – in May. We drove out of Aquihana (my request) to an isolated spot along the road where we sometimes parked when we wanted to be alone together. I thought it would be the perfect spot to propose. She wore jeans and a blue sweater (she looked nice in sweaters). She wore her hair in a ponytail because she knew I liked to undo it. I had been careful not to use too much Brylcreem because I knew she didn't like it. I was surprised how nervous I was, but after I suggested driving to our spot I could think of nothing to say; I couldn't even follow what she said. When she parked the car I felt something was expected but I couldn't think what. She was looking at me with her eyes wider than usual as if she were waiting for my response. "I'm sorry," I said. "What did you say?"

She gave a short laugh. "I said, Home, Dear, that you haven't been listening to a word I've said." I laughed too, I think, self-consciously. "I've got something on my mind, something I wanted to ask you."

Her eyes became cloudy as if she knew what I was going to say. "Yes?"

"Let's take a walk. It's a nice night. We can talk while we are walking."

"Attchha."

She knew it amused me when she spoke in Hindi, but I couldn't even smile. I took my shoes off instead. I thought it would be romantic walking without shoes. When she asked me why I was taking off my shoes I shrugged. "It's a nice night."

"There are stones outside."

"I don't mind. I'm from India."

She didn't laugh at my feeble joke.

There was no sign of life except for the sound of the crickets and a house in the distance with one bright yellow square of light. On either side of the road along which we walked were fields, occasional trees, highlighted in silver as far as I could see. "Look," I said, squinting my eyes, "when the wind blows through the grass you can almost imagine you're at the seashore. It looks like the surf when the tide comes in."

Julie, gamely, squinted. "Yes. I see what you mean."

The glow and the shimmer were unearthly, and at some other time I might have been happy just to watch in silence for a while, but the stones were cutting into my feet and I was aware of other important things that needed to be said. "Look at that house," I said, pointing to the sole visible form of inhabitation in the distance. "Isn't it amazing to think that someone actually lives there, so far away from everything else."

She looked at me as if I were becoming less familiar, as if I might have said something obscene. "It's not so amazing," she said. "It's not that far away. I'm sure they have a car. What are you trying to say?"

I shook my head as if I were clearing it of a spell. "I don't know why everything gets so difficult. I want to marry you. Will you marry me?"

I couldn't look at her but I knew she had stopped walking. She turned me around from behind, held me tightly against her wonderful bosom, kissed my face until it tingled. I kissed her back, tasting wonderful salty tears. "Crying? Why? Does this mean Yes or No?"

She laughed. "Yes! Yes!" She cried some more. "I'm so happy."

"I love you."

More kisses.

"I should have bought a ring. I wasn't thinking."

"It's all right."

"Here, take this instead – just for the time being." I thrust my sandalwood elephant, my good luck charm for so many years, into her hand.

She took her hand away. "That's sweet of you, Home, Dear, but no. It's all right, really. We can get a ring later."

We walked back to the car arm in arm. I felt as if I were moving on ball bearings. I was silent again. She was talking. "Suddenly there's so much to be done – but first things first. We must get you baptised as soon as possible."

The stones began cutting into my feet again. I knew what she meant, perhaps I had even feared it, but I said, "Baptised? Why? What do you mean?"

She clasped her hands around me from the side, kissed my ear. "You know what I mean. You're not a Christian. You have not taken Jesus into your heart."

I held her tightly but I felt myself shrinking from her already. "Why would that make a difference?"

"Why? Well, I couldn't marry a heathen, Home, Dear. You understand that, don't you, Dear?"

"I am not a heathen. If you thought that why didn't you say something before?"

"I thought you understood. You came to all the celebrations. You said you enjoyed them. I thought it was only a question of time."

Yes, yes, yes, of course, and yes again, the misunderstanding between us became increasingly clear, but remained insoluble. I was a Zoroastrian, but not as devout as I might have been because I did not wish to close myself off to what other religions had to offer. That was why I had attended all the celebrations. In Hinduism, the Buddha was the ninth avatar of Vishnu, Jesus the tenth. I liked that.

Gandhi had conducted prayer meetings for Hindus, Muslims, Christians, Sikhs, Jains, Jews, whoever chose to attend. I liked that. It did not make me a heathen. I thought she had understood that about me. I tried to make her understand one more time. She listened patiently but it was a patronizing patience; her face lost its contours appearing like a moon itself in the silver light. I felt as if I were choking. "What about the children?" she said.

I might have thought she was still trying to meet me halfway if not for the flatness in her voice, as if nothing I said would make a difference, but I tried anyway. "In one of the Zoroastrian prayers," I said, "there is a phrase: Manasni, Gavasni, Kunasni. Roughly translated it means good thoughts, good words, good deeds. Zoroaster teaches that good thoughts are necessary, good words are preferred, and good deeds are the most desirable. We have to show our children, by our own example, to do good things and let them make up their own minds what to believe."

"It doesn't mean a thing what you do," Julie said, looking pointedly in front of her, "if you don't believe in Jesus."

"I'm not saying I don't believe in Jesus — but I believe in others also. Jesus would not want me to cut them all off. He is not such an egotist. He is love. We must teach our children about Jesus."

She gave me a sharp sideways look. "And also about the others?"

"Why not?"

She was silent. In the car I massaged my feet. The gravel on the road had made ribbons of my socks. She pretended not to notice. How different was the ride back. I talked about my feet; she kept silence. As we passed the Welcome to Aquihana sign she spoke again. "If you love me, Home, Dear, you will do this for me." She spoke gently, tremblingly, looking at me as if she were afraid I might strike her. "Would you do it, just for me?"

I couldn't look at her. "How can I do it? It would not be real. How could you even want such a thing?"

"It could become real, given time. It would be all right with time. You'll see, Home, Dear. Please? For me?"

A song I had always hated but she had always loved — "Julie, Julie, Julie, do ya love me?" was on the radio. She turned it off. I could only shake my head for a while. "I'm sorry," I said. "I cannot do it."

On the Wings of
a Dragon

I could not believe it; it made no sense; I was no heathen. Something else had to be the matter: I was from India; I had a bum leg; I wasn't sexy – but I was not a heathen. That had to be a red herring. I understood Rusi's phrase, "ethnic anxiety", at which I had scoffed before. During the following month I lost ten pounds, I couldn't sleep, I couldn't work, but when I called her (she was back in Allentown for the summer) she was unwilling to talk unless I saw things her way, and that I could not do. It seemed inevitable that I would meet Candace again (I wanted her, Julie didn't like her, Aquihana was a small town, I felt ready for her) – but this is the recollection of which I am the most afraid because it was the repetition of this recollection (I invented a trip wire mechanism for the memoscan so that I could set it on a repeat cycle) that sent me into the coma from which I was recovering. One more recollection of the event might trigger a relapse, but if I survived, then Dr Horvath's thesis, that proximity with the objects of my long term memory might heal the decaying synapses in my brain, would be proved correct.

I think of my interlude with Candace as a weekend because it took place on a Saturday night, but it was hardly even the entire night. I began frequenting all the places where I had seen her as often as possible (she wasn't listed in the telephone book; I didn't want to ask anyone about her). On the third Saturday of my peregrinations I saw her again on Willow Street where Julie and I had passed her once before. I had thought I would know exactly what to say when I saw her but nothing could have prepared me for the way I felt as she came toward me, her face in darkness from the street lamp behind her, her tranquil walk as if she were being propelled by air, her hips swaying side to side like a bell. An electron microscope trained on my heart would have revealed a thousand minuscule elves working a thousand minuscule pumps. "Well, well, hullo, hullo. I'll be darned if it isn't old Candace. How are you doing? How is it going? What's new with you? Fancy meeting you here."

She walked right by me as if she hadn't seen me. I thought perhaps I had not spoken loudly enough and shouted after her retreating back. "I say, Candace. Hi, I say. How is it all going?"

She continued walking, and I might have let her go, thinking at least there had been no one to witness my mortification, but rage suddenly filled my head as if she had ignored me to safeguard her vanity. "I say," I said, stalking after her, "you don't have to be so bloody rude. You don't have to treat me like a bloody beggar just for saying Hi. It's not going to bloody kill you to say Hi back."

She turned just as I caught up with her. "What do you want?" Her jaw trembled, her eyes were wide.

I did not expect her to be scared. I replied with a chastened tone. "Nothing. Just saying Hi. It just got me mad when you kept on walking."

She searched my face as if for a clue before she spoke. "Do I know you?"

I didn't know what was worse, that she might deliberately ignore me or that she might genuinely have forgotten me; besides, it was dark, the light might have been behind me. "I'm Homi Seervai. We were introduced once, by Dale Schweppenheiser, on the hill going up to Carter Hall, about two years ago. Don't you remember?"

As I watched the unfolding of this scene yet one more time, this scene which I had already played back for myself countless times, I became aware of an additional texture underlying its fabric, Candace's perspective presented as clearly as if it had been my own. I felt her envy, anger, frustration as if it were my own. I understood that she had wanted to attend Ow but had disqualified herself because she didn't think she was good enough. She found it easier to hold the students in contempt. It was promising that I understood how Candace felt because it indicated that instead of blindly tracing my memory once more I was bringing my own faculties to bear on what I was seeing, it indicated a positive prognosis for my malady. "I remember Dale," she said, smiling. "Such a sweet boy. How's he doing?"

I wished she would think of me as wistfully; I would have preferred to have been remembered as a man myself, but I would have been content to have been remembered at all. "Dale's fine. He's in Watsonburg again for the summer. We had just come in for the fall semester. His brother Broderick, Bro-Brod, was with us. He told you I was from Bombay. Dale was to be my big brother. You must remember."

"I remember now," she said, still smiling, but now I felt she was smiling for me. "He said you were a brain."

"A brain, yes, that's me! I'm so glad you remember."

She continued to smile. The lamplight gave a sheen like a halo to her hair, a texture like gossamer to her short sleeveless frock, a glow as of dusk to her downy arms and legs. "Is Bombay in the Middle East?"

"No, no, in India, on the west coast."

"Oh, of course. That's even more exotic than the Middle East."

"Exotic?"

"My astrologer said an exotic would come into my life. She must have meant you."

The qualitative difference between being an exotic for Candace and a heathen for Julie escaped me entirely. "Yes, yes, you might call me an exotic," I said instead, delighted at my good fortune. "For an American, of course, I am an exotic. We consult astrologers all the time in India. I believe strongly in astrology."

"Me too, but most Americans think it's weird – but not me. I believe."

"My ex-girlfriend thinks I'm a heathen," I said, anxious to let her know that I'd been around, that I was free, to know that she was free as well, that she had nothing against heathens. "That was why we broke up."

She laughed, but when she said nothing I persisted. "Do you have anything against heathens? Do you think they're funny?"

"Oh, no, I love heathens. I'm a heathen myself – at least, I think I'm a heathen. Christians are so sanctimonious."

It was my turn to laugh. "I know what you mean. My ex-girlfriend was a Christian. You knew her I think – Julie Clooney. She met you at one of the celebrations on campus. We passed by you once, right here on Willow Street, about two months ago. Do you remember?"

She shook her head. "It doesn't matter," I said, finding it somehow appropriate that Julie had remembered Candace so determinedly while Candace had not remembered Julie at all. "What about your boyfriend?" I said, getting back to the point. "Does he mind that you're a heathen?"

She narrowed her eyes as if she had seen through my question. "How do you know I have a boyfriend?"

"I just assumed. Everyone on campus is so mad about you. Is your boyfriend a heathen?"

She shook her head, still sizing me up with her eyes. "I don't know. It's not something we talk about." She laughed again briefly and the image of someone I had never seen appeared to emanate from her, a scruffy bearded man with a large balding head and soft round belly in a greying undershirt and red and white striped boxer shorts. Surprised, I recognized him from a description Candace had given me later of his pale eyebrows like beer foam and his face the colour of a Bud lite. Even had I known the exact nature of his appearance I would not have admired Candace less; I might have pitied her more, but hindsight diminishes her appeal considerably, that she would consort with such an unappetizing man, that she had so little regard for herself as to live with him as his lover. "So," I said, "where are you going?"

"To the Inn Different, where I work."

"Oh, so you're working tonight?"

"No. It's my night off. But Biff's working. He's tending the bar. I'm just going to keep him company."

"Ah, this Biff, he is your boyfriend?"

She waited, as if she were thinking, before she answered. "Not really. He thinks so, and it doesn't make any difference to me so I let him think what he wants – but I'm thinking of leaving him."

"Leaving him? But why? Is he bad to you?"

She laughed. "No, but he's a jealous fucker. I can't go anywhere without telling him." She stopped laughing. "Still, I suppose that means he loves me – if he's jealous."

"But no, no, no," I said, glad to have won her confidence, wanting to ingratiate myself further. "If he is jealous it means only he doesn't trust you. And if you do not have trust how can you have love?"

She said nothing; I elaborated. "If he is a jealous fucker it means only that he is jealous – and that he is a fucker."

She laughed again; I felt worldly talking to her that way. Already she had broadened my horizons. "I say," I said, "I have got an idea. Supposing I show you my experiments? It won't take long. Biff will not even miss you. No need to tell him anything. What do you say?"

She said nothing but seemed to be thinking. I told her about Magic, the rabbit, whose brain I had mapped so thoroughly that I could make him do what I wanted merely by training the memoscan appropriately. "But that's cruel," she said. "Poor little rabbit."

"But he is not hurt at all. This is a non-invasive technique. That means no surgery. There is not even the need for an anaesthetic. It is completely painless." When she continued to hesitate I said, "Come on, Candace. Biff will never know. You only said you wanted to be free. What do you say?"

I don't know how much she understood of what I said about the memoscan, but at least I had convinced her. "Is it far? Should we take my car?"

"Not too far, maybe twenty minutes walking. You know where the Aquihana Hospital is."

"That's more than twenty minutes. Let me get my car."

"Okay. Good idea."

We walked in the direction from which she had come to an old blue Thunderbird. "Get in," she said. "It's open."

There was a clutter of newspapers, empty Budweiser cans, a large half-empty bag of Wise Owl potato chips. I cleared a space for myself on the seat and wedged my feet between the cans and papers. "Sorry for the mess," she said. "I hate to throw garbage on the street. You know how some people think the street is their garbage can? I'm not like that. I wish I was. Then I wouldn't have such a messy car."

"It is no problem," I said, wanting to put her at her ease. "I'm very comfortable. Let's go."

She drove as if someone were chasing her but I pretended not to notice. The top of the car was down and all I could see were the striations of her lovely blond hair behind her and the imperious tilt of her chin against the wind. "Lovely name you have," I said. "Candace. It suits you."

She missed the compliment – or pretended to. "Most folks call me Candy. I'm used to it – but I prefer Candace. It's more cosmopolitan."

"Yes, yes, of course, absolutely, it is! Candy is like sweets. That is for children – but Candace! A princess would be proud of a name like Candace. Incandescent Candace! It is so appropriate."

She smiled approvingly but she said, "I'm no princess. I'm really more of a Candy than a Candace. I guess that's why everyone calls me Candy."

"But no, no, no. Maybe you are a Candace and you don't even know it yourself."

She continued to smile. "Maybe, but I don't think so."

"Array, but you must think so. You have to believe in yourself first, no? Otherwise, why should anyone else?"

"Maybe. I never thought of it like that."

"But you must. Otherwise, why should anyone else?"

She looked at me sideways, a ribbon of hair flying across her face, as if I had said something unexpected, but then she laughed. "You're right . . . What did you say your name was?"

"Ho-mey Seervai."

"Homi. Yes, you're right, Homi. From now on everyone is to call me Candace – and don't you forget it." She laughed again.

There was a touch of mockery in her laugh, but I took it for world-weariness. I thought only that we were kidding together, that my name was on her lips; my face burned as if with a temperature of a thousand degrees. "I would never have called you anything else anyway."

I was glad it was a Saturday night; the research labs would be empty; I wanted neither to share her presence with nor explain it to anyone. The only person to see us was the guard who knew me and waved, staring at her all the while. It was dark; she seemed scared hovering silently behind me, but I preferred to leave most of the lights off, gathering power from my familiarity with the place in the dark. There was someone in the adjacent lab but I closed my door so we wouldn't be disturbed. She relaxed when I got Magic out of his hutch and let her hold him. Her baby talk while she cuddled Magic made me feel proud, as if we were parents. I showed her the graphs I had mapped of Magic's brain, the adjustable metal plate which would cover his head, the cathode ray tube which would generate the electrical impulse, the memoscan whose screen would guide us through the graphs of Magic's brain. At first she playfully refused to give Magic up to me as if she knew I meant to harm him. I considered that she might have been inviting me to wrestle her for Magic, but didn't dare to take her up on it, choosing instead to explain once more how innocuous the procedure was. She gave him to me then, eyes downcast as if I had scolded her; I took him back furious with myself for being such a prig, but during my demonstration (Magic twitching ears, nose, feet, as I directed) her eyes grew wide as if she were a child at a birthday party and I the magician. "Wow!" was all she said.

After we had returned Magic to his hutch she began looking at me as if I had suddenly come into focus, as if I were newly someone with whom to reckon. "Tell me about India," she said. "It must have been so different growing up there."

I felt uneasy as if her question were a mask for something else. I did not understand it then but from the sanctuary of my bedroom in Mayo House I saw clearly what she had been thinking: the two of us naked on the floor of the lab, she astride me – but a me with a different body, flabbier, a complexion the colour of lite beer, curls of flaxen hair like foam around the nipples, Biff's body! She had imagined me with Biff's body because she hadn't given enough thought to how my own body might look. "Where to begin?" I said in answer to her question. "I think of America as the land of unlimited orange juice – O.J. as you call it. In Bombay, Granny's bearer spent hours squeezing oranges so my brother and I could have one glass of orange juice, only one glass in the whole week.

Here you can get readymade, easily, as much as you want. There, when I was growing up, for two annas, you got a small packet of Victory Wafers or Coronation Wafers which was finished in zero time. Here you can get a big bag and eat chips forever – and so many dips! There we only had tomato sauce."

She was smiling as if she had not heard anything I had said. "Is there some place we can lie down?" she said.

"You are tired?"

She nodded, still smiling.

"There is the lounge."

"Will you lie down with me?"

I pretended to check the lock on Magic's hutch. "I am not tired."

"That's not what I meant."

I knew what she meant, but she had a boyfriend; as far as I was concerned she might as well have been married; my suggestion, stealing a few innocent moments in the laboratory, was merely hijinks; hers suggested irrevocable betrayal; besides, I had not slept with a woman before. "They might see us in the lounge. There is no privacy."

"What about your place?"

I didn't want to take her to the dormitory; I didn't want anyone to know. "That's no good. My room-mate will be there" (I didn't have a room-mate). "What about your place?"

"Someone might see us. They might tell Biff."

I shrugged, smiling weakly, as if to say Well, we gave it our best shot, but more than anything else I was relieved.

"What about a motel?" she said. "Would you spring for a motel?"

"You would not mind going to a motel?"

"No, not if it's the only choice."

I said nothing.

"What's wrong? You don't want to?"

We hadn't even kissed; I couldn't believe it made so little difference to her; her shamelessness galled me but I confessed to her instead that I had no experience in such matters, from which point, of course, there was no going back. I rationalized that the love of one good man might do her good.

We got back into the Thunderbird and she raised the top. She suggested the Come Back Motel where she had been before when she had had "absolutely no other place to go," but she wanted me to get the room because she didn't want to be seen. The subterfuge was not my style, but after Julie had left I wasn't sure any more what was. I was silent for most of the ride but she couldn't stop chattering: I can't believe it's your first time (laugh); it's such a nice night we could just go by the roadside (suggestive smile, sidelong glance, shake of the head from me); not for your first time, of course not, we want everything to be just right (laugh), but it *is* a nice night for a fuck, so warm, don't you think? (big smile, nothing from me); I just can't believe it's your first time (laugh, laugh); I was thirteen my first time, it feels so long ago I can't even think what it was like before (laugh, laugh).

"I don't think it's so funny," I said, more for something to say than to shut her up, more to make an observation than to appear disapproving, but I was hardly convincing, even to myself.

"I'm sorry," she said, immediately concerned, "I wasn't laughing at you. It just seems strange to me, like you were still learning how to walk or something, especially after you had a girlfriend for so long."

I thought about my leg; even when I walked normally I felt as if I were perpetrating a deception, as if I had to hide from everyone that I would always be learning how to walk, as if polio had rendered me fundamentally different; I had not felt that for a long time but after Julie had left the old insecurity had returned as if it were a conscience warning me of my limits. "She was a Christian," I said.

"I know," she said, sympathetically squeezing my knee. "I'm sorry."

She might have meant that she was sorry that Julie was a Christian, but I didn't think so; she had spoken without mockery; she was just sorry. "It's all right," I said. "I'm just nervous."

"Nothing to be nervous about," she said. "You'll see." She leaned over to kiss my cheek and my heart soared as if on the wings of a dragon.

Our roles were reversed the moment I shut the door behind us in the room and turned on the light; I became the child, she the magician, the moment she kicked off her shoes (actually, more like ballet slippers), pulled her dress over her head, and stepped out of her panties as naturally as if she might have been alone. I felt privileged just sharing the room with her naked person, and hardly moved when she turned to me, holding out her arms, slowly undulating her shoulders. Her breasts were smaller than I imagined Julie's might have been, but proportionate with her slim limbs, her sleek torso, and flushed and capped with swollen conchlike nipples. "I want you to remember me like this," she said, turning from me to the bed, drawing her knees to her chin, showing me all her separate parts, her plump pink pudendum, her round rosy buttocks, framing them with her fingers and thumbs as if to focus my attention. My knees felt weak; if she had not spoken they might have given way. "If you wanna get something out of this, Sweetie-pie, you have to do something yourself. Otherwise, it's no fun." She spoke in a low voice, without mirth, her eyes narrow and hard.

I dimmed the lights, took off my clothes. My senses that night were so skilfully woven that I had not imagined such a dense fabric possible: the smell of herbs in her hair, of cloves in the soft sandpaper of her armpits, the taste of salt, the texture of silk in the web of her pubic hair, the smell of rainwater and earth, the texture of peachskin in her complexion, the taste and the smell of a pungent cheese in her feet, the continual moan of the ocean as heard through a shell broken periodically by shrieks as of seabirds. I was quieter, hardly daring to enjoy myself, afraid to disrupt my fortune as if it might have been a house of cards, afraid to bring her suddenly to her senses, aware that Biff's place had been usurped by a pretender with a puny leg, but after I had satisfied her curiosity about my polio she kissed and carressed my leg – my twice naked leg – as if it were a talisman, and I breathed more easily.

"Nice," she said, giggling when it was over as if she were suddenly shy. "You're a sweet fucker, gentle, very nice, nicer than Biff."

"Really? How?"

She giggled. "I just told you. You're also better looking. Biff's fucking ugly."

I snuggled behind her as she described Biff, fitting myself to the curves of her body as we lay on our sides, enfolding her in my arms, hardly daring to believe what she was saying, kissing her to sleep, tracing her breaths with mine until I too was asleep.

The idyll was over. When she awakened me she was slipping into her dress again. "It's almost three o'clock," she said. "We've got to go. Biff's gonna kill me."

I was too chagrined by her disappearing nakedness to hear what she said. "Come on," she said. "I never intended to go to sleep, but you were so sweet with all your kisses."

"Forget Biff," I said. "I will take care of you. I mean it."

She laughed. "Don't be silly. You're sweet to say that, but it would never work."

"Why wouldn't it work? I . . . I love you. I will make it work. You will help me."

She slowed down. "Look. You're sweet. We had a nice evening, but it's over. I'll give you a ride home, but that's it. There's nothing between us."

"Array, but how can you say that? After what happened tonight, how can you say that?"

She spoke patiently, as if I were a child. "Nothing happened. Absolutely nothing happened. We had a sweet evening, but it's over. I'll give you a ride home, but I might never see you again — and that's okay, because we had a nice time, but it's over. Let's not spoil that now."

I couldn't think of anything to say; I got dressed; she drove me to the dormitory, smiled, kissed me goodnight; I said, "I love you"; she smiled; I was sure that she felt guilty about Biff, but that after she had had time to sort things out for herself she would come back to me; she frowned when I pressed my phone number into her hand just in case, but smiled again when I followed it up with my sandalwood elephant "for remembrance's sake", thanking me then, and kissing me once more, quickly.

The denouement came the next Saturday evening. After a week of inactivity, of impossible hopes raised and dashed with each ring of the telephone down the hallway in the dormitory, I decided I had to see her again and headed for Willow Street to take up a vigil by her Thunderbird. I was so immersed in what I would say to her that I almost missed her (her house wasn't as far down the street as her car), but there was no mistaking her walk when I looked up and saw her about to turn the corner on to Main Street. "I say, Candace, wait up, old girl," I shouted, running after her. "It's me, Homi. Wait up, I say."

She stopped a moment but, recognizing me, continued walking, so that when I caught up with her we were on Main Street which was more brightly lit and crowded. She was walking more briskly now; it was difficult for me, out of breath from my dash, to keep up with her, but I matched her stride as well as I could. "Slow down, I say, Candace," I said. "Where's the fire, I say? Something I got to tell you."

She looked at me briefly as if she couldn't understand why I was there, a concession for which I was grateful, before accelerating her pace. "What do you want?"

"Slow down, no, and I'll tell you. I want to tell you something."

She stopped. "What is it?"

Nothing was as I had imagined. There were too many people around, there was too much light, I was breathing like a locomotive, feeling more like a recalcitrant schoolboy than a courting lover, but I didn't know when I would get the chance to see her again. "I say, Candace" (breathing, breathing), "that night we spent" (more breathing), "it was the happiest night of my life" (still breathing, breathing), "the most beautiful . . ."

"Look," she interrupted, "no hard feelings, but it was nothing like that for me, understand? Nothing happened."

I hated to think there were others listening, but there was no help for it; I tried to keep my tone as confidential as I could despite all the heavy breathing. "How can you say that? You were there. You know what happened. You were there. You said it was nice – gentle."

She held up her finger, once more the mother and I the child who could not have any more sweets. "Look, there's nothing more to be said. Nothing happened and that's how it's going to stay, okay? Let's not spoil a good thing, okay? Don't be a shithead, okay? Now let me go."

She turned to leave but I caught her wrist to make her stay; she yanked her hand to free herself; I wouldn't let go but she caught me off balance and yanked me ahead with her hand; I stumbled and (I like to think this was accidental, but I cannot be sure) tripped over her foot, falling to the ground on my side. She got out of my way as I fell and left me behind almost immediately. Still dazed from my fall I heard her shout, "Leave me alone, dammit! Just leave me alone."

Someone came to help me up but I waved them on; I didn't want to talk to anyone; I think I was crying. It seemed women were always leaving me, but this time I did not waste time moping; I set directly about refining the memoscan; if I couldn't be with Candace the way that I wanted I would be with her the only way I could, by repeatedly reliving the memory of my night with her until it became my whole life; I didn't know whether I would die of thirst (attached to the memoscan I would have no access to water) or of the inevitable debilitation of my brain (the convolutions in which the particularized memory was stored, deepened by repeated stimulation, would encroach upon other areas of the brain causing unpredictable dysfunctions), but I didn't care because in either case I would die the happiest of deaths, constantly reliving the happiest moments of my life. I chose the fourth of July weekend to carry out my plan because it gave me more time alone in the lab away from possible interference; I hung up a Do Not Disturb sign for insurance. I didn't even think, as suicides sometimes do, of leaving behind a note of explanation, because I didn't think of it as a suicide; I thanked God instead for providing me with so benevolent an alternative as the memoscan.

Epilogue

When I fell on the sidewalk the needles in my forehead felt as if they were pulling threads of blood like rivers behind them from temple to temple; it was perhaps the strongest attack yet but its etiology, less and less a mystery, was less and less a source of fear; my comprehension gave me the courage I needed to wait out this one final attack. I had thanked God for His gift and then set about abusing it. The potential of the memoscan, by slipping from conscious memory to the collective unconscious, the Memory of the Soul as Bapaiji put it, began only then to dawn on me. I had been granted the power to probe the memory of elephants, to learn the password of whales, to discover no less than the equation to the universe which Einstein had sought, and I had chosen instead to perish so romantically – so foolishly, so pathetically – denying the world wisdom for a selfish, self-destructive love. I might have killed myself had one of the doctors not smashed down my door in answer to my screams (of which I had been unaware), broken the cycle into which I had locked myself, and freed me from the memoscan.

The crowing of a cock outside told me it would soon be dawn. I would soon be talking normally with Mom and Rusi and everyone else, but my brush with the collective unconscious had shown me a way to control the past, at least in my imagination, and I wanted to exercise that control one more time, to prove to myself that I was finally the master, no longer the slave, of what I chose to see. Tableau: Bapaiji and Granny in straight-backed chairs with their husbands (Hormusji and Rustamji) between them, also in straight-backed chairs, on the porch at the top of the stoop of Hill Bungalow in Navsari, dressed and posed stiffly as if for one of the innumerable portraits Bapaiji had framed in her verandah and living room;

321

behind them Mom in a sari, Dad in his Captain's uniform, Jalu Masi and Sohrab Uncle beside Mom, Soli Mama and Farida beside Dad, Jalbhai Pherozshah Cama behind them arms spread proprietarially around them; children arranged decoratively on the steps, Rusi, Zarine, Penny, Cyrus, Anand, Erach, Vijay, among other childhood friends; behind the immediate family the Paymasters, the Bhagats, the Jairazbhoys, the Chibbers, the Davers, the Agteys, among other friends of my parents; around them all, hovering like archangels, ancestors, old men and women, in pious robes and saris, dating back centuries to Bahman and his mother who had fled from the village of Sarosh in Pars in Persia, to Xerxes who had been killed by the Musalman while praying by the well at the edge of the desert. Back still further to Yezdigard III, Khushrow II, Noshirwan, Shapur II, Darius, and Cyrus, the shahanshahs eran ud aneran; all impatient, stiff, angry with the person who, assembling them, kept them waiting, but as I rose from my bed, the focus of all their gazes, their poses relaxed, their faces broke into smiles, and everyone, even the seated old people, got up to give me an ovation; behind them, above them, all around them, a light like a halo, ethereal, ineffable, the face, the presence, of Zoroaster, conferring his blessing. I had done it: I had brought them all together in one place at one time, made a whole of all the scattered pieces.

The cock crew again. As a child I had entertained a recurring dream of a forest beyond the Back Gardens behind Mayo House filled with chickens running from a fox in the night; I was afraid for the chickens, but just when it seemed the fox would catch them a cock would crow, it would be morning, and the fox in retreat. The fox *never* caught the chickens.

Rusi was still in the chair, but slipping, jerking in his sleep as if he were soon to be falling. I got out of bed, set him up from behind, and kissed the top of his head. He awoke with a start, shaking his head to clear it. "Array, Homi? How are you feeling? Are you okay?"

I couldn't stop grinning. "I'm fine, but I have to open the window." I walked across the room. "The air conditioning's making me so claustrophobic."

Rusi leaped to his feet; opening the door behind him he shouted, "Array, Mom, come quickly, no? See for yourself what has happened. Homi is okay again." He walked slowly toward me as if I were a ghost, but he was smiling.

There was a noise of a chair toppling over within; outside, the cock began crowing repeatedly, and the sky became lit, as if with a wash, veined by the first streaks of pink.

Glossary

Achu Michu: Blessing performed during weddings by the in-laws respectively of the bride and groom.

Ahriman: The Evil One, Satan, also known as Angra Mainyu.

Ahura Mazda: The Almighty, the Wise Lord, God, the Creator in the Zoroastrian cosmogony, also known as Ormazd or Hormazd.

Amah: Ayah, nanny (Chinese term).

Array: Catch-all expression to preface indignation, surprise, anger, or other emotions.

Ashem Vohu: A short prayer on the theme of truth.

Attchha: Okay.

Avestan: One of two ancient Persian languages, the other being Pahlavi, in which the sacred books of Zoroastrianism have been written, and in which the Zoroastrian prays.

Ayah: Nanny.

Baba: Boy baby or child.

Babu: A naif.

Baby: Girl baby or child.

Bai: Madam, what a servant might call the mistress of the house.

Baksheesh: Tip, gratuity.

Bania: Shopkeeper, merchant, money lender.

Bapaiji: Paternal grandmother.

Bapavaji: Paternal grandfather.

Bawaji: Appelation to indicate a Parsi, which, depending on the context, might be used affectionately or derisively.

Bearer: Houseboy.

Bhajia: Deep fried snack, filled either with potatoes, onions, or other vegetables.

Bhakhra: A sweet.

Bhel Puri: Mixture of grams and cereals with sweet and spicy sauces.

Biri: Home grown cigarette.

Carom: Game played with round counters on a board with corner pockets.

Chaipi: Tea drinker, used derisively in the sense of a bum or drunk.

Chana: Gram.

Chapatti: Unleavened bread, made of wheat flour, baked on a griddle.

Chappals: Leather sandals, generally with open heels.

Charpoy: Rope cot or bed.

Chhabar: Water splashed indiscriminately creating a mess.

Choli: Blouse worn with a sari.

Chori: Beans, often served with kharia.

Chowkidar: Guard for a private residence or single building.

Chula: Stove; also a pot with hot coals used by chana-wallahs to keep over their chana and sing to keep them warm.

Collector: District Officer, collector of revenues.

Dagla: White cotton overcoat, lighter than the dagli, with bows instead of buttons in front, but serving the same purpose.

Dagli: White silk coat.

Dak Bungalow: Post house.

Dakhma: The Tower of Silence where the Parsis commit their dead.

Darbar: Court of the Indian king.

Dastur: Zoroastrian priest.

Dekchi: Large pot used for cooking.

Dhimmi: Non-Muslim who remained in Iran after its conquest by the Arabs.

Dhobi: Washerman, launderer.

Dhoti: Cotton cloth worn around the waist, loins, and thighs.

Dubras: Servants, labourers..

Fakir: Ascetic, a member of a set of religious mendicants.

Faltu: a slang term meaning "useless".

Fehnta: Stately, semi-conical, custom-made, hat, to be worn with a dagla or dagli, dropped in favour of the paghri in recent years owing to its complicated construction and because the fehnta-makers have disappeared owing to a slackening in business.

Ganga: A working woman, a maid, a labourer.

Ghora Gari: Horse and carriage.

Gujarati: Language of the state of Gujarat on the west coast of India, also the adopted language of the Parsis.

Hindi: National language of India.

Hindu: Follower of Hinduism.

Hisab: List or calculation or sum.

Housie-Housie: Bingo.

Hu-tu-tu: An outdoor game in which teams line up outside the opposite borders of a narrow arena. Each team sends out members in turn to tag one of the members of the opposite team and to return to his own team without being pulled over the line. While he is in the arena the member must hold his breath and demonstrate that he is doing so by muttering Hu-tu-tu over and over without pausing to breathe. The opposite team is not allowed to touch him until he has tagged one of them.

Irani: Iranian.

Jaripuranawallah: Ragman, ragpicker.

Jizya: Tax levied on all non-Muslims who chose to remain in Iran after its conquest by the Arabs.

Katchoubar: Salad primarily of thinly sliced onions sprinkled with lemon.

Khadi: Home grown cloth.

Kharia: Goat trotters.

Khas-khas Tatti: Screen made of grass matting and hung around doors in the hot weather.

Kiddy-kiddy: Game with two teams in which one team bends over against a tree or wall in a long line arms locked around one another's waists, while the other team leaps atop them from behind as boisterously as possible and stays for a count of ten, the point being to get the team holding them up to give way.

Kurta: Long cotton shirt.

Kusti: Cotton thread, one of the articles of the Zoroastrian faith, to be tied around the waist over the sadra, the other article of the faith, while reciting certain prayers.

Lhega: Loose white pajama-like cotton breeches.

Looban: Conical container with a narrow opening at the top in which sandalwood is burned so that its smell may permeate the house.

Maha: Great, as in Mahatma (Great Soul), but also used in a slang sense to indicate, for example, a great time.

Maidan: Park, garden, or field used for recreation, spelled more phonetically as "mydan" than "maidan".

Maiji: Madam, used respectfully.

Malido: A sweet.

Mama: Mother's brother.

Mamaiji: Maternal grandmother.

Mamavaji: Maternal grandfather.

Manja: Glass-encrusted twine which is used in kite fighting to saw and cut through the opposing kite line.

Marere-mua: An imprecation: May the swine die!

Masi: Mother's sister.

Matka: Round earthenware vessel in which water might be stored.

Mehndi: Orange cosmetic applied on the hands of women.

Mem Sahib: Madam, used respectfully; also Bai.

Mithai: Sweets, pastries, desserts.

Mota Bajar: Big Market.

Motabawa: Big Bawa, used respectfully.

Muddum: Corruption of Madam, used derisively to indicate an occidental woman.

Musalman: Another name for the Muslim or Muhammadan.

Navar: Ceremony, only for Zoroastrian males who have had their navjotes, who might wish to study for the priesthood.

Navjote: Investiture ceremony whereby a Zoroastrian child is officiated into the religion, wherein he is initiated with the sadra and kusti.

Paan: Betel nut.

Paghri: Hat, not unlike a derby without its brim, to be worn with a dagla or dagli; also a white cotton head-dress, not unlike a turban, worn by priests.

Pakadav: Indian name for Catching Cook or Tag.

Papeti: The Parsi New Year.

Parsi: Name given to the Persians who fled from Persia to India. The name comes from Pars, one of the Persian provinces.

Patrel: Spicy, pulpy snack.

Pehlwan: Strong man, wrestler, weight lifter, or gymnast.

Pinjda: Literally a cage, also a wire mesh cupboard used as a pantry.

Puja: Hindu prayer ritual.

Puri: Light fried wheat cake.

Raga: Traditional melodic pattern in Indian music, an improvisation on the pattern.

Saakar: Unrefined sugar.

Sadra: Loose white cotton garment worn as an undershirt, one of the articles of faith of the Zoroastrian religion to be worn at all times, around which is tied the other article of faith, the kusti.

Saebji: Parsi greeting.

Sahib: Sir, same as Seth.

Samosa: Deep fried snack filled with ground beef and potatoes.

Seth: Sir, what a servant might call his master.

Sev: A sweet.

Sing: Peanuts.

Tala: Traditional rhythmic pattern in Indian music.

Talao: Well, pond, lake, or other similar small body of water.

Tandaroosti: Health prayer.

Tila: Decorative red dot placed on the forehead for festive occasions.

Tonga: Two-wheeled, two-seater carriage drawn by a pony.

Wadi: Neighborhood enclosed from the rest of the town or village by doors which were closed during times of interfamilial conflicts and sieges.

Wah-wah: Expression which might be used to indicate admiration or praise as well as facetiousness, analogous perhaps to Wow!

Yaar: Meaningless slang term, used primarily as filler, analogous to "man", "you know", and "bloody".

Yatha Ahu Vairyo: A prayer which gains its power, to smite the "violators of truth", by repetition.

Zoroaster: Greek form of Zarathustra, the prophet of the religion of Zoroastrianism.